Throwback

A Novel

Zeia Jameson

Cover Design by Murphy Rae
www.murphyrae.net

Editor
Tee Tate
www.teetate.com

Formatting
Champagne Formatting
www.champagneformats.com

www.zeiajameson.com

Dedication

Dedicated to my grandmother, who initiated and nurtured my love of books, reading and writing.
I miss you and will love you always.

Prologue

I GET INTO MY CAR AND SIT. MY HAND REFUSES TO PUT THE KEY INTO the ignition.

This is dumb. So dumb. Just stay. Go back in there and just say never mind.

I look up and see one of the curtains in the front window of the house flicker. I am being watched. Is she waiting for me to come back in? Is she wondering if I'm really going to go through with this? Does she think that I don't have the balls to leave? Or maybe it's the opposite. Maybe she thinks I'm a chicken shit for leaving.

My hand finally decides it's time to go and shoves the key into the ignition and turns. My eyes are locked on the curtain in the window and before my brain registers what is going on, my hand has put the car into reverse and my foot is hitting the gas pedal. I'm doing it. I'm moving. I am backing away from the house. I am pulling out of the driveway, putting the car into drive and moving away from the house.

Down the street.

Farther and farther away.

My plan has been literally set into motion and my heart wants me to stop and turn around. But the rest of my body keeps going forward. I come to a stop sign. I can turn around or keep going.

Turn or go? Turn or go? At that moment, a car horn beeps at me from behind. I look in the rear view mirror and realize I'm holding up traffic. And when I look into the mirror, I see my reflection. I look at my worn face, dark circles, frown lines.

The realization that I look like absolute shit sits heavy with me.

And then another realization hits me: I am alone. All by myself. I haven't been all by myself in…well, I can't even remember. I am all alone. Most people might consider that a desolate feeling, but for me, for some reason, I'm not upset that I'm alone. I feel…*free*?

The car behind me honks again. I've made up my mind. There will be no U-turns today. I hit the gas and accelerate forward.

Alone.

One

Jeremy

Age 5

"**M**OMMY, ARE WE GOING TO HAVE MY BIRTHDAY PARTY AT THE Jungle Gym House like Dylan did?"

"No, baby, not this year. We are going to have a party here at home."

"But the Jungle Gym House has big slides and trampolines. We don't have any slides or trampolines."

Mommy shakes her hand in my hair and then kisses me on my head. "I know, baby. Maybe we'll do it next year. You'll be bigger and you'll be able to do more of the activities."

Mommy hugs me tight. She says that it doesn't matter where we have the party. As long as we surround ourselves with people who love us and make us smile, we will always have fun.

"I wish Daddy could be at my party," I say. "I miss him."

Mommy squeezes me tighter. "Me too, baby. But he'll be watching us from Heaven. And it will make him happy to know that you are having fun on your birthday."

"Okay. Do you think he'll get me a present?"

Mommy lets me go and moves back a little so she can look at me. She laughs and wipes tears from her face.

"Oh, sweetie. I don't think so."

"Why not?"

"Once you go to Heaven, things like presents don't matter anymore. Only the people you love matter. Daddy will be with all of his friends and family that are with him in Heaven, and he will check in on us and look over us until we get to go to Heaven and see him."

"So, why don't we just go to Heaven now and see him?"

"We don't get to choose when we can go to Heaven. When the time is right, and we've done what we need to do here on Earth, we'll go to Heaven and see Daddy again, okay?"

I nod. "What is Earth, Mommy?"

"It's where we live right now," she answers.

"I thought we lived in Franklin."

Mommy smiles. "We do, baby. Franklin is just one small city on Earth."

"Oh." I want to ask more questions but Mommy hugs me again. Then she looks at me, wipes her face and smiles at me one more time. She kisses my cheek and straightens up my hair.

"Let's get you ready for school, okay? We have to bundle up extra good. It snowed this morning."

"Really? Can we play outside this afternoon? *Please!*"

"I won't be home when you get home, remember? But I'll tell Jenna to go outside with you." She points her finger at me and gives me her serious face. "Don't forget your snow boots this time, okay?"

I smile. I love playing in the snow. "Okay!" I say to Mommy.

Mommy gives me another tight hug. This one lasts a long time.

"I love you, Mommy. So much."

"I love you too, baby boy. So much."

Two

Livy

Age 8

"WHAT ON EARTH ARE YOU EATING?" I CAN'T SEE HER, BUT I can feel my mother sneer down at my plate.

"A hotdog and green beans." I look up at her and she tries to make eye contact with me but she stumbles backwards slightly and clutches one of the other chairs at the small table I'm sitting at in order to steady her balance.

A hotdog, with no bun or ketchup or mustard. A six pack of hot dogs and a family sized can of green beans was all I could afford this weekend at the grocery store after scrounging up a few dollars in change. If I divided it out just right, it would last me for dinner all week until I could figure out a way to get more money.

"Well hurry up so you can clean up the mess you made in the kitchen and go to bed already."

Why does she have to be here tonight? It's so much better when she's not here. When she's home, I'm not allowed to go anywhere but the kitchen with food and drinks. I have to sit at the kitchen table and eat dinner by myself because I'm messy.

Although I've never made a mess before.

When she isn't here, which is most of the time, I eat and drink where ever I want.

My mom walks away to the living room to give Gator, her new boyfriend, a beer.

I don't know why anyone would name a person Gator.

That's worse than being named Olive.

I want to ask him why his name is Gator, but mom told me not to talk to him because she wants him to stick around for a while and kids annoy him, so if I ask him, he will probably leave. Maybe I should go talk to him so he *will* leave. He's not very friendly. Then, Mom could find a friendly boyfriend.

Not that any of her boyfriends have ever been friendly.

I finish my dinner and wash the dishes. When I'm done wiping the counters and sweeping the floor, I turn out the kitchen light and head toward my room. I have to pass through the living room to get to my bedroom. As I walk through the living room, neither Mom nor Gator looks my way. I stop walking, right in front of them both, and look over at Gator. "I think Gator is a stupid name," I say, in an annoying way. A way that I've heard girls at school talk on the playground when they tease other girls.

When they tease girls like me.

I start walking to my room again. As I reach for my bedroom door, my mom comes up behind me and opens the door herself. She pushes me into my room and slams the door shut.

"Why in the hell did you say that?" she yells. She stumbles toward me and I just stare at her. I don't answer her. She slaps me in the face. Hard. It almost makes me fall down.

"Why did you say that, you little bitch? I told you not to talk to him!"

I just stand there and look at her. I want to touch my face to try to make it not hurt anymore. I want to cry but if I do, I know Mom will hit me again. I still don't answer her though. I don't really have an excuse. I just thought it as I was walking by and decided to tell him. But if I say that to Mom, or if I tell her, *"I don't know"*, she will just hit me again. Really, if I say anything, she'll hit me again. Even if I say I'm sorry.

I just stand there. It is really the only chance I have to not get hit again.

"You are so aggravating! Put on your pajamas and go to bed. And you better be up and ready for school in the morning." She puts her finger in my face and shakes it at me. I do not move. I do not blink. I do not breathe. "If you miss that bus…I swear to God, child."

I never miss the bus. I don't know why she even said that. I get up and ready every morning and sit outside to wait for the bus for a long time before the bus even gets there. I'd rather sit outside and wait for the bus than be in the house and risk waking up Mom. Even in the snow. I hate snow. But not so much that I'd choose to be in the house instead, just a few thin walls away from my mom.

Outside is safe, even when it's freezing.

Mom walks out of my bedroom and slams the door again. I put on my pajamas and crawl under my covers with a little flashlight my granddad gave me when we used to live with him. I also have a book that I found on the bus a few weeks ago. It's about a girl named Ramona Quimby. I lost count of how many times I have read it.

If Mom found out I was reading in bed instead of sleeping, she'd probably get mad.

But I don't care.

It's not like she ever comes to check on me at night anyway.

Three

Jeremy

Age 18

"You have the right to remain silent. Anything you say can and will be used against you in a court of law."

"Aw, come on. This is bullshit!"

"You have the right to an attorney. If you cannot afford an attorney, one will be appointed to you."

"I can't believe you are arresting me. I didn't do nothing! Come on, Phil, you know me."

"Do you understand these rights as they have been read to you?"

"I can't believe this is happening. Yes, I understand."

"Good. Now, Mr. Waters, let's get you into the back of the patrol car. Watch your head."

Phil, *Officer Santos*, places his hand on top of my head and guides me into the patrol car. I'm tired. My head is spinning a little. I just want to go to sleep and pretend this day never happened.

"Are you going to call my mom?"

"We'll get in touch with her once we get you settled at the station."

"She's going to be so mad at me." I lean my head back onto the seat and close my eyes. Having your hands cuffed behind your back is really uncomfortable. Phil doesn't respond. The car is quiet and as it starts to move, I doze off. Just before sleep, I remember the last thing Jessie said to me before she ripped my heart out of my chest.

"I'm going to college. You aren't. This can't work. We have to break up."

"Jeremy, I am very sorry about Jessie, but I am really disappointed in what you did."

Mom came and got me at three a.m. I feel like such an asshole. We are in the car on the way home and I know how much I've hurt her. When I first saw her at the station, I could see all of the fear and worry in her eyes. She just hugged me and told me she was glad I was okay. She didn't cry. She never does. Mom always puts on a brave face for me. But she can never hide the truth in her eyes.

I'm such a prick.

"Mom, I'm sorry. I'm so sorry. I went to Caleb's house after school. She broke up with me in the parking lot, Mom. The parking lot! She just said it was over and then she left. Just walked away. I went to Caleb's and we took some beer from his dad's fridge in the garage, and before I knew it, I was walking in the middle of the street, yelling at trees."

From the corner of my eye, I see my mom smile a little. I'm glad she finds humor in the situation. It means that she isn't completely devastated by her derelict son.

"I'm just glad you are okay, sweetie. I was worried, but now that I know you are safe, I'm okay. Don't beat yourself up over it too much. I know you had a hard day. It could have been worse and I'm glad that it wasn't. I'm glad that you weren't driving."

She says the last word very quietly as she grips the steering wheel tighter.

"Mom, I would never do that. Not only because it's dangerous but especially because of Dad…"

She removes her right hand from the steering wheel and holds it flat towards me to signal me to stop talking.

My dad was killed by a drunk driver when I was five. My aunt Jenna told me all about the accident when I was fourteen. But my mom and I have never talked about it. She has told me countless stories of how great my dad was. His reaction when I was born. How he tried to teach me to catch a baseball before I could even walk. The first time he and I saw fireworks together and how I was so scared until he whispered something into my ear and calmed me down. None of us have a clue what he said to me that night. I don't remember it and Mom said she never thought to ask.

I've only mentioned the accident to my mother a few times. Every time she stops me.

It's not something we discuss.

"I'm sorry, Mom, please don't be upset. But please just know I would never do something that stupid. I know I'm a dumba—," I stop myself. I don't want to curse in front of my mother. I've slipped up a couple of times before and she's never reacted to it or said anything about it. But she never uses profanity so I don't feel like I should use it in front of her. I start my sentence over, "I know I'm a dummy sometimes, but I'm not *that* dumb."

She lowers her hand and places in on top of my hand that is resting on the center console. "You aren't a dummy, sweetie. You are just a boy. And sometimes, boys do dumb things. Especially when they get their hearts broken. But you have a good head on your shoulders and even though I still worry, deep down, I know you wouldn't do anything like that."

"Thanks, Mom, for bailing me out. And for understanding."

"Of course, sweetie. But, technically there was no bail out. Phil just wanted you to sleep it off. The only reason he read you your rights is because he had to cuff you and the only reason he had to do that was because you wouldn't calm down. He told me the whole story while we were waiting on you to wake up. You weren't processed though. No record. Phil just wanted you in a safe place until I could get to you."

"Why didn't he just take me home then?"

"Because he didn't want me to have to deal with you being drunk. He thought it'd be best if you sobered up in the clink." She looks over to me and winks.

"I'm sorry, Mom."

She squeezes my hand. "I know, baby."

"She broke up with me, Mom. In the parking lot. She said it was because I wasn't going to college. I told her I wasn't planning to go to college six months ago. Why did she wait until the last day of school to break up with me?"

"Well, baby, I can't answer that for you. Maybe she just woke up today and said 'I don't want to be Jeremy's girlfriend anymore'. Or, maybe she stewed over breaking up with you for a long time and just didn't have the guts to do it until today because she knew she wouldn't have to see you again. Or, maybe she thought you'd change your mind and go to college with her."

Ouch. My mom was good at being brutally honest when the situation called for it. I knew one of her scenarios was probably right—or maybe they all were, but it stung hearing someone say it out loud.

"No matter the reason, though, she is leaving to go to college soon. She'll be nearly on the other side of the country. Long distant relationships are hard, especially for eighteen year olds."

"So, do you think I should have gone with her? To college?"

"No, baby, that isn't what I'm saying at all. You made the decision to not go to college, and to not follow her because that is what your gut told you to do."

My mom has always told me when you listen to your gut, or instincts, you tend to make the best decision when it comes to important moments in your life. Listening to your gut, she'd say, was letting your brain do what it did best, logically, and letting your heart assist in guiding that logic with hope, passion and optimism.

I drop my head and sigh. A brief bolt of panic shoots through my body.

"I just don't know what I want to do, Mom. But I do know that I don't want to sit in a classroom for two years and waste anyone's money just to drop out because I can't figure it out, like Mark did. Aunt Maggie spent so much money to send him to school and then he just quit. I don't want to do that. Plus, I don't want to move away from you and Aunt Jenna and Aunt Maggie."

"Well, let me stop you right there. You know I have told you several times that Jenna, Maggie and I will be fine. You aren't listening to your gut on this one. Your heart is strong arming your head and invading you with thoughts about not wanting to leave us."

I make a feeble attempt at a laugh. "So, what? You gonna kick me out after I graduate?"

"Of course I'm not going to kick you out. But if you think you are going to graduate from high school and piddle the rest of your teens and your twenties away with us old biddies, you've got another thing coming. You are an adult now. It's time for you to start building pieces of your own life. To focus on you. I've done my part and now you have to experience life as a young man should. Be adventurous. Take chances. Have fun. You can start slow and figure things out in time. But you do have to start somewhere or I may just have to put a boot to your butt."

She smiles. I know she'd never kick me out of the house. But, I also know she's right. I can't live with her forever. I certainly wish I could. Her hand is still resting on mine as we pull into the driveway of the house. I place my other hand on top of hers and squeeze.

"I love you, Mom."

"I love you too, baby boy."

Four

Livy

Age 17

"DAMMIT, NANCY, WHY DO YOU EVEN CARE?" I CAN'T REMEMBER how long it's been since I called her Mom. I first called her Nancy sometime in middle school. She didn't react or say anything about it so I've called her Nancy ever since. Now I wonder if she even remembers that I am her daughter. She only ever treats me like a free loading tenant.

"My house, my rules! And as long as I pay the bills around here, you'll do as I say. And, I say your curfew is ten o'clock."

"Whatever, Nancy. It's not like you'll be here to check up on me. You'll be sitting on a bar stool or lying in someone else's bed passed out by ten o'clock tonight."

"What did you say to me, little girl?" Okay, maybe she does remember I'm her daughter. She calls me *little girl* whenever she wants me to understand who is in charge. Although, she hasn't really controlled anything I did since I started high school. And *little girl* is a terrible way to describe me these days. Especially in perspective to Nancy's build. I've got at least seven inches on her petite five foot frame. My shoulders are built like they were designed for a defensive tackle, which I'd happily be if the school would let me play football. And apparently, according to the weirdos around here—who like to put in their two cents worth where pennies aren't appreciated—I've got nice, child bearing hips.

Translation: I'm not going to be squeezing my ass into Nancy's size zero jeans anytime soon.

I highly doubt any man will ever call me his *little woman*, as I've heard so many of Nancy's boyfriends call her. I'm hardly fat, but I'm no small fry either. Some guy in school said to me once that I had "curves in all the right places." But rather than swoon over his words, I rolled my eyes and told him he made me want to vomit.

Not that I'd want anyone calling me *little woman*, anyway. I don't understand why any woman would think that is an endearing phrase.

"You heard me. What difference does it make what time I come home, Nancy? You won't be here. I don't know why you are so adamant about *me* being here."

"I don't want you running the streets, getting knocked up and shit just so I have another mouth to feed."

"Going to a bookstore is hardly running the streets. And not that it's any of your business, but I don't open my legs up for every guy who calls me sweet cheeks and flashes dimples in my direction, like the other people who live in this house!"

That earned me a slap right across the face. Even though I had the advantage on Nancy in height, she was still able to conjure up enough power in her tiny arm to leave a hand print on my cheek every time.

I should know better by now, just to keep my mouth shut. But over the years I learned that irrational arguments with Nancy would only ever end if I chose to walk away from the nonsensical yelling and rambling, or if I spoke up and said something that struck a nerve within her, ending in her hitting me.

Once she hit me, she would shut up and walk away herself. I'd prefer not to get slapped in the face. However, sometimes, Nancy's ridiculous accusations toward me regarding how I was blossoming into some type of tramp, essentially following in her footsteps, infuriated me like nothing else. I'm nothing like Nancy, not even in the slightest. I've never even slept with a guy. Hell, I've only kissed two and haven't gone farther than that.

Guys around here repulse me. There must be normal guys out

there somewhere. Guys who don't try to pinch your ass before they even know your name. Guys who don't spread rumors about having sex with girls they've never even been alone in a room with. Guys who don't treat women like pieces of meat.

Guys like that must exist somewhere because people who write books and make movies create stories about these types of guys all of the time. The ones who are romantic and fight for a girl's love when it is called for. The guys who would risk life and limb for the girl he loved.

I'm not saying I want *that* kind of guy. But I would like to meet someone one day who will actually make eye contact with me when I speak, rather than having his eyes gravitate towards my boobs or my ass. Someone who would like to sit across the dinner table with me and chat while we eat, rather than sit on the same side of the booth and try to grope me and make out with me before the appetizers arrive.

Someone who isn't from this God-awful town.

Someone who doesn't know Nancy.

Someone who doesn't know anything about my childhood.

My face is still stinging. She's staring at me, waiting for the reaction that she's always wanted. She wants me to cry. But I won't. I'm not even sure I can cry. I've become so numb to Nancy's ways that they don't even affect me emotionally. Except when she tries to compare herself to me. That'll get me almost every time. I stare at her, motionless. She stares back with fury in her eyes. She hates that I don't succumb to her physical aggression.

"I can't wait until you turn eighteen, little girl. Your ass is so out of here. And I can finally have this house all to myself again."

I don't respond to her. I want her to leave. I can't stand being in the same room with her for one more second.

She finally turns and leaves. I hear her car crank outside and then barrel down the driveway. I sit on my bed and exhale. A tear falls from each of my eyes. Not from pain and not from anything Nancy said or did. It's from relief. In two weeks, I graduate. Three days later, I turn eighteen. Thanks to my perfect GPA, I've got college in my sights and paid for with scholarships. As soon as I get that diploma in my hand and my ID can validate that I'm old enough to buy a bus ticket on my own, I'm out of this shit hole and far away from Nancy. She has no idea where I'm going, but I don't think she'll even care that I'm gone. I don't know where I'll live when I get there. I don't even know how I'm going to pay for a place to live. But I'll figure it out. I just want to get the fuck out of here and I'm so relieved that that day is right around the corner.

Five

Jeremy

Age 21

A shot through the heart

I DID WHAT MOM TOLD ME TO DO. I DETACHED MYSELF FROM HER and my aunts slowly. It wasn't as hard as I thought it would be. After the night Phil Santos had to call my mother to pick me up from jail, I made a promise to her to keep looking forward and keep my head level.

I took a summer job doing framework and remodels with a construction crew. My Aunt Jenna's boyfriend, Michael, was a general contractor and helped me get the job and showed me the basics. I learned fairly quickly how to swing a hammer, among other things. Toward the end of the summer, I helped Michael organize and lead a crew for two Habitat for Humanity projects. By the beginning of September, I was a pretty savvy carpenter. Michael made the suggestion that if I wanted to escalate my career to a general contractor, like himself, I should take some business classes in the city before I got my license. It wasn't a requirement, but if I didn't like the business part of owning my own company, I wouldn't fully enjoy the other aspects of it either. I really loved carpentry. I enjoyed working with my hands. But, I also really liked the management part of the construction business as well. And, I knew that avenue could take me farther in life than just doing carpentry.

Not that being a carpenter was a bad job to have. But in the short four months that I worked with a crew, I quickly learned that the physical line of the business was most suitable for young, able-bodied men and women. I only worked with a few people while framing houses that were over the age of forty. And while they probably did still enjoy their jobs, I could tell all the years of manual labor had taken a toll on their bodies.

Additionally, general contracting would allow me to be my own boss and that sounded very appealing. Michael made sure that he didn't glamorize his job to me or sugar coat the work load that came with it. He made sure I knew the ugly part of the business as well as the luxuries. He included me in on a lot of his projects and let me shadow him, showing me all of the intricate steps and details that it takes to complete a project. All of the communication that had to be done and all of the multitasking that was required. I quickly understood that if you didn't juggle everything just right, your business could fall apart before you even got it off the ground.

I decided to take Michael's advice and sign up for business classes. He arranged for me to be an apprentice with a business partner of his whose office was located close to campus. It didn't pay much but it was enough for a small apartment. Plus, my mother put away most of the money from my dad's life insurance policy into an account that accrued interest for thirteen years. I had plenty to help pay for classes and anything else I might need until I could stand stable with my own income. When I felt like I was at that point a few years later, I had spent less than ten percent of what was in the account. I told my mother she could have it. She refused to take it back. She told me to let it continue to grow and to use it for milestone expenses—an engagement ring, a new house, decorating a nursery. There was no pressure or insinuation behind that, but she thought I might want these things one day, even if I didn't want them right now.

Truth be told, I was so focused on being the best damned general contractor I could be, I didn't think about sharing my time with anyone else very often. I went on a few dates from time to time, but nothing ever "stuck to the fridge" as my mother would say, referring to how spaghetti noodles stick to the face of the refrigerator door when they are just perfect.

I lived with my mother through the holidays after I graduated from high school and then moved to the city that January. I began my apprenticeship a week after I moved and classes just a few days after that. After about three months, I went back home to visit my mother. I told her all about everything I was learning in school and at work. She told me that she was so proud of me and that she could tell by the happiness in my eyes that I had followed my gut and had done the right thing. She also reminded me that she once told me how easy it would be to move forward with my life once I figured it out. And, of course, she was right. My eighteen year old self was terrified to be anywhere that my mother wasn't. But when I decided to move and take classes, it excited me and the fear completely subsided. It's funny how my mother always seems to know things that I was far from figuring out myself.

I finished taking all of my classes about six months ago. I didn't get an actual degree but I learned a great amount about how to run a business from the classes that I took. And with all of the experience I had already under my belt with work, I would have no problem remaining gainfully employed without an official piece of paper declaring my intelligence. Plus, I was planning to be my own boss one day, and as the boss, I didn't care whether I had a degree. After I finished my classes, the owner of the company I was working for as an apprentice gave me a full time position with a salary and benefits. The job is tough but I look forward to getting up and going to work every day.

It's been a particularly long day at work today, so I decide to stop off for a beer before I head home. A friend recommended I hit up a specific bar when I got a chance because they have a beer that I like on tap and it's close to where I live. He also mentioned something about the place being entertaining or exciting. Enticing? I don't remember what word he used but he talked it up enough to make me want to try it out.

Upon arriving at the location, I realize that the building is kind of in a strange area, and although it is not far from my apartment, I've never even known it was here. I hesitate for a second and evaluate the credibility of the buddy that suggested coming here. I'm sure it's fine.

How bad could it be? And, if it's awful, I'll just leave.

I open the door and walk in. The room is dark, with mostly only the glow of neon signs and a few televisions illuminating the space. I sit at the bar and pick up the plastic, triangular tent of a beer menu to see what's on tap. I peruse the options available for a few moments. Just as I spot the beer that I'd like to get, I look up to see the bartender placing a beverage napkin in front of me. My eyes and head motion up from the napkin on the bar, and I slowly take in the person standing in front of me. As I look up, I'm met with the face of what I can only describe as a mixture of delightfully gorgeous and wildly terrifying. Her eyes are the darkest shade of green I think I've ever seen. Her smile exists, but it's only there to appease customers. She's not genuinely happy to be standing before me, offering me a beverage. If I was an expert at reading faces, which I certainly am not, I'd say what she is really thinking is something along the lines of *"what the fucking fuck do you want, fuckface?"*. She has no intentions of flirting with me for a good tip.

She is tall. Her arms are toned. Her hair is long and brown, braided into pigtails which are hanging down the front of her shoulders, nearly half way down her torso. She's wearing a black t-shirt, with the logo of the bar stamped on the left side of her chest. The sleeves are cut off and the neck is cut into a V, the disrupted thread curled down at the edges. With the V cut, her collarbone is exposed and her olive skin is accentuated with a short, silver necklace that has a small clover charm dangling from it. No, it's a shamrock. A slight, but significant, difference. The charm is so small that you cannot tell what it is at first glance. You have to gaze on it for a moment. I find myself focusing on that particular spot of her skin, where the silver meets her neckline. The sparkle of the jewelry against her skin's hue is mesmerizing. If she's paying any attention, she might be thinking that I'm checking out her cleavage. I should probably stop looking there and make some eye contact but I can't seem to manage to make that small effort. How can jewelry lying on bare skin be so hypnotizing?

"What can I do you for today?" She speaks and my eyes instantly correct themselves and look her in the face properly. Her voice is low. But not manly low. It's low like a jazz singer. *Bluesy*. I wonder if she has a good singing voice. It's certainly a very beautiful speaking voice.

As I'm thinking about how her voice might carry a tune melodically well, in a perfectly open acoustical room, with brass and string instruments playing for her in the background, I discover yet another intriguing thing about her. A splendid scent floats across the bar, broadsides me, and my head begins to spin.

Peaches. A whole orchard of sweet, luscious peaches.

The combination of her voice, the peaches and the head spinning start to make other parts of my body react without my approval. My heart starts beating uncontrollably and my face begins to flush. My brain shuts off and in such, neglects to remind my lungs on the proper operation of breathing.

"Cat got your tongue? You want something to drink?" she asks.

My head wants to move. In any direction. Yes, I want a drink. No, I don't want a drink.

My mouth wants to speak.

My eyes want to blink.

But I remain frozen.

I can't even blink!

"Look, buddy, if you are going to sit there and do nothing but drool all night, you can take your ass elsewhere. That seat is for paying customers only."

She scowls at me. The scowl contorts her beautiful face into something frightening. She means business and I'm suddenly terrified. I've got to pull myself together before she throws my ass out. And by the account of her height, broad shoulders and muscular arms, I believe she could physically remove me from this seat all by herself.

Finally, I clear my throat and attempt to accumulate some moisture in my mouth so I can speak before she makes good on the promise I am assuming her eyes are insinuating.

I look at the menu. "Um, I'll have a pint of ah…um."

Why is this so fucking hard to say?

I want a pint of Stella.

It's the only beer I drink.

"We just tapped a good IPA from Colorado. It's hoppy but since it's distilled at such a high altitude, it's very crisp and clean. Wanna try it?" she asks me with that mellow, rich voice of hers. I don't know how to respond and suddenly the insides of my hands are wet. Really wet. Oh dear God, I think my palms are going to drown everyone in the room with the amount of sweat pouring from them. Why is my body being so rebellious against me right now? I move my hands down to my slacks and wipe them off. I look at her. Her eyes have softened to what they were before. Her gaze, her voice and her scent are melting my entire body, as indicated by my liquefied palms.

Except for one part. That's staying rather firm.

"Yes," I squeak out like a fucking thirteen year old.

What am I doing? What is an IPA? Stella. I want a Stella.

But she walks away before I have a chance to change my mind.

Screw it. What the hell. If I don't like it, I'll just drink it slowly. That'll at least give me an excuse to stay at the bar longer and try to loosen up enough so I can perhaps actually speak to her without sounding and looking like an idiot. I can't leave this place without finding out her name and number. I have to talk to her. I want to know everything about her.

Or maybe I just want to sleep with her.

Well, definitely the latter but I really do feel compelled to ask her a million questions until I know her like no one else does. And I can't even come up with a good enough reason as to why. I've been sitting here less than five minutes and she's only said like seven sentences to me. And not flirty sentences. There were just a few questions, some informational facts and I think a death threat. I shouldn't be turned on right now. At the very most, I should just feel better educated about beer and slightly worried for my life.

I also can't ignore the fact that as she is standing there pouring my beer facing away from me, my eyes drift down toward her ass. In jeans. And it's fucking amazing.

Oh shit, she's coming back with my beer.

I dart and point my glance to the left. Then to the right. She didn't notice me looking at her ass.

She didn't notice.

I'm smooth.

"Here you go. Maybe this'll calm your nerves a little. You seem... pent up." She picks up a small, glass salt shaker with her empty hand and sprinkles the napkin that she put in front of me earlier with a little salt. Then she places my beer, perfectly poured I aptly notice, on top of the napkin. She's looking at me, faintly smiling. It dawns on me that she's making fun of me. She noticed my uneasy reaction towards her and now she's fucking with me.

"Thanks." I straighten my posture, square my shoulders and on some peculiar instinct, release an odd, manly grunt. My pitiable attempt at showing her I'm a *studdly guy* backfires and I end up looking even more like a moron than before. I look her in the eyes and make a valiant effort to give her at least a good smile. Perhaps a smile can save me and make me look adorable and irresistible, and she'll forget the other stupid shit that I've done up to this point. I bring the glass to my lips to sample this IPA from Colorado. She points her thumb over her shoulder toward the beer taps. "Did you enjoy staring at my ass while I was standing over there?" I nearly spit out the first sip of beer that I've taken.

She did notice.

My adorable and irresistible smile just got impaled by her question. I manage to swallow the beer and clear my throat, "Excuse me?"

"You were checking out my ass when I was pouring your beer. Did you like what you saw?" Her eyes change again. They aren't sweet anymore, but they aren't the chilling eyes she gave me before either. They are playful but not even in the way they were just a few seconds ago when she was teasing me about being a bumbling idiot. One might even say her eyes were sinister.

But one definitely wouldn't say that out loud.

She's fucking with me again and trying to make me squirm. She's using confrontation as an intimidation mechanism and I feel like she's testing me to see if I'll forcibly deny that I was checking her out or own up to my automatic masculine tendencies.

I feel like if I'm going to have any chance of getting her number—hell even her name at this point—I should choose option B.

I look at her square in the face and give a good, confident smile. "Actually, I did."

Looking at her, I notice the sinister is fleeting and being replaced with slight surprise and a hint of satisfaction. "Hmmm. A guy who admits that he was checking out the goods. I like that."

"Well I didn't figure you'd be wearing those jeans if you didn't want people taking a peek." I decide to go for a little teasing of my own. "And as long as I'm being honest, you know what else I checked out?"

She looks at me just like I thought she would. Like she knows I'm going to say her boobs. Or rack. Or tits. Or whatever other off color term you could use to describe breasts. The smile leaves her face and she gives me a look of disappointment. I admire that even though she is let down, she still locks eyes with me, awaiting my response. It makes me wonder if she's had this exact same conversation countless times before. She gave me a little honesty and she thinks I'm about to take advantage of that vulnerability.

How the fuck can I tell all of this about her just by looking at her face?

She leans into the bar, and gets closer to my face. At the V of her shirt, the fabric loses connection with her skin and if I were looking in that direction, I'd probably be able to get a great view of what was hidden underneath. But my eyes do not leave hers. "Yeah, what's that, stud?" she says, monotone but enunciates the *d* in the word stud, nearly making it its own syllable. She's indicating that I need to choose my next words wisely.

I wait before I answer and stare at her a few seconds. She looks so sad, like she wanted me to be different. There was a small glimmer of hope in her face before and now it's been extinguished.

I want to reignite it.

Here goes nothing.

"Your eyes," I finally say. And, as I assumed, that takes her by surprise. But her reaction is hardly noticeable. I only see the minor adjustment of her face. Her eyes widen ever so slightly and there is just the tiniest bit of a grin on the left side of her lips. But the best part is that I see the hope again.

"My eyes," she repeats, as she straightens and backs away from the bar. "Well, that's new." She tilts her head to the side slightly as if she's trying to decipher what just happened. "You aren't some weirdo eye fetish guy, are you? You don't have like a bunch of women's eyeballs pickling in a jar under your bathroom sink, do you?"

I chuckle. "Of course not. That would be ridiculous. I keep the jar on my nightstand so I can see it just before I fall asleep."

She laughs and her voice infiltrates my ears. Her eyes smile so much larger than her mouth. Her face at this moment is the most beautiful face I've ever seen. I want to put my hands on either side of that laughing face and kiss those smiling lips.

"Of course. That is entirely more appropriate and acceptable. What was I thinking?" She spins her head and looks over at the corner of the bar. She turns back to me and says, "Well, I hope you enjoy the beer. I'm Livy. I have to take care of those drunk bastards over there. Let me know if you need anything, okay?"

"Sure thing, Livy." I smile uncontrollably and watch her walk away.

Livy and her emerald eyes that have a mind of their own.

I want to see her laugh more.

I want to touch her hair.

I want to hold her hand.

I want to kiss her.

Five minutes with this woman, the bartender of a sketchy sports bar, and I feel more compelled to do things with her, to her, for her, than I have ever felt about any other person of the female population since the second I realized girls didn't have cooties. It is by far the most absurd and simultaneously the most concrete cluster of feelings I have ever had. I've only known her name for fifteen seconds at the most. How is it possible to be so drawn into someone so quickly?

Given these facts and these feelings, I realize at this particular moment, while sipping an IPA from Colorado, that I have to know more about Livy.

Six

Livy

Age 21

Ass Kicking Thursday

I DID EXACTLY WHAT I SET OUT TO DO. I GOT THE FUCK OUT OF DODGE the day I turned eighteen. I packed everything that was important to me, which wasn't much, into a medium sized duffle bag. I headed to the bus station as soon as I woke up, bought a ticket and headed toward the city. I never looked back.

I didn't have a plan. I was never good at planning. Fortunately, I was good at studying, which led to the GPA and the scholarship. There wasn't on-campus housing and the scholarship didn't cover room and board. I had no idea what I was going to do once I reached my destination and stepped off that bus. My single most important priority was to get far away from Nancy and that dirt bag town. I knew I'd be able to figure out everything else once that burden was off my shoulders. I'd have more clarity then and the answers would come to me.

And they did. Just not as easily or as quickly as I thought they would. I had always been good with taking care of myself with very little money. Food. Clothes. In high school, I tutored football players after school. Disgusting, gropey football players. I think the only reason they hired me to tutor them was because they all had a bet on who could get into my pants first. I dealt with the groping and disappointed all of them when it came to having sex with any of them. They all repulsed me. There was no way I'd drop my panties for any of those assholes. But I could tolerate sitting in a room with them for an hour after class every day to have a few bucks in my pocket for the necessities.

The city was different, though. At least in high school I had a roof over my head. The weight of Nancy telling me I was blessed she gave me a roof to sleep under was heaviest at the moment I accepted that I was alone in a city I knew nothing about. And, I was homeless.

But I was resourceful. I found a public library and used their Internet to find some shelters. I made a list of all the shelters the search found so that I wouldn't have to come back to the library if the first shelter I went to didn't work out. For a month, I circulated around four out of the six shelters in the city. Two of the shelters were in areas even I didn't feel comfortable hanging out in, so I avoided them altogether.

After a week of adjusting to the routine of living in a shelter, I decided to get serious about looking for a job. I had two and a half months before school started and I needed to find something lucrative enough to get myself an apartment before then. I knew I wouldn't be able to handle taking classes and being homeless at the same time.

I got a job at a bar. I didn't have any experience but the owner, Joe, said I would brighten the place up. He also didn't seem concerned with the fact that I was only eighteen. He knew how old I was and I certainly didn't ask about the legalities of the situation. I needed money and he was willing to employee me and that was that.

When I first met Joe, I made the incorrect assumption that he was just like all the guys I was used to—a douche bag. Turns out, he's not. He just calls it like he sees it and isn't afraid to pay a fair compliment. As far as the experience was concerned, Joe said I would mostly be pouring beers. He had twenty-three taps and rotated his stock constantly. He showed me how to pour a proper beer, the difference between the types of beer and which glass was best for each type. I told him I was skeptical of a beer tasting differently based on the shape of a glass. So, he proved his point one evening after closing by letting me sample various types in various glasses. He was right.

He also taught me some other basic stuff, like what the terms *"two fingers"* and *"neat"* meant. He said occasionally we'd have someone come in and ask for a liquor drink but people mostly came for the beer. For the summer, I worked every night, seven nights a week and hoarded every single penny I earned.

Just before I started school, Joe hired another girl to pick up shifts that he and I couldn't pick up. Her name was Sara and she worked part time while she went to school full time. I on the other hand worked as many hours as I could and took as few classes as my scholarship would allow. I really needed the money and the fewer classes I took, the less time I needed to study.

I wasn't ashamed to tell anyone about my shelter situation. When Joe found out, he insisted I stay with him but I refused. He was a nice enough guy, but I didn't feel comfortable accepting the offer. When Sara found out, she made the same offer. She only had a one bedroom apartment, but she said we could easily make the living room into a bedroom by standing up some dividers. She was hardly ever home and I knew I would probably be scarce as well. I knew less about her than I knew about Joe but I had a feeling in my gut that living with her would be okay. I told her I'd move in on three conditions:

1. I pay half of everything.

2. When her lease was up, we try to find a two-bedroom we could afford.

3. And, if she turned out crazy, I bailed.

She agreed.

Two people who aren't sleeping together living in a one bedroom apartment is quite the challenge even if you aren't there often. But we made it work for the rest of the time she had her lease. Turns out, she wasn't crazy, so we found something that had two bedrooms. Even with the limited hours I spent there, having my own real bedroom made a world of difference.

We still live in the same two bedroom apartment today. Sara is set to graduate soon but she's hoping she'll get a job in the city so she won't have to move. Otherwise, I'm going have to figure out an alternative solution. But I've decided not to worry about that problem until I have to. Right now I have to focus on studying. I almost have enough credits for an Associate's degree and I'm not sure if I want to continue past that. I'd still have the scholarship, so it makes sense but at the rate I'm going it'll be at least another three years for me to get my Bachelor's.

I had one goal: get away from Nancy and that town. I achieved that and with an Associate's degree, I would have options to make a decent living. But again, I'll cross that bridge when I get there.

One day at a time.

I head into work on a Thursday afternoon. I've spent all day at the library studying. The last thing I want to do is stand on my feet for the next eight hours and deal with drunks. But, it's good money. And I'm not sure I could leave Joe if I wanted to. He's got issues with his back and only comes in if it's necessary. He does the books at home and I take care of inventory and some other managerial concerns. We used to open at noon every day, but now we open at five in the evening. The afternoon business was slow and Joe couldn't handle being on his feet so much anymore.

Sara only works two nights a week now. She's been working on an internship for her degree and doesn't have a lot of time to squeeze in shifts. However, I make plenty of money to cover any household expenses she can't. And I don't mind. We've become decently close. As close as I can let myself get to anyone. Certainly as close as I've ever been to another person. I could even consider her a friend, I suppose.

It's about six-thirty and the crowd is starting to grow. There are three men sitting at the end of the bar who've been here since I opened the doors at five. They are already shitfaced and are beginning to get rowdy. I may have to kick them out.

As I'm considering this, a guy sits down on the opposite side of the bar. He's young. Close to my age, I'd guess. But he looks really worn out. He certainly looks like he needs a beer.

I'll take care of him first before I deal with the rowdies.

I walk over to his end of the bar. At first, he is looking down at a beer menu but when I get closer, his eyes travel north. But only when I speak does he look me in the face. "What can I do you for?" It's a stupid expression of a question, but Joe uses it all of the time and now it's kind of just habit to greet customers that way.

I take notice at what this guy was looking at before I spoke to him. I'm pretty sure he was staring at my tits. But what's new? They all do it. After I place a napkin down onto the bar in front of him, and ask him the question, his entire body freezes. He doesn't answer me. He doesn't move. The look on his face is peculiar. I give him a minute to figure out whatever the fuck it is that is going on in his head.

"Cat got your tongue? You want something to drink?"

No response. Great. Another stupid asshole who is so enamored to have boobs in such close proximity to his face that he's too stunned to order a fucking beer.

Except he's looking me straight in the eye and the look on his face is kind of weird. It's not a look of lust. It's more like he's listening to music in his head and studying every lyric of the song. This is wildly odd and I'm suddenly slightly uncomfortable. But the discomfort doesn't completely overshadow the fact that I'm also annoyed by this guy's refusal to answer a simple fucking question.

"Look, buddy, if you are going to sit there and do nothing but drool all night, you can take your ass elsewhere. That seat is for paying customers only."

I give him a stern glare to signal that I mean business. Finally, he clears his throat and looks at the menu. "Um, I'll have a pint of ah… um."

The rowdies at the other end of the bar are getting louder, so I need to try to hurry this guy along. I didn't know it was going to take him ten minutes to order a drink.

"We just tapped a good IPA from Colorado. Wanna try it?" He moves his hands down to his pants and wipes them off. He's sweating. What is with this guy?

"Yes." He squeaks out, like a little man child. No one his size should make sounds like that.

I head over to the taps and grab a glass. As I'm pouring the beer, I subtly look over my shoulder to find him staring at my ass.

I thought so.

I walk back to his side of the bar. "Here you go. Maybe this'll calm your nerves a little. You seem…pent up." I decide to use a sarcastic line and try to judge his response. I don't know why I even care but I feel like I need to know what is going through his head. I don't get a creepster vibe from him and that is very unusual for me.

Am I so tired that I've lost my scum bag radar senses? Maybe I'm weakened by all of the time I've spent looking at a computer screen while studying. Perhaps he is playing some Jedi mind trick on me.

I salt the napkin before I put down the beer.

"Thanks," he says as he sits up straight, makes some God awful noise, looks at me and smiles. He picks up his beer to taste it. For a moment, I fear I might have a Tyler Durden situation on my hands—he's a schizo. At first he was quiet, nervous and sweaty. Now he's flashing teeth and puffing out his chest like he's the most confident person on the planet.

I can't read him at all. And I also can't figure out why I'm so intrigued. But I don't have time to figure out his mystery. I decide to be brutally blunt. That usually scares them away. He'll finish his beer and leave and then I can get back to my normal.

I point my thumb over my shoulder toward the beer taps. "Did you enjoy staring at my ass while I was standing over there?"

He chokes on his beer, "Excuse me?"

"You were checking out my ass when I was pouring your beer. Did you like what you saw?"

I put more flirt into my voice than I meant to. I'm trying to scare him away not lure him in. Right? I mean, he is a cute one, and I have a sense that he's not the run of the mill arrogant pain in the ass that generally hangs out here. He's quirky, though. I'm interested to see how he answers the question.

"Actually, I did."

Honest.

But it didn't piss me off.

Interesting.

"A guy who admits that he was checking out the goods. I like that."

"Well I didn't figure you'd be wearing those jeans if you didn't want people taking a peek. And as long as I'm being honest, you know what else I checked out?"

Okay, maybe he *is* a douche. I swear if he says I have nice tits, I'm hosing him with the seltzer sprayer. I lean in towards him. "Yeah, what's that, stud?"

I place my left hand on the top of the nozzle, positioned for action.

Ready...

Aim...

"Your eyes," he proclaims, and I have to take a second to register what he actually just said.

Wait. What? Did he say...eyes?

I try not to act shocked. But I am just that. Shocked.

I disengage the sprayer.

"My eyes," I say, as matter of fact as I can, trying to tamp down the surprise. I decide to cover that feeling with a bit of sarcastic, bitchy humor. "Well, that's new. You aren't some weirdo eye fetish guy, are you? You don't have like a bunch of women's eyeballs pickling in a jar under your bathroom sink, do you?"

He laughs. And I catch myself thinking about how beautiful his smile is.

I've never considered a man's smile beautiful before.

And then, as quickly as I finished my humorous accusation of him being a psychopath, he volleys back a response, "Of course not. That would be ridiculous. I keep the jar on my nightstand so I can see it just before I fall asleep." Instantly, I laugh. I can't help it.

Oh my God, he has a beautiful smile and he's good at picking up on my humor.

This is unusual. And quite nice.

What is going on here? My brain is muddled with thoughts that are foreign to me. Thoughts that almost have me tripping over my own tongue.

Keep it together, Livy. He's just a boy, for crying out loud. You have met those before.

I recover from whatever brain prolapse I was having and respond back with a somewhat forced smile. "Of course. That is entirely more appropriate and acceptable. What was I thinking?" I say, not being able to produce a clever retort. Our witty banter has ended all too quickly, by my feeble efforts, nonetheless, which I'm not used to. Normally, I could one up anyone with quick, whippy comebacks, especially the bar patrons.

I hear elevated voices from behind me. I have to go do my job now. But all I want to do is stand here and reconstitute my conversation with this guy. This adorable guy with chocolate brown hair and crystal blue eyes. Eyes that happened to be locked on mine. We've been staring at each other, motionless, wordless for at least thirty seconds now. There is a feeling in my chest. A pounding.

What the fuck?

"Yahtzee!" I hear someone yell behind me and it knocks me back into reality.

What is wrong with you, Livy?

"Well, I hope you enjoy the beer. I'm Livy. I have to take care of those drunk bastards over there. Let me know if you need anything, okay?"

"Sure thing, Livy," he says and smiles that beautiful smile.

I walk back toward the rowdy bunch hoping I can get them to cash out and leave. "You guys ready to call it a night?" They're all laughing at something when the middle guy looks at me.

"Nope. Think we'll have 'nother round," he slurs.

"And shots!" the guy on the right adds.

"Come on, guys, I think you've had plenty." I look at their hands, all of them sporting wedding rings.

"Why don't you head home to those sweet wives of yours?"

Middle Guy's face changes from happy to dark. "We said we want 'nother round. And shots." The last two words come out slow and I hardly understand what he says.

"How about this? I can cash you out and you can either call it a night or go slosh around someone else's bar. Those are your choices." I head toward the cash register.

"I'm the customer, bitch!" Middle Guy says in my direction. "You're the bar wench and the wench gets the customers what they want!"

Great. Fuck it. I'll cash them out later. If any of them dispute an unsigned credit card slip later on I have justification and video footage on my side. I head toward the opening of the bar and walk over to the drunken assholes. I decide to take on Middle Guy first since he seems the least lucid.

"Alright, buddy. Time to go. You don't get to call me names and expect me to let you stay." With his back toward me, I take his right arm and twist it behind his back and I use my other hand to grab his left ear lobe. This generally produces enough discomfort in people to get them to do what you want them to do. Especially drunk people. I pull him off the bar stool and walk backwards to the entrance. "Come on. I'm not putting up with this shit. It's way too early in my night for this."

"Let go of me, you bitch!" Middle Guy loudly slurs.

"Will do, as soon as you're outside," I assure him.

I make it about half way to the door when the other two guys approach me, trying to get me to let go. They start pulling at my arms. Middle Guy yelps. I can hear chairs rustling in the background. People are getting uncomfortable or are wondering if they should help.

"Hey!" I scream at the two trying to pry me away. "Let me explain something. I've got a death grip on your pal here. Anything you try to do to get me to let go is only going to make me squeeze and pull harder on your friend. It would be in *his* best interest if you just follow me to the door and leave with him. "

I wait for some type of acknowledgement of understanding but I get no response.

"You heard the lady, fellows. Now, I suggest you take her advice or you'll have me as a problem too."

I look over my shoulder and it's the boy who couldn't speak. Man, rather. He's tall. Taller than me.

"Fine. *Jesus.* Just fucking let me go. I'm outta here," Middle Guy says. After I take a brief moment to convince myself he's telling the truth and that potential trouble is not imminent, I let him go. He turns and looks at me while massaging his shoulder. "Damn girl, I thought you were going to rip my arm off."

"Good. Don't come in this bar again with that mouth or that attitude. Now go!" I look at his two wingmen letting my eyes deliver the same message to them. At once they all transition their eyes from me to the man behind me and then quickly make their way out the door.

Once they are gone I turn around and look up at this chivalrous man but I make sure that when I look in his eyes I don't let on that I might be swooning. Because that was the nicest thing anyone has ever done for me. No one has ever made an effort to protect me. I try to look generous but not overly enthused.

"Thanks. Not sure I could have handled all three at once."

He smiles. "I think you could have." He points to his empty glass on the bar. "But I needed a refill and I knew lugging all three of those fuckers was going to take some time so I decided to help out."

I don't want to but I smile and let out a tiny chuckle. "Well sir, would you like another IPA?"

"Yes I would. Thank you. My name's Jeremy." He holds his hand out for a shake. I grip his hand firmly and shake once.

"Nice to meet you, Jeremy".

Seven

Jeremy

Nobody expects the Spanish Inquisition

"Come on. A drink? Coffee? Some cheesecake?"
I met Livy last Thursday. I came into her bar and she rendered me speechless by just asking me what I wanted to drink. Then I watched her strong arm a drunk guy from his bar stool and proceed to literally throw him out while his other henchmen gave her shit about it. I have to admit that while that was the single coolest thing I've ever seen a woman do, I couldn't just stand there and watch them treat her that way. I had no doubt she could handle it. Hell, before that happened I was confident she was going to throw me out for not ordering a drink. But I wanted to help. Before I knew it, my whole body had jumped from the bar stool and was hovering over her in no time. I didn't really think through my actions. It was automatic. I wanted to protect her even though I knew she didn't need to be protected. I've never had that kind of feeling in my gut over a girl before. I don't even know her. Saying that she's *my bartender* is as possessive as I can get, but for some reason I wanted those guys to know that she was mine to protect.

That night of the scuffle, I stayed in my barstool until last call. I nursed two beers after my first one and had a few bowls of mixed nuts for dinner. I didn't move from that spot all night. Not even to pee. I passed the time with the sports channel on the TV mounted up behind the bar. Livy came over and chatted me up a few times but she was pretty busy most of the night. I couldn't leave without getting her number. After everyone had filtered out and I was the only one left, Livy walked over to the entrance, dead-bolted the door and turned off the outside neon sign.

"You locking me in for the night?" I asked.

"Seems that way since you haven't moved from that spot in over six hours."

Wow, had it been six hours? I looked at my phone to check the time. One a.m. Shit.

"Um, well, sorry." I stood and my legs nearly gave out because I'd been immobile for so long. As I grabbed the bar's edge for stability, I tried to finish my sentence. "I didn't want to leave without…"

By then, Livy was back behind the bar, bringing up a bottle of brown liquid from a shelf underneath. "You drink bourbon?" she asked, as she grabbed two small glasses from the sink rack. She headed towards me with glasses and bottle in hand.

"It's not my first choice, but I don't hate it."

She poured a generous amount into each glass and slid one my way.

"No ice?" I contested.

She was already in the middle of her first sip. Her eyes looked over her glass at me and she slowly shook her head no. Her mouth was occupied but her eyes said a million words all at once.

It's free booze, douche bag.

This is how you are supposed to drink it, moron.

Drink it like a man, you pussy.

I'm really glad you stayed.

I hope you stick around.

I picked up my glass and tilted it her way first to say cheers. I took a sip. It was smooth but still burned going down. But it wasn't bad.

"So, Jeremy, what's a guy like you doing slumming in my bar?"

"I've never been here before. Someone said you had Stella on tap, usually, so I decided to check it out. Turns out it's just my kind of spot. Great scenery." I smiled.

"We do usually keep Stella on tap. But you didn't drink Stella."

"To be honest, my brain got kind of jumbled when...you...you flustered me somehow. Then you mentioned the IPA. Thought I'd try it. It's very good so I decided to stick with it."

She gave me a little smile. She didn't blush but her eyes told me that she didn't detest me.

After finishing her first glass of bourbon, she pours another. "Well, I gotta clean up so..."

"You want some help?" I asked on impulse. I figured it was either that or I'd have to go home. I didn't want to go home just yet.

"Uh, sure," she replied with a questioning inflection on the last word. "But I keep a clean bar and I don't put up with half-assed work."

Challenge accepted. "That's good because I don't do half-assed work."

So we cleaned and then we both sat at the bar and had a few more drinks. We talked for hours and I laughed harder than I had in a long time. She's got a twisted sense of humor. And her laugh is incredible. We didn't talk about anything serious or personal, just random stuff. Like how many legs a spider would actually have to break before it couldn't walk anymore. We decided on three because four would be at the fifty percent mark and would be too much of a burden on the other legs. Or, how the city came up with the crazy design of the little vehicle that the parking meter enforcer rides around in. It seriously looks like some kind of bubble pod that would be jettisoned from a space shuttle.

The only personal details I learned about her are that she's going to school and she has a roommate named Sara that also works at the bar. But even though we talked about nothing in particular, it was the best conversation I had ever had with anyone. Period.

Livy looked at her watch. "I should get going. I've got class in like four hours."

"Damn. I'm sorry I kept you." I felt bad for keeping her, but I still didn't want to leave.

"Don't worry about it. I'm a big girl. I can handle a late night and still manage class. I'm twenty-one not fifty-eight."

She looked at me but I couldn't tell if she was teasing me or giving me the what for. Then her eyes softened just as they had done a few times that night. "Besides, I had fun. It was nice to talk to someone who wasn't fall down drunk for a change. "

"It was fun. But I may be borderline fall down drunk. That bourbon was pretty good but I'm not used to drinking liquor."

"You gonna make it home okay?" she asked. *Well shit*, I thought to myself. I was the one who was supposed to be asking those kinds of questions to her.

"Oh yeah. I don't live far from here and I'm not that bad off. The beer nuts soaked up most of the alcohol."

"You didn't even eat dinner, did you?"

"Like I said, I was enjoying the scenery too much."

She smiled again. Absolutely the most beautiful smile. "Well, *you* are a big boy so if you say you're fine then I believe you."

She started walking towards the door to let me out. I suddenly remembered why I stayed there so long to begin with. She opened the door and stood to the side to let me walk through.

"Do you need me to walk you to your car?" I asked, hoping for a few more minutes with her.

"No thanks. I've got some things to shut down before I leave."

"Okay. I had fun. Thank you. Do you think I could call you some time, Livy?"

She smiled but put her hand on my chest and gently pushed me out the door. "Goodnight, Jeremy. Please be safe."

And she shot me down.

"You too, Livy," I said and walked away.

She closed and locked the door behind me.

That was Thursday. Now I'm here almost a week later and I can't even get her to have a slice of cheesecake with me. Since Thursday, I've been back every night. I've sat here until she closes, same seat as the first night. I help her clean and then we sit and talk just like the first night. I've asked her a few times for her number or if she'd go to dinner with me. Every night she says no or doesn't answer me at all.

"Jeremy, please. I can't. I don't have time to date anyone or go out. School and this bar consume nearly every moment I've got." She must have forgotten that she told me she had the night off tomorrow.

"So what do you do when you have the night off?" I ask.

"Study, usually."

"Livy, when is the last time you went out to eat or to the movies… or bowling…clubbing? Anything that doesn't involve work or school?"

She looks up to the sky as if she's thinking. "Well, the last time I went to a restaurant was when I first started working here and Joe insisted he take me to dinner for helping out so much. The last time I went to the movies I think I was five."

"Are you serious?" I ask, with a little more shock in my voice than I meant to let out. Her eyes go slightly wide with my reaction. She looks at me and nods. There is sadness in her eyes. I want to ask her why that makes her sad but she continues. "I went clubbing once with Sara a few months ago. She begged me for weeks to go with her so I finally did. She made me put on a dress and makeup. I hate both of those things."

She doesn't smile but it makes me laugh that she doesn't like to wear dresses or makeup. I've ever only seen her in jeans and she certainly doesn't need anything to enhance her beautiful face.

"I hated it." She continues. "I was uncomfortable all night. The music was too loud and a lot of drunk guys hit on me, which was extremely annoying. It was terrible. I will never do that again. I asked Sara not to try to force me to have fun again. I make my own fun just fine."

Until now, I've never met a twenty-one year old woman who didn't like to go out dancing with the sole purpose of making drunk guys drool.

"And also, I've never been bowling."

"What? How is that possible?"

She shrugs her shoulders. Getting information out of this girl is what I imagine to be the equivalent of interrogating a double agent spy.

"So. What do you do for fun?"

"I like to read."

"You like to read? For fun?"

"Mmmhmmm." She nods.

"What else?"

"Jeremy, I told you. Work. School. No time for fun."

"Oh for heaven's sake, you are twenty-one. There are plenty of college students who balance work, school *and* fun."

"Yep, that's what Sara said too. But I'm kind of content just doing what I do. What's wrong with that?"

"Nothing. You are right. If you are living your life the way you want to then there isn't anything wrong. But my biggest issue is that I'd like to spend time with you outside of the bar. In case you haven't noticed, I kind of like hanging out with you."

She smiles, "I've noticed."

"I'm not a bad guy, Livy. "

"I've noticed that too."

"So why the hesitation?"

She stares at me like she's trying to read my expression. Her eyes are so sad. She inhales.

"I really like you. And I'm scared I'll hurt you."

"It's just one date. "

"But it could be more. I've never met a guy like you. You aren't like all the handsy douche bags that I grew up with or that sit at this bar. You are kind and I appreciate that, but it scares the hell out of me."

She looks back up at the ceiling. She's pushing back tears. I've seen that maneuver from my mother before. With her eyes still pointing upward she confesses, "I have a terrible past and I don't want to tell you about any of it because I don't...well, I don't want to talk about it. And I certainly don't want your pity."

As she completes the last sentence she looks back at me with glassy eyes. There is so much sorrow. But her look also tells me she's not joking. She absolutely doesn't want sympathy from anyone.

"Well, we can solve that problem. I can take you to dinner and I promise not to ask you any personal questions about your past."

She shakes her head immediately. "No. One date might lead to two and three and eventually you are going to want to know and I don't want to talk about it."

I sigh. She's sitting here waving red flags right in front of my face telling me she's trouble, but I couldn't care less.

All I think about is her.

Her face, her hair, her eyes.

Her scent, her laugh.

Every moment I've spent with her plays on repeat in my brain 24/7. Even when I dream.

I don't want to quit her.

"Okay. How about this? Is it okay if I ask you three questions that are very generic and will not pressure you to divulge details about your past?"

"You can ask but I am not promising an answer."

I nod with understanding. She sits up straight, bracing for my inquisition.

"Ok. Are you running from the law?"

She chuckles, "No."

"Are you a convicted felon?"

"No."

"Are you an illegal alien, a murderer of any sort, or some type of prior drug king pin, Mafioso, or ex-gambling addict that owes some thug a lot of money?"

She smile big and laughs. "That was like five questions in one."

"I know. I was trying to cover all bases and I was running out of questions. Well?"

"No. I am none of those things."

"Okay then. If you are none of those things then I don't care about anything else. We can go on a million dates and I won't ask. If you want to tell me I will listen. My mom taught me how to be a good listener."

I smile but she winces just slightly. I've said something that struck a nerve. But I persist. "I like you. I really like talking to you. I don't know if I've ever laughed as much with anyone else. And you aren't bad to look at *and* you smell kind of nice."

I wink and she smiles back and actually blushes a little. I take a chance and reach out to her hand that's sitting on her lap. I squeeze it just a little. There is surprise in her face but I don't think she's going to smack me.

"Please, Livy. Let me take you to dinner. You don't have to dress up and I promise we'll have fun. No loud music. No drunk guys. Just you, me and some delicious food."

Please say yes, please say yes.

I feel like I wait an eternity for her to respond.

In the smallest voice I think she could possibly make she whispers, "Okay."

"Okay?" I have to confirm that I heard correctly. She nods. The physical confirmation is much clearer. I squeeze her hand a tad harder and I smile the biggest smile that my face has ever produced.

My heart nearly leaps from my body.

Calm down. It's just a date, you knucklehead.

Yep. Just a date. With the most beautiful, down to earth, badass and mysterious woman I've ever met.

We're both in trouble.

I know I'm never going to want to let her go and I get a sense she is going to try to convince me, or herself, why she can't stay.

Eight

Livy

Defrost

JEREMY. IS. AMAZING.

Women all over the planet profess that about the guy their smitten with but Jeremy.

Is.

Truly.

Amazing.

And I really hate using the word *amazing* to describe him. That term is too common in conversations these days. Sara uses the word *amazing* like most people use the word *the*. Maybe she's rubbing off on me finally. I don't know, but *amazing* is the only word I can think of to describe him. There has to be a better word—*adorable, hilarious, courteous*? But with *amazing* you kind of roll all of those other adjectives into three easy syllables.

And yes, I also used the word *smitten*. Another word I have scoffed at every time I've seen it in a book I've read. *Smitten. Psssh.* Dumbest fucking word in the dictionary if you ask me. Correction—if you had asked me a few weeks ago, that is. Now, I understand that *smitten* is for real.

And I feel like the biggest fucking idiot for feeling this way. *Smitten* and I are not friends. A guy walks into my bar and in under a week, I am all googley eyes and puppy love. I can't stop smiling. All I think about is his stupid adorable face and his annoying beautiful eyes and his wickedly large, strong masculine hands.

I'm Livy, the girl who never smiles. The girl who uses the word *fuck* more than Sara uses the word *amazing*, if for no other reason than to just scare people so they'll stay away. The girl with no soul.

And now I'm *smitten*.

Fuck me.

After a week of his persistence and habitual presence at the bar, I finally caved. I agreed to go out with him. He was more stubborn than me and it pissed me off a little. But it was also a little appealing. He got my humor and understood my point of view. He always had a positive counterpoint to any negative argument I had about the world from my eyes. He was easy to talk to and fun to laugh with. Laughing with anyone wasn't something I normally took part in but it's fun with Jeremy. The laughter mixed with the shallow conversations on general broad topics felt nice. It was like we had been old friends who hadn't seen each other in years and picked up right where we left off.

On our first date, I asked if he'd pick me up at the bar. Even though I felt like I knew him better than anyone else I knew already, he was still technically a stranger and I didn't want him picking me up at the apartment. Not to mention it was kind of a hot mess since Sara and I are there only long enough to make a mess but not clean. I can't remember the last time I did laundry. We try to keep dirty dishes to a minimum. Since I left Nancy, I've become kind of averse to doing chores. I was the one who did everything around that house. Laundry, dishes, floors—you name it. From the time I was about five years old, I was the sole chore-doer.

Now, I couldn't care less if the bed is made or the bathroom floor has hair on it. I turned into a tiny bit of a slob. But Sara doesn't protest so why make the effort? With Joe's bar though, I'm a neat freak. Spilled beer gets gross and smelly if it lingers too long. And it's hard to have a busy shift without spilling a little beer here and there. Plus, it's Joe's business and livelihood. And if I don't take pride in it, the bar could lose customers and I could lose my job. I wasn't joking with Jeremy when

I told him I don't clean half-assed. With the exception of the financial investment Joe has in it, this bar is mine just as much as it is his. I'd be lost without it.

Jeremy met me at the bar around seven. I assumed we'd leave right away but he suggested we sit and have a drink first. It wasn't too busy since it was the middle of the week. I kind of felt weird sitting on the other side of the bar, being a customer and having Sara wait on me. But she said she didn't mind at all. So we sat and had a pint each. I asked him if he liked Porter, a rich, dark beer, and he shrugged and said he didn't think he'd ever tried one. So Sara poured us a couple of Porters and we sat at the bar and chatted just as we'd done so many times before over the past couple of days. But this time was different. We were on a date and we were surrounded by other people.

Prior to the date, I told him I was going to wear jeans and he seemed okay with that. I wore the extra snug ones though and a cute top in my favorite color that accentuated my curves and my eyes. Jeremy came in wearing a blue button down shirt, untucked, sleeves rolled up and khakis. I think he was conveying the notion that he was okay with us both being casual. The days he had come into the bar before that night, he also wore button downs and slacks, but he was a little tidier with his shirt tucked in and his sleeves rolled down and buttoned properly. Even though there was nothing wrong with his normal, straight laced attire, I kind of dug the more casual Jeremy.

His shirt also emphasized his dark, crystal blue eyes as my green shirt did mine. He had a five o'clock shadow so his face was surrounded by his dark, chocolate hair which made his eyes the focal point of my attention even more.

Jeremy was handsome. Extremely handsome. I would never admit it out loud, but I've imagined many times what was under those clothes. Arms. Abs. Ass. Dick.

Nope, I would never say that out loud. If anyone paid close attention they'd see me blush slightly when I thought about what Jeremy looked like naked. I've never fantasized about a man's penis. Hell, I've never even fantasized about having a man naked in my bed. Sure, there were plenty of good looking men that came into the bar. Men of all kinds—suits, blue collar, meat heads. But I never imagined what it would be like to have sex with any of them.

After the Porters, he paid and left Sara a generous tip. He stood and lifted his arm, elbow pointed in my direction signaling for me to stand and wrap my arm around his. I did and we headed out for what turned out to be the absolute best night of my life. At that point anyway. I would soon discover that every moment I spent with Jeremy was the best moment of my life.

We headed to the bowling alley. Something I'd never done before. The town I grew up in didn't have a bowling alley. Jeremy gave me the run down on how it worked and how the game was scored. He suggested I start with an eight-pound ball. The first time I rolled it, it went air born more than half the length of the lane before it hit the ground landing with a deafening bang. I was so embarrassed Jeremy assured me it was ok and handed me a ten-pound ball. After a few rolls down the lane, I settled for a fourteen-pound ball. Jeremy said he was a little impressed but not surprised after the altercation with the assholes I had the first night we met. Even though I was more comfortable with the weight of the ball, I still managed to make about half a dozen gutter balls. I think it wasn't until the fifth frame that I actually knocked down three pins. I was elated. I jumped and clapped and spun around like I'd won a game show. Jeremy ran up to me without hesitation and hugged me. I didn't hesitate to let him hug me either. In that embrace I got a good inhale of his earthy cologne and his scruffy face brushed up against my cheek. His hold on me was strong but endearing. It was like we had known and loved each other for an eternity. It was weird but it was also comfortable. The best part about it was that interaction between Jeremy and me was automatic. There wasn't awkwardness and I didn't shy away from his subtle hand touches. I was never a *touchy feely* kind of person but with Jeremy it was natural.

But this hug. It was warm. It made my insides feel like I had just drunk hot cider. I wasn't used to hugs and maybe the unfamiliarity made it seem that much more special. I don't know, but I loved that hug and I knew that I would cherish the first time Jeremy hugged me forever. Even though it was a hug over knocking down stupid bowling pins. After that hug I started wondering what it would be like to kiss Jeremy. What it would be like to make out with him in the car until the windows fogged up. What it would be like to have his hand up my shirt while he was kissing my neck.

Not until the end of that date, however, had I started thinking about our bodies wrapped around each other naked, tangled in sheets, sweaty and out of breath.

After bowling, we went to dinner at an Italian trattoria. I only call it a trattoria, because it had the word *trattoria* in the name of the restaurant. I mentioned to Jeremy that I always thought that word was a bit pretentious, despite the meaning of the word translating to something along the lines of "small, quaint restaurant". Jeremy told me to relax and that this place was old, and indeed small and casual. It had been owned by generations of the same Italian family and the food was to die for. He also told me there was nothing more romantic than pasta, wine and tiramisu. Jeremy was talking about romance. Never in my life had I heard a guy say the word "*romantic*". Maybe on TV, but certainly not in real life.

The hostess motioned to the direction of our seat and Jeremy followed me with his hand at the small of my back the entire time. She led us to a booth and I sighed a little. I wasn't a fan of dates that involved booths. However, when we sat down, he sat across from me. I don't know why I was surprised but of course he did. That's what normal guys that don't live in the freakville town I grew up in do.

And that's when it hit me. He's that guy. The one I envisioned years ago, sitting on the edge of my bed while counting the days to turn eighteen. The guy I'd finally find that would want to look me in the eyes and talk to me instead of pinning me in between him and the wall and trying to cop a feel the whole evening.

I wasn't ignorant enough to believe he was *the one*, as in we would run off into the sunset and live happily ever after. But I did begin to feel a glimmer of hope that he could help me see and understand aspects of humanity that I'd never witnessed in real life, only in fiction. He was civil and he treated me like a person. Not to mention, he made me laugh. I cannot reiterate that enough. It has truly only been since I met

Jeremy, that I understood how good it felt to laugh. And that feeling is a large part of the reason that I'm smitten. Now that I've got a taste of that feeling, I would be distraught if I knew I would not get to have that again if I stopped hanging out with him.

The dinner was fabulous. We stuffed ourselves with the absolute best pasta, bread, salad and red wine. And tiramisu! Something else I had never experienced before. The waiter said it had just been made that day. It was decadent and heavenly. Chocolate coffee flavored silk. I don't know if filling yourself to the brink of explosion is really romantic but I do know I enjoyed every sip and every bite. And every word that Jeremy and I exchanged. Every laugh. Every gaze. Every moment with him at that restaurant, as he sat across from me at the booth, never once touching me. Just food, wine and conversation.

After dinner, I asked Jeremy to take me back to the bar so I could help Sara close up. It was a weeknight so the bar closed a little earlier than on the weekends. He obliged and even stayed to help clean like he had done every other night for a week. I told Sara to go home and we would lock up because she not so subtly mentioned she was dead tired and had to get up early. I really think she didn't want to be our third wheel and Jeremy insisted on staying and walking me home.

She winked at me slyly as she walked out the door.

Jeremy and I sat down and had our traditional few glasses of bourbon.

Well, if you call doing the same thing every night for a week tradition.

We talked some more and laughed so much. And after we finally locked up, he walked me home.

There was no way he was seeing the inside of my apartment just yet. Not until I made an effort to clean it. But a walk to the front door would be harmless.

On the way, Jeremy explained to me where he lived. It was only a few blocks from the bar but in the opposite direction of my house. Mine was only a few blocks away as well. Midway through our stroll, Jeremy grabbed my hand and held it while we walked. He didn't ask but he didn't demand it either. He just did it and I didn't waver. When his fingers touched mine, I swear there was a blue arc of electricity between our palms before our hands joined together completely. It was probably just static from the crisp night's air, but either way, it put my heart into over drive and I was thankful it was dark because as hot as my face felt, I'm certain it was at red as it's ever been. I felt like such a juvenile for feeling this way over a boy at my age, but I tried to keep my humility in check. I would think about why he made me feel this way later, in the comfort of my own quiet, dark room, when thoughts of that curious nature always seem to swirl in my head. We walked hand in hand for what seemed like hours. But in reality the walk to my house was only about ten minutes.

We stopped at my stoop. And even though there was a brief moment of silence between us, there was still no awkwardness. It was more like we were both just taking it all in and savoring the moment. We were facing each other and although I was cherishing every second, my mind was racing about what would happen next, in between this moment and the moment we said goodnight to each other and I closed my front door behind me.

Jeremy, still holding my hand and facing me, grabbed my other hand. My legs began to feel gelatinous. He smiled and even in the dark, I could see the sparkle in his blue eyes.

"Livy," he said, and I think I began holding my breath.

My mind was still racing. My heart was pounding and my legs were melting. All more things to consider when I'm trying to fall asleep tonight.

"I don't know about you but I had such a great time tonight," he said.

Still holding breath. Heart still pounding. Legs disintegrating.

"I really like you, Livy. When I'm around you I feel like no one else exists. Nothing else exists. It's hard to really put into words how you make me feel because it's so new to me. I've never felt this way about anyone. When I'm away from you, you are all I think about. But not in a lusty, I wanna jump your bones kind of way."

That was blunt.

"I mean, not that I don't want to jump your bones because you are fucking sexy as hell."

Holding. Pounding. Jell-O.

His brazenness was turning me on and at that moment, I began tingling.

"But what I think about most is your laugh and your hair and the way it smells like peaches. I think about how hilarious you are and how I could talk to you for days without thinking about doing anything else. I think about how hard you work and study and I definitely think about how glad I was to have walked into your bar that day to get to witness you dragging a guy by his ear out the door because you were tired of his shit."

Holding. Pounding. Jell-O. Tingling.

I think I smiled but I'm really not sure. It was hard to move but I drank in every word he said. No one had ever said anything like that to me before. Telling me what he likes about me that doesn't include comments about my plump ass or my nice tits. Telling me that he noticed my hard work and my sense of humor. That he liked ME and not just my body, although I can't say I didn't like him calling me sexy. Countless men, and boys thinking they were men, had called me sexy in my lifetime and I had always scoffed at that sentiment. But the word sexy coming from Jeremy's lips was well received by my ears as well as the rest of my body.

"I really hope I get to spend more time with you, Livy. I'll hang out with you every night after the bar closes if that's all you want. But I really would love to take you out again."

I finally exhaled. My heart calmed but only just a little. My legs were surprisingly still solid and standing but they were buckled and I feared I could pass out at any minute. I half way thought about jumping up and wrapping my legs around his waist, and kissing him until we both had no air left in our bodies. But I didn't.

I squeezed his hands, "You can still come to the bar any night you'd like. I do enjoy the company."

I could tell he was getting nervous about what I was going to say next.

I smiled a big toothy, dorky smile. I bowed my head and kicked my leg out a little like a school girl. All of my actions were strictly involuntary and I was surprised I could even speak correctly. I think I even batted my eyelashes a little bit. What the fuck?

I took a deep breath to compose myself. "But I would also very much like to go out with you again, Jeremy." I was being honest. I looked up at him, "I had so much fun. Thank you."

Then he smiled the big toothy, dorky grin. "I'm glad to hear you say that. And I am also very relieved that I can tell you are being honest because I can see it in your eyes."

I wasn't sure how to respond to that but I didn't have to. He leaned towards me and before I knew what was happening he kissed me.

But not on the lips. He kissed me on the side of my face, near the corner of my left eye. It was a light peck that lasted less than a second. It was unexpected and caused me to exhale sharply. Jeremy pulled back, seemingly unaffected by my reaction. "Have a good night, Livy. I will see you tomorrow." He released my hands and I instantly felt empty.

"You too, Jeremy."

He turned and walked away. He looked back twice before he rounded the corner at the end of the street. I just stood there for a few moments—relishing the lingering feeling of his lips on my face. I finally headed up the stairs and was relieved that Sara was not awake because I didn't think I could put into words the night I just had until I had time to process it for myself.

In my bed, before I fell asleep was the first time I really truly fantasized about Jeremy being naked. As I was lying in bed trying to calm down enough to sleep, analyzing why Jeremy turned me into this strange acting girl I'd never met before, my thoughts kept drifting only to him. I guess I couldn't really focus on why I acted as I did, because I didn't really care all that much. All I could see in my mind was Jeremy. The things he said to me on our first date stole my heart. He didn't want me just for my physical assets. He admired my mind and my strength and my determination. All the things he said he enjoyed about me switched on something carnal in me and all I could think of from that point on was Jeremy. Naked. With white hot lust in his eyes for no one but me.

It's been two weeks since the night Jeremy tapped on my heart and warmed it up. Before I met him I thought I was fine. I had school and a job I loved and I had Joe and Sara. I thought I was pretty complete. I had no idea what I was missing. It was something I'd never had so I didn't know I was lacking. It was laughter and sincerity and…and…well, I don't know. But what I do know is that I never knew how vacant my life was before I met Jeremy. My heart feels two times larger and I think the muscles in my face have strengthened three fold because of how much I've smiled lately. Even the regulars at the bar have taken notice. Some say I may have been replaced with an android because they didn't recognize me with the new facial expressions I had.

Sara told me once I had a resting bitch face and that it took quite a grand gesture to get me to smile.

"But not anymore," she teases. "Now you have a resting *in love* face". I look at her and roll my eyes. She's helping me clean up the apartment before she goes to work. Jeremy is coming over tonight and I'm going to cook him dinner. "I'm not in love, Sara. I've only known him like a month."

"So what? You love him and it's clear as day all over your face. There are no rules when it comes to who your heart decides to love."

"Sara, stop. I really do like him. But it's not love. I can't love him."

I'm lying through my teeth. I could love him. Maybe. But I don't know how it could last. I don't know how to be in a relationship. I don't know what love feels like. I don't know what it's like to love someone unconditionally or have that from someone in return. Growing up, I was either looked at as being a burden or an object. Never as a person worthy of love. But I moved on from that, and until I met Jeremy, I thought I was okay. As it turns out, I was really just a shell that was methodically wandering through life. I thought I had exactly what I wanted but I realize now that I was merely complacent.

Now there's Jeremy and I really don't know if what my heart feels is love or just elation that someone has come into my life for once that brings me what I can only describe as authentic joy. Whatever it is, I am absolutely terrified. I'm terrified I'm going to lose him but I'm also terrified about a future with him. There's no marriage or children in my future—I decided that a long time ago—and if whatever this is between us goes further I'm going to have to tell him that.

"It's not up to you who you love," Sara interrupts my thoughts. "And whatever you are thinking right now, stop. You are over analyzing something. I can see it all in your face. Just have fun with your handsome man and go where it goes. I don't know what screwed up your head in your past, but you are a good person, Livy. You are good to me and good to Joe. You deserve to be happy and if that boy makes you happy, just let him do it. Everything else will fall into place. I promise."

I nod at her. Sometimes I wonder if she can read minds. Or if thinking about Jeremy is weakening my ability to hide my feelings.

"Jeremy has gotten rid of your resting bitch face and that's worth more than your weight in gold." She points and winks at me. "Alright. I'm getting out of here unless you need anything else," she says, walking toward the door.

"I'm good. Thank you for helping."

"Of course! Have fun tonight. And stay out of my room."

"But your sheets are so soft." I wink.

"I'll buy you a set of your own for Christmas. "

"Seriously, you really have nothing to worry about," I say. "After what I've heard going on in there, I'm not setting foot in your hanky-panky room."

"Good to know. See you later."

As I'm dicing tomatoes, I hear a knock at the door. I nearly slice off my finger because my heart starts pounding and my breath hitches.

He's here.

I run to the door but compose myself before I check the peephole and open the door.

"Hi," he says, after I open the door. I catch his smile, then the flowers in his hand The bouquet is a mixture of flowers, but I can't even begin to tell you what kind they were.

"Hey. Come in." I can't. Stop. Smiling.

"I brought you these. I don't know if you like flowers but my mother says you can never go wrong with flowers."

He talks about his mom a lot. They are so close. I try not to let my disdain for Nancy show when he talks about his mom but it stings a little every time.

I take the flowers from him and smell them. "Thank you. They are beautiful. No one has ever given me flowers before."

He doesn't respond but I can tell he wants to ask me something. I turn and head toward the kitchen to find a vase. I'm not even really sure how to tend to flowers. I put some water in the vase, remove the ribbon from the stems and place the flowers in the vase. Maybe Sara will know what to do with them.

"How was your day?" he asks. I don't know what it is about the simple little questions like that he asks but they mean so much. He is asking me to tell him something because he wants to listen. He wants to know.

After I place the flowers on the dining table, I wash my hands and resume with the tomatoes. "It was good. I went to the bar early this morning to do inventory and did shopping for dinner. It's been sort of relaxing. How about your day?"

"Do you need some help with anything?" he asks.

"Um, sure. You can chop these veggies while I get the rest of dinner ready."

"Sure thing," he says. "My day was good. We are finishing up a business office renovation and my boss said I might get a bonus for completing the project two weeks early."

I head to the utility closet and grab the bag of charcoal I bought today. I pass back through the kitchen to make my way to the patio and stop. "That is great! It sounds like your boss really appreciates you."

"Yes, I think he does." He looks up at me. "Hey, what are you doing?"

"Going to get the grill ready," I explain. I want to ask him—*doesn't it seem obvious what I'm doing, given the charcoal and the direction I'm walking?* —but I let it slide and stay silent.

He seems perplexed. "Um, need any help with that?" Jeremy stops chopping and moves toward me.

"No, I've got it, thanks." I slide open the patio door and walk toward the grill.

He proceeds to follow me out the back door anyway. I pour the charcoal into the base of the grill and Jeremy is standing next to me with his arms crossed. He's smiling.

"Something funny?" I ask while lighting the coal.

"No." He chuckles and shifts his weight to the other leg. "What's on the menu tonight, grill master?"

"Steak. Filet," I answer.

"Sounds delicious," he says.

I smile and head back into the house now that the grill is started. He follows and returns to his chopping station. I check on the potatoes that are baking in the oven and pull out a bottle of wine from the pantry.

"Hey. That's the same wine from the restaurant we went to," he says.

"Yes, it is. It was so good. I'm not much of a wine person but I thought it would be good with dinner. I knew this label was a sure thing and I didn't want to try to guess on anything else."

"Good plan. I'm not really a wine person either but you're right. It'll be good with filet. "I grab the steaks out of the fridge and unwrap them from the butcher paper.

"You think the grill's ready?" he asks. He's not going to come out and say it, but he doesn't think I can handle a grill.

"No," I reply. "It won't be ready for another fifteen minutes or so. These have to sit and rest first. You shouldn't put cold filets on a grill. It'll make them tough."

Jeremy is looking at me funny. Like I have two noses or I've lost an eyeball. "What's wrong?"

"Nothing." He smiles and lets out a tiny, breathy laugh. "You surprise me every time we're together. You bounce drunk guys out of your bar. You drink whiskey and your favorite thing to wear is jeans, which I very much appreciate by the way."

I blush. In twenty-one years, I think Jeremy is the only person that has ever gotten me to blush.

"And now you are standing here, giving me pointers on how to prep a steak. I don't know if I can handle any more of these surprises. Granted it's all good stuff, but you just seem too good to be true."

Did he really just say that? I'm as ordinary as they come.

"What else is there? Just lay it all out for me."

"But won't that ruin the mystery?" I say jokingly.

He doesn't respond. He's four feet away and looking straight into my eyes. He has a half smile and I have no idea what he's thinking. I turn and walk over to the TV remote and hit the power button to turn on the flat screen that is hanging on my wall. Once the screen comes alive, I point to it and say, "This is my favorite channel."

He looks up at the TV and then back to me. Back to the TV. Back to me.

"You're fucking with me," he says.

I smile and shake my head no. "I watched SportsCenter this morning before I went to the bar. I've heard this is something most girls don't like. At least according to Sara, who points it out to me every time I watch it in her presence," I say, the last part a bit facetiously. "But I don't know why you are so surprised about it. It's always on at the bar."

"That's because it's a bar."

"No. It's because I like to watch it."

He takes four large strides to reach me and stops. He's so close to me I can see his pupils as they begin to dilate. I can hear my own heart pound in my ears. And maybe even his heart as well. He cups my face with his hands and grips my jaw. He pulls me in and kisses me. It's forceful. His hand moves back and his fingers tangle with my hair. His lips are pressed hard against mine. It hurts but I'm enjoying every second. I drop the remote and my hands start at his neck and make their way into his hair. It's so soft and I've imagined running my fingers through it a million times.

It's just as I envisioned.

Better.

Jeremy pulls me closer and our chests clash into each other. He moves one hand from my hair but keeps the other in place as if he's afraid to let me go. His other hand makes a journey to my shoulder then my arm and my side and lands itself on my ass with a gentle squeeze.

Oh dear God!

His mouth and his taste and his hands are spinning me high. I don't want this to end but if I don't regain control I'm going to rip his clothes off in one single movement. I clutch his hair and kiss him hard. He responds even harder. After this continues for what seems to be a lifetime, I place my hands gently on his chest and push. He resists and I nearly cave.

Fuck dinner.

But I push again and he releases me from his amazing death grip lip lock.

I'm breathing so heavy that it's making me light-headed. I'm hyperventilating over a kiss.

"Well. Shit. If I'd had known ESPN was such a turn on for you, I'd have mentioned it sooner."

Jeremy smiles his beautiful smile. He brushes hair from my face. "You are the most gorgeous woman I have ever known." He places his hand over my heart. "All the way through," he finishes in a whisper. I'm glad he still has his arm wrapped around me cupping my butt cheek because if not I think I would have passed out and fell straight to the floor.

With his hand on my chest I know he can feel my heart trying to push through my sternum.

Deep breaths, Livy.

I want to tell him thank you but I can't manage to speak. I just stare into his crystal blues.

"I hope you like me hanging around because I'm not going anywhere. You are one of a kind, Livy, and I want you all to myself."

Stay positive, Livy. Remember what Sara said. Have fun. Don't dwell on negative.

"I think I'm okay with that, Jeremy." I smile.

Stay in the moment.

Jeremy hugs me. It's a hug like the one from the bowling alley. He envelops me and I feel like it's just him and me and nothing else exists.

It's peace.

There is no past.

No future.

Just us.

Just now.

I wrap my arms around him and bury my face into his chest. We stay that way for a few moments until the oven timer beeps at us.

"Potatoes are done." I speak into his chest and the words come out muffled.

"Sounds that way."

"I gotta get the steaks on the grill."

"Okay." He doesn't move and neither do I.

Another minute passes and the timer beeps again. We finally let each other go and finish making dinner. Jeremy follows me out to the patio and watches every move I make with the steaks and the grill.

"You okay with medium rare?" I ask.

"That's perfect," he says. I look in his direction and he grins and covers his mouth with his hand.

"What now?" I ask.

"ESPN and mid-rare steaks? Are you sure you're not a guy? Are we going to have a belching contest later?"

I hang the tongs I have in my hand on the grill. Without a second thought, I use both hands to raise the bottom of my shirt up to my chin. "No. I'm positive I'm not a guy. If you want more proof I'll be happy to show you."

Jeremy freezes and I put my shirt down.

"We can have a burping contest if you'd like, but I'll have to switch out the wine with Guinness to even have a chance."

Jeremy remains frozen. I take the steaks off the grill and walk past him to go inside. He doesn't budge.

"Livy, this was the best steak I've had in my life. Color me impressed."

Jeremy wipes his mouth with a napkin and reaches across the table to grab my hand. "Everything was delicious. I may have to request lessons. The sauce you made for the steaks and the salad dressing you made were phenomenal. Did you bake that bread from scratch?" He's teasing me.

"No." I smile. "That came from the bakery across the street. Very fresh. I've never tried to make bread before but I don't think I could make anything like this."

"Are you serious? All this food you made yourself and it was so good."

"But that was easy. Making bread can't be that easy."

"So who taught you how to grill steaks and make salad dressing and mushroom sauce from scratch?"

"Food Network and YouTube."

"Seriously?"

I nod.

"So you are telling me that you learned how to grill from a video?" Jeremy asks, skeptically.

"A couple of videos actually. My granddad used to make steaks and they were my favorite. I watched videos on what kind of grill to get, what kind of meat to buy, how to let it rest, before and after you cook it, and how to tell the temperature by touch. It took me about half a dozen tries, but I finally got it right."

"Wow. That is amazing." Jeremy still has hold of my hand and gives it a squeeze. "Why didn't you just ask your granddad to show you how?"

I snatch my hand away immediately and begin gathering dishes as fast as I can. I don't want to answer him. And the thought of Nancy taking me away from my granddad all those years ago rushes to my brain. It makes me so angry that my hand begins to tremble and I drop a plate. Jeremy looks at me, concerned. I put everything I've collected into my hands back on the table. "Excuse me." I run to the bathroom and slam the door. I can't breathe and my face flushes.

Do. Not. Cry.

Do not ruin this date. Pull yourself together. Don't scare him away.

Or maybe you should tell him to go. He's going to ask questions you don't want to answer. What's the point? It's not going to go any further than this.

I start to cry. I slide down the wall and put my hands to my face, trying hard not to make a sound.

I don't know how long we lived with my granddad but it was the happiest I ever remember being. I was too young. We left his house in the middle of the night. I don't even know if he lived in the same state as where I grew up. I asked about him once, but Nancy told me to never ask again. I don't know his first name and I wouldn't even begin to know how to look him up. He's the only person besides Jeremy who's ever hugged me. We did a lot of fun things together too. He took me to the movies, to the park and to the library. He gave me the flashlight that I still have today and told me if I was ever scared in the dark to use the flashlight to chase the fears away. I miss him so much.

I stand up and pull myself together. I look in the mirror and freshen up my face.

My gut is telling me to tell Jeremy to leave, but I can still hear Sara in my head.

Just walk out there and go with your instinct.

I don't want to hurt Jeremy. But I'm so addicted to him.

I walk out of the bathroom undecided.

Jeremy is no longer in the dining room and the mess has been cleaned up. I look over into the kitchen and see him in front of the sink. Washing dishes. My heart swells.

"You don't have to do that. I have a dishwasher."

He looks up at me, smiles and winks. "I noticed. It was full. Of dirty dishes."

Shit. Busted.

"Well you still don't have to wash those. I can do it later."

"It's fine. It's just a few. Plus, I feel obligated after the magnificent feast you prepared for me."

"It was hardly a feast. But thank you. For the kudos and the dishes."

"You are welcome. I didn't know where your vacuum was. You may want to go over that spot by the table where the plate broke."

"I'll do that now before I forget." I head to the utility closet to grab the vacuum when Jeremy turns off the water. "Hey, Livy."

I pause at the sound of my name coming from his lips. I love hearing him say my name. "Yeah?"

"You okay? I'm sorry if I said something…"

"It's fine Jeremy. I'm fine."

He walks from around the counter and I see his hands. I burst out into laughter.

Uncontrollable laughter.

I snorted. "Oh my God, where did you get those?" I point to his hands which are fitted with pink, floral rubber gloves.

He looks down at his hands and turns them over a few times. "What? They were under the sink. My mom has some just like this. I worked hard getting the calluses I have on these hands. I don't want to ruin them with conditioning dish soap." He air quotes the last three words. I begin my belly laugh all over again. Another snort emerges. He shrugs his shoulders and returns to the sink, continuing with the washing. I give the floor a quick vacuum and then head into the kitchen to help him finish up the cleaning.

"Do you want some more wine?" I ask as I grab our two glasses.

"Sure," he says, wiping the counter top. I pour some wine and hand him his glass. He's leaning against the counter facing me with his legs crossed and his sleeves rolled up. Sexy as hell. I try not to make it obvious how much I want him to be naked. I sip my wine.

"Livy," he starts.

Say it a thousand more times please.

"I am really sorry. I feel terrible. I shouldn't have asked. I was just trying to make conversation. Not trying to pry about your past."

I inhale and hold my breath a second or two before I exhale. "It's okay. Really. My family is a sore subject. I'd rather not talk about it. But, you didn't know."

He sets down his glass and begins moving toward me. I put my glass down as well because I don't know what's about to happen. But I do know that I don't want spilled red wine or more shattered dishes.

He's right in front of me. He places a hand on my cheek. "Are we okay?"

Be happy. Have fun.

I look up at him and nod, but I'm lying. I don't know if I can do this. I'm so scared.

"I think it's okay to be scared, Livy."

Seriously? How is everyone a mind reader all of a sudden?

"I'm scared," he admits. "I know we haven't known each other that long, but I know I don't want to lose you. You are pretty awesome and you have no clue how much."

There it is again. The breath holding, heart pounding, wobbly knees syndrome. How does he do this to me? I really want to tell him how he makes me feel too. He's so open about how he feels about me and I'm standing here thinking about what it would be like to put my hand around his...

"Livy?"

"Yes?"

"Are you listening to me?"

Be honest.

"I'm trying to, Jeremy. And I want to tell you how you make me feel but I can't seem to put words together."

He removes his hand from my cheek "Try. I'm really interested to know."

Inhale. Exhale.

"Okay."

Inhale. Exhale.

"I've never really dated anyone because I learned pretty quickly that most guys attracted to me are only interested in what's underneath the threads." I place my hands on my boobs for articulation. Jeremy's eyes go wide.

I'm such an idiot.

I clear my throat.

"But you talk about how you like things about me that aren't physical. And I really like that. It..."

I have his full attention, but I can't say it.

"It what?" he asks

Inhale. Exhale.

"Before our first date I liked you because you were so easy to talk to and you never once tried to make moves on me. It was nice. But it was nice like he's-a-great-pal kind of nice."

"Um?" he begins.

"Let me finish, please. At the end of our first date you told me how you liked my laugh and my work ethic and it seriously threw me for a loop. And since then…"

"Since then?" Jeremy repeats.

God, I can't believe I'm about to say this. I look into his eyes, unwavering.

"Well it really kind of…turned me on."

His eyebrows raise.

"I mean, I've never been really turned on by guys before. I thought I had but once you said those things I knew what I felt at that moment was the real thing. You were standing there telling me all those sweet things about how you were attracted to my mind, while being as non-physical as possible and I was standing there thinking how I wanted to throttle you and rip our clothes off."

Jeremy audibly swallows and clears his throat.

Is he sweating?

Wrap it up, Livy, so he can run away.

"And that's all I've thought about since. You in my bed. Or the couch. Or the countertop. I like your sense of humor too. And your smile. And I like that you listen to me when I talk. But I love your cologne and the way your hair feels in my fingers and you are lucky that damn timer beeped before dinner because otherwise we'd be on that living room floor right now, naked and hungry."

That should have done it. Too much information. He's terrified. Exit stage left.

Instead of doing an about face and bolting, Jeremy picks me up and sits me on the counter. He locks his gaze with mine briefly, then kisses me with the same magnitude as before. I throw my arms over his shoulders, fingers instantly in his hair. I wrap my legs around him and pull him as close as I possibly can. He smells so good. My hands decided to explore and slide down to his biceps, which are quite exquisite. I reach down and grab his ass. Holy Jesus, it's such a nice ass. Jeremy groans and lifts me off the counter and begins walking towards the living room. He breaks our kiss momentarily and tilts his head. "This floor?"

I nod. No time for words. Back to kissing please. He gets the message and kisses me again. His lips move away from mine and to my jaw line and neck as he lowers me to the floor. My whole body is tingling and my heart may just literally explode. What a mess that would be. The first guy that actually makes me feel this way and I might just die before we even do anything serious.

He puts his hand under my shirt and brushes it over my stomach.

"I've wanted to touch you since the first time I saw you, but I was scared you'd kick my ass."

I laugh.

"And when you flashed me in the back yard earlier, I thought I was going to lose it."

"What's a girl to do? You were questioning my femininity." I bat my eyelashes.

He kisses my neck again and moves to my collarbone. He moves his hand up, still under my shirt and runs his fingers over my bra. The sensation I have from the kissing and from his hands working simultaneously is overwhelming. I let out a tiny groan of my own.

"God, Livy. You are so fucking sexy."

He said my name.

He's kissing my chest just above the neckline of my shirt.

His hands are inching their way under my bra.

My body is going to burst into flames.

Noises are coming from my mouth that I'm not sure I've made before.

My fingers are in his hair, writhing and begging him for more.

I never want this to end.

I hear the front door unlock.

"Livy?"

It's Sara and she sounds upset.

Jeremy bolts upright and straightens his shirt. And then my shirt.

He grabs my hand and pulls me up. I look at the clock on the wall.

It's only eight. She shouldn't be here. She should be working.

Something is wrong.

"Sara?" I make my way towards her. I see her face and she's been crying, but her look makes it obvious that she knows what she walked in on. She puts her hand to her mouth and begins to cry. "I'm so sorry," she murmurs softly. "I tried to call you like a hundred times."

"My phone is charging in my room. I never heard it ring. Sara, what's wrong? You are scaring me. Are you okay? Are you hurt?"

She shakes her head and I instantly feel relief.

"It's Joe. He was at the bar tonight doing some kind of paperwork. I mentioned to him that one of the taps was floated and he said he'd change it out. I told him I'd do it, but he insisted. Twenty minutes later, the tap was still empty so I went back to change it myself. I figured Joe just forgot or something. But when I got back to the storage room…"

Sara starts crying harder. I hug her and stroke her hair. Jeremy is in the room with us now and he places a hand on my shoulder. "Shhhh. Sara, what happened?"

She pulls back. "Joe was lying on the floor. Unconscious. With a full keg sitting on his chest." She could barely manage to get the words out.

"Oh my God, is he okay?" Something in my brain triggers and I go on autopilot looking for my keys. I don't really know what Sara says after that. I hear "9-1-1" and "hospital" and "alive". That's it. Then I hear Jeremy say my name a few times while I'm rummaging around the coffee table for my car keys.

Jeremy grabs my arm and I recoil.

"Livy," he says gently.

"What?" I scream, still rummaging.

"What are you looking for?"

"I'm looking for my goddamned car keys! I have to go see Joe!"

Jeremy takes my arm again and I try to break away from his grip, which stiffens. He pulls me into him and hugs me tight.

"Please calm down. It's going to be okay."

I inhale his cologne and it soothes me.

I look up at him. "I have to go to the hospital," I say quietly.

"Okay. I'll drive you and Sara to the hospital. Both of you are a too upset to drive. Let's go."

I let go of him and head toward Sara and the door.

We get to the hospital in less than ten minutes but it is hours before they let us see Joe. At first it was because of the whole *we're not family* issue, but after I pleaded with the nurse and explained to her that we were the only family he had, she grew sympathetic and told us she'd let us know what she could find out. After a while, she called me to the counter and said that they were doing X-rays and cat scans to see the extent of the damage. She told me that Joe was conscious and stable and that she would let Sara and I go back as soon as she could. After three hours, the nurse finally let us back. I told Jeremy he could leave and we'd get a cab home. Then, I nearly ran down the hall to Joe's room. When I saw him, I thought I was going to cry. He looked so frail and puny. I sucked it up though because I didn't want to him to see the pain in my face and make him feel worse.

"Joe." I grabbed his hand and sat beside his bed.

"Livy. Hey, darlin'. You didn't have to come down here and check on me." His fingers wrapped around my hand.

And I cried. Dammit.

"Aw, hun. Don't be upset. I'm okay. I'll be up and about in no time."

I wipe my face. "What happened? Sara said she found you in the storage room KO'd with a full keg on your chest."

"Shit. Is she alright?"

"Yeah. She's here. She'll be in soon."

"You gals are too good to me."

"You are good to us too, Joe. Now spill it."

"Well you know I'm a stubborn old fart."

I raise an eyebrow and nod.

"Sara said she had a keg blown. She's such an itty bitty thing. I just wanted to help. Hell, it's *my* bar, for crying out loud. Anyways, I lifted the keg from the crate and my back went out and I fell backwards. The keg landed on me and strait up knocked the wind outta me."

"Oh Joe, you daft old bastard."

"I know. It was stupid."

"So…how'd you end up passed out?"

"Well, I tried to yell for help with what little breath I had. I tried to roll the keg off me but my back just wouldn't let me move. After a few minutes I got dizzy and that's the last I remember until they put the oxygen mask on me and loaded me on the stretcher."

"Please don't ever do that again. I'm so glad you are okay."

"Thanks, hun. Now I want you to go on home back to that boy of yours. Sara said you had a date tonight with that fella that sits around my bar all the time."

Dammit, Sara!

"It's fine, Joe. He went home. It's okay, really."

"Well, go get some rest then. You need it. You look like shit."

"Thanks. You really are a charmer, Joe."

"The ladies love me." He winks.

"Joe?" Sara pops her head in. When she catches sight of Joe, she immediately starts to cry.

"Aw hun, not you too," he says.

I kiss Joe on the forehead. "I'm gonna step out and give you two a minute."

I walk down the hallway and back to the nurse's station. I thank her a hundred times and then ask her if she knew where I could use a phone to call a cab. In the panic of it all, I didn't grab my phone out of my room before we left.

"Sure," she says. "There's a phone in the waiting room where you were before."

"Thank you." I hadn't even noticed. I turn the corner to make my way to the waiting room and I stop so suddenly that my tennis shoes squeaked against the linoleum of the floor.

"I thought you left."

Jeremy smiles and walks toward me, giving me his amazingly comforting bowling alley hug.

"Nope," he says with his chin on my head. "I wanted to make sure you two got home okay."

I squeeze my arms around him so tight. I'm falling for him. Hard. And I know that there is nothing I can do about it. I still want to rip his clothes off at some point. But right now I'm not thinking about that. I'm thinking about his kindness and altruism. I'm thinking about everything he likes about me and how I like those same things about him.

I told him my stupid rant about me going all feral after he said he liked my personality. He saw me go into full on rage mode when I couldn't find my car keys and he watched me pace this very floor beneath our feet for hours worrying about Joe.

He has witnessed a little of my crazy.

I told him to leave.

But he stayed.

"Thank you," I say to him and clutch my arms around him as tight as I can.

I can't let him go.

Ever.

He's amazing and I'm smitten.

Nine

Jeremy

One month later

JOE WAS IN THE HOSPITAL FOR A WEEK. HE HAD A CRACKED RIB AND a dislocated shoulder. The doctors also recommended that once he recovered from the injuries he sustained in the fall, he should have surgery on his back to fix the pain that caused him to fall in the first place.

Joe appeased the doctors by saying he would follow up. However, Livy told me that she had a feeling he never would. She said he's very stubborn and would die before he set foot inside an operating room.

Since Joe's accident, Livy has been going nonstop. For the week Joe was in the hospital, she stayed with him every free moment she had. She went to school, worked, studied and did the books for Joe. She barely slept or ate. I tried to remind her to do both, but she was very quick to tell me it wasn't my place to tell her what to do. She was wearing herself thin but never stopped. She had the focus of one of those guys at the town market who paint flowers on rice with a tiny toothpick of a paint brush. She made sure everything and everyone else was taken care of before she took care of herself, which was very seldom.

After Joe was released, Livy spent most of her time taking care of him, making sure he ate, got his meds right and even bathed properly. I went over there with her once. He was tired of being coddled and he called her a "wretched woman." She didn't care. She called him a "grumpy, ungrateful fuck" and carried on about her business of giving him the best care possible. She forced him to eat soup and bread. Then she told him that he smelled like a dead fish and threatened him with a sponge bath if he didn't get in there and shower himself.

At a distance, the words exchanged were harsh and cruel. But under the surface, if you examined their behavior well enough, you could tell she was trying to do what was best for him and he really did appreciate it.

Livy and I haven't spent any time together. I mean, there has been plenty of time spent in the same vicinity of each other. I still come by the bar after work, but instead of us talking, I clean the bar while she does closeout paperwork in an effort to crunch time so she can check on Joe before she goes home to study. Twice, I've convinced her to let me come home with her just so I could make sure she slept.

Tonight, we are at Joe's to make sure he's good for the night. Joe seems to be recovered nicely but Livy is continuing her over protective role.

"Livy," Joe says. "I'm fine. Look." He twists his torso and raises his arms over his head.

"Joe," Livy replies. "Don't be an ass. I can see you wince every time you move."

"Livy, I appreciate everything you've done for me, I really do. But if you come to my house one more time to check on me, I *will* fire you."

"Yeah, right. "

"No joke."

"Joe…" Livy huffs, and is ramping up for one of her epic protests. I've witnessed many over the weeks, having spent so much time with her and Joe.

"Livy, I'm fine. You have finals coming up and if you fuck those up because you refuse to listen to me, not only will I fire you, but I will put my foot in your ass, young lady."

"Who told you I had finals?" She glares at me and I raise my hands in innocence.

"Sara. She's worried about you. So am I. So is Jeremy." He points to me. "I can see it in your face, boy." Joe looks back at Livy and then at me again. "Jeremy, take this pretty little tired thing home, threaten *her* with a sponge bath if she doesn't shower on her own, and put her stubborn butt to bed."

"Yes, sir." I reach for Livy's arm and she extends it in my direction.

Joe looks back at Livy. "Come here, girl, before you go." He holds his arms out and she lunges to him for a hug.

"Thank you so much, Livy, for everything. Even though you are annoying as shit. It would have been really tough getting through this without you." He squeezes her and she squeezes back. Joe lets out a *hmmf* noise. His eyes squint a little as if he's in pain.

"See, old man. You aren't fine, but I'll leave you alone if that's what you want."

Joe places his hand on her shoulder. "Yes, you get back to being you. You've done so much for me, but it's come at a cost to you. You've lost weight, your eyes are so dark and you smile even less than you did when I first met you. I want the old Livy back." He pauses and looks up at me. "Not even the old Livy. I want the Livy that showed up when this guy started coming around." Joe points his thumb in my direction.

"Now go. Sleep. Get those finals done. And let Jeremy spend some time with you."

I'm feeling a little uncomfortable that he's talking about me like I'm not in the room, but I don't disagree with him. I miss Livy and I want her back so badly.

I get Livy home. We didn't speak in the car. I'm pretty sure she fell asleep but she would never admit it. She remains silent even now that we are in her apartment.

"Livy, let's get you to bed."

She turns to me and wraps her arms around me. "Thank you, Jeremy. I'm so sorry I haven't said that sooner. We are practically strangers and you have been here every day. I really can't describe how grateful I am for all that you've done."

"We aren't strangers, Livy. "

She nods into my chest but doesn't say anything.

"Come on, time to sleep," I say. I still have my arm around her and we begin walking towards the bed when she speaks again, with a small, squeaky voice, "Jeremy?"

We continue walking and make our way into the bedroom, "Yeah?"

"If you don't want to, please be honest." She pauses and is looking at me with her beautiful, tired eyes. "But...would you stay with me tonight?"

"Of course I will."

"Here, in the same bed with me, I mean."

"Sounds even better."

"I have an extra toothbrush."

"Bonus!" I firm my grip around her before I let her go.

She heads to her dresser and pulls out a t-shirt and shorts, then heads to the bathroom. "I won't be long."

After she closes the bathroom door behind her, I get lost in my own thoughts. I hate that she considers us still strangers. Maybe it's just her exhaustion making her wear the literal hat. I mean I know we still don't know a lot about each other. Strike that. I don't know a lot about her, but I've made sure to plug in bits and pieces about myself when I can. She never asks me, but I have a hunch that it's not because she doesn't want to know but because she doesn't want me to ask back. I don't care. I already know everything I need to about her. When she accepted my plea to let me take her out, she affirmed that she wasn't some sort of sociopath or criminal. And everything I've discovered about Livy through just spending time with her is good. Great, even.

Sara snuck in some comments about Livy when Livy wasn't looking. Once she told me that she thought Livy was the strongest woman she'd ever met—physically and emotionally. There are no games or drama with her. Sara had lived with her for a few years and from what she could tell—because even Sara hadn't had the privilege of being told about Livy's past—Livy was a *no-bullshit* kind of gal. All of her cards were on the table. She told you how she felt with not much regard to whether it hurt your feelings or pissed you off. For the most part, I already knew that. However, I've also seen how Livy's words don't match the expression on her face sometimes. She puts up a good front that most people can't see. But I've seen it. I've seen her lips smile while her eyes are sad, and I've heard her say she's fine while everything on the exterior is screaming she's not. But I know she's strong, in both ways that Sara mentioned. And that's what I love about Livy.

Love?

Well, whatever it is, I don't care what it's called. If wanting to be around a woman who fascinates you on a daily basis, for every moment of the rest of your days is love, then fine. I love her. I've known her two months and our relationship has been anything but typical. However, Livy is also far from typical in what my pathetic stereotype of a woman should be.

That's why I need her. And why I am certain no one else will ever compare.

Or maybe that's why I am a massive tool and I don't deserve her at all.

Either way, I'm not going away unless she tells me to.

Another thing that Sara said to me that has resonated loudly in my brain, and my heart, is that Livy is remarkable. She's Wonder Woman for all intents and purposes. But, she's like that *because* of whatever fucked up shit happened before Sara met her. Sara made it clear that Livy doesn't let people in and I should consider myself very lucky that she's let me see past her wall, even if it's only a slight peek.

I do feel fortunate. Extremely fortunate. And I am more than fully aware that Livy is unique. She's not just the most unique woman I've ever met, but quite frankly the most unique person I've ever met.

Sara also assured me that if I broke Livy's heart she would severely kick my ass. *She* being Sara, and that beating would probably come second in line to Livy's own tortuous thrashing. I told her not to worry because if I broke Livy's heart I would lie down and take the beating and thrashing willingly.

Livy comes out of the bathroom and I instantly smell peaches. I snap out of my trance and look up at her.

Dear God.

It feels like my heart just disconnected from my body and there's a little commotion going on in my pants.

I can't sleep in here with her tonight.

She's wearing an oversized, baggy t-shirt. If she has on the shorts that she took in the bathroom with her I can't tell because the shirt's too big. All I can see are her long toned, tanned legs. Those legs look fantastic in jeans, but Jesus H. Christ they are even more incredible bare.

I want to touch them and run my hands up and down them while she's underneath me.

I want to kiss them and watch goose bumps appear in response.

I want to bite them and tease her until she screams my name in ecstasy.

I want to…

"Hey, lusty boy. Covet much?"

Shit.

I look her in the eye, somewhat embarrassed. She can tell that I'm thinking of her with desire on the brain.

I shift my legs a little to adjust.

"You gonna brush up or is that not your thing?" she asks. It's just a simple question but I feel like her subtext reads something like, *Go brush your goddamn teeth or you aren't sleeping in my bed.*

I point to the bathroom in an effort to help my brain find words. "Uh. Yeah. Toothbrush in there?"

Walk, legs! Dammit!

She smiles and nods at me.

She's laughing at me.

Awesome.

I go into the bathroom and try to remember how to brush my teeth.

Calm down, you idiot.

How am I going to sleep in the same bed with her?

In my boxers?

Without physical evidence of what I really want to do instead of sleep?

I'll just lay with my back to her. Okay. Problem solved. She's tired and she won't give a shit how I'm sleeping.

As I rinse, my head clears and my nerves and body parts chill out.

I make my way into the bedroom. Livy is already lying in bed. Maybe she's already asleep. I go to the other side of the bed and try to pull the covers back so not to disturb her. I ease into the bed and turn away from her.

"Jeremy?"

Crap.

I clear my throat. "Yeah, Livy?"

"Did I ever tell you that I think you give the most amazing hugs?"

"No."

"Well, you do. When you hug me, everything goes away. It's just you and me."

"I feel that way too."

She's quiet for a moment. I begin to wonder if that was the extent of the final conversation of the evening.

"Well..." she says finally, "I'm not much of a cuddler, but, I was wondering if you'd..."

She pauses again as if she doesn't want to finish the sentence. I raise my head and turn to her.

"What is it, Livy? Anything. "

"Would you snuggle up with me? I'm dead tired but I don't think I can sleep. Although I might if you give me one of those awesome hugs...in cuddle form."

I hesitate. Of course I want to wrap my arms around her. But that would require physical contact.

From head to toe.

"Jeremy, I don't care if you have a hard-on."

She said it so matter of fact, like she was saying, *"Jeremy, tomorrow is Tuesday"* or *"Jeremy, pick up some apples from the market."*

"I want you too, Jeremy," she continues. "You know that. We'll get there. Just not tonight. I'm too exhausted to make a decent effort. However, it would mean a lot to me if you came over here and hugged me."

I don't know what to say. There's nothing left to say. She just put it all out there. I remain silent. I roll over and nestle in as close to her as I can possibly get. I wrap my arm around her and secure our connection. I bury my face in her hair and inhale. Peaches. Best goddamned peaches on the planet.

"Thank you, Jeremy. This is nice. Peaceful."

"It is. I'm glad you asked me to stay over to do this." I give her a little bear hug squeeze. "I hope it helps you sleep."

"Thank you. I hope so too. Good night, Jeremy."

"Good night, Livy." I close my eyes and try to think of anything that would make me go to sleep.

Counting sheep.

Reading classical literature.

Listening to Coldplay.

But all I can think of is her smell that is traveling through my nasal cavity. Or the fact there is nothing but a thin cotton shirt between my arm and her stomach. Or that her gorgeous ass is in full contact with my dick and it's trying to do a happy dance.

"Jeremy?"

I clear my throat again. In the failed attempt at falling asleep my mouth has grown astoundingly dry. "Yeah?"

Livy moves back towards me. There was no space between us before but now there's even less. She wiggles her ass just a little and faintly giggles.

"Nice package."

Bright light hits my face. I squint one eye open. Although I'm not facing a window, the sun is forcing me awake by reflecting itself in a dresser mirror and coming right back in my direction.

I smell peaches.

And then I realize where I am.

I'm no longer spooning Livy, though. Now, I'm on my back and Livy is lying halfway on top of me with her head in the crook of my arm and her leg draped over my stomach. My fingers are tangled in her hair.

Much of my body is numb and my boxers are tented.

I don't care. I never want to move.

However, a yawn surfaces itself from my chest. I try extremely hard to suppress it because I don't want to wake Livy.

But I do anyway.

She stirs and stretches her arm out and makes a tiny moan. Her eyes stay closed until she realizes her pillow is my chest and arm. Her head pops up and she looks at me and smiles.

"Good morning."

"Good morning," I reply. "How did you sleep?"

"Amazingly well. That is the best sleep I've had in…well, forever. I don't think I've ever slept that well."

I take my poor numb arm, hug her and lift up a little to kiss her on the side of her face. "I slept pretty great too."

She smiles bigger. "You're a little odd," she says. "Who kisses people on the side of the face like that?"

I shrug. "I don't know. I've only ever done that with you."

"Well I do like it. It's sweet. The first time you did it, you gave my stomach butterflies."

"That night I wanted to give you a real kiss. But I didn't want to move too fast and scare you away. But I wanted to do something. I think that maybe I was aiming for the cheek, but then at the last moment, my brain forced me to go a little higher." I bring her in closer and kiss her on the side of her face again. "It was impulsive and not well thought out."

She looks at me and a peculiar feeling overcomes my body. It's a little bit of fear mixed with a touch of nervousness and large amount of lust. The way her eyes are boring into mine, I feel like we are about to begin a pretty hot and heavy make out session.

Then, I feel her hand slide down my stomach and she moves her leg a little.

She makes her way to her destination and she's still staring me in the face. She takes a firm hold of me and I inhale sharply. While her hand is still in place, she leans in and kisses me. I grab the back of her head and I kiss her back.

We may just do a little more than make out.

This epiphany causes my heart to pump faster.

Before I know what's happening, she climbs on top of me. She straddles me and sits on my stomach. And I realize that the only thing she is wearing is that t-shirt.

Holy hell.

Livy finally breaks our kiss and sits up. She places her hands on my chest and seductively runs her fingers down my chest and over my abs.

"Damn, Jeremy. I have imagined what this chest and these abs looked like more times than I'd like to admit. I assumed based on your bulky biceps, this was pretty chiseled too, but *wow*! It's even more magnificent than I imagined."

She leans down and kisses me again. I kiss back but I'm hung up on her words. I know I've got a pretty good physique but hearing her say it kicks my libido directly from first to sixth gear, and quite swiftly, I might add. Livy sits back up, crosses her arms and grips the bottom of her shirt. She hesitates and smiles. She rolls back her hips a little so that she's now sitting on top of my boxers, creating more pressure than what was already there.

"I dreamed about us again last night. Being naked. It was pretty hot," she says slowly, in a low, sultry voice.

She rolls back a little more.

"And you were poking me in the ass with this thing most of the night." She giggles. But then her smile fades a little and she tilts her head, looking me in the eye.

"I know the last few weeks have been crazy and I've probably been a class-A bitch..."

I shake my head no. I can't speak.

"But on the nights I actually slept, I still dreamed about you."

She lets go of her shirt and leans down for another brief kiss. She brings her lips to my ear and whispers, "I don't think I can wait another second. I'd really like for these dreams I've been having to become a reality. Think you can help me out?"

Stop being a doofus and speak to this sexy creature who's propositioning you!

I slide my hands up her thighs and grab her ass. I nod my head and smile at her. "I think I can assist."

She kisses me and I squeeze her plump cheeks. She sits up once again and removes her shirt.

Sweet baby Jesus.

I remove one hand from its current, comfy position and touch her collarbone. I graze the side of my hand from that spot and trail down the middle of her chest. I make my way down to her stomach and over to her hip bone where there's a tattoo. I trace my fingers over the design. It looks Celtic. It's circular and there are words that are not English, following the perimeter of the symbol.

Livy says, "The symbol is supposed to mean strength. The writing is Gaelic. It means *your life is only yours to live.* It's from a book I read."

I smile, "Of course it is."

I trace my fingers over the tattoo once again. "Got any more of these?"

"No. It was an impulse purchase. Hurt like hell."

I take another look at the tattoo and then back at her face. "You are so fucking beautiful. How did I get so lucky?"

"Funny," Livy replies. "I was just thinking the same thing about you. It's almost too good to be true."

"But it *is* true," I assure her.

She leans down and we kiss again. Instantly, our hands are all over each other. We are exploring every square inch of one another. Livy moves to the side of my face and kisses my cheek. Then she makes her way down to my jaw. She's performing some sort of kissing/licking/nibbling combo and it's driving me wild. Almost over the edge. I close my eyes and try to think about random stuff in order to keep this experience from ending prematurely.

Baseball.

Current events.

The Walking Dead.

But my hands are roaming everywhere and images of naked Livy are flooding my brain.

She continues her endeavor down my neck and makes her way to my chest. I point my chin down to look at her and she almost simultaneously raises her eyes up to meet mine. She smiles and moves over to one nipple which she proceeds to bite. I squirm. Goddamn, that hurt but it felt amazing. She looks back up at me and snickers.

Red Sox

Politics

Zombies

I don't know how much longer I can take this euphoric mouth torture she's giving me.

But I also don't want it to stop.

Dead, disgusting brain eaters.

She's at my stomach now. She stops the kissing and places a finger just below my navel. She looks at me again and that feeling of frightening, anxious lust reemerges. I have no idea what is about to happen.

I can't wait to find out.

With one fingernail, she gently trails down to the edge of my boxers. She brushes her finger back and forth on my skin just above the elastic. Livy looks up at me once more. She's taking her time and she's teasing the hell out of me. And I'm fucking loving every minute of it. With both hands, she grabs the waistband. I lift my hips a little and in less than a second, I too am naked and exposed in broad daylight.

Her eyes grow wide and she's grinning from ear to ear. "Sweet Mary Mother of Joseph."

Before I know what's happening, she's moved her hips and positioned herself over me. She takes me into one hand and then lowers herself onto me with full eye contact. She descends slowly. My eyes roll into the back of my head and maybe hers do to. I have no idea. But we both let out a desperate groan. I open my eyes and look at her. Her head is thrown back and her chest is arched. Her long, brown hair is cascading behind her and light from the mirror's reflection of the sun in the window is peeking through the strands. It's the most beautiful sight I've ever seen. She begins moving, and for I don't know how long, I'm in another world. I'm disconnected from reality and there is no clarity. All that exists is the most wonderful sensation I've ever experienced. No reasoning. No rationale. No logic.

I'm making my way to the edge when Livy begins to moan. Repeatedly. With each of her movements, the moans get louder and louder. Finally, I can feel her tighten around me and she lets out the loudest one of all. It's low and animalistic. My instincts are to release with her, but I don't want to be done yet. I want this connection between us to last forever. Livy leans down and puts her hands on either side of my face. Our eyes connect and she kisses me fervently. I hook my arms around her waist and flip positions so that I'm hovering over her now. Still kissing and still connected.

I move inside her while kissing her everywhere: her neck, her shoulders, her breasts, her mouth. I can't take in enough. Her peachy scent, her soft skin and her sensual noises are spinning me into oblivion. I rise up and lift her leg so that it is resting on my chest. I put one arm underneath her back to raise her hips slightly. Keeping a steady rhythm, I turn my head and begin kissing her leg just as I had imagined doing the night before. I open my eyes and see the goose bumps. I shift my gaze to her and she is looking back at me. I kiss again and then very gently, I bite her calf.

"Jeremy," she says, in a husky whisper. Hearing her say my name enhances every sensation in my body. With her leg still resting on my chest and my arm around her back, I bring her as close to me as I can. I escalate my pace and she begins to breathe heavier. My breathing increases as well. I'm very close to losing control and I want Livy to come right along with me. I take my free hand and beginning at her ankle, I slide it down her leg, until there is no more leg, and I put my hand to work.

"Oh my God!" Livy screams as she arches her back higher.

"Livy," is all I can reply. Increasing my pace and intensity even more, I again lose clarity. All I can focus on now is each moan that accompanies every breath Livy exhales.

"Jeremy!" she screams and I can feel her tighten around me once again. With that, all control is lost and I let go. Livy's perpetual noises and her pulsating squeeze take me so high that I might not ever come down. I don't think I can. The feeling that has built and is escaping me is every feeling and emotion I have ever had, magnified by ten thousand. I lean down to Livy and kiss her hard. She wraps her legs around my back and hooks her feet at the ankles. Her grip is strong like she never wants to let go. And I never want her to.

I break our kiss. We are both panting and sweating. I put my forehead against hers.

"You fucking sucked at that," she says, breathless and smiling.

"So did you. I guess we'll need more practice," I say, mimicking her sarcasm.

She exhales a quick laugh and then looks at me with abstraction. "Jeremy, that was amazing. Better than amazing. As many times as I've dreamed and imagined us doing this I could have never envisioned it to be that unbelievable. It was more than sex. I felt like we were one person. Or that we fit perfectly together. I don't know. Saying it out loud sounds corny." She closes her eyes, as if she's ashamed.

"It does sound corny," I tease. "But I feel the same way."

Livy's eyes open and focus on me. "Really?"

I nod my head, my forehead still touching hers. "Mmmmhmm." I move down and kiss her gently. "This may sound corny too, but I have never felt this way with anyone. I know people use that as a line all of the time, but I'm sincere, and I really don't know how else to put it. "

"Oh yeah, I've heard that line before." She smiles. "But lines like that are used to get laid, not after the fact. So, your sincerity seems legit." She winks and clicks her tongue at me. Then she lets out a small huff. "I have definitely never felt this way. Not even close," she says and rolls her eyes up to our adjoined foreheads. "Jeez. We sound like two mushy losers from some dumbass chick flick. What have you done to me?"

I laugh. "Calling it a chick flick is just perpetuating a stereotype."

"Well, they are called that for a reason. When's the last time you watched one?"

"Good point."

Livy smiles. Her legs are still wrapped around me. We are still embraced fully. Still connected.

I never want to move.

"I wish we could stay like this forever," Livy says. The fact that we often seem to know what each other is thinking is weird but interesting at the same time.

"It would be nice," I respond. "But we'd probably get hungry." I lean down and kiss her on the side of her face.

"Jeremy," she says in a matter of fact way. Her tone has changed. I look at her. "I don't ever want to get married. Or have children."

I'm perplexed. This seems out-of-left-field random.

"I...I just. Jeremy, I feel things with you, around you, that I've never felt before. I even act differently when I'm with you. It scares me but at the same time it excites me. I don't want to let you go because I miss you when we aren't together. It sounds so lame but it's the truth. But I feel like I needed to tell you *that* because I feel very strongly about it. I wanted to tell you this before we got involved further but I just didn't. And I didn't expect *this* to happen this morning but I couldn't resist you, being in my bed, both of us half naked. I thought I could but I was fooling myself and being selfish because I wanted so badly to fall asleep in your arms." She pauses and looks at me even more seriously than before. "If you want to bail then I'll completely understand. It'll hurt me like hell, but it's not right for me to hide that from you and lead you on to false expectations. "

I'm speechless. I don't know how to respond.

Livy turns her head away from me. "I'm sorry," she says. "I just ruined an absolutely perfect moment by dropping that on you. I should have at least waited until we got dressed, I suppose."

My heart is aching. But not because I'm upset. It's because there is so much pain in Livy's words. I want to take all of her pain away. I look at Livy and see this woman who deserves everything she's ever desired primarily for the sole fact that she never wants for anything. Whatever has happened to Livy weighs heavy on her and floats over her like a dark cloud insisting that she isn't allowed to be happy.

"Livy, you didn't ruin anything. And I'm not going anywhere." I say nothing further and keep my promise to her not to ask questions. Although I want to. I want to know. So badly. And only because I want her to tell me so I can bottle it up and toss it away and help her understand that it is perfectly fine for her to be happy.

With me.

Forever.

I roll over onto my side and I wrap her up into my arms and bring her into me. "Let's lay here awhile."

"Don't you have to work?"

"Nope. Let's relax. Then later I'll take you for breakfast. Or brunch. Lunch. Whatever you want. And then we will spend the rest of the day doing whatever you want."

"I have to work tonight."

"Nope again." I kiss her on top of the head. "Sara is working."

"You sneaky devil you." She taps me lightly on the ribs.

"I thought if I asked you, you'd give me resistance. So I just decided to take charge of the situation so you wouldn't have the opportunity to say no."

"Well, I guess since you are holding me hostage, I'll try to make the best of it." She looks up at me and winks again.

"I know it'll be tough." I look back at her. "But I think if you try really hard, you just might have some fun." I swoop down for a quick kiss.

"Challenge accepted." She smiles.

I smile back.

I love her smiles. I want to see them more often. And I want to spend all the time I can keeping a smile on her face.

Livy deserves to be happy.

I hope I can get her to understand that.

Challenge accepted.

Ten

Livy

Three months later

EVER SINCE THE MORNING I MADE THE SUPERLATIVE DECISION TO basically assault Jeremy in my bed, every day after has been more perfect than the previous. Jeremy still helps me close up the bar on the nights I work. The other nights not working were, for a few weeks, filled with studying for finals to finish up the credits I needed to obtain an Associate's degree. Two weeks ago, I finished my last class and I am officially a college graduate.

A week after my last final was the graduation ceremony and although I had no yearning to participate, Jeremy, Joe and Sara all pushed me to do it until I caved. Joe closed up the bar that evening, so the three of them could all attend and see me walk across that stage. The evening was equipped with cameras, videos, gifts, flowers, and dinner with three people who exuded so much pride in me I didn't quite know how to take it all in. The evening was really more for them than it was for me. But I was totally fine with that. I was glad to have finished the degree, but I didn't know what I'd do with it. I still didn't see myself leaving Joe's bar. I was perfectly happy staying there.

The best part of that evening though was Jeremy.

After the evening ended we parted ways with Joe and Sara and we went to his place. He barely had the door unlocked before he grabbed me around the waist and pulled me into the apartment. Shutting the door, he pushed me up against it and I gasped. He kissed me hard.

"Damn it, Livy, that dress looks amazing on you."

I rolled my eyes while his mouth was all over my neck. "Don't start, Jeremy. Never again. I swear."

I had made the mistake of telling Sara that I intended to wear slacks under my graduation gown and her exact words in response were, "Oh hell to the motherfucking no." She told me that I was wearing a dress if for no other reason than to let Jeremy have the privilege of getting to see my *smokin'* legs in a dress at least once.

So—I wore a dress.

When Jeremy saw me for the first time that evening when picking me up, he had whispered in my ear professing how fucking hot he thought I was. *Fucking hot* were his words, not mine. He also threatened to pull over onto the side of the road and take me in the back seat of his car on the ride to the ceremony. I told him to cool it and at least try to make it through the evening without his tongue hanging out of his mouth and his eyes all bugged out like some silly cartoon character.

I put up a tough front. But listening to him whisper those words to me almost made my knees buckle and I'd be a liar if I said I didn't want him to do everything he described he wanted to do to me on the shoulder of a two lane road in a cramped back seat.

The first time we had sex released something in the both of us that neither of us knew we had been keeping locked away. We couldn't keep our hands off of each other. Every time Jeremy touched me, I was instantly stimulated. He didn't even have to touch me, really. Every time he spoke, my core would twinge. Hell, when he walked into a room and my nose caught a trace of his cologne my entire body pinged and pointed to Jeremy like a spaniel tracking a hunted bird. Sometimes, closing up the bar, we couldn't even wait to finish and get home. We'd have to take a sex intermission before finalizing the cleaning and paperwork.

This attraction to Jeremy hit me like a ton of bricks. I don't know how to make heads or tails of the way I feel about him. But I'm not looking for explanations. I'm just enjoying what's in front of me.

Jeremy.

"Your legs in this fucking dress are driving me insane. I can't wait another second," he said to me. He pressed me up against the door harder and he put his hand under my ass. He lifted me and I wrapped my legs around his waist.

Locked tightly onto him, he spun us around and took a few steps to the kitchen and set me down on the counter.

"What are you doing?" I asked.

He reached underneath my dress, snatched off my panties and tossed them over his shoulder.

"Taking full advantage of this dress." He pressed his lips to mine and scooted me to the edge of the counter. He fiddled around with his belt buckle and pants and I heard them fall to the ground. Jeremy kissed my neck and I threw my head back. He moved his hands and mouth on me like there was a five alarm fire. I felt his hand graze up between my thighs motioning to part my legs. I writhed with pleasure when he placed his fingers exactly where he wanted them.

"Holy fuck, Jeremy!" I let out.

"Yeah," is all he replied. My palms were both pressed flat on the counter. I moved one hand in his direction to touch his hair but he reached over and grabbed my wrist only to reposition my hand back on the counter.

"Not yet," he said. Our eyes connected. "Let me enjoy the dress." His assertiveness was making my insides shutter. In a good way. I could only nod in response. The hand he used to put my arm back to its apparently rightful position was now on my shoulder, eagerly pulling down the straps of my dress and bra. His right hand was still in between my legs, winding me up tighter than a pin coil as he brought his other hand up to my exposed breast and squeezed.

"So beautiful," he said, before he placed the handful of my bare skin in his mouth. *Oh God.*

He was teasing the most sensitive spots of my body and I suddenly left the atmosphere. "Jesus, Jeremy. Please don't stop." On that command, he exhaled and turned up the teasing a few notches. It was then that I felt his own excitement tapping itself against my leg.

"Jeremy," I said once again, perhaps a little louder. My wound up pin coil shattered into infinite pieces and floated ever so pleasantly back into the atmosphere. Jeremy kissed me and positioned himself to enter me. Once he did, he lifted me up and spun us around again. He found the closest wall available and crashed me into it. His thrusts were quick and impatient but it felt incredible. I let out a moan as he was working his mouth on my breasts again. I grabbed his hair with both my hands and pulled like I was trying to rip his hair out. His head angled back and we looked at each other for a short second. Then I crashed my mouth into his. It was rough, but so hot. My nerve endings had never been so sensitive and the feelings from them had never been so intense. His thrusts became harder and our lips stayed connected. I briefly feared we were going to go through the wall. I felt myself going to the edge again.

"I'm so close Jeremy," I whispered. After my back hit the wall a few more times I came undone. I cried out and not too far after Jeremy chimed in with his own grunty noises. He smashed me into the wall one final time and kissed me. We were both breathing way too hard to speak. We just looked at each other as our chests rose and fell in unison. Jeremy took a step back with a firm grip around me and managed to squat down and lower us both to the ground. He kissed me once more before laying back onto the tile floor and stretched his arms over his head.

"Holy fuck," he panted out.

"Yeah," I feebly retorted. My body was numb. I was sitting up, straddled over him. I eased up and created space between us keeping in mind that while I may have been numb, Jeremy's nether area was still at a quite delicate state. He made a small fuss as I moved away. I only had energy enough to lie on the floor beside him. On my back. With my dress only half way on. But the cool tile floor felt nice against my uncovered skin.

"Please, please, please. I beg you, and will give you or do anything you want. It is imperative that this is not the last time I see you in a dress," Jeremy said to me after he turned his head in my direction.

"Well, if the outcome is even remotely similar to what just happened, I'll wear a dress every fucking day."

"Good."

After lying on the floor for nearly an hour, finally recovered enough to make any gesture that wasn't just being still and breathing, I spoke. "I don't understand what you do to me."

"Do you have to understand it?" Jeremy mumbled. I considered his question and continued to be still and just breathe for a few moments. It was a simple *Yes* or *No* question to which I couldn't provide an answer. Of course I wanted to understand how a single individual could make me make decisions I wouldn't normally make, act in ways I wouldn't normally act and have feelings I wouldn't normally feel. If it hadn't been for Jeremy, I probably would have told Joe and Sara to politely fuck off in regards to attending my graduation ceremony. And if it hadn't been for how I had imagined Jeremy's reaction to be when Sara suggested my attire for the evening, it would have taken nothing short of my own funeral to get me to wear a dress.

But perhaps I didn't want to understand. Maybe the explanation was that I was so subconsciously desperate and wanting for companionship, I took everything Jeremy was willing to offer without abandon and that I could very possibly be setting myself up for a disaster of epic magnitude.

My mind swirled with post-coital endorphins and a scattering of words to formulate an appeasing and appropriate answer to Jeremy's question. The best and most honest answer I could come up with was, "These past few months have been good to you and me. I guess I should just leave well enough alone and not attempt to break what's not broken just to see how it was put together in the first place…right?" I questioned. Not just to Jeremy but also to myself.

Jeremy rolled his entire body over to face me. Still lying flat on the floor, I only turned my head in response. He bent his arm and supported his head in his hand. With his other hand, he moved my dress around to cover up all of the exposed skin of my chest which had been lying there, unabashed, for at least forty-five minutes. He looked me in the eye and smiled.

"I think you are exactly right." He leaned in and kissed me gently. Then, Jeremy helped me up from the floor and led me into the bedroom, where he slowly and strategically undressed me and proceeded to worship my body like a deity until we both passed out from exhaustion.

I'm off from work today and am sitting around my apartment, trying to find something to occupy my time until Jeremy gets off work. I've found that my free time has become more common and more unsettling now that I don't have to attend class or study so often. I should be relieved that I no longer have to spend my precious time cramming useless knowledge into my brain until I'm cross-eyed. But the reality is that even when I'm curled up in my comfortable oversized chair with an enticing book, I'm restless. I feel this strong, overbearing urge to move around and be productive. And that, for some reason makes me feel anxious. I'm in the process of wiping down the kitchen counter for the third time today, when I realize I'm acting like a crazy person and I halt my cleaning frenzy.

Jeremy and I are going out tonight. He wants to take me dancing. Not like sleazy, night club dancing. Jazzy, blues club dancing. I'm intrigued. It's something I'd always fantasized over after reading about it in books or seeing scenes as such take place on a television screen—a low lit dance floor with a substantial, brassy band in the background and someone like Louis Armstrong or Etta James rasping out lyrics involving heartache and longing. It always seemed brutally romantic and stunningly inviting to think of people dancing to someone else's sadness. I, of course, never envisioned myself being the one dancing. That would have required that I ever imagined myself garbed up in dancing attire. I always thought about Fred Astaire and Rita Hayworth or Humphrey Bogart and Ingrid Bergman. I've even often thought of Heathcliff and Catherine dancing out there on the floor, and eerily enough, as an elderly couple.

I say I never envisioned myself, but that is a lie. I had mentioned to Jeremy my fascination with this seemingly antiquated form of evening entertainment and he vowed to take me. After that, I caught myself lying in bed well after Jeremy had fallen asleep for the night, with fantasies of Jeremy and I, dressed to the nines, snuggled tightly to one another, swaying on a dance floor.

Sara helped me pick out a dress and heels that aren't too terribly uncomfortable. Dresses and heels still aren't my thing but after my graduation night I'll wear whatever the fuck Jeremy wants just to make him happy. Because I love making him happy. It is my most favorite thing to do lately. Sara should be leaving for work shortly and I'll begin getting ready. Jeremy will be here in about two hours so I'll have time to take a long bath—a nice presoak for my feet as an advanced *thank you for not hating me after a long night in heels*. And hopefully the bath will also ease my urges to stay perpetually in motion.

Sara comes out of her room with her phone in hand. She looks scared shitless. "Sara?" I ask, "What's the matter?"

She looks at me and immediately begins crying. "I got a job."

"That's awesome. Why are you crying?"

"It's in Connecticut. "

I look at her puzzled, probably for longer than I should have. But then, realization hits me.

She's crying because she's leaving.

She's crying because she's leaving me.

I have to find a new roommate.

I have to find a new bar employee.

Fuck.

"Sara, why are you upset?" I ask as I push away all of the thoughts that are cramming my head.

"I've been trying really hard to find something here, but I heard about the Connecticut job working with a clinical therapist who has been in my field for twenty-five years. He has like fifty publications in American Science Journal. I would have been stupid not to apply. And I really didn't think I'd have a shot." She's looking down at her feet like she's remorseful.

"Sara. If this is your dream job or your chance of a lifetime then you have no reason to be upset. I'm happy for you. Really. I hate that you'll be leaving but I'll be fine. I'll figure it out. You can't stop your life for me. I'm just the roommate."

Sara hugs me tight, still crying. And I make a feeble attempt to hug her back. "Thank you, Livy. I'm really excited. But, I am going to miss you so much. You aren't just a roommate."

I pat her on the back lightly. "I'm going to miss you too," I return.

"You are the best roommate I could have asked for. You are so mature and drama free. And you knew how to do all the manly shit around here. Fix the sink when it was clogged. Change out the ceiling fan when the old one broke. Hang the mirror in the hallway."

I release her from my embrace. "Uh, thanks?"

"You know that's a compliment. You are self-sufficient. I'm not even close. I don't know how I'm going to survive without you."

"I'm sure you'll manage just fine."

"Probably." She wipes her face and rights herself. "Now, go get ready for your man. That stud of yours is going to break his jaw when it falls to the floor seeing you in that dress we picked out. And those heels? Whoa mama!"

I roll my eyes. But truthfully, I *am* looking forward to the look on his face.

"Have fun tonight. Stay out of my room!" Ever since the first night Jeremy came over, it's become a running joke.

"No worries, soon enough you'll be in Connecticut and I'll have both rooms to myself."

Sara smiles but I can tell she's still a little sad. "You sure will," she says. I think she's going to start crying again. But instead she turns so she's no longer facing me and grabs her purse. "I have to go. See you later." Before I have a chance to respond, she's out the door.

I head to my bedroom and sit on the edge of my bed to take in the news Sara just delivered. I'm not sure what to think. I mean it's not like we're *BFFs*. Hardly. She's night clubs and lipstick and designer heels, when she can find them on sale. I'm Friday night books in my favorite chair, haven't cut my hair in three years and shove as much money into my Roth IRA that I can manage. Not sisters from different misters by any means. We don't even really hang out with each other. Except for the very few occasions our schedules align and we find ourselves occupying the apartment on the same afternoon. But we had coexisted in the same apartment without complication. Neither of us ever bitched at the other for being messy or hogging the shower or disturbing the peace in the middle of the night. It helped me transition in my move to the city with one less stressor to deal with. And I will forever be grateful for that. That's something I should probably tell Sara.

A car horn beeps outside my window and I snap out of my nostalgic rumination. I look at the clock.

Shit! I've got to get these feet soaking!

There's a knock at the door and as always my heart flutters. But I can't run to the door as usual because of these insane heels. I make my way from the bedroom to the door, probably looking like a baby ostrich just learning to walk. I could have very easily waited to put my shoes on after I let Jeremy in, but I needed the heel-walking practice and I wanted Jeremy to see the whole get up at first sight. I make it to the door and grab the handle, more for balance than for being the prompt, courteous hostess.

I open the door.

Jeremy has his head down and lifts it as I reveal myself from behind the door.

He's holding wildflowers.

He *was* holding wildflowers.

Now they're on the floor and he has his hands engulfing my face. His lips on mine.

We stand in the threshold of the doorway and kiss for quite some time, until one of the neighbors walks by and clears her throat as if we are ruining her day. Jeremy pushes me inside. His hands are fumbling around the back of my dress. "This dress is amazing, but it has to come off. Now. "

I turn so he has full visibility of the zipper. He unzips my dress and it falls to the floor. I step out of it, making conscience effort to appear sexy and not *ostrich-y*. I turn and face him. All I have left on is a black push up bustier and matching black lace panties.

And tall, spiky *fuck me* heels.

"God. Dammit. Do you moonlight as a porn star?"

I grin as devilishly as I can. "Not anymore."

He leaps towards me and puts one hand on the back of my head and closes in for a sharp, breathtaking kiss. His other hand is under my ass lifting me up. I wrap my legs around his waist.

"I never thought I'd have something this sexy wrapped around me."

"But we've been in this exact predicament before," I respond in amused confusion. "Or don't you recall?"

"Oh yeah. I remember. But you are dressed in all black and those shoes…you look like some kind of dominatrix. You are so fucking hot. Jesus Christ, Livy, I feel like the luckiest man on earth right now."

His words are crude. But his reaction is really turning me on.

He kisses me once more and then looks to the left and right, seemingly planning his next move. He walks us over to the small dining table where we once ate steaks.

"Do you know what these heels are good for?" Jeremy asks. My arms are draped loosely around his neck. I smile my devilish grin again and slowly shake my head no.

Jeremy motions me to uncross my legs and stand. I take my time so not to wobble. He kisses me and then makes his way down to my neck. He kisses my collarbone and I groan softly. He puts his hands on my waist and spins me around. Now I'm facing the table with Jeremy at my back. He places one hand around my stomach and one hand on my back, near my neck, and gently pushes so that I'm bent over the table.

Holy mother.

I spread my arms out over the table and let him take full control. He places his hand on my ass and squeezes. "Just as I suspected. These heels make you the perfect height."

My hearts jumps out of my throat right onto the table.

Dinner is fucking served.

I can't see him. But I can feel Jeremy move. His hands are on my calves. "Your legs are so fucking beautiful." His hands slowly move upward and I have chill bumps on top of my chill bumps. He's back up to my ass now. He gives another good squeeze on each cheek and grabs my panties. He pulls them down and I feel them fall to the floor to my ankles.

"My God, what a view. I'm going to have to take a picture and show all my friends."

He's joking, I know.

"Well if you must," I say with my head turned sideways, partially compressed by the table. "But only close friends, please."

His hands move up my legs again and they smooth over my ass once more. He places both hands in between my legs and motions me to move them farther apart. I abide.

His hands move up to the center and meet. His fingers move. Taunting. Teasing. I moan and writhe on the table. I feel completely exposed and vulnerable but I like it. I trust Jeremy, and I am wholly contented with allowing him to do whatever he wants. As he does. His fingers cease in their movements and I feel an instant void. But as quickly as the fingers are gone, they are replaced with his hot breath. And tongue.

"Oh, God, Jeremy!" I'm searching the table with my hands for something to grab on to. I come up with nothing. He continues this glorious torture on me and I rise and fall into oblivion. I'm shouting and panting. My legs are shaking. I feel like I'm going to crumble to the ground when Jeremy stands and grabs my hips to steady me.

He leans over me and whispers into my ear. "You okay?"

I nod, face still contorted by the table. I am so uncomfortably comfortable.

Jeremy kisses the side of my face and stands up. I hear the sounds of his zipper and then belt clanging to the floor. He grabs my hips and I feel him kiss my back.

"So fucking sexy," I hear him whisper. He firms his grip on my hips and he enters me. Slowly and gently at first. Even in the first few motions, I feel as though I'm going to explode again. He picks up his stride and fervency. Noises are coming from us both that might sound murderous out of context. Each thrust is powerful and electric. The sensation is beginning to build up.

"Jeremy," I exhale.

"Livy," he responds.

Hearing my name depart his throat sends me over the edge. "Oh my God!" I've yet to find anything my hands can grasp for leverage, so I press my fists into the flat surface of the table. Jeremy's final movements are so vigorous, we move the damn table a good six inches.

Jeremy leans over me and kisses my back between my shoulder blades. "Wow."

"Yeah," I say.

Jeremy stands, lifts me up to a standing position and turns me around to face him. I wobble and try to gather my bearings. Between the heels, being plastered to a dining table and the multiple orgasms, I'm a little off kilter. Jeremy wraps his arms around me and chuckles. "I can't get enough of you. You are like a fucking drug. I'm a Livy junkie."

"Ditto." I raise my hand as if I'm taking an oath. "Jeremy junkie."

"You still want to go dancing?" he asks.

"No chance," I confess. I'm not even sure I'd be able to stand if he lets me go. Dancing is out of the question. We will not be Fred and Rita tonight.

"Stay in and order take out?" he asks.

"Sounds perfect." The fact that we are discussing dinner options while half naked is not lost on me.

Jeremy kisses me. While he's kissing me, I notice his legs wiggling around. He's stepping out of his pants and removing his shoes. Then, still kissing, he sweeps me up and begins carrying me toward the bathroom. In the bathroom he sets me down on the counter.

"Shower first, then food." I say nothing but nod in agreement. I just took a bath thirty minutes ago. I have on makeup and hairspray in my hair. But, I don't give a fuck about any of those things. A shower with Jeremy sounds more delightful than any restaurant food or jazz club music I could ever imagine existed.

Jeremy looks at my bustier, completely stupefied. "Now, how do we get this damn thing off?"

After giving Jeremy a lesson on disassembling lingerie and another marvelous romp in the shower, we settle on the sofa waiting for our take out to arrive. Jeremy is wearing his slacks, sans belt, and the solid white t-shirt he was previously wearing under his button up. I am wearing his button up and boy short lacy underwear. Jeremy selected, and insisted on, my wardrobe for the rest of the evening. I obliged with no resistance.

His shirt smelled like nothing other than Jeremy, and I had no problem having it envelop me the rest of the night.

"Do you want to watch a movie?" I ask. "We have lots of options." I point over to our flimsy excuse of a media shelf. They are mostly Sara's, which I guess I'll be losing soon, but we've picked up a few extras along the years. I'm suddenly wondering how we'll split up the collection. And what about the dishes we bought together? Or the area rug? I feel like I'm going through a divorce. It gives me chills.

"Which is your favorite?" Jeremy asks. I forego my separation concerns and smile. "*The Rocky Horror Picture Show*." I lean over and grab the movie and hand it to him.

"Never seen it. But by the look of the cover I'd say you are a weirdo."

"You asked. It's amusingly terrifying. And it's a musical of inappropriate proportions."

"Sounds great." His voice is sarcastic and his eyebrow is raised. He does not look sold.

"You choose then," I say.

"No. If this is your favorite, I want to see it no matter how crazy it is. But I have to warn you, this could be a deal breaker."

"I'll have to take my chances. If you aren't on board with *The Rocky Horror Picture Show*, I might be breaking the deal first."

Jeremy puts the movie in and I set up the television to communicate with the DVD player. Jeremy leans back on the couch and reaches over to pull me into him. He pulls the blanket off of the back of the sofa and covers me with it. I'm snuggled against his side and his arm is draped around me. This is my new favorite movie watching seat.

We get about twenty minutes into the movie when the doorbell rings. I stand up and out of, I guess, instinct I head toward the door.

Jeremy grabs my wrist. "Uh, Livy, you aren't wearing pants."

Oh yeah.

"I've got it," he says. "Unless you mind me answering your door." I shake my head, sit back down and cover my bare legs with the blanket. Jeremy retrieves the take out, grabs some plates from the kitchen, along with a couple of beers, and brings everything into the living room.

"I don't need a plate," I say.

"You aren't going to share?" Jeremy asks.

"Wasn't planning to." I wink. "But I guess I could."

I search through the containers. I can't even remember what we ordered. I dump a little from each container onto a plate. I lean back and prop my feet on the coffee table and begin to eat.

I pause before my first bite because I can sense Jeremy staring at me. I look over at him and, sure thing, he is looking at me as though I'm an alien.

"What?" I question. I have no idea why he seems so puzzled.

"Your feet are on the coffee table."

I look at my feet then back at him. "Yeah?"

"The food is on the coffee table."

I take the bite of food and with a full mouth, I say, "I'm not connecting the dots here, buddy."

"You don't think that it's gross to have your feet in such close proximity to food you are about to consume?"

I don't understand this question.

"No. My feet are clean. You washed them yourself, or don't you recall?"

"But you've walked on them since."

"Does this put you off? Did you lose your appetite because my toes might waft gunk in the direction of your take out box?"

"No."

"Then what is it?"

"Nothing, I guess. I just have to keep reminding myself you aren't a typical girl."

I feel like I should be slightly insulted. Or offended at best. It causes me to sit up straighter from the sofa and glare a little at Jeremy. "What the fuck does that mean?"

"Hey. Calm down there, Firestarter. I'm not trying to offend you. It's just that my Aunt Jenna almost chopped my feet off once for putting them on the coffee table near her bowl of popcorn."

"Why do you insist on comparing me to other people?"

Now he looks hurt.

"I'm sorry. I don't know. I have three other significant women in my life. My mother and my aunts. I love them and I trust and respect them and I guess I compare everyone to them. Especially women that I think I might…"

He stops. I don't know what the end of the sentence was going to be, but I'm not going to press for it.

Jeremy picks up his beer and takes a long exaggerated swig. The detachment of the bottle from his lips makes a noise that seems loud mostly because it's the only noise in the room. "I think I might love you, Livy."

I didn't press. But he gave it to me anyway. My heart and brain both stop. My face flushes. I can feel tears surface. I don't quite know why I'm reacting this way. This is a good thing deep down I know but I'm terrified of what he just said. I can't move because I know if I do the tears will fall and that is the last thing I want Jeremy to see. I don't want him to remember that he said he might love me and it made me cry.

"Livy. I've gone out with other girls. Some, not many. But with each of them, I never made it past a second date. There was nothing. But the moment I saw you, something inside of me reached out and grabbed something inside of you and I know you feel it too. I…I love you, Livy. I know I do. And I know you love me too even if you don't want to say it. You don't have to say anything. Every moment I've had with you right up to this very second says enough. I don't need words. So don't feel pressured. Don't freak out. I love you. And I love that you think that feet and food can comingle happily together on one table."

I still haven't moved. I close my eyes and take a deep breath willing the tears to subside. Then I open my eyes and look at him. I heard every word he just said and I have no idea how to react. But he said I didn't have to. So I am going to put it on a shelf and address it later.

"Well, it's not like I'm eating with my toes," I say and smile.

He leans in and kisses me.

We both turn toward the food and TV, resume the movie and eat dinner in comfort, with our feet on the coffee table.

The movie credits begin to roll. I lost myself in thought somewhere during the "Time Warp" song. The entire day came to the forefront of my brain. After we finished eating, I tried to compartmentalize what Sara and Jeremy both told me and store it away to process later. But apparently later is now.

Sara is leaving.

Jeremy loves me.

I'm going to be all alone in this stupid apartment I convinced Sara to move into, probably without dishes and a rug.

How can Jeremy love me? He doesn't even know me. He's being foolish.

Foolishness is so unbecoming.

But I'm addicted to him nonetheless.

How do I know if I love him?

How can I? No one before now has shown me any semblance of love. How can I love someone when I don't know how to? I don't know what it feels like. Of course I'm infatuated with this boy. He's intoxicating and I *want* to love him. Is it that easy? You want to love someone so you just do? He loves me and *wants* me to love him back so why shouldn't I?

"Earth to Livy." Jeremy is snapping his fingers in my face and I break free of my trance.

"Did you hear me?" he asks as I try to focus on what's going on.

"Uh. No, I guess not."

"That was a pretty twisted movie. But it's not a deal breaker as long as I don't ever have to watch it again."

"Whatever. You know you loved it. It's a seventies movie. Hippies and drugs produced this great cult classic." I point to the TV. "Just you wait. You'll get Tim Curry and Meatloaf stuck singing in your head and you'll be begging for more."

"Highly doubt that."

I begin to sing the words to "Whatever Happened to Saturday Night." He leans over and covers my mouth. I giggle.

"You are playing unfairly." He moves his hand.

"I always do. Get used to it."

He kisses me quickly and gently.

"So what had you deep in the think tank? You didn't watch most of the movie."

I'm not ready to talk about my thoughts and feelings on the subject of love just yet with Jeremy. Not sure I ever will be. Which is what scares me the most. But I don't want to shut him out completely so I decided to talk about the other issue.

"Sara is leaving. She's moving to Connecticut. "

"When? Why?"

"Not sure when yet, but she got a job with some doctor who is a legend. She applied thinking it was a long shot. But of course she got it. She's awesome."

"She is that. Are you okay?"

"Yeah, I guess. I mean I'll be fine. I'm just shocked. She gave me the news and left. We'll talk about it more I'm sure. But I just feel a little blindsided I guess."

"Well, will you be okay? Financially?"

"Oh yeah. I'll be fine. But I'll probably downgrade to a one bedroom after the lease is up. This is too much apartment for just me. No need in wasting money."

"You could move in with me," Jeremy says, before I could even finish my own sentence.

"What? No. Don't be ridiculous," I scoff.

"Why not? When was the last time we spent the night apart? Why shouldn't we live together?"

"I won't have my own space. I need my own space," I immediately counter without hesitation.

"I have the spare room. You can make it your space. Whatever you want."

"But that won't be *my* space. It'll be space for me in *your* apartment."

"Our apartment," he defends.

"I don't know," I say, shaking my head.

"Look, it's just a place to live, right? Come give it a trial and if you don't like it, I'll help you look for something else."

"But if I don't like living with you, wouldn't that be a bad thing for our relationship?" I question and I'm a little nervous as to what his answer might be.

"Wouldn't it be better to find out sooner than later? Besides I'm not worried. I have confidence you'll love living with me."

How can I say no to the huge smile gleaming at me?

"You're right. It's best you find out now how horrible it is to live with me before I sink my claws in deeper," I say and look over at him, "But don't say I didn't warn you."

"Noted. So. That's a yes?"

I look into his crystal blues, beaming with excitement and anxiety. His eyes are my Kryptonite and I can't say no. I don't *want* to say no because that Kryptonite also warms my heart.

The Kryptonite makes me weak. But weakness doesn't seem so bad in Jeremy's presence.

"That's a yes," I finally say. "But that may just be the beer talking. I may reconsider in the morning."

"I'm okay with that." He leans in for another kiss. "You ready for bed?"

"I'm not tired, really."

Another kiss. "Me neither."

I smile, getting his not so subtle hint. "Definitely ready."

He scoops me from the couch and heads to the bedroom.

For a long night of no sleep.

In the best of ways.

The next morning, I didn't reconsider my decision to move in with him for a second.

Eleven

Jeremy

Two months later

SARA LEFT THREE WEEKS AFTER SHE BROKE THE NEWS TO LIVY. WE all went out to dinner the night before she packed up and headed to Connecticut. Sara cried. A lot. She cried when she thanked Joe and Livy for everything they'd done for her. She cried when she apologized to Livy (for the fifth time) for leaving her. She cried when she'd promised she'd visit as often as she could. She even cried when they brought out her salad because she claimed there was no way Connecticut would have salad dressing as good.

In true Livy fashion, surprising the hell out of me yet again, she took Sara's hands into her own and said, "Sara, I know you are scared to be in a new place all alone. But remember, you've done it before and you came out of that just fine. You are headed toward something you want to do. Stay focused on that. Everything else will fall into place. And Joe and I will be fine. We'll miss you like crazy but we know you are going to get to Connecticut and conquer the world."

And just like that, Sara was pacified. How does Livy come up with just the right words? She knew exactly what to say to make Sara feel better.

She reminded me of my mother.

Was that good or bad?

Definitely good.

Right?

The next day we all helped Sara pack up her car and a small moving trailer she rented. Well, Joe "supervised" because Livy wouldn't let him help. We said our goodbyes and even though I thought she would, Sara didn't cry. She hugged Livy last, thanked her again, no tear shed. She promised she'd come back for Christmas. Then she got into her loaded down car with the trailer attached and set off onto her new life journey. Livy never showed any emotion other than pride and happiness toward Sara. But I could tell she was a little sad to see Sara go.

Livy still has one month left on her apartment lease. However, we haven't spent a night apart since Sara left. Actually, we hadn't spent a night apart since that first night I slept in her bed. We alternated between her apartment and mine. She was still on board with moving in with me. After our first conversation about it, she never gave me anymore push back. I had asked her twice if she was sure and both times she told me yes. I decided not to ask a third time.

One night, I showed her that I had cleared out the spare bedroom. There wasn't much in there to begin with—a bed and a desk—but I took everything out and told her she could do with it whatever she wanted. We moved her reading chair into the room, by the window. We also moved in her bookshelves and her hundreds of books.

"That's it?" I asked once we got everything situated "That's all you wanted was a place to read?"

"Yep."

"Well that was almost too easy."

"Easy for you, maybe. All you had to do was move a chair and shelves." She reached out to some old leather bound books. "I had to pack these very carefully and strategically. That was quite a task. My collection has grown a great deal since the last time I had to move. I only brought two books with me when I came to the city. And I only had about a quarter of these when we moved to the two bedroom apartment."

I look at the shelves. There has to be at least three hundred books. "So you've bought all of these since you lived in the city?"

She nods. "I visit the used bookstore down the street once a week. Rarely do I leave empty handed."

"And you've read all of these?"

"Yep. Some twice."

"And this is fun to you?"

"The best kind of fun. Until I met you." She winks.

"Well that's a relief to hear," I say.

Later that evening, after work, I head to the bar to help Livy close, just as I do every night that she works. Which has been every single night since Sara left. Joe made the executive decision to close completely on Mondays just to give Livy a break. I asked Livy why Joe hadn't found anyone to replace Sara yet and she said that she hadn't asked and he hadn't brought it up.

Ladies and gentlemen, introducing the two most stubborn people in the world—Joe and Livy.

I don't know of Joe's reasoning, but I knew Livy didn't want to work with anyone else. Anytime I brought up the subject she immediately changed topic. She didn't trust people and this bar was her pride and joy even if it was a small alley dive on a downtown side street.

I walk in and there are two regulars at the bar nursing their domestic drafts. Henry and Ben. No sign of Livy.

Then I hear yelling.

Livy yelling.

"She's been carrying on like that for twenty minutes now," Henry says. "Might want to pour yourself a cold one and catch up on this game we're watching."

I glance up at the T.V. Baseball. Red Sox and Rays. Any other night I might have done exactly what Henry suggested, but I need to find out why Livy is yelling.

"Who is she yelling at?" I ask the duo.

"Poor old Joe. He came in about an hour ago and went back to his office. Then Livy went back to check up on him. Then the yelling started. She said a bunch of *how dare yous* and a couple of *bullshits*," Henry says.

"She even called him a motherfucker," Ben chimes in and Henry nods in agreement.

"This sounds serious." I begin my way back to the office.

"You might want to stay out of this, son. It's pretty damn tough breaking up two pit bulls. You might lose some fingers."

"Taking my chances," I bellow, still walking towards the office. The door is open. I approach the room and Livy has her back to me.

"How the fuck can you do this? What am I supposed to do now?" Livy screams.

"Livy, you have a degree. There's plenty you can do. I'm not going to let you waste your life away here in this trash dump," Joe answers calmly.

"This *isn't* a trash dump!" Livy screams, barely letting Joe get his words out. "It's my *job* and I happen to like it. A lot! And you are taking it from me!"

"Livy, you need to go find something that you are passionate about. Go change the world. Make a difference. You have that in you and you can't do it from behind that bar."

"Goddammit, Joe, why are you doing this? Stop trying to run my life! Who the fuck do you think you are?"

"Someone who cares about you enough to not let you get stuck here forever. I don't want you waking up a forty year old wishing you'd gotten out when you had the chance."

Joe looks over Livy's shoulder at me. Livy turns and looks at me. The look on her face isn't one I've ever seen. It's homicidal. I'm terrified.

"Perfect," Livy says in my direction. "Did you have a hand in this? Is this some kind of ploy between the two of you to micromanage my life for me?"

"Livy, I have no idea what I just walked into. What is going on?" I ask.

Livy points at Joe. "This son of a bitch is selling the bar!"

"What?" I look at Joe and he gives me a confirming look. "Someone made me an offer three times its value. They want to turn it into a TGIFridays or some shit."

"You are a selfish son of a bitch, Joe! I can't believe you did this without talking to me about it. I've put almost four years into this place!"

I've held this place together when you couldn't. And now you are just going to what? Just pull the rug out from under me, slap me on my ass and say have a nice life?"

Livy's breathing is labored. I think she might hyperventilate. "Livy," I say softly, "maybe you should…"

"Stay out of this Jeremy. This is none of your fucking business!" she snaps and Joe immediately grabs her by the shoulders and turns her square to his stance so that they are eye to eye. I can't see her face but her posture stiffens like she's shocked by his actions.

"Don't you dare talk to him like that, Livy. You can say what you want to me, but if I ever hear you talk to Jeremy like that again, I'll hang you upside down by your ankles and shake the stupid out of you, girl. That boy has done nothing but be wonderful to you. Don't let that mouth of yours run him off."

There he goes talking about me again like I'm not here. I clear my throat just to alert them I'm still standing in the doorway.

Livy's posture relaxes and she hangs her head. Joe places his hand under her chin and lifts her face. "Now. If you would shut the fuck up for two seconds, young lady, I can tell you the rest of the story. Some guys in suits came in a few weeks ago saying they want to buy this whole block of buildings. Offered me a shit ton of money. *A shit ton.* I'm old, Livy. Having some money in the bank without having to worry about this bar, or *you*, is exactly how I want to spend the rest of my days."

Even from the angle I have, I can tell Livy is about to say something. Joe puts his hand over her mouth. "Stop. Let me finish for fuck's sake." She nods and he removes his hand. "I'm giving you forty percent, Livy."

"What?" Livy whispers, tilting her head to the side.

"I'm giving you forty percent of the shit ton. This bar wouldn't have survived without you and I have no problems admitting that. Sixty percent is plenty for me. You deserve the rest. You can take your time and figure out what you want to do with your life. That's what I want for you."

Now is the part in a regular scenario where the grateful girl hugs the big burly man that she sees as a father figure and thanks him relentlessly. He hugs her back and all is right with the world.

Except, this is Livy we are talking about here.

She steps back from Joe. Then, before I even know it's happening, she slaps him across the face. Hard. The sound of hand meeting face is like a baseball colliding with a wooden bat.

"Fuck you, Joe. I don't want your goddamned money."

Livy turns and walks in my direction. She pushes past me in the doorway and continues to walk toward the front door.

I look at Joe who who's rubbing his face with his hand.

"You okay?" I ask.

"I'm fine. I just wish that girl wasn't so goddamned hard headed."

"I better go catch her. She'll come around, I'm sure."

"You be careful with her, Jeremy. Don't let her words hurt you. She says dumb shit when she's angry like this. But she doesn't mean it. Don't let her run you off. She's a good girl. And you're good for her."

"I know. Thanks, Joe."

"Sure thing, kid," he says, still rubbing his face.

I make my way past Henry and Ben, who both give me a curious look, and I head outside. She is too far ahead of me. I have no idea which way she went. I decide to head to her house. On the way there I think of a million things to try to say to her to get her to calm down.

This is a good thing, Livy.

Joe just wants to take care of you.

It's what's best for you both.

You terrify me when you're angry, but it's also kind of hot.

Okay, maybe that last line won't be the one I'll lead with.

I get to Livy's building and there are no lights from her window. I head up anyway and knock.

"Livy?"

I wait. And I knock again.

"Livy?"

Nothing.

I decide to use the key she gave me and unlock the door. I open it just slightly.

"Livy, it's Jeremy. I'm coming in. Please don't attack me."

Silence.

I open the door all of the way and go in. I check her bedroom first. Then the bathroom and even Sara's room.

"Livy?" I call out into the dark and apparently empty apartment. There is no answer.

I pull out my phone and try to call her. Straight to voicemail.

Damn woman. She's turned off her phone.

I leave her apartment and lock up. My next stop is the bookstore she told me about earlier today. I honestly can't think of anywhere else she would go. I pray that she doesn't end up in some other bar. As angry as she is, if she gets some drinks in her she's likely to beat the crap out of the first guy who speaks to her.

The bookstore is closed. Shit. I take out my phone and text Sara.

<When Livy's pissed, where would she go to cool off?>

I start walking, waiting for an answer. I peek into the windows of a few bars and restaurants that I pass. No luck.

My phone buzzes. It's Sara.

<What did you do?>

I roll my eyes.

<Nothing. She's mad at Joe. He's selling the bar. She ran out and I can't find her.>
<Shut the fuck up! No way! Why is he selling? >
<Sara! Focus! I need to find Livy. I'll fill you in on the rest later.>
<Right. Sorry. Try the park near the footbridge. She goes there sometimes.>
<Thanks!>

I put my phone away not waiting for a response. I'm jogging and I don't really realize it until I get to the footbridge and I'm out of breath. I look around. It's dark but there is lighting around the bridge. I don't see her. I cup my hands around my mouth. "Livy!" After no response I call out once more.

"She ain't here."

I turn to see a man lying on a bench with a newspaper covering his shoulders.

"Excuse me?"

"You looking for Livy, right?"

"Yeah," is all I can say. I'm bewildered.

"She ain't here. If she was I woulda seen her. She would have said hi."

"Do you know Livy?"

"Sure do. We used to live together. She comes by every once in a while and brings me a sandwich."

I may have just entered the Twilight Zone. I think I can hear the macabre theme music in the background.

"I'm sorry. Did you say you used to live together? With Livy?"

"Sure did. We were at the south side shelter together for a while. Sweet girl."

I want to ask him so many questions, but I'd be wasting time I need to spend on finding Livy.

"So you haven't seen her tonight?"

"No. Sorry."

"Thanks for letting me know. Here." I take a couple of twenties out of my wallet. "I appreciate your help. I hope this helps you get a few good hot meals."

"Thanks." He takes the money and looks up at me. "She told me she found a good one. Take care of her."

"Sure thing. I just need to find her first. Have a good night."

"You too. I'm sure you'll find her soon. If there's any place you can think of where she can park herself with a book, go there. That's where I'd look. But, of course, I assume that's why you came here."

Well he *definitely* knows Livy.

"Okay. Thanks again." I need to get very far away from the weirdest moment of my life. I'm jogging again. Then it hits me.

Her chair.

But that's too easy. She couldn't have just gone home.

My home.

Our home.

I head to my house. I'm there in five minutes. Lights are on. Good sign.

I get to my door and unlock it as fast as I can. "Livy!"

The spare bedroom door is closed. I open it and see Livy in her chair. But she isn't reading. She's passed out. Her face is red and swollen as if she's been crying. There's a bottle of bourbon at her feet. Half empty.

I rush over to her and kneel beside her.

"Livy. Wake up. Livy." I tap her cheek very gently.

She jumps and her head shoots up, eyes wide. "What the fuck?" she yells.

I grab one of her hands. "Shhh. Hey. It's just me."

She looks at me and it takes her a moment to get her bearings.

Then she starts to cry.

Hard.

I grab her and pull her down to the floor with me. I hold onto her as tightly as I can. "Hey. It's okay. It's okay." But every word I say is just making her cry harder. I stop talking and just hold her.

"Why do you have to love me, Jeremy? I'm a horrible person! Just like my mother. You don't want me! Joe was just trying to do the right thing and I slapped him. I slapped him! Just like my mother. I'm just like her. Sara left. Joe's kicking me out and surely he hates me now. You're next. Just go ahead and leave already. It's what I deserve! I don't deserve anyone. I deserve to be alone because I'm just like her. I can't love anybody! It's all her fault." She screams the last few words and then she sobs. Harder than I've ever seen anyone cry. I want to cry for her. I squeeze her so tight.

"I'm not letting you go," I whisper. She continues to cry, saying no more words. We stay that way for at least half an hour until she falls asleep.

With her still in my arms, I try to lift us both off the floor without waking her. I figured the half a bottle of bourbon would have assisted in putting her into a deeper sleep, so my awkward jerky movements wouldn't bother her too much. However, of course, I was wrong.

Livy turns her head and moans. Then she opens her eyes and looks at me. "What time is it?"

There is no clock in the room and my phone is in my pocket. I am highly aware that my phone is in my pocket because it's been vibrating my leg all night with calls from, I'm sure, Sara. Or Joe. Or both. But because of the same reason I haven't answered those calls, I also can't check what time it is. My hands are full with Livy. But I don't care because only Livy matters regardless the time.

"Not sure," I answer. "But I'll guess it's probably 11:30." I'm still trying to manage getting us both off the floor. She's making it a little more difficult now that she's wriggling about.

"Here, let me help." She motions to stand up on her own when she realizes I'm struggling a bit.

She keeps her arms around my neck and plants her feet on the floor. Then we stand together.

"You okay, Livy?" I ask, worried what her answer might be.

She nods. "Yes. I have a bitch of a headache and I'm a little embarrassed, but otherwise I'm fine."

"No need to be embarrassed. Stupid shit happens sometimes when your heart hurts. Did I ever tell you about the time I got arrested?"

She lifts her head and looks at me "What? No! You've failed to mention your criminal history, mister." She smiles and I smile back.

"Well, let's get you to bed and perhaps we'll discuss in the morning."

Livy shakes her head at me. Her hair is a tousled mess, but she is still so fucking beautiful. "Nuh, uh. You are spilling now. Come on, I need aspirin and coffee." She walks out of the room and I follow. She makes her way to the kitchen and begins making coffee.

I sit at the table and watch her as she brews the coffee and reaches for the aspirin and a water glass. After she pops the pills and chases them with water, she grabs two coffee mugs and turns toward the fridge.

Either she is still half asleep or she's entered into her own little world. There is a glaze over her eyes and she's staring off into space. She pours a little milk into both mugs and heads back over to the coffee maker. The coffee is still percolating but she quickly replaces the pot with a mug. Then she replaces the first mug with the second mug and finally repositions the coffee pot in its proper place. All without spilling a drop.

"You know you ruin the whole pot doing that."

"Who cares?" she says flatly.

"No one in this room."

She brings the mugs over to the table and sits sliding one mug in my direction.

She takes a sip and sighs with her eyes closed. "Perfect." Livy opens her eyes and looks in my direction. "Now. Tell me about your time in the clink."

I laugh. I think that is the same term my mother used when she picked me up. *The clink.*

"Is it a funny story?" she asks, responding to my laughter.

"It is, but I was laughing because you reminded me of my mother. She used that same term when she bailed me out. *The clink.*"

"Interesting. Is she a George Orwell fan?"

And the most random question award goes to Livy.

I shrug. "I have no idea."

"George Orwell once tried to get arrested on purpose to see what it was like to spend Christmas in prison. The cops wouldn't send him because they said he wasn't drunk and disorderly enough to be sent to prison and they released him. He later wrote an essay about it and titled it *Clink.* I think that's the first time jail was referred to as *the clink* in a literary reference. After that, I think they started using it in movies…"

I'm not even really sure who George Orwell is, but hearing Livy ramble on about the origins of the phrase, *the clink,* is mind-blowingly fascinating. *Mind-blowingly?* Is that even word? Probably not. I may be watching too much ESPN with Livy. I've tripled my viewing time of that channel since she and I met. They create their own words all of the time. *Trickeration. Heismanology. Escapability.* It must be rubbing off. But word or no word, *mind-blowingly* is an accurate depiction of how I feel about Livy's awesome randomness.

However, I must be looking at her as though I'm completely uninterested because the moment she makes eye contact with me, she stops mid-sentence. "You know what? Never mind. I took a tangent there. Sorry. We were discussing your criminal deviance." She motions her hand towards me to continue. I proceed to tell her about Jessie and how she broke my heart and how I got drunk and detained.

"Technically, not arrested," I made clear.

Livy laughs "Oh! You poor thing! I guess it's good that you had people in your community looking out for you. And your mother..." Livy looks down at her coffee mug. Her grip tightens around it and her eyebrows dip together in the center of her forehead. "If that had been me..." She stops and inhales, "I probably would have been patted down inappropriately by the arresting officer and my mother would have let me rot in jail."

That is the first time Livy has ever mentioned her mother or her past. Sober, at least.

She looks up at me. "You want to know, don't you?"

"Of course I do, but not so I can feel bad or sorry for you. I'd like to help you move past it if I can. Your past hurts you. I can tell. You don't deserve that, Livy. You don't. If I can help mend that, I'll try my damnedest to. But I'm not going to force you to tell me."

Still looking at her mug and gripping it tightly, Livy parts her lips to speak. At first there is no noise. I don't move. I don't want to give her any excuse or opportunity to back out of anything she might be about to tell me.

I want her to trust me. I want her to have faith in me that I won't see her in any other light than the one I see her in now. She is *my* Livy. My tough-as-nails, tells-it-like-it-is, knows-everything-about-everything, one-of-a-kind Livy.

"My mother is...my mother is an alcoholic and a drug addict. I'm fairly sure she was both long before she had me. I'm not even sure how I survived to the point where I could take care of myself, which was about age five. I know we lived with my grandfather at some point, but I don't know how long and I only remember small fragments of that time. I grew up alone. My mother was home sometimes but there was usually some random guy with her that couldn't care less that I existed. My mother was a hateful person. She hit me when she was angry. Even if I didn't provoke it. And there was really no one I could tell. I didn't trust anyone.

"Our town was very small and everyone seemed to have a layer of scum covering them. I tried to give people the benefit of the doubt, but once you've done that a few times and it's bitten you in the ass, you build a wall and keep everyone at a distance. I didn't have friends. I drudged through high school in the shadows, staying away from attention. I let my guard down a few times and went out with guys but none of them ever really wanted *me*—to talk to me or get to know me. They all knew who my mother was and they assumed I was just as easy. They wanted to be the one to uncover the mystery of what I looked like naked. After they discovered it wasn't going to happen, they left me alone for the most part but they all said they'd slept with me anyway…and that I was lousy in bed. I built my wall higher and thicker and just became numb. I knew that if I didn't get out of there I would drown or waste away. Or eventually crack and become my mother. That realization scared the shit out of me. So I began planning my escape. I kept my grades up and applied for scholarships at schools all over the country. I didn't give a shit where I went, I just wanted to go. And I felt like going to college was a better step in the right direction than just running away with no plan at all. I didn't want to move away just to fall on my face in a strange city and end up like my mother anyway. And that's how I ended up here. I got a full scholarship. So, on my eighteenth birthday, I bought a bus ticket and left. And I never looked back." She exhales again, her head hanging, waiting for judgment.

"And you lived in a shelter?" I ask.

Her head snaps up and she looks at me, confused. "I asked Sara and Joe not to say anything about that," she says. "I wanted to be the one to tell you that, if I ever decided to."

I shake my head. "They didn't spill your beans. I met a guy earlier. In the park, when I was looking for you. He said he used to live with you at the south side shelter."

Livy smiles, "That was probably Marcus. You talked to him?"

"Yeah. I was at the footbridge calling out your name and he told me he knew you and hadn't seen you around."

"He's a nice guy. He lost his whole family in a house fire and he just gave up. I don't really blame him. I go talk to him sometimes. I feel like it brightens his day a little."

I grab Livy's hand and smile at her. She continues, "So when I came to the city, I didn't have a place to live or much money. I stayed in a few shelters for a couple of months. I got the job at the bar, Joe hired Sara and she convinced me that taking up space in the tiny living room of her one bedroom apartment would be better than staying in a shelter. And that's pretty much it. So. Now you know. I don't like talking about it because it's all bad and I've moved past it. I didn't want you to pity me because there's nothing to pity. I'm where I am right now because of everything that happened. I am who I am because of all of it. I like where I am and who I am, so I have no grudges or bitterness about it."

"But, Livy, you do," I have to interrupt. I'm not sure who she's trying to fool here. Me or herself. "You do have something. Otherwise you wouldn't have drunk half a bottle of bourbon and told me not to love you because you were unlovable and that it was all your mother's fault."

She looks at me surprised.

"I don't pity you, Livy. Not even a little. I don't look at you any different now that I know what you've held back from me for so long. I hate that you had to go through that, but you are right. All of that has made you who you are. The person I fell in love with. *My* Livy." I lean toward her and place her hand, covered with mine, over my heart.

"So now that we have that established, Livy, you also have to understand that you will never be like your mother. You are not hateful. I watched the way you nursed Joe back to health, and the way you nearly killed yourself to keep the bar straight. I watched the way you looked at Sara the night before she left and told her exactly what she needed to hear to calm her down. And you just told me that you keep a homeless man company sometimes because you see something in him that he doesn't see in himself. Livy, you have a huge heart and you don't even know it's there. You have compassion. Hateful people don't have that."

Livy looks at me as though I am telling her something she seriously does not know. She stares at me and I wait to see if she has anything to say. She shakes her head.

"I don't know what to say about any of that, Jeremy. Marcus, Joe and Sara all helped me when I needed it most. Marcus told me where to look for a job, Joe gave me a job and Sara gave me a stable place to live. I felt the need to reciprocate."

"Maybe. But it's more than that. You care, Livy. Your heart isn't made of ice. You care about people who care about you. Do you not understand that?"

Livy leans back in her chair and let's go of my hand. She doesn't respond. For minutes we sit there in silence. She just sits there staring at her mug again.

"I don't know how to love you, Jeremy," she says, finally.

And then she just changes the subject completely.

"I don't understand what you mean," I reply.

"I have avoided being in a relationship this long because I don't know how to have a relationship with anyone. I tried so hard not to start this with you but I couldn't stop myself. I want to love you, but I'm terrified I'm going to fuck it up. And like I told you before, marriage and kids are completely off the table for me. I think marriage consists of a bullshit piece of paper and vows people never intend to honor. And there is no way in hell I would allow myself to be a mother when I have absolutely zero examples to follow in that department. And if that is something you are aspiring toward, then we have to end this. As much as it kills me to think about that, you have to understand I am serious. No marriage. No kids."

"Livy, look at me." Her eyes shift up to mine. "I want you. *You*. For as long as you'll have me. I love you. I don't know what to tell you about anything else. What I do know about you, Livy, is that you do know how to love me. It probably helps tremendously that I have a mother and two aunts who raised me and treated me like a prince while simultaneously brainwashing me to believe that women are angels sent to earth to keep men from regressing to Neanderthals."

Livy laughs.

"I was smothered with love, Livy. I kinda know how it works. Just… let *me* love *you*. Trust me. If you do, I think you'll figure it out and you'll realize you've loved me all along. Everything else? We'll figure it out. What do you think?"

She looks at me for a long time. I wonder what she's thinking. Is she trying to decide whether she can trust me? Whether I'm telling the truth? Is she going to say *"fuck off"* and walk out the door? I have no clue. I can't read her at all.

"Okay," is all she says.

"Okay?"

She nods "Okay. I trust you, Jeremy. More than I've ever trusted anyone. That trust was instantaneous. You didn't have to earn it. I don't know why that is, but I generally listen to instinct, and my instinct told me to trust you the first night I met you. When you stood behind me with those men at the bar. You let me handle my business, but you had my back just in case. You didn't try to rescue me. I don't know why, but that meant a lot to me. That one single action hooked me and I've been hooked since. You sunk your hook in even farther when you said you liked me for me, but that first night…deep down, I really already knew."

She is staring at me and she says nothing else for a few minutes. Her eyes are locked on mine. It's as if we are trying to read each other's minds. Then she finally speaks again.

The six most fabulous words I have ever heard.

"So. Okay. Go ahead. Love me."

Twelve

Livy

Thirty-seven days later

Meeting the family

I LET HIM LOVE ME. I PUT ALL RESERVATIONS, DOUBTS AND SKEPTICISM regarding relationships aside and just...let him love me.

And he did it so well. My lease ran out and I took up permanent residence at his apartment. Each morning, he woke me with gentle kisses on the back of my neck and shoulder. He wouldn't let me get out of bed until he hugged me for at least a good five minutes.

In the mornings, we cooked breakfast. Together. We did dishes. Together. In the evenings, we cuddled up on the sofa and watched a selection from what Jeremy calls my strange cult collection, (turns out Sara let me keep all of the movies). I've opened his horizons to several movies I thought every red blooded American had seen. *Good Morning Vietnam, The Sandlot, Pulp Fiction, Top Gun* and *The Shining*, so far. He hadn't seen any of these. When we first met, he razzed me for never having gone to the movies in my adult life. However, it turns out my movie prowess was somewhat more expansive than his.

When we weren't watching movies, we were going out on the town. We had finally made it out to the blues club. We danced all night and it was incredible. Jeremy took me to places I didn't know existed. Gastro pubs. Tapas restaurants. Art galleries. To him, the fancier the event, the better, because it called for me wearing a dress and heels. Both of which I still hated. However, the way Jeremy's eyes grew dark when he looked at me in a dress, and the all-night bedroom activities that took place afterward, were most definitely worth the temporary discomfort.

One night, he took me to a book signing. Let me repeat that. A book signing! A receptionist at Jeremy's office heard that George R. R. Martin was having a reading at the bookstore on Fifth. Jeremy was familiar with Martin from the television show derived from his books, but I had been reading his work for years before the show existed.

We attended the reading and when it was my turn for him to sign my copy of his first publication, he balked at the age and wear of the book.

"Would you like a new copy for me to sign?" he asked me.

"No thank you," I replied respectfully. "This is one of the first books I bought when I came to the city. You were in town for a reading then also. I read in an article written about you in the news that your work was inspired by Ivanhoe. I love Ivanhoe. I decided to give you a try." I forced a smile because he looked at me funny. I was trying *not* to come off as a critical know-it-all bitch, but I think I did it anyway.

"I love your writing," I attempted to salvage my end of the conversation "This particular copy of your book is very special to me." I tapped my finger on the ragged edged book.

"Very well, young lady. I am glad you enjoy my work."

"My favorite aspect is that even though your world is completely fictitious and dabbles with fantasy and mythology, you tie in actual real historical notes such as caste systems and political tyranny. It's like you took medieval England and gave it a little LSD."

"Ha! That is quite an interesting perspective."

I smiled, "I call it like I see it."

He chuckled and looked to his left and then to his right. His head disappeared under the table he was sitting behind for a brief moment and reemerged quickly with a paperback in his hand. "Here. It's one of my new novellas. On me. What is your name?"

"Livy. L-I-V-Y," I spelled out.

"Livy," he said as he signed my old, ratty book and also the fresh new book. "I hope you continue to enjoy." He handed me both books and then extended his hand for a shake. I held out my arm and clutched his hand. "It was a pleasure to meet you, Livy. You are a breath of fresh air."

"Pleasure to meet you as well. I am honored to have met you."

"Thank you, dear."

I headed over to Jeremy who watched my entire encounter with Martin. "You two were chatty."

"Jealous?"

"Absolutely," he smiled.

"He gave me a copy of his new novella."

"You dialed up your sexy charm for free swag?"

"Hardly. I just told him what I thought about his books and he thought it was an accurate account. I won the door prize for hitting bingo." I winked.

He wrapped his arms around me and kissed the side of my face. "Did you have fun?"

"The best fun," I responded.

I certainly could get used to being loved.

It's Thanksgiving. I knew the day would come when I'd have to meet his mom and the aunts. We were an official couple now, so I couldn't back out of holiday events.

But not for lack of trying.

The day after I slapped Joe, I went to him as soon as I could and apologized. He accepted, called me a stubborn girl and told me more details about the sale. Once the deal was done, a check with more zeroes than I was comfortable with was cut in my name. At first, the fact that I had no job was foreign to me. The first few days seemed like a vacation. Then as the days passed and began to merge together, I got cabin fever and became a little stir crazy. I remembered the anxious paranoia I had when I first finished school and had more free time than I was used to. Now, all of my time was free and the need to fulfill my days with something meaningful grew even more important. I had to find something to do.

I decided to go to the shelters, which I had once called my home, and volunteer until I figured out something else. I washed linens, cooked food in the kitchen and pitched in however I thought I was needed.

I had told Macy, the manager at the south side shelter, that I would help out on Thanksgiving before Jeremy mentioned going to his mom's for dinner. When he did mention it, I told him I couldn't because I had a commitment already.

He looked at me quizzically then shifted his eyes at me as if he'd figured out a riddle and simply said, "No worries. We eat dinner late at my mom's. We can help out at the shelter for most of the day and then go to Mom's after."

His offering to participate at the south side soup kitchen Thanksgiving service made my heart swell a million times its original size. How could I possibly say no to meeting his mother—on flipping Thanksgiving—now?

"You really didn't have to cook anything. I promise, my mom will have enough to feed a hundred people."

"I don't care. I'm not meeting your mother for the first time—on a holiday—without bringing something."

I had made two pies, apple and pecan, as well as cranberry tart.

Jeremy kisses me on the side of my face in the same spot of his first kiss ever to me. "You are truly amazing, Livy. Truly amazing."

I look at Jeremy and my heart sinks a little at a thought that's been ricocheting in my head. "She can't *not* like me, Jeremy. Never in my life have I been concerned about what anyone thinks about me. But your mother. She can't *not* like me. When you talk about her your eyes sparkle. You two have a bond that I will never comprehend. If she doesn't like me, I won't be good enough for you…" I trail off, spinning one of the pie trays, as if giving it a final quality assurance inspection.

Jeremy puts his hands on either side of my face. "Livy. She already loves you. There is nothing you can do to change her mind. I promise, you will be fine. Just be yourself."

I nod.

Be myself.

"Livy! It is so nice to finally meet you!" Jeremy's mother embraces me with her full body. She pulls back and kisses me on the forehead. "I am so delighted that you have tolerated Jeremy for this long!"

Just as with Jeremy, when his mother comes into my personal space, I don't shutter or recoil. Her hug is comforting and warm and my arms go on autopilot. They reach around this tiny, stout woman and hug her back. Her hug is like Jeremy's. I don't get totally lost in it like I do with Jeremy, but her hug speaks to me. It says: *It's all going to be okay, Livy. You are going to be okay.*

I pull back and say, "Thank you. But I must admit that it's Jeremy that has done most of the tolerating." I look to Jeremy and wink. He winks back.

"Well, whichever it is," his mother starts, "I know my baby boy is just head over heels for you. Before he met you, when we'd talk on the phone all he talked about was *work, work, work.* Now, all he talks about is *you, you, you.*" She squeezes each of my arms at the shoulders and says the last three words between her teeth like she's so happy she might just explode from the elation.

I know Jeremy talks about me to his mother. However, her saying it out loud is a little more than I was ready to hear.

"Mom. Please. Let's let Livy stick her toes in first…get used to the water. If you and Jenna and Maggie submerge her completely at once she might jump out and run away." He leans over and kisses her on the side of the head, hair and all.

His mother looks at me and smiles the kindest smile I've ever seen. "Very well. But you're a good one, Livy. I can tell just by looking into your eyes. My gut tells me so. It'll take more than us three old biddies cackling about to scare you off."

I smile. She's right. I fully understood the dynamic I was walking into. Three women that adore their baby boy to the point of ad nauseam and his girlfriend, a spectacle they aren't used to dealing with. I knew I would get the third degree. I just kept Jeremy's words in my head—*be yourself.*

"You're right." I look at Jeremy. "I'm not going anywhere."

Dinner. Was. Fabulous. As Jeremy predicted, there was enough food for a small army. Turkey, ham, every vegetable that ever existed, most of them slathered in butter or wrapped in bacon, four types of breads. And the desserts. My Lord, at the desserts! Pies, cakes, muffins, strudels, cookies. There was definitely no need for my offerings. However, they were very well received.

"Livy, that cranberry tart is to die for. You have to share the recipe," Jeremy's Aunt Jenna, who insisted I just call her Jenna (*we're all adults here*), said. She was the youngest sister of the triad at only eight years older than Jeremy. Jeremy said Jenna was the one who practically raised him because his mother worked third shift a lot.

"Absolutely. I found it online. Saved the link in case it was a keeper. I'm glad you enjoyed it."

Jeremy's family was warm. They were exactly like what you'd picture on a holiday greeting card. All gathered around the festive dinner table, jovially eating, laughing and catching up on life in conversation. The greeting card with the soft amber light that surrounded the group as if there was a kindled fireplace somewhere in the background. It was fun. I should feel like an outsider but I feel nothing even close. I feel like I've known these people all of my life.

Jeremy told me to go with the flow and soak it all in. Enjoy the good moments. Instead of dwelling on why my crappy past should dictate and solidify a crappy future, I should be focusing on why my crappy past is the exact reason I deserve a happy future.

Deserve.

I deserve to be happy.

Most people might think it an odd concept for someone not to re-alize that they deserve to be happy. But it is foreign to me. It's a mantra that I literally have to repeat to myself every day.

I deserve to be happy.

I am worthy of love.

As I sit around the table, watching everyone's interactions with one another, I do drink it all in. Let it absorb. These people are genuinely happy. They aren't rich. They aren't perfect. But they are filled with love for one another. And they've allowed me to be a part of it.

I let Jeremy love me.

And I let his family love me too.

It's the most satisfying feeling I've ever felt. My whole body feels it. From the tip-top of my skull to the tiny edge of my pinky toenail.

Jeremy's family consists of his mother, Rosalie, of course. His aunt Jenna who is not quite yet thirty. His aunt Maggie, who is the oldest of the three but only a few years older than Jeremy's mother. Jenna and Maggie are both happily married to Mike and Stanley, respectively. Jen-na and Mike have a little girl, Mia, who is two, and Maggie and Stanley have two children—Mark, who is twenty-four and Tabitha who is fif-teen.

Dinner is over and I'm helping Jeremy's mother clean the dish-es. She insisted that I didn't but I insisted harder that I did. She relin-quished, with a hefty grin. It's just the two of is in the kitchen.

"Livy, Jeremy tells me that you don't want to get married or have children."

Here we go.

The *when are you going to make an honest man out of my son and give me millions of beautiful grandbabies* speech.

The speech I never wanted to hear or argue against.

I clear my throat and try to mask my disdain on the topic. My back is turned to her and she's facing the island. I'm at the sink. She can't see my face, so I'm safer in hiding how I really feel. "That's correct."

"So you don't think you'd ever want to marry Jeremy?"

"I don't believe in marriage. It's just a piece of paper and vows that no one honors."

"That isn't entirely true. I'd like to think that if Jeremy's father were still alive, we'd still be happily married. And Maggie and Jenna seem to be doing it right, also."

"You guys are the lucky ones," I retort, maybe a little too surly.

"We are very blessed. All of us are. Jeremy too. He is very blessed to have found you."

I turn to her, still hoping to not get too emotional over the conversation. "Rosalie, Jeremy is the most polite, most caring, humorous, genuine man I've ever met. I'm…I'm rough around the edges. I have… issues. Issues that Jeremy is helping me to acknowledge and resolve, but issues nonetheless. I can't help but think that one day Jeremy will tire of me and want to move on and I certainly don't want that to happen after we make vows before God, family and the state, claiming our ever resilient love for one another. I just want to enjoy the time I spend with Jeremy and not worry about any pressure of being legally bound to him. "

"You don't want to be legally bound to him so you have the opportunity to run and bail, without guilt, if you get scared?" Her words shock me but Jeremy told me that she didn't hold back her thoughts, similar to me. But, she spoke it in a tone that kept the energy of the conversation light.

"I just don't think that vows are real," I pathetically try to defend my convictions.

"I understand your hesitation, Livy. But please keep in mind that Jeremy is a loyal creature. He would never ask you to be his one and only for eternity if he didn't really mean it. If he didn't feel it in his gut."

"Most people have those intentions when they say *I do*."

"You are right. But those people aren't Jeremy. He's practical and analytical. Even if he loves you, he won't ask you for that kind of commitment until he knows for sure that both of you will be on board for the long haul. After you've lived together and can handle each other's quirky living behaviors. After you had arguments over stupid stuff and both come out on top and stronger than before. After your lives have intertwined with each other so much that being separate from one another is unspeakable."

"But I've told Jeremy I don't want to get married." A chill runs up my spine and breaks me out into a cold sweat. "Oh my God, he's not..."

"He's not going to propose if that's what you're asking. I think he would have told me at least."

My heart slows back down to resting rate. "But I will say this. Jeremy is a romantic. He likes the idea of marriage. He doesn't want to be a bachelor forever. You may have discussed your feelings about marriage with him, but my best guess is that he feels eventually you'll change your mind."

I don't know what to say. Jeremy said he understood. Didn't he? Or did he just say something along the lines of *"one day at a time"*? Should I be mad? Or worried? Before I decide on either, Jeremy bolts through the kitchen door in an appearance that he may have had one too many glasses of wine.

"Come beautifuls," he says, slightly slurring, addressing both his mother and me. "It's time for wine and board games." His half lidded eyes and quirky grin are so adorable. I smile, wipe my hands dry and look at his mom. She returns my glance and her eyes are filled with concern. For me. For Jeremy. *"Please don't break his heart"* I feel like she's saying.

"I promise," I try to silently say back.

We all head into the den and play board games well into the night and imbibe on exorbitant amounts of wine. I listen to his mom and aunts tell stories of Jeremy when he was a boy. We all laugh until we cry. It was good, clean family fun and I enjoyed every precious second of it.

The best night of my life...yet.

Thirteen

Jeremy

One month later

Christmas

"JEREMY, WHERE ARE WE GOING?"

"It's a surprise. Part of your Christmas gift."

Livy smiles. "So you figured it out, huh?"

A few weeks ago I had asked her what she wanted for Christmas. She said there was nothing that she could think she wanted. And then she gave me a brow beating about the meaning of the holiday.

"Besides, if I told you I wanted a paperclip for Christmas and the time comes to open gifts and low and behold you got me a paperclip, where's the fun in that? Where's the Christmas spirit? And of course you know if I wanted a paperclip I'd just go out and buy one. Not wait around for you to buy it for me."

"Livy, I feel like you are really hinting around at me getting you a paperclip for Christmas," I had replied sarcastically.

She swatted at my arm gently and rolled her eyes. "Yes. That is exactly what I'm doing. But seriously if you want to get me something so badly, *you* figure it out. I already figured out what I'm getting you and I know you are going to love it. And it wasn't that difficult rubbing some brain cells together to come up with the idea." She smiled and reached

out her arm again to me in an attempt to give my stomach a playful
pinch. I darted backward out of reach just before she made contact and
laughed. "Hey now, no need to resort to physical violence. I just wanted
to know what you wanted for Christmas. But I get it, you're right. It'll
mean more if I figure it out on my own."

"Besides, how can I even think of wanting anything for Christmas
when I see people at the shelter—children—who aren't going to get anything more than a hot meal and maybe a warm blanket?"

Livy had been volunteering at the shelter since Joe closed the bar.
She had even donated a substantial amount of money from her share
of the sell to the shelter, in hopes they could start up some counseling
sessions and job fairs for those that really wanted to try at a fresh start.
She cared so much about those people. All she wanted to do was help.
She had once told me that she didn't know how to love, but Livy's heart
was filled with nothing but just that. She had so much compassion for
those that were left with no option but to be homeless, especially the
women that ran away from their abusive husbands with the sole mind-
set of saving their children from harm.

And those children. She knew them all by name. Their ages. She
loved every single one of them. I could hear the passion in her voice and
see the light that danced in her eyes when she talked about them. How
she would make them smile with just the slightest of gestures. She wanted them all to be saved, happy and free from distress. And she tried her
damnedest to do just that. With every single child. Livy was definitely
capable of love. And I hoped one day that I could convince her that she
was capable of loving children of her own.

My children.

Our children.

But I'm going to take it one day at a time. I have all the patience in
the world.

I hugged her. "Livy, you work so hard at helping the people that
want to be helped. And they may not have a Rockefeller Christmas this
year but they might some day. Because of your help. Because of your
heart. That is exactly the reason you deserve every gift that's ever been
given."

Livy sighed. "I know. It's just that I look into those kids' eyes and all I see is sadness and worry. I just want them to have the childhood they deserve. No child should be homeless. Children should be happy and carefree. No child deserves to have those looks in their eyes that I see every day. What did they ever do to anyone?"

And just then, Livy answers my question. I know exactly what I'm getting her for Christmas.

"We're taking the car?" Livy asks, as the apartment building elevator opens to the parking garage.

"Mmmhmm," is all I reply.

"You are a mysterious man, Jeremy Waters."

"Why thank you, Livy."

We get in the car and head to our destination. While I drive, Livy remains silent and she is dissecting our route, trying to figure out where we are going.

Finally, I pull into a small parking lot behind a two story building.

"Jeremy…" Livy looks at me. "This is…this is the shelter. What are we doing here?"

"Get out and help me unload the back, will ya?"

"The back? What the f…?"

"Come on then," I say, heading toward the hatch of the car.

Livy meets me at the hatch and I open it just as I'm finishing up a text message to Roscoe, a volunteer at the shelter who is going to meet us outside with a rolling cart.

Livy peers inside the hatch. "Jeremy! What is this?"

"Gifts for the kids, of course." There are about four dozen gifts, wrapped with shiny Christmas paper and ribbons and bows. All shapes and sizes. Three for each child at the shelter. I called the manager, Macy, who is good friends with Livy, and asked if I could get the first names, gender and ages of all the children intending to stay there that night, which happened to be Christmas Eve. She gave me the names of twelve children. I had taken up a collection at work and mom and the aunts chipped in as well. I went out shopping and purchased three toys for each child. Mom and the aunts volunteered to wrap the gifts and they did a beautiful job. We're talking Martha Stewart professionalism level.

"Jeremy, tell me. What is all this?" Livy asks, just as Roscoe comes out with the cart.

"I asked some people at work to chip in a few bucks for some Christmas presents for the homeless children where you volunteered. I also told mom about it in passing conversation and she insisted that she, Jenna and Maggie would chip in too. And they wrapped everything. After I collected the money, I called Macy this morning and got the names and ages of all the kids. Each kid has three gifts here, labeled with their names. Macy said there is a tree set up in the chapel so Roscoe here is going to help us load these onto the cart and we are going to put them under the tree. Then, we are going to gather the children and their parents and hand out gifts. Oh, and Mom also made Christmas cookies."

Livy is staring at me, speechless. I can tell she's speechless because her mouth is agape as if she wants to speak but she's just unable to.

"Merry Christmas, Livy."

She inhales a quick deep breath. Then, she exhales a quick deep breath. By the dim light of the bulbs illuminating the parking lot, I can see her eyes are getting glassy.

"Jeremy," she finally lets out in a breathy tone. "Oh...my...God. I don't even...how did you?"

"I pulled some strings. You know, you've got a lot of clout around here, missy. I pitched the idea to Macy and she loved it. These people that work here would move heaven and earth for you. They absolutely adore you."

"It's true," Roscoe confirms.

Livy looks at Roscoe briefly and then back at me. She lurches toward me and gives me a big bear hug. She whispers in my ear, "Tell those brain cells of yours *good job*. You figured out the perfect gift indeed. Thank you, Jeremy. Thank you so much!"

"You are most welcome. I knew this would mean a lot to you."

"You have no idea."

She lets me go. "Let's get this party started." Once we get the gifts loaded onto the cart, I reach into the hatch and grab two large duffle bags that were hiding behind the gifts.

"What are those?" Livy asks.

I looked down at my hands each holding a duffle bag weighing, I'd say, a good fifteen pounds. "Well, after asking people at work for money for the kids at your shelter, a number of them got together and decided to donate clothes as well. There are clothes in here of all sizes. Women's clothes. Kid's clothes. Baby clothes, if you ever need them. In the back seat, I've also got a box of blankets, two boxes of women's shoes, a box of children's shoes and a suit bag that has three women's suits that you could maybe loan out for job interviews for the mothers."

Livy lifts her hands and cups her mouth, fingers pointing toward her nose as if she's saying a silent prayer. "Holy fuck, Jeremy! This is just...so...amazing! I seriously cannot believe this is happening." She hugs me again and I'm forced to drop the duffle bags. "Thank you!" she says again.

I hug her back. We engage in one of those comforting, solace hugs she's always referring to and we stay there for a long time. Roscoe clears his throat to break our spell. "Sorry, Roscoe," I say.

"No worries," he replies. "It's pretty chilly out here. Best we get inside."

"Absolutely," Livy says. Roscoe begins to walk in with the cart. Livy follows behind, cookies in hand, with what appears to be a skip in her step. I pick up the duffle bags and decide to retrieve the rest that's in the back seat later. There's no way I'm going to delay Livy's fun any longer.

The children were thrilled and the parents were so very grateful. Roscoe and I made another trip to the car with the cart and retrieved the donated clothes. After all the gifts were opened and all the clothes were given a once over, Livy and I decided to head home. We thank Roscoe and everyone at the shelter that was involved with helping. Making our way out the door, in the parking lot toward the car, Livy grabs my hand and stops walking. I stop and turn to her. "What is it, Livy?"

She stares into my eyes and then puts her hands on either side of my face. She slowly runs both of her thumbs up and down my cheekbones, still staring. I wait for her to speak. Instead she kisses me. A hard, passionate, breathtaking kiss. With her hands still on my face, she releases my lips from hers. Her eyes hone in on mine once more.

"I love you, Jeremy."

I smile the biggest smile I've ever smiled in my history of smiling smiles.

I wrap my arms around her waist and lift her off of her feet. She wraps her arms around my neck and I attempt to kiss her. It's difficult, however, for my lips to make any sort of simulation of the position they should be while kissing because they are too busy smiling.

I can't stop smiling.

She loves me.

My heart feels so big that I feel like I want to…

Cry?

I put her back down on the ground and envelope her into a hug. One of *those* hugs.

She said she loved me. I knew she would eventually, but finally hearing it after waiting all this time, waiting for her to be ready to admit she loved me is…it's quite an overwhelming feeling.

Blood is rushing to my head, which is suddenly spinning. My heart is volleying itself between my chest and the bottom of my shoulder blade. My face is stuck in eternal smile mode. My hands are sweating.

All because she said she loves me. My body may be shutting down on me, yet I want to hear it again.

With her head still resting against my chest and our arms locked tightly around each other, I say, "Say it again. Please."

There's silence. Did I imagine it? Wait, am I dreaming?

"I love you, Jeremy."

Ah. There it is. The pinch I needed. Not dreaming.

I squeeze Livy tighter. "I love you too. So much."

"Good morning," I say to Livy as I roll over to wake her up. She's lying on her stomach, naked with the covers only covering her from the waist down. Her back might be my favorite part of her body. The curve of her shoulders, her olive skin and the dimples at the bottom, just above her ass, all drive me wild. It's a blank canvas that I want to paint with kisses. Which is what I do. I start at her neck and work my way down.

"Mmm. Good morning to you too," she says. She lets me kiss her on the back a few more times and then she rolls over, takes my face into her hands and kisses me. "I love you," she whispers.

"You better watch out," I say with a smile. "You are going to wear it out."

I say this, jokingly, considering we stayed up for many hours last night after we got home, stripped naked, and I was able to get her to say *I love you* about fifteen to twenty more times.

"I doubt that," she says and kisses me again. I lean into her a little, suggesting perhaps a little morning delight before we get up to open our gifts.

"What time is it?" she asks.

"A little after nine."

Livy pushes me away and rolls out of bed. She stands, nude.

For the love of God, how did I get so lucky?

She throws on a t-shirt and runs out into the living room yelling, "It's time to open your gift!"

I fall flat, face down onto the bed.

Shot down.

I get up and lazily put on my pajama pants and head into the living room.

Livy is sitting by the tree on the floor with her legs tucked under her knees. I can't believe she's sitting there in nothing but a long t-shirt. In her lap is a small, white envelope. She pats the floor in front of me, "Come here! Sit." I obey and sit on the floor in front of her. She picks up the envelope, leans in for a kiss and then passes the envelope to me.

"Merry Christmas."

I look down at the envelope and flip it over a few times. The flat, unsealed side has my name on it. "I don't have very high expectations about this," I joke.

"Oh, just open it already," she says blithely.

"Impatient much?" I ask her.

Her eyes give me the middle finger and tell me to knock off the shenanigans and open it.

So, I tear in and pull out a slip of thick, glossy paper and take a moment to read.

Holy shit. No fucking way!

"Livy! This is…how? I didn't even know this was a thing."

"That's what she said," she replies.

"Seriously? A tour of the ESPN news room? And lunch with the anchors? I cannot believe this. This is the best gift ever. How did you even know that this was possible?"

"Well, I remember at Thanksgiving how you and Mike were talking about how cool it would be to go there. So, I used this magic tool called Google to see if I could make it happen. And it turns out, I could."

I lean over to hug her. And then I pull her over into my lap and kiss her. "Thank you. So much. This is really pretty amazing."

"That's what she said."

I laugh. "That's a bit inappropriate for Christmas morning, don't you think?" I tease.

She snickers. "That's what she said!" and continues to laugh.

"That one didn't even make sense" and before she can continue her silly *that's what she said* loop, I kiss her again.

She pulls back. "I don't know if you noticed but that tour is for two. I mean, I know you would probably want to take Mike considering your conversation and all…"

"Fuck Mike. I'm taking you. If it weren't for ESPN, we might not be with each other right now. I wouldn't dream of taking anyone else."

"Yay," she exclaims while making little baby claps with her finger-tips.

"So, you really think if I hadn't told you that I like to watch ESPN, you wouldn't have made that first move that night?" she asks, smiling.

"Well…you know, I was on the fence. *Is Livy cool enough?*" I say with my hand in the air, flat out, tipping it back and forth as if weighing the thought.

She taps me on the chest with the back of her hand. "Shut the fuck up. You are so full of shit," she laughs. She clasps her hands together, tilts her head to the side and bats her eyes with much exaggeration "I had you at hellooo…" she says in a high pitch, melodic voice.

I chuckle. "Actually, I think the words were 'what can I do you for?'"

She smiles and her eyes sparkle. "I love you," she says and darts in for a quick peck on the lips.

"I love you too." I smile back "Now. Time for your gift." I peek under the tree and grab a small box I hid in the branches a few days ago.

I present the box to Livy and her eyes go wide. Very wide. "First of all, you already gave me my gift last night with what you organized at the shelter. That was way more than enough." She points at the box, her eyes still wide, "Second of all, what the fuck is that?"

"Livy. Just open the box."

She looks at me. Then the box. Then back at me. She shakes her head no.

She's starting to freak out which was not my intention at all. I push my hand out to her further.

"Livy, just open the box."

Fourteen

Livy

New Year's Eve

"**L**IVY, JUST OPEN THE BOX."
    No. I know what's in it. It's a black felt box. One with a little hinge on the back so it snaps open and shut. A jewelry box. A ring box.

A. Fucking. Ring. Box.

I shake my head no. *I can't. I can't.*

He's going to ask me a question and I'm going to have to say no. And then it'll be over. No more Jeremy and Livy.

"Livy, come on. Don't be afraid."

I continue to shake my head no.

Jeremy rolls his eyes at me. "Holy cow. I really didn't think you would react this way."

I've told him I don't want to get married. How did he not think I would react this way? And what about what his mother said at Thanksgiving after dinner? About him not doing this unless he was sure and we were basically molded together and inseparable? We have barely lived together. We are not at that point that his mother explained. Does he think we are? Maybe he does and maybe I'm just never going to have that feeling because of my conviction and lack of need to get married.

Is it because I said I loved him?

I do love him.

Jeremy places his free hand on top of the box and begins opening it. It literally creeks as he slowly opens it. Soooo…slowly. I'm frozen. Time is frozen. The whole world is frozen with the exception of Jeremy's hand opening the box. I want to protest and snatch the box from his hand and throw it out of the window or flush it down the toilet. But I'm frozen and everything is happening in high-speed-camera-slow-motion.

The box finally pops completely open.

In it lies a small

Shiny

Silver

Metal

Paperclip.

I take a moment to register this. It's a paperclip. Not a ring. A paperclip.

"A paperclip?" I ask. I just had an anxiety attack over a fucking paperclip? Jeremy was fucking with me. If it weren't for that damn adorable smile on his face, I might have gotten angry. Instead, I internalize my panic and annoyance and focus on the fact that it was a good joke and he made a comical point regarding the reference I had made weeks earlier about the paperclip. Besides, I couldn't be mad at him on Christmas day.

"You were pretty adamant about getting a paperclip," he says. "You ask. I deliver. Merry Christmas." Jeremy smiles and leans in to kiss me on the side of my face.

I try to keep the mood light and not let on that my heart was still at a rapid pace because I thought thirty seconds ago there was a ring in that box. I smile and layer my words with thick, sultry sarcasm. "Wow. It's perfect."

Jeremy chuckles and returns, "That's what she said." I let out a genuine laugh. I love how absolutely perfectly juvenile we both are. Pranks and dick jokes all before breakfast on Christmas morning.

Jeremy has planned quite the evening for New Year's Eve. It was a *dress and heels* kind of event. I anticipate our festivities will carry on well into January 1st of the next year.

We began with dinner downtown at a sushi restaurant of all places—a revolving sushi restaurant at the top of a hotel with a fantastic view of the city. What says fun more than raw fish and spinning thirty stories up in the air, right?

I'd never had sushi before, but I figured what the heck, I'd end the year with a bang and be adventurous. As it turns out, I'm in love with spicy tuna and any other roll as long as it's drizzled with wasabi vinaigrette. That shit is amazing! I'm going to have to figure that recipe out. I'd eat that with cardboard!

I wasn't too keen on the Sake, though. However, it did pack quite a punch. One tiny, warm cup was plenty for me.

After dinner, the plan was to head to another floor of the hotel where they opened up a ball room for a New Year's Eve party. There was supposed to be a swing band playing. Neither Jeremy nor I can swing dance, but we thought it would be fun to try. These heels might give me a fit, but we'll see.

Adventurous…

Before we head down to phase two of the evening, I feel the need to get something off my chest. Something that's been nagging me since Christmas morning. Something I've thought about no less than fifty million times in the week that has passed.

I grab Jeremy's hand across the table. "Jeremy, I'm sorry about the way I acted when you gave me the paperclip. I was an asshole. I shouldn't have just assumed that you would…propose." That last word was very difficult to spit out. "I should have…trusted you more. I mean. I do trust you. I guess…I don't know…red flags and sirens went off in my head screaming *danger Will Robinson* and I didn't get a chance to think clearly."

Jeremy squeezes my hand and smiles. "Danger Will Robinson? That's what your brains says when you get freaked out?"

I nod.

"Well shit," Jeremy laughs. "I don't blame you then. I'd freak out too if my head screamed that. Is it like in the robot voice and everything?"

I giggle. "Yes it is, as a matter of fact. But, Jeremy, I'm serious. I'm sorry."

"It's okay, Livy. Really, don't worry about it. I have a confession. I put the paperclip in the ring box on purpose. I just wanted to see your face. It was supposed to be a joke, but I guess I just didn't think it through. I'm the asshole. I'm sorry too."

"Well I'm glad we cleared the air on that," I say.

"Me too."

We squeeze hands again.

I wonder if my reaction to the joke proposal scared him off enough to never actually propose. I hope so.

Don't I?

Wait, what? Where did that thought come from? How did those two tiny little words pop into my head? Before I can assess, Jeremy says, "So. Ready to head downstairs and dance like idiots?"

I smile and nod. I'll worry about those two tiny little words later. Right now, it is time for fun. "Absolutely."

And we did dance like idiots. Right up until midnight. I had to take my shoes off to keep dancing, but I promised Jeremy I'd put them back on later. We toasted with champagne and kissed when the countdown reached zero. Jeremy lifted me up and spun me around. We were having the time of our lives.

"I love you," he says.

"I love you too," I reply.

We had survived our first holiday trifecta together. And I have to say, hands down, that it was the best holiday trifecta I'd ever had.

Jeremy makes everything better.

I could do this forever.

I could do this forever.

Forever.

We've had quite the mixture of champagne, tequila shots and beer. The onslaught of booze to my brain is making me contemplate thoughts of forever. Can forever really exist with one person? Happily ever after? Sure, there are couples out there who have been married to each other for fifty, fifty-five, sixty years. But are they happy? Is it really possible? And on top of all of these thoughts, I'm wondering why the fuck am I thinking these thoughts at all?

Jeremy pulls a key card out if his wallet. "Ready to take this party to our suite?" He slurs a little.

The final phase of the evening was to take place in a luxurious suite that Jeremy had reserved. A fun filled evening of dinner, dancing and… other extracurricular activities, all wrapped up in one location. It was a brilliant idea. One that Jeremy had come up with and executed masterfully.

I turn up my champagne glass and empty it. "Yep. Very ready. Let's go," I slur a little too, in return.

We head to the room, drunk on champagne and maybe even love. We can't keep our hands off of each other in the elevator. We stumble and giggle down the hall until we reach our door. Jeremy slides the key and opens the door.

"Ladies first," he says, holding the door open and motioning for me to enter ahead of him.

I walk in and instantly head to the bedroom, hoping Jeremy is following close behind. I walk in the bedroom and my eyes immediately focus on the center of the bed.

"What the fuck is all this?" I turn to ask Jeremy.

He smiles. "Thought we could have a little kinky start to the first day of the year."

I turn back to take stock of the items on the bed. Handcuffs. An assortment of sex toys. Oils, for his *and* her pleasure. A bottle of chocolate syrup and a bowl of red, luscious strawberries. And a silver tray with two crystal flutes and a bucket filled with ice and chilled champagne.

"Thought we could maybe start with the champagne." He's right behind me now. He moves my hair away from my neck and kisses the back of it.

"You are a dirty, dirty boy, Jeremy."

I tilt my head to the side and he begins unzipping my dress.

"Will you leave the heels on?" he asks.

"Whatever you want." I bring my arm up and wrap it around the side of his face and grab his hair. His lips on my neck always make me shudder. My heartbeat quickens.

I am so very ready to be delightfully tortured.

Cheers and Happy New Year to me. Here's to being adventurous.

Fifteen

Jeremy

Four months later

One-year anniversary

L IVY IS THE LOVE OF MY LIFE.
   One year ago today, I stumbled into a bar and met the love of my life.

We've been living together for nearly half a year, now. It's been an interesting adjustment. When Livy said she needed her own space, she wasn't joking. A few times, she's gotten pissed off for what seems to be no reason whatsoever. The first time, I tried to confront her about it while she was still angry. And that, I quickly learned, was a terrible idea. Now, I know that when she seems frazzled or overwhelmed about something, I should not say a word to her until she is calm and regrouped. Generally, she'll retreat to her book room until aforementioned regrouping has commenced. Then, when she's ready, she'll tell me why she was upset. If I deviate from that pattern, it just prolongs her anger and I get an earful of a few colorful words.

We've also argued about mundane things. Dirty dishes. Control of the remote. Sharing a bathroom.

Speaking of bathrooms, I have to admit, sharing one with Livy is quite nice, when we aren't arguing over the lack of space there is for two people to be in there simultaneously. It's nice because it always smells like peaches and since I met Livy, that is my most favorite smell.

The other great thing about sharing a bathroom is Livy's singing. She sings in the shower. The first time I caught her singing in the shower, I stood outside the door for nearly twenty minutes listening. She has a great, low raspy voice which was befitting to the song she was singing. She was singing the Janis Joplin song about Bobby McGee. She sang it two or three times while I stood outside the door listening. I knew this song from when my mother listened to it when I was a child. Livy knew every word and sang it just like Janis. It was beautiful and sexy as hell. Shortly after witnessing that encounter, I downloaded that song onto my iPod and played it one night while we were sitting on our living room floor playing cards around the coffee table. She smiled when the first few notes played through the speakers.

She looked up at me from her hand of cards and asked, "How do you know this song?"

I shrugged my shoulders and smiled back. "Something my mother used to listen to."

"Is that right?" she replied accusingly.

"Mmhm," is all I offered.

After a few verses played, "How do *you* know this song?" I asked.

"People used to play it on the jukebox at the bar all of the time. Her voice is so unique. Joe got me one of her CDs for Christmas one year after he said he'd seen me singing one of her songs while cleaning the bar one night."

"So you sing her songs?"

She gave me an intense look. I wasn't fooling her one bit, but then again, I wasn't trying very hard to fool her. "I think we both know the answer to that question," she said.

"You have a beautiful voice."

"I know." She smiled.

"Will you sing for me?"

"Right now?"

I nodded.

She gave me a half smile without looking up from her cards. "Sure."

I reached over to my iPod and hit the back button so that the song could start from the beginning. She sang and we continued to play cards. I played the song twice before she threw down her cards and climbed over the coffee table and straddled my lap, running her fingers through my hair and kissing me until I didn't think I could breathe anymore.

And so began the tradition of me eavesdropping in on her shower singing and me downloading the song to have her sing it for me. Her voice turned me on and for her, watching me watching her sing turned her on. I never interrupted her shower singing sessions, although I certainly wanted to. But it was a game. A fun game. A game that always ended with sex and that was a win for all parties involved.

All in all, I love living with Livy. I love waking up to her peachy scent every morning. And being able to have breakfast with her before I go to work. I love falling asleep on the sofa with her in the middle of a movie. All of these things, essentially we did before she moved in but now it just seems more official or permanent. I don't want anything to change. I can't imagine *not* living with Livy or *not* being in a relationship with Livy. She is the air in my lungs, the blood in my veins, the beat of my heart. I was made for Livy and she was made for me. And all of that other Shakespearean stuff that we learned about in high school. Those words exist because they are true. You hear the cheesy, chestnut, antiquated proclamations of love like that and you think that no one person can feel that way about another human being. But, in fact, they can. It's how I feel about Livy.

It's our anniversary. Livy hasn't mentioned it and I'm not sure if she even knows that it's been a year. This evening I am going to take her to the park, by the bridge, which is her favorite spot in the city. I'm getting takeout from the restaurant where we had our first date—which happened a week after we first met so technically *that* is our anniversary but that's all just semantics. I have wine. The same wine from our first date. I have cozy blankets, music and battery powered LED candles. I am hoping the sky will produce enough ambiance to set the mood I'm trying to portray.

Because I'm going to propose.

"Livy, my mother has a saying about listening to your gut to make important life decisions. I want you to know I've thought about this a lot and I'm listening to my gut. I know you want to say no but just hear me out before you say anything.

"To you, marriage is just a piece of paper and vows people don't take seriously. To me, marriage is about wanting to *proudly* call you my wife and to be able to *proudly* call myself your husband. To *me*, a husband and wife are two people who have found one another and want to make the commitment to be there for each other no matter what.

"I know in my heart and with every fiber of my being that I want to be with you for the rest of my life. I want to wake up to your beautiful face every morning. I only want to kiss your lips and look into your eyes. My heart has never felt anything the way it feels when I'm with you. We live together, we get along just fine. We tolerate and accept each other's differences and idiosyncrasies. I am totally, one-hundred-and-thirty percent comfortable around you. I think about you all day. The way you laugh. The way you smell. The way you are completely different from any woman I've ever met and the way I love every single thing about what makes you unique. I love you, Livy. I can't be without you. You are my best friend. If you would grant me the opportunity of letting me call you my wife, I swear to you that I will honor every word I say to you, up at that altar, until the day I take my last breath. You have to believe me. I want to have what my mom and dad had. I want to have what my aunts and their husbands have. I want *you*. Forever.

"Livy, will you marry me?"

Sixteen

Livy

The proposal

"I HAVE TO TELL YOU SOMETHING," SARA SAID TO ME OVER THE phone.

"What is it? You are worrying me. It's the middle of the day. On a Friday. Shouldn't you be researching something or writing about some medical breakthrough right now?"

"Yes," Sara exclaims. "I should be in the lab right now but I have to tell you something. It's about Jeremy. I'm a horrible person for telling you, but I am afraid that you are going to freak out on Jeremy and ruin everything."

I can feel my face flush with anxiety as my heart begins to pick up pace. "Sara what are you talking about? What is wrong with Jeremy?"

He's hurt.

He's dead.

He's cheating.

He's a spy.

All things that rush through my brain. But I focus on the part that Sara said I would ruin something and I am instantly confused. There is silence on the phone. "Sara? Just spit it out. You called me in a panic and now you are not speaking. What is it?"

I pause.

"Sara? Dammit, Sara if you don't say something I am going to hang up on you and…"

"He's going to propose!" she blurts out.

My mind takes a minute to translate those four words.

He's going to propose.

I have full understanding of the definition of each of those words, but as Sara said them, all lumped together in one sentence, I am finding difficulty comprehending them.

"Livy! Now you say something."

"I…" is all that comes out. And then there's silence.

Finally, Sara speaks. "Look, I know it's supposed to be a surprise and I tried to explain to Jeremy that it wasn't a good idea to surprise you with something like this, but he wouldn't listen. He said he had it handled. But I know you, Livy. I knew if he got down on one knee without you having any notion of what was about to happen, you would run. And I'm calling to tell you not to run. Don't freak out. Listen to him, Livy. Listen to what he has to say. And remember that this is Jeremy we are talking about. Sweet, funny, rock hard abs, Jeremy. Loyal Jeremy. Trustworthy Jeremy. If you don't want to marry him, fine. But don't run away from him. He's good for you, Livy. I know you know that."

Rosalie did tell me that when he knew it was right, he would ask, even though I told him I never would.

"Livy, I wish I could be there in person to read your face right now. What are you thinking?"

"When is he doing this, Sara?"

"Livy?"

"When?"

"Tonight."

"Thank you. I have to go."

"Livy, wait!" I hang up before she can say anything else.

My initial instinct is to go find Jeremy and ask him *what the fuck?* But I lean back in my chair and stare at the wall for at least two hours. My phone rings three times, before I put it on silent, all calls from Sara. I've freaked her out. Rightfully so, but fair retaliation for her freaking me out.

Jeremy is going to propose. Tonight. What am I going to do? What am I going to say? The fact that I even have to consider that I may not immediately say no worries and relieves me simultaneously. It worries me because I'm considering accepting his proposal, which means I'm vacillating on my firm opinion of never getting married. But it relieves me because it means that I may see things in a different perspective. Maybe being married to Jeremy wouldn't be so bad. And, if I said no to his proposal, then what? He wants to get married and if I don't then what? Will we break up? Will he find someone else who does want to get married and live happily ever after with *her*? I don't want to lose Jeremy. He makes me happy. I love him. To be without him would devastate me.

From the second he knelt in front of me, my head began to spin. I heard every word he said. I understood. He wants to spend the rest of his life with me.

His life.

My life.

Our lives.

What part of *I don't want to get married* didn't he grasp?

I'm a terrible girlfriend. I didn't even register that we'd been together for a year. I can't be a fiancé, let alone a wife.

Negativity infiltrates my brain.

Can't do it.

Not possible.

No sir.

However, as he is kneeling there, professing his love, telling me that he swears to love me forever, under all circumstances, I look into his eyes.

Jeremy has never lied to me.

He is open and honest. Not as blunt and brash as me, but honest all the same.

He wants to love me forever through whatever thick and thin we may face.

He says he doesn't want to be without me.

I don't want to be without him.

We already live together. We've had minor ups and downs. If he wants to be legally bound to me, *until his last breath*, why shouldn't I want to make him happy?

Why didn't I want to ever get married again?

Oh yeah, I didn't want to be stuck with someone who turned out to be a douche bag later down the road and decide he didn't want me anymore because I'm such a pain in the ass.

But Jeremy won't do that. I know it.

He is telling me this. His voice is begging me to believe him.

And I do. I do believe him. Because I know Jeremy. Really, truly know him. His words are genuine.

I want to spend the rest of my life with him.

"Livy, will you marry me?" He's holding his breath, terrified that I'll protest and say no.

And before I know that it's happening, my head begins to nod and I'm crying.

Big fat tears.

Jeremy's eyes grow big in shock. "Livy?"

My head still nodding, I open my mouth. "Yes," I squeak out. "Yes, Jeremy, I will marry you."

Seventeen

Livy

Three months later

The wedding

I HAD ABSOLUTELY NO REASON TO WASTE MONEY ON ANYTHING FANCY. Jeremy wanted to do everything traditional. Getting married in a church was his top request. Specifically, the church his parents were married in.

I agreed and asked his mother if she would make those arrangements. She was thrilled.

She, along with Jenna and Maggie, took care of nearly all the details. And they've been frantic. Planning a wedding in three months, after all, is tough business, so I've been told. But I stressed to them that I wanted everything as simple and inexpensive as possible. I absolutely refused to spend money on things like flowers or tiny little candies with our names on them.

No hearts on everything.

No mushy, romantic music.

No rice to be thrown at me.

All of that was dumb and a pure waste of money. And I made sure the ladies understood.

Jeremy wanted to get married in a church and he wanted all of his family there and I was happy to do it for him. Since the day he proposed his demeanor has become more jovial than I've ever seen it before.

He says it because I've made him the happiest man alive by agreeing to marry him.

When his mother told us that the only available date for the church was only three months away, she thought we'd be concerned. However, Jeremy and I both were pretty happy about the news. Him more than me, maybe. He said the sooner the better. I agreed but not really for the same reasons. If it had been up to me, we would have just gone to the courthouse and made things legally official. I'm not too eager to walk down an isle while all of his family—and Joe and Sara, of course—stare at me.

Jeremy's mother insisted we go dress shopping right away. "*Three months is not much time at all to not only find a dress but have it altered,*" she kept reminding me.

I had to put the brakes on the crazy dress talk.

"I am happy to let you go dress shopping with me but I'm going vintage. As in *used.* I'm not spending the next six weekends twirling around in some fancy dress boutique pretending I care about anything like that. Sara told me about a few places that sell vintage gowns. She's going to be in town in two weeks and she wanted to be a part of the dress shopping as well. Is that ok?"

"Of course, my love," Jeremy's mother says as she clasps her hands together and smiles. "We will all go together."

And that we did. Sara came home. She got to meet Jeremy's trio and they all instantly clicked. She showed us three stores and at the third one, after trying on a myriad of beaded and laced gowns, I found a dress that I thought Jeremy would love.

This was all for him, after all. I'd get married in a tank top and yoga pants. This dress was for Jeremy.

It was short but not *tacky short.* It came to my knees, short enough to show off my legs. The color was off-white and there was a mixture of lace and beads covering the majority of the fabric. It was sleeveless with thick shoulder straps. The front had a modest scooped neckline, I assume to make up for the nearly nonexistent back. It plunged almost to my waist. The skirt of the dress had multiple layers of fabric but it wasn't poufy. *Flowy* I think was the word Sara used. It was a beautiful dress and I knew Jeremy would love it.

"It's perfect," I said while wearing it and checking myself out in the mirror. All the ladies of my entourage agreed.

Today is the day. From all of the accounts I've read about or seen on TV, brides are supposed to be bundles of nerves. But I'm not really. I'm just sitting. Waiting. Looking in the mirror at myself in the vanity. Sara and the trio insisted on doing my nails, hair and makeup. I don't even look like myself. I look like an amazingly beautiful android of myself. They did a hell of a job. It's the first time this face has seen foundation and blush. Quite a transformation.

Now I'm sitting here alone waiting on everything to start. I'm not allowed to move until I'm summoned. Sara has been in twice, stopping herself from crying both times.

"I cannot believe you are getting married, Livy. I am so happy for you. Jeremy is…" Sara pauses and looks up at the ceiling for a second and then looks back at me. "He was put on this earth just for you, Livy."

I smile. It's a good theory, but highly unlikely. "He is perfect," I say, "And I hope I can be perfect for him too."

"Livy, you've never shown him anything but exactly who you are and he loves you. Every bit of you."

"I know. I know," I concur.

In thinking back on our last conversation before she left and promised not to return, Sara is absolutely right. Jeremy loves me for me. And I love him for just that reason. I never thought I'd find something like this but for some reason or another, it fell right into my lap. I didn't even have to try.

And maybe that's what it's all about. Just letting it happen.

There is a rap at my door and then the door creaks open a little.

"Livy, girl?"

It's Joe. "Come in, Joe."

"Oh, Livy, you look absolutely stunning." I stand up and he hugs me. He's wearing a freaking suit. Neck tie and all. "Thank you, Joe. You clean up pretty nice yourself."

Joe looks down at himself and runs his hands down his jacket. "Yeah, well I got all gussied up cuz I figured I'd be walking ya down the aisle."

"What? Joe…"

He puts up his hand, palm facing me. "Now before you get all in a twist, it was Jeremy's idea. We were gonna surprise ya. He didn't want you walking down that aisle all by yourself. He said that wasn't fair."

I open my mouth to respond but before I can, Joe continues. "So that was the plan. But then it changed a bit. Well, I mean. It's up to you. You'll see." Joe clears his throat.

"Joe. I don't understand."

"Livy. There's someone here. Jeremy invited someone today. Some…of your family…"

What? I don't have any family.

My immediate thought goes to Nancy. There is no way in fucking hell that Jeremy would invite her. No fucking way.

"Joe, what are you talking about? I don't have any family?"

Joe shifts his weight to his other leg. "Apparently, you do. Just… wait here."

He walks out of the door and leaves it slightly open. My heart is racing. I swear to God if Nancy is on the other side of that door, I am out of here. No wedding. No Jeremy. If he thought inviting her here was somehow acceptable in the least, then he doesn't know me at all and this marriage is done before it begins.

I see a hand grasp the open door. It's an old hand. Wrinkled, with age spots. And it's not a feminine hand. It's very much male.

"Livy?"

What do I say? Who is this? "Yes?"

The door opens and a man of about sixty stands there in the door-way. His hair is white and he's wearing a black tuxedo.

Is this the minister Rosalie hired? He looks awfully familiar. Is he the one who was sent to retrieve me to start the wedding?

Wait. Where is Nancy?

I'm so confused.

"Livy," the man repeats. And then he puts his balled fist up to his mouth. He begins to cry. "Oh my dear, precious, Livy. I have waited so long to see you again."

See me again? If this is the minister, we have issues. He is way too emotional for this job.

"I'm sorry. But who are you, exactly?"

With his hand still at his mouth his lets out a sobby exhale. "Oh, Livy. I'm your grandfather. My name is Maxwell and I am your mother's father."

Eighteen

Jeremy

The wedding

"JEREMY! COME QUICK! IT'S LIVY! SHE PASSED OUT!" JENNA IS running and waving at me. I can hardly make out the words.

"What? What do you mean? What happened?"

"You tried to do a good thing, sweet boy, but you surprised the shit out of her and now she's lying on the floor unconscious."

Oh shit.

I jump up and follow Jenna.

I've been trying to find Livy's grandfather since the night she told me about her mother. I had my old pal Officer Santos speak to some of his detective friends. Turns out, Livy's mother had been arrested a few times some years back and once, a man named Maxwell Jenkins bailed her out. Seeing as he had the same last name as Livy and her mother, the detectives rightfully assumed he was family of some sort and after digging a little, they found out he was Livy's grandfather. They found his current address and I went to visit him a month ago. I told him that I was engaged to Livy and that I didn't know much about her past, but I knew that her mother didn't treat her well and her fondest childhood memories were of her granddad.

Maxwell cried when I told him that. And he was so very grateful that I reached out to him. He said he had tried to find Nancy and Livy for years but couldn't. He also said that he had convinced Nancy to live with him and help her raise Livy, but that only lasted a few months. Nancy couldn't keep herself away from the drugs and left with Livy in the middle of the night. He had been heartbroken to find they were gone the next morning.

"If only she had asked me. She could have left and let Livy stay with me. She was the most precious child." He cried more. Then he showed me a few pictures he had of Livy when she was four.

I stayed with Maxwell an entire afternoon. I told him how I met Livy and I showed him some pictures I had of her on my phone. Then I told him we were getting married in a month and that the best gift I could give my bride was for him to be there and possibly walk her down the aisle.

He was thrilled.

I was thrilled.

However, I think Livy was something other than thrilled.

I followed Jenna into the room where Livy was. All of our guests were surrounding her as she was lying there on the floor in a gorgeous dress.

Shit. I'm not supposed to see her before the wedding.

My mother is fanning Livy's face. Maxwell looks up at me with much concern.

I see Livy's eyes open and look around at everyone circling her. "What the fuck is going on?" she says. My mother laughs and kisses her on the forehead. My mother loves Livy's matter-of-fact demeanor.

"You passed out, sweet girl. Probably just nerves. Best it happens now than when you are standing at the altar, in front of everyone."

Livy looks at me and then her eyes lock on Maxwell.

"No. That's not it at all." She sits up and rests on her elbows. She points at Maxwell. "This man says he's my granddad."

Maxwell does not respond. Livy looks around the room and eyeballs Joe first. Then Sara. Finally, she tags me.

"I found him, Livy," I say. "I thought it would be important to you if he was here today. And maybe even if he…walked you down the aisle. If you wanted."

Livy sits up farther and then stands. Her eyes shift to Maxwell. He nods. Then she looks back at me. "Jeremy?" she starts. "Is this…is this for real?"

I go to her.

Fuck bad luck. That shit's overrated.

I hug her.

"Yes. I had some friends try to find him. I knew he meant a lot to you. I went to visit him and told him all about us. All about you."

She looks into my eyes for a long time. Then she wraps her arms around me. "Oh my God, Jeremy! This is the most amazing…" She begins to cry into my tux jacket. I never intended to make her cry. "Thank you, Jeremy." She looks up at me with dewy eyes. "Thank you. So much." She kisses me. I am pretty sure that is bad luck too, but everyone in the background is clapping and cheering so it can't be all bad.

She releases me and turns to Maxwell. She wipes her eyes. "I can't believe you are here. I never thought I'd see you again. Thank you for coming."

Maxwell tilts his head. "Oh, Livy. I never thought I'd see you again either. After your mother ran off with you that night, I tried to find you but I just couldn't. I couldn't."

Livy hugs him. "I know," she says. "I'm glad you are here."

Everyone allows Livy and Maxwell their moment. Then my mom claps her hands and says, "Okay, now, let's get these two married."

Maxwell says, "Yes! Let's. Livy, you and I can catch up later. This is your day. Now, Jeremy suggested I walk you down the aisle. But I understand you are very close to Joe. It's your choice, of course."

Livy looks at Joe. She never intended on anyone walking her down the aisle. Now she has two contenders waiting on her to decide. She shifts her gaze between the two of them.

"Why not both?" Livy asks. "There is no way I could decide. I'd be honored to have you both do it. That is if you're up for it."

Joe nods. "'Course, kiddo. It's your day. Whatever you want."

Maxwell nods as well. "It'd be my pleasure."

Nineteen

Livy

The wedding

JEREMY FOUND MY GRANDFATHER. NO WORDS COULD EVER DESCRIBE my gratitude.

Jeremy is my hero. He gave me a piece of my past back. A good piece.

The ceremony was beautiful. Rosalie, Maggie and Jenna did a phenomenal job of making everything gorgeous but still simple.

I asked Jeremy if we could write our own vows. Usually, when I hear that people want to write their own vows, I consider it the dumbest idea on the planet. Just repeat after the minister and get on with it. However, as much as I pitched a fit about vows being unrealistic, I figured that if we said things from the heart, it would be less likely that we'd break the vows down the road.

Jeremy had no problem with my request.

Standing there facing Jeremy, I was up to bat first. I had words planned but the bombshell of a grandfather that Jeremy just landed on me made me rethink my whole spiel.

"Jeremy, I spent many years thinking I was happy. But you walked into my life one day and proved how wrong I was. Since the day I met you, you have shown me nothing but love, just as you promised you would. I trusted you and gave you my heart. You have sheltered it and nourished it and now my heart has completely transformed. You've shown me what love is and how it heals. And even up to this very day, where we promise to commit to each other for our eternity, you have shown me just how far your love can reach." I look over at my grandfather. "You don't have to prove anything to me anymore. You love me and I understand. I understand. I promise to love you back, each and every day. I promise to do everything in my power to make you happy, so you can always proudly call me your wife." I say the final words looking directly in his eyes. He smiles.

"Livy, it only took you about thirty seconds to steal my heart. And you did it without even trying. Everything about you is magical. I'm not going to stand up here and profess *'til death do us part* or ask you to *obey and honor me* because I know that's not what you want to hear. What I will tell you is that everything about you is unique. And everything about you, I love. All the parts. All the pieces. I will do whatever it takes to make sure I put a smile on that gorgeous face every day for the rest of my life, because that is what you deserve."

His words were simple. He promised to make me happy. A single vow. An effortless declaration.

Twenty

Jeremy

Halfway through the honeymoon

WE'VE SPENT FIVE DAYS IN ARUBA. MOM SUGGESTED THAT WE GO to the beach, since neither of us had ever been. A co-worker of mine suggested Aruba. There was an all-inclusive resort that he took his wife to for their anniversary. He said it was magnificent.

And it was.

It was stunning.

White sand. Blue water. Tropical flowers and wildlife. Sunsets and waterfalls.

It was like nothing you could appropriately describe with words or pictures even. You had to live it first hand to truly understand the beauty.

However, my favorite part was just being with Livy. We spent most of our time lying in a hammock, limbs entwined and talking about stupid, random stuff like we have a tendency to do.

"What do think would happen if Mike Myers found himself in the middle of a zombie apocalypse?" Livy asked one afternoon while in our comfortable lounging state.

"Do you mean Mike Myers or Michael Myers?" I ask.

"I forget, which one is which."

"Mike Myers is Shrek. Michael Myers is the dramatically disgruntled dead brother that wants to kill his sister and everyone in his path along the way."

"Ah. Michael Myers, then."

"Isn't Michael Myers technically a zombie already?" I ask in response.

"Hmm. No. I think he is undead but his actions are driven by evil. The zombies are just dead and infected with some unnatural microbe that keeps them moving and upright."

"Well if that's the case, Michael would singlehandedly wipe out the zombie infestation. Evil always prevails."

"Good argument." She twists her head to look up at me. She brings her arm up and curves it around the side of my face and top of my head.

"What if...one of the zombies happened to take a chunk out of Michael? Would he turn into an infested zombie and lose his evilness or would the zombie that bit him turn evil?"

I take my hand and run it through her hair. Then I move her hair away from her neck and arch down to kiss it. Her head tilts back into my chest and she giggles slightly.

"What if..." I say, "I were to bite you on the neck right now? What would happen?"

I kiss her again and her arm around the side of my face tightens slightly. She giggles again.

"Depends," she exhales. I kiss her neck again and she lets out a slight moan. "Are you an evil dead murderous zombie guy?"

My heart is racing as I kiss her again. And again. She reaches between us with her other hand and gently squeezes. "Nope. Definitely not dead," she confirms.

I plant both of my feet into the sand. In one swift move, I have her on the ground, in the sand underneath me. I kiss her and she puts her hands in my hair, pulling me closer to her. My lips move from her mouth to the side of her face, to her jaw, neck and chest. My mouth suddenly cannot get enough of her and my hands are making their way beneath her bikini top and bottom.

Making love to my *wife* in the sand has definitely become my most favorite thing to do.

Twenty-One

Livy

Honeymoon

MAKING LOVE TO JEREMY...MY *HUSBAND*...IN THE SAND IS BY FAR my favorite new pastime. Yes, there is a lot of aftercare involved with getting sand out of places sand should never be, but that is all totally worth it.

Jeremy and I are married, and I am happy. I never thought this day would exist. I never thought I could be this happy, let alone with a guy, let alone with a *husband*. I have never felt so free and uninhibited as I do in this moment on our honeymoon. We have done much of nothing besides lie around and talk and feed each other fruit.

There was also a new experience with champagne a few nights ago in the insanely huge Jacuzzi bathtub, which proved to be something we'll have to try to make a repeat performance of once we make it back to our normal lives in civilization.

I never want to feel anything else but as happy as I feel right now.

Twenty-Two

Livy

Three years, five months and four days later...

IT IS HARD TO DESCRIBE HOW MY LIFE IS RIGHT NOW. If I had to use only one word it would be abso-fucking-loute-ly-fantastastically-amazing.

Being married is nothing as my previously negatively clouded brain envisioned. It is seven hundred times better. I get to wake up next to a beautiful man every day. One who adores me. And I use the word adore because that is how I feel every second I am with my husband. Adored. Not smothered with ooey-gooey, sickening, gushy, touchy feely stuff all the time. But every touch, every word, every glance we exchange is filled with what I can now comfortably describe as love.

My heart is overflowing.

A year ago, Jeremy decided to branch out and open his own business. The startup was difficult for him but he worked very hard and finally achieved what his original strategy for his entire career was—to be his own boss. He was home a lot less, but I knew his work gave him satisfaction and made him happy.

I continued volunteering for the shelter and a few months after Jeremy and I got married, I was asked by Macy to come on board as a paid employee to organize a program to help battered women and their children get back on their feet. The shelter administrators had some strategies in place, since I donated the money to them, but they just couldn't get proper traction on details. So, I agreed to help. I knew I had to. Because seeing an ostensibly broken woman smile after she's been assisted in making a step in the right direction gave me an elevated sense of purpose. Joe was right all those years ago. I was meant to do something besides tend bar. I wasn't really changing the world, but I was helping people who had a hard time finding a way to help themselves, and I felt like I was making a difference even if on a small scale.

Although Jeremy and I both stayed very busy with our jobs, we always made sure to carve out time for each other. Often, Jeremy would come home, late at night, well after I had gone to sleep, and wake me with kisses. I never once denied his request for two a.m. sex. I never wanted to. Being awakened by his gentle, calloused touch and his *hard-at-work-all-day* scent always pleasantly raised me from even the deepest of sleeps. No event of the next day that may have required a good night's sleep ever took priority over being caressed and held by the man I called husband.

On a number of occasions, Jeremy and I traveled. Yes, I was busy at my job when I was there, but I had the fortunate flexibility of a lump sum in my bank account and an employer who didn't necessarily need my input eight hours a day, five days a week. I could take time off when I needed to, for however long I wanted. Macy always vocalized that the administration of the shelter felt very fortunate to have me on board to help when I could and that I should never feel any pressure or guilt when I wanted to take extended leaves of absence. My position was open ended.

On the other hand of my marriage, however, was Jeremy. He worked himself to the bone in an effort to prove that he was good at being a company owner. He took oversight on everything, nearly to the point of micromanagement. He couldn't let anything slip through the cracks. He couldn't fail. I took it in stride. I understood his point of view. He took a big leap and I supported his decision. He wanted his dream to come true and I was adamantly on board. I didn't really have any dreams to follow. My dream had come true the moment I stepped on that bus when I turned eighteen. I had made it out of the hell my life had been for so many years and in the process, I had picked up a few people in my life that really mattered to me. Especially Jeremy. I never set out to find someone to spend a future of bliss with. I realize how truly blessed I am and I have no complaints with how my life unfolded. But truth be told, I missed Jeremy a great deal. He worked long hours and weekends. He was consumed. However, there was no way I was going to do something so selfish as show any signs of how much I missed him because I knew it would make him feel guilty. And I didn't want him to feel guilty for pursuing his dream.

But we did make it work. We always made sure we ate dinner together at least twice a week, one of those nights being at home with take out and a DVD, or something we had recorded on the DVR. We took a shower together every morning, without fail, so that if nothing else we could at least talk about how our days might play out. Every Sunday, Jeremy made us breakfast. Every single Sunday.

It was always very exciting when Jeremy announced that he had to travel for work, because I always got to go with him. We hadn't taken a true vacation since our honeymoon. Once, one of Jeremy's clients offered him a house for the weekend on the coast. We took full advantage of the offer, and it was delightful, despite the fact that Jeremy spent most of the time wining and dining with the owner of our weekend getaway house, who conveniently had a second home just a few paces down the shoreline and opted to take up residence in that home the very same weekend. Jeremy said it was the way of the business.

The extended travels though were much more one-on-one for us, and resembled as much of a vacation as anyone could have while still working. Being the boss, there were a lot of conventions, trade shows and seminars Jeremy had to attend. That is what he told himself, anyway. He probably could have had someone else go in his stead, but I didn't argue. I was happy to pack up and head off to New York, or Seattle, or Dallas whenever he felt his presence was necessary. I enjoyed traveling and seeing new sites. And I enjoyed mostly that I got Jeremy all to myself. Traveling seemed to be the only time Jeremy would turn work completely off. Aside from attending whatever event he was in town for, all other minutes he gave to me. Back at home, even when looking me in the face in the shower every morning, discussing our to-do lists, or sitting across from me at Sunday breakfast, enjoying the French toast, or sitting on the sofa next to me, cuddled and catching up on episodes of Breaking Bad, I could tell his mind was always in work. It was only when we were far away from our home that his focus returned back to me fully. I took and enjoyed what I could because I loved Jeremy with every molecule of my heart, and seeing him succeed at his business was part of what made me happy. Because it made Jeremy happy. It exhausted him, but it made him happy.

While Jeremy and I were cocooned in our own little married-life bubble, the world outside of it continued to turn.

Joe met a woman named Vicky when he was out shopping for fertilizer for the garden that he shouldn't be working in. It gives his back fits, but after I fussed at him about it, he told me to mind my own business, so I did. He was bored and needed to fill his time with something productive. Vicky was working at one of those massive do-it-yourself stores the day Joe stepped in to shop. She helped him find something he was looking for and I don't know how she was able to strike up a conversation with him, because he does not take too kindly to talking to strangers, but she did. Now, Joe and Vicky are quite…*friendly.* They see each other every day. He likes to cook her dinner. He even got her a gift for her birthday. *It's pretty serious.*

Sara is doing well also. It took her five months to acclimate to Connecticut. She really hated it at first, but then she got submerged into her job. So submerged, she didn't take notice of the man working in her research group that was so very desperately trying to get her attention. His name is Craig, and Jeremy and I met him one weekend when he and Sara came to town. From Craig's account, Sara didn't even notice that he existed for the first two months that she worked there. Apparently, they had to do research together and she was so devoted to her part of the research that she didn't even notice the way he watched her from across the room when they were working during the same shifts. After he realized there may be no end to Sara's obliviousness toward him, Craig decided to strike up a conversation with her about a local deli nearby. But even then she still didn't get the hint. He finally just came out and asked her out and she was very surprised. She accepted, however, and had a wonderful time on their first lunch date at the deli. So much so, that they went out again for an official nighttime dinner and dancing date. He seems to be a really great guy for Sara. He treats her well. They have a great deal in common. He makes her happy. They've officially been a couple just about as long as Jeremy and I have been married. I wouldn't be surprised if he didn't put a ring on it soon.

All of Jeremy's family members are just as they were before. Loving. Supportive. Inviting, whenever we get the chance to visit. Jenna and I meet for lunch or coffee quite a bit. Sometimes, she comes by the apartment and we just chat. We've gotten moderately close. She calls me her sister. Not sister-in-law. *Sister.* We ran into one of her friends from work while out one afternoon and she introduced me as her sister. I never asked her about it, but I took note of the sentiment. She often tells me that she's worried about me and about Jeremy working so much. I reassure her every time that we are ok and she always affirms that he won't always be working so hard. It will pay off in the long run. She has living proof in her husband, Mike, who used to work longs hours, days on end. But now, he's home a lot and his company just kinds of runs itself. I always thank her for reminding me that she and Mike were once in a similar situation and that she understands. I have never once mentioned to her that I miss Jeremy sometimes, but I guess I don't have to. She gets it.

My life is whole and rich with bliss.

Jeremy and I are married.

Our life together is full and enjoyable.

We're very happy.

Sara is happy.

Even Joe's happy.

Everybody is just one big ball of happy.

And all of that makes me very happy.

What doesn't make me happy is waiting on test results.
Because I am pretty sure that I am pregnant.

Twenty-Three

Livy

YEP. THAT'S RIGHT. PREGNANT. THE DOCTOR MADE IT OFFICIAL. After three mornings of hanging my head over the toilet, I assumed there could be no other explanation. I was too chicken, or too much in denial, to buy a test and confirm it in the privacy of my own home. I made an appointment with the doctor because I wanted someone with lots of medical experience to look me in the eye and verbally confirm that I was knocked up. I had to have the vision of someone's lips—preferably someone with a white coat with his or her name monogrammed on the chest, peeking through the stethoscope draped around his or her neck—uttering the words *you are pregnant.* That way, I can replay it in my head over and over in slow motion in order to come to terms with this information.

How can I be pregnant? A question I thought I only said in my head to myself.

"Well, Mrs. Waters, oral contraceptives are not always one hundred percent effective."

I looked up at the doctor. Did he just read my mind or did I ask that question out loud?

"But we were careful. I don't want children. I can't...I can't."

"Mrs. Waters, if you don't want to keep this baby, you have options that you and your husband should discuss..."

"What? No. That's not what I...you don't understand. Never

mind…you are right. I need to talk to my husband."

That revelation became the most urgent thing in the world. I need to tell Jeremy. He will make this better. He'll wake me up from this nightmare and laugh and say something like: *"Don't be ridiculous. It's not possible. We are careful. It was just a faulty (100 percent accurate) blood test. The doctor made a mistake. He's an idiot. That's all."*

Leaving the doctor's office, I call him on the phone, "Jeremy, where are you?"

"Livy, I'm at a site. What is wrong? You never call me."

He's right. I never call him. I hate talking on the phone. Communication with him when we aren't together is usually done through texts.

"I'm uh…in town right now. Can you meet me at home?"

"Of course. Are you okay? I'm kinda freaking out. I'll come home right now but please tell me everything's okay."

"Yeah. Yeah, I'm fine. I just need to see you. I'll see you at home."

"Okay. I love you."

"Love you too." I barely get the last word out before I hang up. I'm going to hyperventilate. I can't take another step farther. I look around to find a place to sit. There's a nearby bench on the sidewalk. I use all of my effort to get to the bench and throw myself onto it once I get there.

How can this happen?

Not a hundred percent effective.

I can't be a mother. I can't. I can't!

My hands are clenched to the bottom of the bench seat and I'm shaking my bent head back and forth, eyes closed, hair fallen forward over my face. To the passersby, I must look like a nut case.

What the *hell* am I going to do?

I can't do this.

I CAN'T have a baby!

I. Can't!

Those two words suddenly become my only vocabulary.

Shaking my head, repeating those two words, I look up and there is, in fact, a woman looking at me like I may be the antichrist.

"Hun, are you okay?" she asks.

I straighten up immediately. The last thing I need is for someone to call authorities on me because I look delusional.

I nod. "Yes. I'm fine. Thank you."

I stand and smooth over my clothes.

Get it together. Get home to Jeremy and everything will be ok.

I begin to walk home. The words *I can't* still pulsating in my head.

I got home before Jeremy. As soon as the front door closes behind me, I drop my keys and purse and slump to the floor as if my knee caps and hip joints have simultaneously disappeared from my body. A noise releases from the back of my throat that I'm not sure how to describe. It's half sob, half scream.

Jeremy and I had been so careful. This makes no sense. I'm not emotionally equipped to bring a child into this world. I have no motherly genes or skills. No instincts. I've never once in my life looked at a child and thought, *I can't wait to have a few of those someday.* Never. Ever. Hell, even this woman Marissa at work invited me—twice—to come to her home to see her new baby and I told her I couldn't make it.

I lied to get out of seeing a baby.

A baby.

I can't have my own kid.

I can't.

I can't.

My chest is heaving and I cannot really tell if I am actually breathing.

My cheeks and chin and even chest are drenched from tears.

I don't know how to love a child.

I don't know how to raise a child.

How do you put a bow in a girl's hair?

How to you teach a boy how to throw a ball?

How do you teach either how to tie their shoe?

What do you do when they cry?

When they're sick?

What if they break?

What if they hate you?

My mind is spinning. It's making me lightheaded. I'm taking in the appreciation that I'm already on the floor.

The door opens. "Livy? Oh God! Livy! What is wrong, baby? Baby? Livy?"

He kneels down next to me and wraps me in his arms, hugging me. He brushes my hair back from my face. My eyes are closed. I can't look at him.

I can't.

"I can't! I can't!" I manage to verbalize.

"You can't what, babe? Oh, Livy, you are breaking my heart. Sweetie, please tell me. What is going on?"

I try to slow my breathing. I try to stop crying. I can't manage to do either. I try to say something but it comes out sounding like blubbering gibberish.

Jeremy puts both of his hands on each side of my face. "Livy, open your eyes. Please look at me. Please."

The urgency in his voice is gone. He is whispering to me trying to get me to calm down. I use all the brain power that is repeating *I can't* and push it aside long enough to open my eyes. But then, I see his crystal blues directly in front of me. They are full of hurt and worry and even though I manage to keep my eyes locked on his, my mouth goes back on autopilot, "I can't. I can't." I shake my head slowly back and forth in between his hands.

"Baby. You can't what? Just. Look at me." He leans in a little closer, still whispering, "Just tell me. Like a Band-Aid. One quick tug. Blurt it out."

Zeroing in on his advice, without pause behind his last word I say, "I'm pregnant!"

My body is almost forcing me to snap and squeeze my eyes back shut and resume the crying and the breathing and the *I can't* chant.

But before my eyelids force themselves down, I see Jeremy's eyes go wide. Very wide. Wider than any human's eyes have ever gone. His crystal blues become enormous orbs of...

Excitement.

He smiles an insanely abnormal wide smile. The features of his face look like they've been stretched out by one of those weird phone apps that lets you distort a picture.

Through these oversized facial expressions, he somehow manages to say, "Livy? Did you...did you just say you were...pregnant?"

One solitary nod of affirmation is all I can provide.

"Oh my God! Oh my God! Livy!" He swoops me up into his arms and carries me to the couch where he sits downs and sits me on top of him, my legs hanging over his. He hugs me and presses my head into his chest sideways, kissing my head. "This is so amazing!"

He's so happy.

So happy.

But all I can imagine is that one day this kid is going to look at me and think *"What kind of mother are you?"* That phrase immediately comes to mind because that is the same phrase I thought about Nancy thousands of times.

I begin to cry again. Hard. My sobs are forceful enough that they are shaking both of our bodies.

"Livy, babe, why are you crying? Shhh. Please don't be upset. Whatever you are thinking, it's going to be okay."

I shake my head into his chest. I speak, but my words are muffled. "No! I can't do this. I can't be a mother. I have no idea how to do that!"

He squeezes me tighter and holds me for a long time. He doesn't say anything in response. He gives me the occasional *"shh"* and slightly rocks me back and forth. I wonder what he's thinking. If he even recalls the whole *"I don't want to have kids speech"* I gave him, or the *"my mother was a really shitty person and I have no business having a kid of my own"* talk we had.

I wake up in his arms

At first, I think he's sleeping too but he's really only just got his head tilted back and his eyes closed. I lift my head and try to remember why we're sitting on the couch in this position.

And why my face hurts.

And why my stomach is doing flips.

Oh yeah.

Fuck.

Before I can ramp back up to panic mode, Jeremy hugs me and says, "Hey."

He takes his hand and turns my chin up toward his face. I lock on to his eyes. Crystal blues. This time when I look at him, I'm immediately at peace. The acid in my throat subsides and my head stops spinning.

At peace, but still terrified. I force a smile and return, "Hey."

"I love you," he says.

"I love you, too," I breathe out.

"Are you okay?"

The *I can't* is lurking in the back of my thoughts. I have to be honest with him and act like a big girl. Even though I don't know how being honest about how I feel is going to help. I still need to say it.

"I can't do this, Jeremy. We were so careful. Why is this happening? I did everything right. I don't want children. I can't. I can't do it."

And with the truth now out there lingering in the air between us, I begin to cry again.

Jeremy hugs me.

"Livy, baby, listen. It's going to be okay. We can do this. You can do this. Remember? Who gives a fuck about your past? I believe in us. We can do this."

"But I don't know how to be a mother..."

"And I don't know how to be a father, Livy."

A point I've never considered and one he's also never brought up. Jeremy doesn't have enough of a memory of his father to know what to do. He doesn't have someone to look up to either to get advice and ask questions like *"How did you do this when I was a baby?"* in regards to a son asking a father. In all my stupid, selfish self-wallowing, I never even thought about Jeremy's point of view about having an absent parent, (absent, not by choice).

Of course the reason I probably never thought about it is because I never dwelled on Jeremy's ability to be a father.

Because this wasn't supposed to happen.

"I'm sorry, Jeremy. I never thought about that..."

"It's okay. It's just that I have a different perspective. A positive one. I don't want to rub in it but..." I look up at him again.

"But?" I repeat.

"Well, you didn't want to date me and look how that turned out." He leans down to me slightly and kisses the side of my face. "And, you didn't want to get married but look where we are now. Not too shabby so far."

"Not too shabby so far," I say, turning up a tiny smile.

"Now you know I can't promise everything will be perfect, but let me tell you what I do know." He gives me another small peck on the side of my face.

"I know that you are an amazing woman that loves me very much."

"That is true," I interject.

"I know that we have a great, solid relationship."

"True."

"I know that we have a remarkable group of people that are going to support us and will be ecstatic to know we're pregnant."

We're pregnant.

I don't respond.

"And I know that you are my very beautiful wife, who is carrying my baby and that makes me so happy. It makes me want to be the best father in the world."

My heart bursts and the remnants flow down and warm my entire body.

The look in his eyes.

The love that he has for a child that he's only known about for a few hours.

That love overshadows any negative thoughts I have.

I CAN do this.

I can do this.

Jeremy wants this baby so badly and his face isn't holding any bit of that back. He wants a baby. A child.

He just never mentioned it because that's how much he loves me. He wants me to be happy even if he doesn't get everything he wants.

Which is exactly why I can do this.

I can have a baby. A child.

I can be a mother.

And at this moment, I vow to do the exact opposite of what Nancy did.

I vow to be the best mother my mind, body and heart will give me the capability to be.

Twenty-Four

Jeremy

The announcement

"GOOD MORNING, MY LOVE." I ROLL TOWARD LIVY AND KISS HER on the cheek. I put my hand on her belly. "My other love."

Livy reaches her arm back and plays with my hair.

"Good morning to you, too."

"I'm going to make breakfast. You want eggs?" I ask. It's been almost two months since Livy told me about our baby. *Our baby*. I cannot believe I am going to be a father. I am going to have a child. I am going to have the opportunity to share things with our child that I craved I could have shared with my father when I was a boy.

Livy's appetite went from nonexistent to ravaging in the course of thirty days. I've tried to do my best to accommodate her nourishment needs as best I could.

"And bacon?" she asks.

"Of course, and bacon." I kiss her on the cheek and head to the kitchen.

I hope that the day she found out she was pregnant was her only emotional meltdown regarding her doubts of being a good mother. I know she has all of the elements necessary to be up for the task. I have reassured her every day that I have faith in her. I know our future with a child (or children) will be wonderful. I know it.

I've wanted to tell my mother. For two months, I've talked to her and it took everything inside me not to blurt out that Livy is pregnant. But Livy asked that we not tell anyone until we were in the *safe zone*.

Today is that day. We are going to Mom's tonight for dinner. Jenna and Maggie will be there too. And we are going to make the announcement. I know my mom is going to be over the moon ecstatic. More so than me when I found out, if that is possible.

"Mmmm, smells good," Livy murmurs, padding into the kitchen. She's wearing a pair of my old flannel pajama pants and a tank top.

She is *so* beautiful.

I put down the spatula and walk over to her. I hug and kiss her. "You are my most beautiful baby-momma." I smile. She lightly swats at my chest.

"So there are multiple." She winks, "I had my suspicions."

"Well you're my favorite by far," I joke.

She snickers before sitting at the breakfast bar. "Feed me, baby-daddy, before this mama-bear gets cranky."

"Yes, ma'am." I load up her plate with cheesy eggs and crispy bacon and pass it to her. "You ready for tonight?" I can hardly contain my enthusiasm.

While she takes her first large bite of eggs she looks up at me. She hesitates before she nods with her mouth full of food. After a second of chewing she says, "I'm as ready as I think I'll ever be. Your mother is going to smother me with hugs. I might not survive her excitement."

I don't disagree with her. "I'll be your body guard. I'll make sure she keeps the smothering to a minimum. "

"These eggs are so good! What did you do different?"

"I added Easy Cheese." Livy's been craving canned spray cheese for a week.

"Ha!" She laughs loud, mouth wide open, her chewed food almost falling. She puts the backside of her hand up to her mouth to prevent such from happening. "Figures. It's fantastic."

I grab the can of cheese from the counter and shake. "Want more?" I ask, holding the can upside down over her plate.

She slowly shakes her head no.

Then, she lifts her non-fork holding hand in the air and pinches her thumb and index finger close together. "Maybe a little."

I chuckle and oblige. She is so adorable.

So beautiful.

So amazing.

She is going to have my baby.

I love this woman so much.

I'll buy a whole fucking pallet of Easy Cheese for her if she wants it.

"Hey, Mom, we're here," I say as I let myself and Livy into Mom's house.

"Jeremy!" My mom rounds the corner of the foyer. She brings her hands to each side of my face and kisses me on the cheek. "It's so good to see you, baby boy."

I hug her, "Good to see you too."

Livy is behind me. I'm trying to play the role of bodyguard the best I can by letting her stay directly behind me. But my role is quickly compromised when mom maneuvers under my left arm and outstretches her arms to Livy.

I need to up my defensive game.

"Livy! Sweet girl!" She hugs Livy and Livy hugs back.

"Rosalie."

My mother releases Livy and looks her square in the eyes. She is still for close to a minute. The silence is growing awkward and Livy refuses to lose the stare off. I am behind my mom so I can't see her face but Livy's is becoming worrisome. Finally, without breaking eye contact, Livy crinkles her eyebrows. "Rosalie?"

Mom puts a hand up to her mouth and I move around so I can see her face.

There are tears in her eyes, on the brink of spilling over.

"Mom?" I place a hand on her shoulder which seems to break her out of her odd reverie.

She reaches out to hug Livy again and whispers loudly into Livy's ear, "You're pregnant."

Livy puts her hands on my mom's shoulder and breaks the hug to produce space between the two of them, "What?"

Mom looks at me and then back at Livy. "You are pregnant, right?"

Livy looks utterly confused and she glances my way questioningly. I raise my brow and shake my head. I'm just as confused.

"It's all over your face, Livy. You are glowing. My God, you are pregnant!"

Livy nods slightly. "Well shit, Rosalie, we can't get anything past you, can we? We were going to tell you all after dinner."

Mom hugs Livy again. "Oh my God! Livy, Livy, Livy!" And then my mom begins to cry. Happy tears, I can tell, but crying nonetheless. She finally pulls back and kisses Livy on the cheek and then uses both hands to wipe her eyes. She turns to me and bear hugs me. She extends her arm and brings Livy into our hug. "You guys. I am so excited for you. And proud of you. It's going to be amazing. Congratulations, baby boy and sweet girl! I am so happy!"

"Thank you, Mom," I say.

In the same moment Livy says, "Thank you, Rosalie."

Mom releases us from her embrace and tidies her hair. "I promise not to say a word. I didn't mean to ruin your moment."

"It's okay, Rosalie. No harm done." Livy smiles warmly at my mother. I love that they get along so well.

"I made pork roast and sweet potatoes, Livy, is that okay?"

Livy nods and smiles. "Sounds perfect."

My mom makes some sort of happy, high pitched noise, "Mmm, mmm, mmm!" and pinches Livy's smiling cheeks before spinning on her heels and floating to the kitchen.

"Dinner was delicious, Mom. Thank you," I say.

"It really was," Livy concurs.

We are gathered around the table with Mom, Jenna, Maggie, their husbands and Jenna's children.

I look over to Livy who is sitting beside me. I take her hand under the table and arch my eyebrows to say *"You ready?"* She gives me a slight nod and smile.

I turn my head toward the rest of the group who are engulfed in heavy conversation. Even my mom. She hasn't even let off any hint to anyone else that she knows our secret.

I clear my throat. "Hey, guys." Everyone turns their attention to me and I get a small case of nervousness. "So, Livy and I were wondering what everyone was doing this summer. Say, July? Because we've got this thing we'd like you all to come to." I'm trying really hard to pass this off as casual conversation to assist with the surprise. However, if anyone could see my heart racing or the sweat beading down the back of my neck, I'd be caught.

"Oh, what is it Jeremy? A vacation?" Jenna says.

"Not quite. More exciting than that."

Dramatic pause.

"Well." I look at Livy and can't contain my smile. She smiles back.

"Livy's on this weight program where she's intending to gain about, mmm, thirty pounds. And in the summer, she's going to lose a good portion of it all in one day. And we want you to all be there!"

Crickets.

I figured I'd be lost on the guys but I thought the women would at least understand the clues.

No one says a word and I can tell my mother is about to explode and let the cat out of the bag.

"We're pregnant!" Livy says before my mom seizes the opportunity.

Suddenly, the room erupts with noise and Livy and I are instantaneously engulfed in hugging arms from every direction. I manage to peer over to Livy to make sure she is ok. There is no nervousness or anxiety in her facial expressions. Her smile is genuine and receptive to every congratulatory hug she gets. She looks over at me and I wink at her. She winks right back.

Twenty-Five

Livy

Four hours into labor

WE ARE HAVING A GIRL. WE ARE GOING TO NAME HER AMELIA Grace.

Now, if she'd just get here already. I'm two weeks late as it is. I went into labor at 2:30 this morning. Not that I was sleeping or anything. I don't think I've slept in a month.

"Get all the sleep you can, while you can."

Every woman I've been in the vicinity of has told me this magnificent little tidbit of advice. Even a lady at the super market said it to me.

A random woman passing onto me her motherly advice.

But it's really hard to sleep when you have a kid in your womb stretching her legs into your ribs and spine.

I'm over it.

So over it.

This child needs. To. Be. Born. Now.

"Oh my God," I scream as I squeeze Jeremy's hand through another contraction. Once it subsides, I turn to the nurse who is reviewing the monitor. "Could I please have some drugs now? It's been a really tough morning."

She reaches over to check all the gadgets that are attached to me. "They've been ordered, sweetie. Just waiting on the doctor to get here.

It shouldn't be too long now."

But before the anesthesiologist could come with the drugs, Amelia decided to make her debut. My delivery doctor said it was uncanny the rate things progressed so swiftly. But before we knew it, I was dilated, effaced and all those other odd birthing terms that I still don't quite understand. After four hours of uneventful labor and thirty minutes of pushing, Amelia Grace was born.

Without drugs.

To say the least, it was quite painful. By the time I gave my final push, I'm certain I would have been capable of murder if it would have guaranteed me freedom from the pain.

However, the second I heard Amelia cry, before I could even see her tiny little face, I fell in love with her.

For months, I had doubted how I was going to have a bond with a child. I worried how I was going to keep another human being alive. Jeremy reassured me every step of the way but I still had hesitations. I had to feed her and keep her clean. I had to clothe her and keep her warm. This baby was going to be completely helpless and I was going to be responsible for her 24/7. I had no clue how I was going to be able to be a mother. No freaking clue.

But the moment I heard her cry, all of my trepidation subsided. Her tiny wail clenched my heart and all I wanted to do was hold her and make her feel safe.

"She's beautiful. So perfect," Jeremy said, leaning over her while the nurses cleaned and weighed her. I looked at Jeremy and he returned my gaze.

He was crying.

And then I was crying.

He immediately walked over to me and kissed me, tears rolling down both of our faces.

"Thank you. Thank you. You are so amazing. Thank you," he says before kissing me again.

"Here she is," the nurse said. Jeremy moved aside and the nurse placed Amelia into my arms. She was snugly swaddled and her head was covered with a pink, cotton cap. Her face was rosy.

"Hi, Amelia."

She opened her eyes ever so slightly and I got a glimpse of her crystal blues.

Just like her daddy.

My heart melted.

I had a daughter.

I was a mother.

I had never felt any better feeling in the world.

Twenty-Six

Jeremy

EVERYTHING WAS SET TO BRING AMELIA HOME. SHE WAS LATE, SO I had the nursery set up, and rearranged a few times, before Livy went into labor. We had swings and bouncy seats and tiny bathtubs. We had breast pumps and bottle sterilizers and high chairs. Car seats and strollers. Diapers, wipes and butt cream. Never in my life could I have imagined how much stuff one little six-pound baby needed.

I stayed home with Livy for two weeks after Amelia was born. Amelia cried nonstop for three days after we brought her home. It was exhausting. But we formed a routine and Amelia adjusted well.

Livy adjusted well too. Because of everything Livy worried about before Amelia was born, I thought motherhood would be harder on her. Not that it hasn't been hard, but she's taking it all in stride. Not once has she complained about lack of sleep or the frequency at which Amelia has to eat or be changed.

I feel bad about going to work and leaving her home. I want to stay home with them and spend as much time with Amelia as Livy does. But running your own business leaves little room for time off. Being gone for two weeks was really difficult. I snuck in phone calls and emails to the office and to clients when I could, just to make sure I didn't fall behind on the status of everything too much.

Livy says she's fine but I know she's not. She's tired and has no energy to take care of herself. It's like when she took care of Joe but on a completely higher level. I'm not sure when she last changed her clothes or showered. Or even ate. I know she's eating because she has to nurse Amelia but I don't know if she's eating enough.

I worry about the postpartum depression her doctor talked to us about. I've been watching out for symptoms but I haven't witnessed any. Livy shows nothing toward Amelia but love. Even when Amelia is screaming bloody murder for no reason, Livy never breaks. As Livy does, in true Livy fashion, she surprises the hell out of me at how much patience and resolve she has with Amelia. I have to admit that I've been frustrated on more than one occasion, which I later feel terrible about because Livy has not once faltered and I'm doing half the work she is.

Not for lack of trying. I help out how I can but before I even realize that helping hands are needed Livy's already taken care of it. I've asked her countless times to let me know if she needs help, or a break or anything at all. All she ever does in response is nods.

It's my second day back to work and to play catch-up, I was in the office nearly twelve hours. I had not even realized it until I noticed the sun going down.

When I get home, there is a note on the kitchen counter:

Jeremy, there are some leftovers in the red bowls in the fridge.
Sorry, I tried to stay up for you but I have to get up with Amelia soon.
I love you. I will see you in the morning.

My heart sank. I feel like an asshole. She cooked dinner for me and I didn't even call to check up on her.

As I heated up my leftovers, I checked to see if there was any pumped milk in the fridge for Amelia. I could stay up and feed Amelia and let Livy sleep. However, I didn't see any. But I could stay up and wait for Livy to get up so I could try to help. Or at least see my wife. I miss her. She's Zombie Livy. Or maybe more like Robot Livy. Or maybe both. Zombie-Robot Livy. She is mechanical and simultaneously always half asleep. She goes through the motions of feeding and changing. I only see her smile when she's talking to Amelia. She hugs me and tells me she loves me but I know she has no more energy to spend on me.

I'm hoping as time moves on and we adjust to being parents, I'll get my Livy back.

My Livy.

Right now, she is Amelia's Livy.

I sit on the couch in front of the TV with my leftovers and a beer and count down the minutes until Livy and Amelia are awake.

"Jeremy. Jeremy." I hear Livy's sweet voice. My brain instantly goes to the day we first met.

That melodic voice that kidnapped my heart.

"Jeremy, wake up."

I'm shaking. Someone is shaking my shoulder.

Am I asleep?

"Jeremy, babe, wake up."

I open my eyes and see Livy's beautiful, tired face. I smile and yawn.

"Hey, babe," I say in a raspy voice.

"You want to come to bed?"

I nod and stand. I wrap my arms around Livy and kiss her. She pulls away. "I look and smell like death. Certainly you don't want to kiss me."

"I don't care." I kiss her again and she kisses me back and squeezes her arms around me. "I'm so sorry I didn't call. The time seriously got away from me today."

"It's okay. I figured you had to play catch up from being gone."

I love her so much. She doesn't give me the business about not calling or working late. She understands.

I kiss her on the side of her face. "I love you so much."

She smiles. "Amelia ate well. Let's go to bed."

"Let's," I agree. I don't focus too much on the fact that she didn't say *I love you* back. Or that her immediate reply was regarding Amelia. I chalk it up to it being 1am and an attempt to sleep is probably her main priority right now.

I follow her to the bedroom, strip to my boxers and crawl into bed with her. I pull her into my chest. "If you have time and think about it, put some extra milk in the fridge tomorrow and I'll feed Amelia tomorrow night." I hug her.

"Okay," she says.

She wraps her arms around my chest.

I kiss the top of her head. "Good night, my love."

"Good night."

I listen and wait for her to fall asleep. I follow suit not far behind.

Twenty-Seven

Livy

Six months later

I'M EXHAUSTED. AMELIA HATES TO SLEEP. I STILL CAN'T GET HER TO sleep through the night. I haven't slept a full night since...well, definitely before Amelia was born.

Lack of sleep has many side effects. Two things mostly being that I can't concentrate on a singular thought for more than three seconds, and that my memory has turned to total shit. I can't remember anything about what I did the previous day or better yet, what I did five minutes ago. I'm constantly writing things down on post-it notes. Often, however, I forget where I've left the post-it notes and find them days, or even weeks, later, when the reminder is no longer even relevant. I've gone to the store for milk and eggs, only to come back with just potatoes and laundry detergent. I've gone out in public wearing my shirt inside out and two completely different shoes on my feet. I lost my keys once and completely turned everything in my house over to find them, only to discover that I'd set them in the freezer. I found my hairbrush in the freezer once too. Now, if I lose anything, the freezer is my go-to usual suspect.

Amelia is in constant motion, scooting around like an inchworm or rolling through the apartment like tumbleweed. When she's awake, she's moving, and, unfortunately, so am I. During her adventures, Amelia scopes out anything she can grab, and everything she touches goes into her mouth. I thought I had *baby-proofed* adequately, but she's always finding something to try to shove into her face to soothe her achy gums. For instance, the TV remote that I thought was out of her reach, yet she somehow *Houdini-ed* into her clutches. One of Jeremy's socks that she found in an *under the sofa* exploration. Was it clean? Nope. And thankfully I caught her before she had a mouthful of dusty, foot germs. My favorite though was when I caught her gnawing on a leg of one of the dining room chairs. I had to give her accolades for creativity. I don't know what I'm doing wrong because I keep ample teething toys in her vicinity but she refuses them all. And I feel like I watch her like a hawk, but I swear, I blink and she sees it as an opportunity to rebel and find something uncharted to chew on.

Second in contention to the downsides of motherhood, right underneath exhaustion, is loneliness. I see people all of the time. But I'm living in a bubble and taking on this task of being a mother while everyone else goes about their normal, daily routine. And when people are around, it's constant discussions about Amelia and, where Jeremy's family is concerned, all other children that have been birthed in the Waters family before Amelia. I'd give anything to talk to an adult about any subject other than diaper rashes or breast feeding. I talk to Jeremy's mother and aunts often, but that's all they want to talk about...*how's the baby?* Or, *when Jeremy was a baby he blah, blah, blah*...I generally tune out. When Jenna and I used to hang out, we'd talk about future travel destinations, or books or sports—light, general interest conversation. But, not anymore. Now, all dialogue with her somehow ends up being comparative prattle on how Amelia is progressing based on how her own kids developed. Even when I attempt to change the subject, it always leads back to that. Maxwell has visited a few times and so have Joe and Vicky—all time spent doting on Amelia. Sara came to visit once to meet Amelia when she was first born. But her research has her swamped with work, and when she does have free time, she and Craig try to make the most of it spending every second they can with each other.

I remember those days.

Jeremy is never home. Not even on weekends. He works all of the time. I've done all of Amelia's doctor's appointments alone. Grocery shopping with Amelia—alone. And yes, I say going to the store *with Amelia—alone*—because when you are in a store with a child that can't quite yet comprehend the English language and all she wants to do is throw a tantrum because she's hungry or tired, or whatever, you feel absolutely alone.

Doing household chores with a baby strapped to my chest.

Making dinner for Jeremy, just to put it in the fridge for him to eat later.

I shouldn't make him dinner every night, right? He's a big boy. He can fend for himself.

But I feel guilty. *About everything.* If I think about not making him dinner or not doing that last load of laundry or not cleaning the dishes in the sink, I feel guilty. I can't even really explain why, but I do. And I feel guilty about how I'm raising Amelia. Am I doing it right? Is it enough? I have no clue about a lot of things, and God forbid I ask Rosalie. I get schooled about how perfect of a mother she is. And I know she doesn't do it to be mean. Her intentions are good. But I don't really give a crap about what kind of shampoo she used on Jeremy when he was a baby. Half of the things she suggests do not even exist anymore or have been overshadowed by something more technologically advanced. And then of course I feel guilty for having negative thoughts about Rosalie's advice because I know she's only trying to help.

I just wish Jeremy was here. He keeps telling me that as soon as this project is done, his workload will slack off and he'll be home more. He assures me that it's only a few more weeks.

I can do this a few more weeks. I can tough it out.

But I'm so tired and when you are as tired as I am, things break down on a mental level. No concentration. No memory. And very little ability to just tough it out. I'm on the verge of a meltdown. I can feel it. And I'm scared and worried because I don't know what to do about it. I don't have a plan nailed down to be strong until Jeremy can jump into the trenches with me. I'm afraid of what might happen if I hit that point. That point of where I can't take anymore and just lose it.

Let me point out that I would *never, ever* do anything harmful to

Amelia. That is not what I mean at all. I love that baby girl way too much to ever hurt her. She is the light of my life and the most precious little person ever created. It amazes me to watch her learn *everything*. How to blink and coo and how to control her arms and legs. You would have thought I was watching scientists split atoms when Amelia learned how to roll from her stomach to her back. I hooted and cheered and cried like I had just witnessed a miracle. But the fact of the matter is that I *had* witnessed a miracle. Amelia is a miracle. One that I thank God for every day. Watching her learn how to live is genuinely the most amazing experience of my life.

But there are some moments when I have a glimpse of what Nancy may have gone through. The difficulties of having to care for someone and relinquish your own wants and needs. The drugs and alcohol gave her an outlet and an excuse not to give a fuck about my wellbeing. I'm terrified about whether I'll ever reach that breaking point. The point where I'll pick up a bottle of something and drink it until everything is blurred and my worries and guilt fly out the window. I haven't had a drop of alcohol since Amelia was born. At first, because I was nursing but then because I was afraid that one may lead to two which would lead to too many if I drank when I was stressed. I've done that a few times before. Like the time I drank half a bottle of Jim Beam when I wanted to tell Jeremy to leave me because I didn't think I deserved him. I know I can't do that now because for one it's stupid, but also because I have a baby. A baby that needs me and I can't just hide away in a room with a bottle and check out. I'm a responsible adult now with a husband and a child and I have to be a pillar. Stand strong. Suck it up.

But dammit, all I want to do is crumble.

It's a Friday. Amelia and I have eaten dinner. She's bathed and in bed and I'm praying she'll sleep at least a few hours.

Have I mentioned just how little that kid likes to sleep?

I've tried everything. She has the most comfortable mattress I could find. A snuggly blanket. Lullaby music. Lavender bedtime lotion. Blackout curtains on her window. Soft, footie pajamas. A twelve hour, no leak diaper (that we've yet to be able to prove its claim), a binky and a teddy bear. If I could buy the kid ear plugs and an eye mask I would, but I assume that since they don't make either of those items in infant size, it's probably frowned upon.

I've put Jeremy's dinner in the fridge and am cleaning the kitchen when I hear the locks on the front door turn. I'm startled at first but then I peek around the corner and see Jeremy. I dry my hands off and run to him.

"You're home!" I plant my lips on his. I feel like I haven't seen him in a month. I've seen him, in passing in the middle of the night. He usually sleeps on the couch when he gets home until I get up with Amelia and I wake him and drag him to bed. But I haven't had a conversation with him for…weeks? We talk through texts. A quick *"love you, miss you"* or *"omg look at what Amelia is doing now."* I honestly can't believe he is standing before me right now, in the flesh.

Wait. Am I dreaming? I reach out to his arm and pinch him gently.

"Ow." He smiles. "What was that about?" he asks while rubbing his arm.

"Just want to see if you are real," I smile back. "Make sure I wasn't dreaming."

He pinches me back playfully. "You're supposed to pinch yourself, I think." He winks.

"Oh right. Well, no matter. You are real and I'm not dreaming. I'm so glad you are home." I hug him and I don't want to let go ever. "I made you dinner. I just put it in the fridge."

He leans down and kisses me. "I don't care. Is Amelia asleep?" He picks me up and I wrap my legs around him and he walks toward our bedroom.

Our clothes are off in seconds. I'm lying there on the bed completely exposed and I suddenly feel very insecure.

When's the last time I washed my hair? Or shaved my legs? Or shaved my…

"Livy? You okay?"

I look Jeremy in the eye and nod. It's been quite some time since Jeremy and I have had sex. I certainly didn't expect him home so early tonight or I might have groomed myself better. I feel like a wooly mammoth and not very sexy at all. For some reason my left hand instinctively slides down to my stomach and grazes over my stretch marks.

Jeremy is kissing me and I blank out. My mind completely leaves the scene. I'm supposed to be elated that my husband is home and we are naked together. However, not only has my confidence in my body waned, but my mind, as tired and attention deficient as it's become, is thinking about a whirlwind assortment of other things. Not one of them is sex.

Twenty-Eight

Jeremy

I HAVEN'T HAD SEX WITH MY WIFE IN TWO MONTHS.

Yes. Let me repeat that.

I haven't had sex with my wife in two months.

I've thought about having sex with her at least a hundred times every day. Sometimes, more often than I'd like to admit really, I have to excuse myself at work for privacy to attempt to satisfy the desire I have for wanting to have sex with Livy and not being able to.

I miss her so much. I want to take this opportunity to make up for all the time we've spent apart. I often question whether opening my own firm was a good idea. It's been lucrative, yes, but I am *never* home. I told Livy this current project was rounding down to an end. However, I can't promise that the next project won't be bigger and more involved. I love my company and the work we do, but it's killing me inside to be away from Livy and Amelia. I feel like I made a selfish decision and put myself before Livy. Of course, I didn't know we would be expanding our family at the time I made the decision. But I did know I'd be working a lot more. I knew I would be spending less time with Livy going in. And now we have a baby girl that is growing faster than I ever imagined and Livy is doing it all on her own. And I feel like an asshole for that. But I really don't know what I can do about it right now.

I tried all day to get everything squared away so that I could get home before Livy went to bed. Coming through our front door to see her smiling face and feeling her arms around me made my head spin and my body instantly aroused. I carry her to the bedroom and get us both undressed as quickly as my hands allow.

I'm hovering over her, impatiently, and trying to make solid eye contact with her. I want to be inside of Livy more than I want to take another breath right now, but I want her to look at me. I want to see the look on her face. I want to see her eyes. I miss her eyes.

"You okay?" I ask. She seems a little too pensive for our current predicament. But she looks at me and I see her beautiful eyes. She gives me a small grin and a nod. I lean up and give her a long, sensual kiss. I want her to feel just how much I've missed her. I make my way over to her neck and eventually down to her chest. My head is clouded with lust and all I want to do is have sex with my wife.

My brain shuts down and another part of my body takes control. Before I realize what is really happening I am pushing my way inside of her, eagerly wanting the release I've fantasized about for so many days.

The fantasy to have sex with my beautiful, sexy wife.

I am looking at her beneath me. Her eyes are closed and her brow is wrinkled, as if she's trying to concentrate. I need to slow down and help her get there too. She probably needs and wants this as much as I do, perhaps even more. But the thoughts about what I could do to make her writhe in pleasure and the look on her face from past encounters sit in my imagination and before I'm able to make any moves to bring her along for the ride, my body revolts against me and I feel everything rushing to one central location.

And I'm done.

Fuck.

Livy never even made a sound. Not one moan or whimper of pleasure.

The fantastic sensation I had moments ago quickly subsides and I immediately feel like an asshole.

Livy's eyes are still closed. I kiss her gently. "Babe. You okay?"

She opens her eyes and looks at me. I can't tell exactly what emotion is lying behind her gorgeous green pupils but it's far from satisfaction.

I have to make this right. I kiss her again while I formulate a plan but just as I'm about to put that plan into action, Amelia squeals through the monitor. Livy puts her hands to each side of my face and looks at me. She smiles but, it's weak. "I need to go check on her."

I try to read her eyes once more but I can't. I resign and simply nod in response. I move over to let Livy up. She grabs a t-shirt, throws it on and walks out the door.

I wake up, lying on top of the comforter of the bed. Naked. The blanket that usually takes residence on the back of the sofa in the living room is covering about half of my body. I lift my head and look around. Livy is not in bed with me. I jump up and throw on some boxers and sweatpants. Livy is in the living room, lying on the floor next to Amelia who is laughing at a stuffed animal that's playing music. I look at the clock on the wall. It's almost 4:30 in the morning.

"What are you guys doing up so early?" Livy looks up at me and blinks as if she's trying to stay awake.

"We're always up this early. I'm almost used to it. Amelia hates to sleep."

Livy and I had gotten into a routine where I would come home, eat my leftovers, fall asleep on the couch so that I didn't disturb Livy sleeping, Livy would wake me up around one or two and we'd go to bed together, us both being so tired that all we did when in the bed was sleep. I had offered several times to feed Amelia at night. At first, Livy said that it was just too cumbersome to try to pump during the day in order for me to be able to feed Amelia and let Livy sleep. Then, after Livy was done with nursing, I offered again and she told me that it was less of an effort to just get up and feed Amelia than it was to try to wake me up first to go feed her. Once I was asleep in the bed, I was dead to the world until my alarm went off. I couldn't help it; I had always been a hard sleeper. I told her I felt bad about that but she waved it off and told me not to worry about it. She said I needed sleep more than she needed help because I had to get up and run a company all day, every

day. When she told me that, I thought I detected a hint of passive ag-
gressiveness in her voice, but I didn't think on it too long. Livy wasn't a
passive aggressive person. She was always very direct and to the point,
so I let it go and assured myself that I was mistaken.

It had never dawned on me that Livy and Amelia got up so early
in the morning. I suppose I just assumed that they got up around six or
six-thirty, only a short time before I got up at seven. Livy never divulged
that information to me until just now and I guess I just never thought
to ask.

I sit down on the floor beside her and move my hand through her
hair. "Have you slept at all?" I ask.

She nods, "I did. After I checked on Amelia, I came back to the
bedroom and you were already asleep." She looks over at me and smiles.
"You were on your stomach and taking up the entire bed. I took a moment and stared at that gorgeous ass of yours and then I covered you up
and came and slept on the couch. You looked so peaceful, I didn't want
bother you."

At that moment I was riddled with guilt. Because what I felt like
she should have said was, *"After your three-minute performance, where
only one of us got off, I couldn't stand to be in the same room with you. I'd
rather sleep uncomfortably on this ratty old couch than share a bed with
you, you prick."*

But, she did care enough to give me a blanket, so I guess maybe
that's not what she's actually thinking.

I clear my throat. "I uh...I'm sorry about last night. I was so excited
to see you. To be with you. To be naked with you. It's been so long. I
miss you so much."

"I miss you too," she says. "So much. And I know it's been a while,
but honestly I think I'm so tired that I just can't get into it like I used
to. It's not the same as it was before Amelia was born. My body feels
and looks different. I don't feel sexy. My hygiene these days is sub-par
at best. I don't even know how you can even look at me and get excited
to have sex."

Her words break my heart. She doesn't think I'm an asshole. She
thinks I shouldn't be attracted to her. I pull on her arm, attempting to

get her to come over to me. She responds and complies. I wrap her up in my arms.

"Hey. I wouldn't care if you quit shaving completely, banned deodorant from your medicine cabinet and took a daily bath in pig shit and skunk spray. You would still be my beautiful, sexy, amazing wife, who gave me this adorable little chunky baby girl. I love you, Livy. All of you. And if you could only imagine how many times a day I think about you naked, you wouldn't doubt your sexiness for a second."

Livy turns her head and looks up at me. "Pig shit and skunk spray? Oh you are so full of shit. But I get your point. Thank you."

I kiss the top of her head. "Now, I want *you* to go get some sleep. As much as you want. Then, I want you to take a long, hot bath. Relax. Take your time. Amelia and I will hang out, eat a bunch of junk food and watch some R rated movies. And I'll call Mom later and see if she will come over and stay with Amelia while you and I go out to dinner or something. Whatever you want to do. What do you think?"

"Amelia usually eats at six. And then every four hours after. Eight-ounce bottle of formula plus baby food, which is in the freezer. To thaw it out, you put the container halfway into hot water for about five minutes. There's apples, bananas, carrots, peas..." She's looking up at the ceiling, thinking, listing the food on her fingers.

"Hey." I grab her hand. "I got this. We will be fine. You go sleep." I kiss her again, this time on the mouth. "Go. I love you. You need sleep. You need to reboot."

She nods her head. "I love you too. Thank you. For what you said and for being so sweet. You are a pretty awesome dad." She looks down at the floor. "I miss you so much."

"I miss you too. Both of you. I promise as soon as this project is done, I'm taking a break."

"That sounds nice. I can't wait." She stands up from the floor. "You two have fun," she says, as she heads to the bedroom and closes the door behind her.

I can't wait to spend time with her tonight. I'm hoping I can reach in and pull out the old Livy. *My Livy.* Pre-Amelia Livy. I need to reassure her that everything is going to be ok and work out in the long run.

I know it's not something I can do in one conversation over dinner, but I'm hoping it'll at least be a start.

Twenty-Nine

Livy

I SLEPT FOR EIGHT HOURS. STRAIGHT THROUGH. WHEN I WOKE UP, AT first I panicked. I had forgotten that Jeremy was home and spending time with Amelia. Then the memories of the early morning conversation came back to me and I exhaled. I looked over at the bedside clock. It was ten minutes until one o'clock in the afternoon.

The comprehension that I had been sleeping in the middle of the day was difficult to drink in. I stretch my arms and yawn and throw my feet over the side of the bed. I feel so rested. Recharged. Better than I've felt in quite some time. I stand up and move to the door to go check on Jeremy and Amelia. I don't hear any playing or crying. I don't hear any noise at all and once again panic begins to set in. I open the bedroom door only to be relieved a second time. I am looking at the most precious sight I have ever witnessed. Jeremy is sleeping on the couch with Amelia sleeping on top of his chest. She's lying on her stomach and one of her chunky little cheeks is pressed against his chest, enough so that her mouth is forced open. Her lips are pressed outward like she's making a fish face. And there is a little bit of drool coming out of the side of her mouth and spreading onto Jeremy's skin.

My heart melts. I very quietly search for my phone and take a picture. Then I head back to the bedroom and run a bath, just as Jeremy instructed. I'm going to go all out. Pedicure. Manicure. Eyebrows. Facial. Deep hair conditioning. I'm going to shave places I haven't shaved in months. I am going to come out of this bathroom smelling like peaches and looking like sin and I am going to spend a long, sexy evening with my husband. Maybe we'll get wrapped up in one of our random strange conversations like we used to. We haven't done that in forever.

I miss that.

I miss him.

I miss us.

It's taken me about two hours but I'm finally ready. I haven't gotten dressed yet but everything else is done. Hair, makeup, nails—the works. Before I figure out what to wear, I head out to the living room to ask Jeremy where he wants to go tonight so I can choose something appropriate to put on. I'll probably just end up wearing a t-shirt and jeans, but if he wants to do something fancier, I wouldn't be completely opposed to wearing a dress and heels. I am just in that kind of mood right now and I know what kind of mood a dress and heels would put Jeremy into.

As I exit the bedroom, I peer out into the living area and see Jeremy sitting at the breakfast table with Amelia in her high chair. By the orange ring of food around her lips, I'd say she's eating carrots. She's giggling and waving her hands in the air, her eyes fixed on Jeremy. It appears as though they are having a great time together. Except when I look to Jeremy, I notice he's got his cell phone pinched between his shoulder and his ear. He's not speaking but listening, either to someone talking or to a voicemail. He's trying to manage the phone and spoon food into Amelia's mouth at the same time. I walk over and take the food from Jeremy's hand and take over. Jeremy looks up at me and his facial expression is not a positive one.

He stands from the chair and walks away before he begins speaking. "Are you sure? I don't even want to entertain this idea if we don't have a shot. There is no point wasting time on this if there's not a chance."

He pauses and listens again. Finally, he lets out a loud huff and says "Fine. Yeah, yeah. You are right. This could be a big deal. I know. I know! Okay. I will see you there." He hangs up his phone and tosses it on the couch. And he just stands there looking at the floor.

He won't look at me.

I give Amelia another spoonful of carrot and watch Jeremy for a second, trying to read his stance and his facial expression. I'm waiting for him to say something but it's almost as if he can't blurt out what's in his head.

"Jeremy? What was that about, babe? Is everything okay?"

He continues to stand there, looking at the floor and saying nothing.

"Jeremy?" I ask again in a normal tone. When he still doesn't respond, I say his name again. Not yelling, but in a stern voice. "Jeremy!"

He looks up at me as if he's been pulled out of a trance. His eyes immediately express worry. I'm beginning to get nervous about what that phone call was about.

"What is it, Jeremy? You are freaking me out a little."

He hesitates but finally says, "I have to go to Chicago."

Jeremy's been out of town three times since Amelia was born. The first two times, he asked me to come along. The first time, Amelia was less than two months old. There was no way I was leaving her with someone to spend multiple days, miles away from her. Plus, there was the nursing issue. No one would be able to feed her but me. So Jeremy suggested that we take her with us, and I explained my anxiety about having a fussy child on a plane, or in a hotel room. There was also the nursing issue again. I didn't want to have to nurse in front of people on a plane.

So, Jeremy went without me. The second trip, he invited me again. Amelia was four months old. He said that he was comfortable leaving Amelia with Rosalie for four days. I wasn't nursing her anymore, so that issue was dead. But I still had reservations about leaving Amelia for that long and being so far away. What if something happened?

So, Jeremy went without me again. The third trip was three weeks ago and Jeremy didn't even bring up the subject of me coming along. He just went without me. But I think if he'd asked me that time, I might have said yes. I desperately needed a break. And I needed Jeremy all to myself without having *"tired mommy brain syndrome"*—it was a phrase that had been coined in a book I read about handling motherhood in the first year.

"Chicago? What for?"

"That was Marcus on the phone."

Marcus. Yes, Marcus. As in *homeless* Marcus that Jeremy met at the park after my meltdown about the bar being sold. The man who also helped me find the job at Joe's when I didn't have a single clue about the city.

After Jeremy opened his own business, I had gone to visit Marcus at some point and when I mentioned it to Jeremy, he asked me if I thought Marcus might be interested in a job. He could start out doing odds and ends, making enough money to get on his feet. And, if it worked out, he'd consider perhaps giving him something more permanent or teaching him something about any aspect of general contracting that Marcus might want to learn more about specifically. Jeremy said that if I trusted Marcus, then he trusted Marcus, and he could always use some extra, trustworthy helping hands on sites.

So I proposed the idea to Marcus one afternoon. I told him no pressure. If he didn't want to, no judgment. But I did remind him of how he helped me and I gave him my *"look at me now"* speech. I told him he could change if he wanted to. If he was finally tired of feeling sorry for himself. I told him he could be happy again one day. He just had to try.

Marcus accepted Jeremy's offer and started out working at sites, setting out and packing up tools for the crews, doing coffee and lunch runs, performing basic, menial tasks. Once Jeremy realized that Marcus was a pretty hard worker and fast learner, and that he actually seemed to be enjoying working with others, Jeremy asked Marcus if he thought he'd ever want to be a site supervisor. Marcus liked the idea of being a site supervisor so Jeremy set him up to follow another site supervisor for a few months to learn the ropes. Once he did, Jeremy made Marcus a site supervisor and the rest is history. Jeremy has had nothing but great things to say about Marcus and his work ethic.

When we actually get to talk to each other, that is.

"What did Marcus have to say?"

Jeremy runs a hand over his face. "Marcus has connections with an architect in Chicago that is looking for a team to renovate a loft apartment complex in the middle of downtown. It's a multi-million-dollar project and Marcus thinks if he and I go to Chicago to meet with the architect, we have a good chance of getting the contract. This could be huge. If we got this job, and it went well, we could potentially expand the business to Chicago."

"Jeremy, that is amazing. I am really excited for you, but why do you look so worried? Are you worried about going to Chicago?"

"We have to leave tonight. Marcus says this guy he wants us to meet only does business on the golf course. We have an eight a.m. tee-time tomorrow. I have to fly out tonight."

"Tonight! What? Are you serious? You said we were spending the night out together. And now you are just up and leaving to go to Chicago to play golf with some guy who *might* give you a job? Golf, Jeremy? Really? You don't even play golf."

I realize that I'm yelling. I'm yelling in front of Amelia and I immediately stop. The fact that I just yelled at my husband in front of my child makes my stomach turn. I set the bowl of mashed carrots and spoon down on the breakfast table and walk over to the sink. I may vomit. I'm pissed. Livid might be a better word. But I'm also hurt and most importantly humiliated. Jeremy just got done this morning telling me how much he misses me—us. And how he wants to take a break. Now, he wants to jet set off in hopes to expand his business. How is he going to have time for us if he's going back and forth between two cities?

And I can't believe that I just yelled at him in front of Amelia. Something I promised myself I'd never do. Something I made Jeremy promise as well. Not that we were the yelling type. But we'd had a few arguments before Amelia was born that had ended with raised voices and door slamming. I didn't ever want Amelia to see us argue. I wanted her to always know that Jeremy and I loved each other even if we were struggling a little behind the scenes.

But leave it to me to be the first one to break our pact. The pact I came up with in the first place and made Jeremy agree to. The pact that I was certain I'd never waver on.

But I just did and it happened before I could even catch myself. That thought terrifies me.

So many emotions are bubbling internally right now. Fear, anger, guilt, sadness. I want to cry and throw something and kick and scream. But I can't. I don't want Jeremy to see me cry and I'm certainly not throwing a juvenile tantrum in front of my baby. I can't do anything. I'm stuck here, in front of the sink wanting to vomit and I can't.

Those two words that always seem to find themselves a way into my brain.

I can't

I can't

I can't

I can't do this. I can't be a mother to a child and raise her all alone while Jeremy is off wheeling and dealing and making a name for himself.

And suddenly, I'm also jealous. Jeremy gets to go out into the world and make a name for himself while I sit here and be the stay-at-home mommy, unappreciated. I get to watch cartoons about ABCs and read books about big red dogs and curious monkeys. I get to listen to the same toys make the same squeaks and honks over and over again. I get to change dirty diapers and bathe dirty Amelia and listen to cranky Amelia scream and fuss and refuse sleep. I don't get to talk to adults and make some imprint on the world. That's Jeremy's job.

I chose to be a mother. Because I wanted to make Jeremy happy.

He promised me it'd all be ok. And it's not okay.

He promised me he'd spend every living day making me happy. I'm not happy.

This is that moment. This is the moment that people reach their breaking point. Because their other half made them a promise, a vow, and then they failed to keep it.

I'm gripping the edge of the sink with both of my hands. I notice my knuckles are turning white. I'm furious and I don't know how to calm down.

I just need to calm down but I don't know how.

Before I know it, Jeremy is beside me. "Livy? Please. Please don't be mad. I'm really sorry…"

"Stop," I say as calmly as I can.

Don't yell

Don't yell

Don't yell

Do not yell in front of your child again.

I look up at Jeremy. "I don't want to hear anything you have to say right now. Nothing." He doesn't say another word. I continue, and begin pointing my index finger to the floor. "When we got married you promised that this moment, right now, wouldn't happen. You promised that you would make me happy. I believed you. You convinced me. We had a wonderful honeymoon and a great couple of months. Then you started your own business and I never see you anymore. Never."

Don't yell.

"You've worked 12-16 hour days for over two years, Jeremy. You've missed holidays. You've missed our anniversary and my birthday. And I told you when you missed those things that it didn't matter. And it didn't. Until I got pregnant. You promised you would slow down. But you didn't, Jeremy. You missed sonograms and doctor's appointments. You missed her first smile and her first clap. You are never here and now it matters. Amelia is going to be a year old soon and you've hardly been here to see how fast she's changing every day. It doesn't bother me so much really that you are missing out on me, but you are missing out on her. You promised me it would be okay and it's not okay, Jeremy!"

Don't yell.

"Do you know what it's like to be surrounded by nothing but *baby* all day, every day?" I air quote the word *baby*. "Baby cartoons. Baby books. Baby toys. Baby food. Baby poop? You have no clue because you are never here. All my mind thinks about is Amelia and everything on Amelia's level. Do you have any idea when the last time was that I talked to an adult about a conversation that didn't involve Amelia? No, you don't. You get to talk to adults all day about everything but Amelia."

Don't yell.

I raise my hand slightly, finger still pointing to the floor and point down again, quite forcefully. "And just this morning you told me how much you missed us and how you were going to slow down after the project you are working on. And not twelve hours later, you are telling me that you have to fly to Chicago, to *golf* and make a bid in order to try to expand your business." I grit my teeth. I'm getting worked up. Jeremy is staring at me intensely. I need to stop before I say something I don't mean. I can feel the words making their way up my vocal cords.

Stop talking, Livy. Enough. You've made your point.

"How the fuck do you plan on being here with us if you are juggling a business in two cities, Jeremy? You are choosing your job over us. If you really missed us, you'd figure out a way to be home. It's *your* goddamn company for crying out loud. You could figure it out. You are choosing your business over us. I've tried to be patient and I've tried doing all of this by myself. But I'm exhausted."

I'm not going to yell.

So, instead I guess I'll cry.

Better crying in front of Jeremy instead of yelling in front of Amelia.

"You made me a promise, Jeremy. And you broke it. You broke it. Just like I told you people do. People make promises and they can't keep them. And now, what can I do about it, huh?"

Stop talking. Don't say it.

"Nothing. There is nothing I can do about it. I have a child that I have to raise. And I don't have a choice anymore. I have to take care of Amelia. I am her mother. I don't get an opt-out. I don't get to whoosh of to Chicago and do whatever the fuck I want. Nope. My only option is to be Amelia's mother. And apparently I'm going to continue to do it alone. You promised me we were in this together but clearly we are not. I thought I meant the world to you. You told me that. Yet, I'm standing here, so angry at you that I could spit nails because you are never here. You keep making promises that you can't keep. How do I even know I mean anything to you anymore? You told me you'd love me no matter what but how am I supposed to believe you?"

I pause because I can't control my crying. Jeremy doesn't say a thing.

"Your actions don't match your words, Jeremy. You said we'd be happy if we got married. You said it'd be ok becoming parents. But I'm not happy. And it's not ok. I trusted you and we built this life together, this path that I can't back out on now." I point to Amelia who is cooing in her high chair, oblivious to the fury that is five feet away from her. So much fury inside of me that I can't stop talking. I don't even know if I'm making any sense at this point. The *piece de resistance* is coming up. The straw that may break our relationship's back. Yet, I can't stop it from coming, no matter how hard I try.

"You've left me here to raise our daughter alone. *Alone.* You are missing every fleeting, precious moment of her life. You have no idea the things you've missed out on. And it's just flying by. You keep saying you'll slow down, but you are full of shit, Jeremy. One day you are going to turn around and she's going to be a teenager and you are going to regret your choices. And each day you choose your job over her, I am going to love you a little less, until I don't have anything left to give you."

I inhale. Tears are dripping from my face onto my bare feet. I'm sure the makeup that I previously so very meticulously applied is beyond ruined.

"You made me a promise. I trusted you. I wanted you to be right. But right now you are breaking my fucking heart and what am I supposed to do about it? I can't leave you. I'm not taking Amelia away from you, even though you hardly ever see her anyway. And I'm sure as shit not leaving her, so my only option is to stay here and put on a good face for Amelia all the while really being numb inside because you took my heart and skillfully mended it back together, just to turn around and smash it back into a million pieces."

And that's how you rip off a band aid on an old festering wound that just won't heal.

Jeremy stares at me for a long time. Amelia makes a noise and I look around Jeremy to check on her. Her arms are stretched out, reaching for one of us to pick her up. I move toward her, but before I get past Jeremy, he grabs my arm. I look up at him and his face is contorted in pain. "Leave me? You want to…leave me?"

He's hurt. He's scared. And he's surprised. Now that I've stopped talking, I take a moment to think about what I've just said. He genuinely had no clue that I felt this way. For a second I think that I should ease up because I've just lashed out at him and he had no idea I had all of this bottled up inside me. But, then, I think, *well fuck*. How could he NOT know I'd feel that way? Does he not feel guilty for being so absent? My fury resumes. Amelia and I are just accessories. He'll work and make money and achieve goals and be successful and when he's done and satisfied, we'll be here waiting. Like the picture perfect family, he always wanted—me, the homemaker wife and Amelia, the dutiful child.

In the back of my brain I have a thought. *"No, Livy, Jeremy isn't like that and you know it."* But the fury in the forefront is feeding fuel into my hateful thoughts and my negativity wins out.

He gets his career and his family. All he ever wanted.

What did I want? To stay single and childless.

Did I get what I wanted? No.

How is this fair?

I stare at him for a long time. Long enough for Amelia to start to get fussy and I'm snapped back to reality. Jeremy squeezes my arm slightly. "Livy? Please answer me. Do you want to leave me?"

I want to say: *"No, Jeremy, I don't want to leave you. I want to spend the happy life together that you promised me."*

But instead I say: "How the fuck can I leave someone who is never here?" I turn and grab Amelia out of her high chair. "I'm going to give her a bath. You should go pack for your trip. I hear it's windy in Chicago this time of year. Be sure to take a jacket." I head to the spare bathroom without looking back. I can't look at him after what I just said. I may have just ripped Jeremy's heart out of his chest but I was too much of a coward to see the look on his face after that last sentence.

I am a horrible, evil bitch.

I begin running the bath water and I sit Amelia into the tub. As she kicks and splashes water with her feet, I begin to cry again. I know I told Jeremy that he broke the promise. But deep down I feel like it's me that let him down. I knew I wasn't strong enough for a relationship like this—to be a mother. I should have held my ground and just left Jeremy before he convinced me to marry him. He would have been better off without me. Better off with someone who wanted a family and could handle the stressors of being a wife and stay-at-home mom. Someone who had friends and book clubs and play dates. Someone who could entertain herself as well as her kid and not worry that her husband was never there because he was trying to provide for his family.

I feel so selfish.

I cry harder. I don't know what to do now. I can't fix what's broke. I have no idea how. I'm not even sure what's broke to fix. I finish up Amelia's bath and I take her into her room to dress her. Then, I decide that we'll stay in her room to play. I don't want to go out into the living room right now.

The mixture of anger and guilt is a dangerous combination because it leads to a feeling of helplessness. And helplessness isn't a feeling I'd wish on my own worst enemy.

"Knock, knock." It's Jeremy. The door is open but I get a sense that he wanted to make his presence known without startling me. He comes in, picks up Amelia and sits down in the rocking chair in the corner and places her on his lap. She has a teething toy clutched in both of her hands and in her mouth. She's gnawing away happily, trying to ease the pain of new teeth cutting through. Today should be a victory for me because I finally got Amelia to use a teething toy. But there will be no celebrating today, at least not right now.

Jeremy looks at me. "Livy, I have to go. And I hate that you don't understand that I have to do this. What you said to me in the kitchen really stung. But that doesn't change the fact that I have to go do this. I have to. It really upsets me that you feel the way you do. And I don't know what to say right now because I don't want to fight with you. It kills me to think that you don't think I care about you or Amelia. You are all I think about. Maybe I just haven't told you that enough. I don't know. But I am hoping that when I get back on Tuesday, we can talk about this some more." I look up at him but I don't respond. He's hugging Amelia and giving her kisses, saying he'll miss her.

He's playing this cool and calm. And maybe it is because he doesn't want to start up another argument, but his demeanor is coming off as smug. Like I'm the one that just turned into a hurricane and he's the one that's keeping it all together in the eye of the storm.

He puts Amelia back down onto the floor and she resumes playing. He leans down and kisses me on top of the head and then ruffles my hair slightly as if he's consoling a child. He's treating me like a child.

"I love you," he says. "I'll be back on Tuesday."

Still looking up at him, I say flatly, "I love you too, Jeremy. Have a safe trip."

If this is his way of trying to diffuse a situation, then he has no idea how nuclear I am.

Thirty

Jeremy

I HAVE NO IDEA WHAT JUST HAPPENED. MY WIFE JUST WENT BAT SHIT crazy on me. I mean, I figured she'd be disappointed that I had to cancel our plans but…fuck! She went *way* out in left field.

She wants to leave me?

I thought we were happy. I thought she was happy. She has never once complained to me about having to take care of Amelia full time. She has never once given me any indication that me working this much has had an effect on her. I mean, fuck, she is right. I am never there. But I'm never there now so that I can get this set in stone and I can be there later when it matters more. When Amelia can actually remember who I am and I can be there for her first day of school and for plays and t-ball or ballet or whatever she wants to be a part of. Yes, I missed them both like crazy and I knew Amelia was growing fast, but it never even dawned on me that I was missing her first smile or tooth or whatever the hell Livy was fussing at me about.

I feel like such a dick.

And Livy yelled. Granted only for a split second but she made me swear that we would never, ever do that in front of Amelia. She broke her own code.

And she says she wants to leave me.

What the fuck?

My heart hurts so much. If she really meant all of those things, then she is really hurting. And, I had no clue.

Because I'm never there.

And she has no clue that I've been busting my ass and micromanaging everything with plans to turn leadership over to one of my site supervisors. My plans are to pull back eventually and let the business run itself. But she doesn't know that because I've never told her.

Because I'm never there.

Goddammit, I feel like such an asshole.

But why didn't she just tell me? Why didn't she just say, "Hey, Jeremy, come home please."

Because she's Livy, you idiot, that's why.

This is what Livy does. She keeps it to herself and toughs it out. Except this time she couldn't take it anymore. The trip to Chicago made her snap. And now I'm sitting at the airport waiting to board a fucking flight to a meeting I don't want to go to and all I want to do is hold my wife and tell her I love her.

She thinks I broke my promise to her. I promised her I'd make her happy and that everything would be ok. And up until an hour ago, I thought I was still keeping that promise. But Livy doesn't think so. And knowing that makes my chest physically ache. I feel like I've been stabbed. She is unhappy and she thinks I'm neglecting Amelia. I put my elbows to my knees and my head into my hands.

The plane isn't boarding for another twenty minutes. I try to call Livy. No answer. I leave a voicemail.

"Livy, I love you. I am so sorry. I had no idea you felt this way. I am an idiot. I will try to call you again later. I'll be home Tuesday and we will figure this all out." I hang up and then scroll through my contacts to find and dial the number of the one person that can help me make heads or tails of this.

"Hey, my sweet baby boy. How are you?"

"Mom. Livy says she wants to leave me. I don't know what to do."

Thirty-One

Livy

Tuesday

I MISSED THE CALL FROM JEREMY SATURDAY NIGHT BECAUSE I WAS trying to get Amelia to sleep. When I heard his voicemail, it was only then I started to calm down. He apologized and called himself an idiot. I could hear sincerity in his voice, even in a message. He had no idea I was unhappy because I put up a front. It was a front that normally he could see through when no one else could. But maybe he'd been so busy at work that my front had even worked on him. Or maybe I was trying so hard to be the strong, loving housewife that my front was just that good. He had no clue I was unhappy. But that does not disregard the fact that he's still never here for Amelia. I can't imagine any justification he could provide that would be good enough to excuse him not being here for her.

However, hearing him on that voicemail made me believe that he had a reason he thought was good enough.

Did I overreact?

Probably.

Is there something going on in his mind that he has failed to share with me?

Also, probably.

It's Tuesday. Jeremy says he'll be home for dinner. I'll cook us something comforting. We'll have a drink after dinner and we'll talk. We'll fix this. I'm confident that we can fix this.

Rosalie called me while Amelia and I were shopping for groceries. It's the fourth time she's called me since Saturday. The first time, I ignored it completely. The second time, I answered, but pretended I was busy so I could get off the phone. The third time, I legitimately missed the call because I was feeding Amelia.

I answer the phone hoping that being in public will somehow assist me in keeping the conversation short. I know Jeremy has told her about our fight. I figured that out after the first missed phone call when she left me a message that said, "Livy, sweet girl, please give me a call. I miss that baby girl so much and if you need some time to yourself, I just want you to know I am more than happy to come over and have a play date with Amelia."

Yeah, real subtle, Rosalie.

I hit the answer button on my phone screen. "Hi, Rosalie."

"Hi, sweet girl, how are you?" Her words are *very* syrupy.

"I'm okay. Just doing a little shopping for dinner. I'm making chicken parmesan for Jeremy tonight."

"Oh, that is his favorite," she exclaims.

"Indeed, it is," I respond.

"What time do you expect Jeremy home, hun?" Rosalie asks.

"Not quite sure. He just said he'd be home for dinner. I'm just going to have everything prepped and then cook it when he gets home."

"Sounds like a lovely plan, hun. So, I know you two haven't spent a lot of...*grown up time* with each other in a while. What would you think about bringing Amelia over here to stay the night? I would love to have a sleep over with her. That way, you and Jeremy could have some...*quiet time.*"

Her sugary words are giving me a toothache. As much as I want to take her up on her offer, I feel like she and Jeremy have come up with some plan behind my back and she's going to hold Amelia hostage until I sort things out with Jeremy.

"Thanks, Rosalie, but maybe another night this week. I know Jeremy really misses Amelia and I'm sure he'd like to spend a little time with her." Rosalie doesn't respond for some time. "Rosalie, are you there?"

"Yes, hun. Of course, that makes perfect sense. Another night, then. Soon, I hope."

"Yes, that sounds great. I would love to have a quiet evening with Jeremy very soon."

"Lovely," she says, as if she is trying to come up with something else to say. Before she can, I say, "Rosalie, I am in the checkout line, about to pay. I need to go. I will call you later, Okay?"

"Absolutely, sweet girl. Talk to you soon."

Situation averted.

That was three hours ago. Now, I'm at home, waiting for Jeremy to arrive. I've got all of the ingredients for dinner prepped. All that needs to happen now is for him to walk through that door.

Or for him to call and tell me where he is.

It's 6:30 for crying out loud. What time does he think we eat dinner around here?

Calm down, Livy.

Just when I pick up the phone to call him, my phone rings. It's Jeremy. Fantastic! He must be on his way.

"Hey, babe," I answer.

"Hey, Livy." He doesn't sound enthused.

"What's wrong, Jeremy?"

Silence

"Jeremy?"

"Livy, I'm not going to be home tonight. I am only calling you just now because at first I thought I'd be able to just get a later flight. But it's already six-thirty, your time, so I just wanted to call and tell you I won't be home until tomorrow. The architect liked our pitch and decided to go ahead and hire us. They drew up the paper work this morning and we were supposed to sign it before lunch and head out. However, there was some wording in the documents that needed to be adjusted and they are just now sending those back over to us to revise. We'll probably be here another hour before we're done, so we just now decided to stay the night."

All I see is red. I want to throw my phone across the room or drop it on the ground and stomp on it a few times.

"That is great, babe. Congratulations." I try to have some excitement in my voice. I mean I am happy for him. I guess.

"Thank you. Look, are you upset? I am really sorry. My flight leaves at nine in the morning and I'm not even going into the office when I land. I'm coming straight to you. I know we have so much to talk about, but when they offered to accept our bid, I had to jump on it. I couldn't hesitate."

"It's fine, Jeremy. I will see you tomorrow."

"Okay. I love you."

"I love you."

I hang up. The chicken parm is ruined. It won't last in the fridge another day. I take it out of the fridge and toss it in the garbage, baking dish and all.

Fuck. This. Shit.

I look over at Amelia who is gumming some fruity, puffy snack in her high chair. She smiles at me. I kiss her on her forehead. "Stay right here. I'll be right back." I head into her room and grab her diaper bag. I start filling it with clothes, diapers, butt cream, and anything else I can think of for an extended trip. I go back into the living room and check on her. Still good. I go back into her room and fill another bag full of toys and I grab her pack-n-play. I take that into the living room. Eyes on Amelia. Still good. I go into my own room and very quickly pack a bag for myself. Back into the living room. Amelia. Check.

In the kitchen, I grab food for her. Bottles, a spoon, plate and anything else I deem essential.

I grab Amelia, head down stairs to the lobby of the complex. Grab a loading cart. Head back upstairs. Set Amelia on the floor to play while I load the cart. Grab her and drag the cart back downstairs to my car. Secure Amelia in the car seat and load up the car.

This may be a knee jerk reaction, but I have to leave. I cannot stay here for one more second.

I knock on Rosalie's door, Amelia resting on my hip. If she refuses me, I don't know what I'll do. I can't just go back home.

The door knob turns and I stand up straight. I have to convince her to help me. Any other outcome is not an option.

"Livy! My sweet girl! You decided to bring Amelia. When is Jeremy getting in?"

"He's not. Rosalie, can I come in?"

The smile on Rosalie's face disappears. "Of course." She steps aside and motions for us to come in with her arm.

I head to the dining room and sit Amelia in the high chair Rosalie has for her. I need to keep her in one spot while I explain to Rosalie what I'm about to do.

"Livy, you look quite upset. What is wrong, love?"

I turn to her and stare her directly in the eye. For a moment I don't respond. I'm not sure I can go through with this.

But if you don't, nothing will ever change.

I stiffen my resolve. I have to do this.

"Rosalie, Jeremy isn't coming home until tomorrow. He called and said something about a deal he's making. I don't know. He is supposed to be back tomorrow."

"Oh, you poor dear," Rosalie interrupts and she moves in for a hug. I hold up my hand for her to stop. If she hugs me I won't be able to go through with this.

"Will you please watch Amelia for me until he gets home tomorrow?"

"Absolutely, love. Where are you going?"

"I don't know, but I have to leave. I have to go. I cannot sit in that apartment one more day and watch Amelia grow up without her father. I can't sit at home wondering when the next time I'm going to see my husband will be. I didn't sign up to be a single parent. I refuse to let this be my life. I am miserable. And I've tried to keep that misery at bay so it doesn't rub off on Amelia, but I know that if I don't do something, it will eventually and we'll just be two miserable peas in one lonely pod."

I exhale. Rosalie has a stone face, but there are tears falling from both of her eyes. She remains silent as if she is anticipating that I have more to say.

"I have to leave. I don't know where I am going to go, but I have to leave. But, please know, that I'm not leaving forever. I just need a break. I need a break, Rosalie. I have to go or I am going to crack and I don't know what that will look like. I'm terrified. I have to go." The last four words are barely audible and now there are tears falling from my eyes.

Before I can defend, Rosalie rushes in for the hug. "My poor, sweet girl. I wish you would have told me sooner. I could have helped you with Amelia."

I pull back. "I don't need your help, Rosalie. I need my husband to make good on his promises. He convinced me that marriage and a child were good things. And don't get me wrong, Amelia *is* a good thing. She is a wonderful thing. She is precious and I love her more than I thought I could love anything. But, I came into this accord thinking I wouldn't be doing this alone. This is so hard, Rosalie. It's so hard and there is no end in sight as to when it's going to get easier."

"Livy, being a mother is hard. So hard. And you are absolutely right it is very hard to do it alone. I cannot even imagine what it would have been like to raise Jeremy alone at Amelia's age. It was hard enough as it was when he was five. Just please, don't give up on Jeremy. Not yet. Please."

"Rosalie, I'm not giving up. I just need to go away. I don't know for how long but I have to go. And when I come back, I don't know where Jeremy and I will land, but I will say this, if he's not willing to put in the effort, to pull his weight, then why should I?"

Rosalie nods her head, more tears emerging. "I will watch Amelia until Jeremy comes home." She puts her hands on my arms. "Jeremy is a good boy. Whatever he is doing, I know he's not doing it to hurt you, Livy. He keeps his promises. Maybe he didn't realize that he was breaking a promise."

"Rosalie, look. I don't want to have this conversation with you. I'm not going to stand here and tell you why I am upset with your son. I just want to go, okay? Please, just…" I turn my head and look down at Amelia. My heart aches because I've gotten myself into a situation that has escalated to a point where I feel like I have to leave my daughter behind. "Just…have some fun with Amelia," I whisper. "Jeremy should be home tomorrow and I will be back…later. I have my cell if there is an emergency. And please only call if there is an emergency." I look back at Rosalie, "And tell Jeremy the same. I don't want to spend time with either of you on the phone while you try to convince me to come home. I know you two." And now I put my hands on Rosalie's arms, "I just need a break, okay? I need to go. I will be back. I promise. Okay?"

Rosalie hugs me again, very tightly. "Okay, sweet girl. I know you will be back. Jeremy and I will leave you to yourself. I promise. Please be safe, whatever you do."

"I will." I turn to pick up Amelia. I hug her tight and give her a thousand kisses. "I love you, baby girl. Have fun with Nana, okay? I'll be back soon." The last words come out choked behind a sob. I don't want to leave her but in the pit of my stomach and in the depths of the chambers of my heart, I know that I have to. I hand Amelia over to Rosalie and give her one final kiss on the forehead. I look at Rosalie. "Thank you, Rosalie. Thank you."

"Of course," is all she says.

"I'll get all of her stuff from the car and leave it in the foyer. It might be best if you two stay in here while I do that."

"Okay, hun. We'll do that."

I head out to my car to get all of Amelia's things. I leave everything in the foyer and when the final item is unpacked, I get into my car and sit. My hand refuses to put the key into the ignition.

This is dumb, Livy. So dumb. Just stay. Go back in there and tell Rosalie never mind.

I look up and see one of the curtains in the front window of the house flicker. Rosalie is watching me. Is she waiting for me to come back in? Is she wondering if I'm really going to go through with this? Does she think that I don't have the balls to leave my child behind? Leave my husband? Or maybe it's the opposite. Maybe she thinks I'm a chicken shit *for* leaving my family.

My hand finally decides it's time to go and shoves the key into the ignition and turns. My eyes are locked on the curtain in the window and before my brain registers what is going on, my hand has put the car into reverse and my foot is hitting the gas pedal. I'm doing it. I'm moving. I am backing away from the house. I am pulling out of the driveway, putting the car into drive and moving away from the house. Down the street. Farther and farther away. My plan has been literally set into motion and my heart wants me to stop and turn around. But the rest of my body keeps going forward. I come to a stop sign. I can turn around or keep going.

Turn or go? Turn or go? At that moment, a car horn beeps at me from behind. I look in the rear view mirror and realize I'm holding up traffic. And when I look into the mirror, I see my reflection. I look at my worn face, dark circles, frown lines. Splotchy and unevenly colored from lack of care. And my hair. Jesus Christ, my hair. It's a rat's nest. I've worn it twirled up on top of my head almost every day since Amelia was born. Aside from the thorough washing I gave it a few days ago, I've not paid attention to the state of my hair. It's gotten *really* long and I found that swooping it up into a bun is just easier when you have a demanding little person always in your presence.

The realization that I look like absolute shit sits heavy with me. I was going to cook dinner for Jeremy tonight and I didn't even put forth any effort to look presentable when he got home. What does that mean?

Still looking in the mirror, my eyes shift to the empty spot in the back seat where Amelia's car seat generally sits. And another realization hits me. I am alone. All by myself. I haven't been all by myself in…. well, I can't even remember. I am all alone. Most people might consider that a desolate feeling but for me, for some reason, I'm not upset that I'm alone. I feel…free?

The car behind me honks again. I've made up my mind. There will be no U-turns today. I hit the gas and accelerate forward. Alone.

My first stop, without even thinking about where I would go, is the bookstore. I used to go to this bookstore at least once a week. Presently, I haven't been to this bookstore in at least a year. I walk through the front door and the dusty air mixed with the smell of leather bounds and printed paper fill my lungs.

Hello, old friend.

I walk over to one of the shelves and run my fingers over the spines of the books that are lined up. The touch ignites something inside of me and I suddenly want to read every single book in this building. I inhale deep and close my eyes. The aroma again fills my lungs and I am high. So high. I look around. My eyes shift and dart from shelf to shelf. What am I in the mood for? Something classic? Shakespeare? Tolstoy? A Bronte sister perhaps? Something poetic? Frost? Keats? Something darker? Poe? How about some Hemingway or Vonnegut? Maybe some Kerouac? Seems appropriate.

I continue to walk the isles and peruse. Stephen King, Dean Koontz. Michael Crichton. Grisham. Dan Brown. I turn the corner. Jane Austen, Harper Lee, Mary Shelley, Maya Angelou. The selections are endless. I'm alone with myself for the first time in months and I feel like the very first book I choose to read should be significant. As though I will look back at this moment and realize that it was a moment of transcendence.

That the book I select will have changed me and turned the path of my life in a completely opposite and upward direction.

I continue to stroll, touching nearly every single book that I pass. How am I supposed to decide this? What if I choose incorrectly? What if my brain tricks me into choosing something that I will regret and it will haunt me for the rest of my life?

Chill the fuck out, Livy. It's just a goddamn book.

I take my time and I end up choosing three books: *Flowers for Algernon*, *The Hitchhikers Guide to the Galaxy Anthology* and *A Clockwork Orange*. I have no reasoning behind any of them. They just stuck out at me. Perhaps it's because I'm progressively blossoming out of my ignorance and need to take a journey of some sort to be rebellious and reckless?

I'm stretching, I know.

And I already have copies of all three. But sadly, they are wasting away in a storage unit, three blocks from my house. We packed them all up, along with my reading chair, in order to give Amelia a nursery.

I purchase the books and leave the bookstore. But before I go to my car, I walk over to the bakery and I grab a few bagels and a bottle of water.

I head to the park. It's getting dark, but I know the perfect spot that is lit and if I sit positioned just right, no one will be able to see me. And I know Marcus won't be there. He is in Chicago with my husband. I will be completely undisturbed.

Alone.

Thirty-Two

Jeremy

MY WIFE LEFT ME.
        I got home on Wednesday afternoon but instead of heading straight to the house as I had originally planned, I headed to my mother's house to pick up my daughter. My mother called me last night after Livy left Amelia there. I had just finished dinner, and after a long day of hurry up and wait to sign what seemed like thousands of documents for a contract on the downtown loft projects, I was exhausted.

She just left. She didn't tell me. She didn't call me or text me. She didn't even ask me if it was okay to just dump my daughter onto my mother and just vanish. I'm furious at her. I'm also devastated. And I'm worried about her. And sadly, I'm not entirely surprised by this. This seems exactly like something Livy would do. Just freak out and up and leave with no warning.

Livy left and I have no idea when she is coming back.

My mom assured me she'd be back.

But when she comes back what are we going to do? Livy's lost faith in me, and to be honest, after this stunt, I've kind of lost a little in her as well. One day she is sweet, tired, loving Livy, who I was certain was happy with holding down the fort until things eased up for me at work. The next day, she is saying all of these horrible things about being unhappy and stressed and neglected. Then, when I think things are settled and we were going to talk it out, she just leaves and now I have no idea why, or what she is upset about or if she even still wants to be married to me.

I have so many questions that I want to ask her and it's killing me that I can't talk to her. My mom very sternly told me not to try to get in touch with Livy. "She's needs space and time to think and process."

"Think and process what?"

"I'm not sure, baby boy, but from my perspective, you guys are not communicating. She thinks one thing and you think another. And you need to talk to each other."

"That's exactly what I wanted to do! I was going to come home and talk it out!" I'm so frustrated right now.

"Jeremy, calm down. You were too late. From what I can tell, Livy has been unhappy for some time and she has done a stellar job with hiding it. I'm guessing she was trying to be strong and wait out the end of the project you were working on. And, maybe when you told her about Chicago, she broke a little. And then when you didn't come home yesterday, because of work, that was it. She shattered."

I sit down on my mother's sofa, trying to not be too loud in my frantic state. Amelia is napping just one room over. I put my head in my hands. My heart hurts and my wife is gone. And I have no idea how to make anything right. I do the only thing my body will allow me to do at that moment. I cry. With my head in my hands, sitting on my mother's sofa, I cry. "What am I supposed to do, Mom?"

Mom comes to sit beside me, wraps one arm around me and pulls me into her. Her other hand is wrapped around the side of my face. "Oh, my baby boy. Shh. It's going to be okay. It's going to be okay." Her voice is shaky. I can't see her face because I'm looking down at the floor but I can tell she's crying too. I can count on one hand the number of times I've seen my mother cry. My heart is breaking and it's breaking her heart too.

We sit that way for awhile. From the outside, I imagine it's a pretty pathetic site. A mother holding, rocking and consoling her grown, adult son. But in the moment, her comforting embrace is keeping me together. It's probably the only thing that would keep me together in this situation. I worry that if her arms, which are so snugly wrapped around me, let go that I might literally fall apart right there on her sofa.

Amelia starts to cry. My mother does release me and I manage to stay whole. I motion to get up and go get Amelia. My mother wipes her eyes and says, "Stay here. I'll get her. Just sit here for a minute and relax."

She kisses me on my forehead and I exhale.

Mom brings Amelia out and when Amelia sees me, she immediately reaches out in my direction. My heart swells with pride and love for this beautiful baby girl. The baby girl that looks like a Mini-Livy, with the exception of her blue eyes. And my heart immediately breaks all over again.

My wife is gone.

Livy brought this precious baby into this world. Amelia is a gift like no other I have ever received. Every day she changes and grows and learns. Every day she gets more beautiful. Every day, she's becoming more and more a replica of Livy.

I want my family back.

I bounce Amelia on my knee and cry again.

Thirty-Three

Livy

I've been gone for four days.

The first night, I sat in the park and read all three books. I rationed out my bagels and water so I wouldn't have lack of sustenance as an excuse to leave my spot. I was there, alone and reading, for almost eight hours. It was well until the very early hours of the next morning before I stood up, legs and ass completely numb, and walked out of the park.

I went to a hotel and checked in around three a.m. For payment, I used a card that was attached to an account that had only my name on it so that Jeremy could not log in to a website and check the activity to find me. Not that I set the account up for that purpose. It was just an old account from when Joe gave me the money from selling the bar. I left a pretty good sum of it in that account after Jeremy and I got married.

Just in case. In case my job at the shelter didn't work out and I needed money—I wouldn't have to be solely dependent on Jeremy. In case there was any reason whatsoever that I needed money that wasn't comingled with Jeremy's money, say like for a big surprise birthday gift for him.

In case I wanted to leave my husband and not be found.

Seriously, that particular thought had never crossed my mind. But the account has certainly come in handy for my current quandary.

I decided to pay for two nights, for now. I didn't know how long I would actually stay here, but I figured I'd give myself at least two days. Once checked in, I took a forty-five-minute shower and then headed straight to bed.

I kept waking up, thinking of Jeremy and Amelia. I would dream that something bad happened to one of them and I would shoot up out of bed. I was all alone with no responsibility and I couldn't even sleep. It was 6am before I gave up trying. I put on some yoga pants and a hooded sweatshirt and headed out. There had to be a liquor store open somewhere around this stupid city. I knew there were a few twenty-four hour joints that catered to the late night partiers, shift workers and sadly, the homeless when they found a way to buy any.

And apparently to the wives who leave their husbands and need a bottle of booze just before sunrise.

I did manage to find one of those types of stores and bought a big bottle of Jim Beam. I returned back to the hotel, brown paper bag in tote. In my room, I opened the bottle, at 6:30 in the morning, and unwrapped one of the plastic cups beside the ice bucket that was positioned to the right of the television. I hadn't drank since I found out I was pregnant with Amelia. I was terrified what rabbit hole it was going to take me down. But now, being all alone, I think it was time for me to find out.

I hovered the full bottle, titled, over the empty plastic cup. Should I do this? Should I stop? Should I just lie back down and let all the nightmares keep me awake? Should I just go back home and give up?

No.

I poured the bourbon into the cup until it was almost full. I set the bottle down, picked up the cup and sat on the edge of the bed. I was going to take my chances. If this cup of brown liquor was going to be the end of me, I had to know. Because none of the other choices I could conjure were looking all too positive either. I lifted the cup to my mouth, tilted my head back and swallowed about half of the contents of the cup. It burned. I coughed and my eyes began to water. I set the rest of what was in the cup on the nightstand and grabbed the remote control to the TV. I hit power and began vacantly flipping through the channels, waiting on the liquor to settle into my stomach and move through my blood stream. Waiting for it to go to my head so I could relax.

Relax.

All I wanted to do was relax.

I find ESPN and leave it. I remembered when I used to like this channel. When I used to watch it every day.

That seemed like a lifetime ago.

I finished the rest of my cup and poured another. And then another. And one more. I methodically drank while I watched the TV, not hearing one word that was being said. My mind got lost in thought but no thought in particular. I thought about Joe and Sara and the bar. I thought about how content I was back then. I thought about Jeremy uprooting my life and it sounding like a good idea at the time. It made me feel guilty and angry but I couldn't really decipher why. And as I filled each cupful and emptied it down my throat, the guilt and anger subsided and all thoughts became a blur.

And then, finally, I slept.

I woke up around 4:30 in the afternoon. I sat up and clutched my head. Fuck! I was in agony. Every square centimeter of all parts of me from the neck up was pounding. My head, my eyes, hell even my teeth hurt. How is that even possible? My ears were ringing and any movement that wasn't slow and calculated sent my equilibrium spinning out of control.

I needed water and Ibuprophen and neither were anywhere in my vicinity. I had to navigate my way down to the hotel pantry and get what I required. That may have been an overpriced option, but there was no way I was stepping foot outside the hotel doors in this condition. I was really very worried that I might not even make it downstairs.

I grabbed three bottles of water, some Ibuprophen, chips and some beef jerky. I slowly made my way back up to the room. I chugged one full bottle of water before I even considered popping the pills. Then I started on the second bottle of water and the beef jerky. After bottle number two and the bag of jerky was empty, I crawled back under the covers and closed my eyes. I was waiting on the pills to kick in.

Then what?

I didn't know exactly. I didn't have a plan. But my main priority at that particular moment was to get rid of the worst hangover I had ever had in my life.

After the extremely vivid images of someone kidnapping Amelia and me screaming *"NO!"* over and over again played through my head, I shot straight up from the bed. The room was pitch-black except for the digital glow of the alarm clock to my left. It read 12:42. As in a.m.

I reached over and flipped on the lamp. Then, I took a look at my phone. No one had tried to call.

No one.

But why was I so surprised by that? Those were my instructions. And true to her word, Rosalie somehow managed to make sure those instructions were followed.

Jeremy must be worried sick.

And the guilt reappeared.

But this is all his fault.

And the anger reemerged.

I looked over at the half drunk bottle of Beam. I considered finishing it off. But then I remembered how insanely awful I felt not just a few short hours before. I had made a full recovery even though at the time I had no idea how that would be possible.

I didn't drink the rest of the bottle. I could have but I didn't. I knew the moment that bottle hit my lips the guilt and anger would flush away again. But I also knew that as soon the alcohol cleared my system, both would come right back.

A vicious cycle.

Just like Nancy.

A chill ran up my spine and I shuddered.

It was at that moment I realized something profound.

I could be just like Nancy if I wanted to. If I were weaker. If I just wanted to be numb. If I didn't care.

But I do care and I don't want to be numb. And I am stronger than her. Because in the moment that I am staring at that bottle and it's calling my name, I say *no*. I want the guilt and the anger to go away but not with booze. I have to figure out a solution—a way that I can continue to live my life and be at peace and not have to medicate myself into a stupor with alcohol.

I leaned back onto the headboard and crossed my arms over my chest. I smiled. I was pretty damn proud that I had come to that epiphany. I almost felt a little sanctimonious.

I've come to a crossroads and I have chosen the right path. I'm not going to spend the rest of my days submerged in bourbon. I'm going to figure this out. I don't know how but I'm going to do it. I'm going to fight and I'm not going to give up.

I'm better than Nancy.

Fuck yeah, I am.

I turned on the TV and begin flipping through the channels again, still smiling. I remained that way until the sun came up. Then, I showered, got dressed and checked out of the hotel. I was in my car before nine o'clock. I knew where I had to go. I knew what I wanted to do. I set up the Garmin for the address I had written down in the planner that I kept in my purse.

Destination: 350 miles

Estimated time of travel: 5 hours, 16 minutes

I was going to see my granddad.

About three hours into the drive, I stopped to eat. I checked my phone. Still no calls. While I was eating, I began to get nervous about going to see my grandfather unannounced. I haven't talked to him in a few weeks.

Ever since Jeremy found him, my grandfather and I had really taken the time to get to know each other. I visited him as much as I could and he did the same.

To this day, I still can't believe that Jeremy found him. Jeremy did that for me.

But that was old Jeremy. New Jeremy is not the same thoughtful, attentive man I knew back then. New Jeremy is work hungry and career oriented.

I haven't talked to my grandfather in a few weeks so I begin to wonder if he'll even be home when I get there. It's a Thursday. Did he work on Thursdays? I couldn't remember.

I shouldn't have done this. I'm being too spontaneous.

I finished my meal and head back out to the car. For a second I thought I should just turn around and go home. I should have called first. Maybe I should call and plan to go another day. But I remembered I had a reason I wanted to go see him. And since I was taking a sabbatical from my life, I should take the opportunity to make the journey.

I continued to follow the GPS directions that were being dispensed to me.

Two hours and some change later, I am standing on my granddad's front porch. His car is in the driveway, so I assume he must be home. I rang the doorbell and waited. My granddad opens the door. "Livy! Oh my goodness what a pleasant surprise! Come in, my dear. Come in!"

I walked over the threshold and he wraps me up in his arms. "What brings you all the way out here? Why didn't you bring that beautiful great-granddaughter of mine?"

With my face still pressed up against his chest as the result of the hug, I began to cry. I had come to see my grandfather to talk about Nancy and lift those demons from my soul. They stuck to me like tarred feathers and no matter how hard I had tried, I could not get rid of them.

But that morning, when I thought of how much different I really was from Nancy, I thought maybe I could go to my grandfather and he could help me get rid of them once and for all. I went there strong but immediately turned to mush the moment he hugged me.

"Oh my dear, Livy. What has gotten you so upset? Is everything okay with Amelia and Jeremy?"

We stand there for a moment before I respond. "Everything is so screwed up. Jeremy…he…and I…I just don't know what to do anymore."

"Shh, calm down. It's okay. It's okay. Let's go sit." We go to the living room and I sit in the first spot I find, on a chair by a window.

"Do you want something to drink? Tea? Water?"

"Got any bourbon?" I just needed to take the edge off. Nothing like the night before.

"I've got scotch."

"Perfect. No ice."

Moments later, he brings me a glass and I take a sip. I lean my head against the back of the chair and look up at the ceiling. "Everything is so fucked up." I cover my mouth with my hand and immediately look over to my granddad. I'm not sure if I've ever cursed in front of him before. Jesus.

"It's okay, Livy," he says. "You are obviously spun up about something. A little foul language is bound to happen. Can you tell me what is going on?"

I exhale, sip on my scotch again and begin to tell him everything. I even mention the way I don't feel attractive anymore and mine and Jeremy's pitiful excuse of a sex life. I figured if I was putting it all out there, I may as well be honest. After about an hour of talking, I had an empty glass and a grandfather sitting across from me with a very strange look on his face. He gets up and walks over to a piano that he has in the corner of his living room. He grabs a framed picture that is sitting on top of it. He then turns and walks my way and hands me the picture.

"Your grandmother was so lovely. The love of my life. We were only married eighteen years before she passed away. Your mother was fifteen when her mother died. I believe that is what started the uncontrollable snow ball that became your mother's life."

All the times he and I had spoken, he had never mentioned my grandmother. And I don't really know why, but I had failed to ask. I look down at the black and white picture of a woman who looks insanely similar to...*me.*

"You are the spitting image of her, Livy. It baffles me. I guess your mother had more *me* in her because she never really looked like her mother. But you? You are your grandmother right down to those piercing green eyes. And boy was she a pistol, just like you. When she was determined to do something, she wouldn't take no for an answer. She was stubborn as a mule but that is what I loved most about her." There is a gleam in his eye. A tear, perhaps.

"My point, Livy, is this. Jeremy is one of the good ones. I can tell. It honestly just sounds to me that you two need to work on communication. And it has to start with you. You can't just bottle it all up, spit it out to him all at once and just leave. It doesn't work like that. You talk about it. Argue about it if you have to but you do it together until you have a compromise. You have to respect one another and also understand that both of you are human and not perfect. If you don't keep that in focus, you'll lose each other before you know what hit you. Go back to him. Talk to him. Figure it out with him. Jeremy is a blessing to you. All of the mess that your mother put you through, I don't even know the half of it, I'm sure, but I know it was not pleasant growing up with her. And you were lucky enough to find Jeremy. He is a good one and he loves you. I see it in his eyes. He looks at you the way I used to look at your grandmother. You have to go home and make this right because you never know when one of you will lose the other for good." He points at the picture.

I look up at him and nod, "You're right."

At that moment, I felt more like a selfish idiot than I had through this entire ordeal. I would be devastated if something happened to Jeremy and I never got to see him again. And that feeling, the despair I know I would have if I ever lost him, overshadows and is heavier than anything else that I've felt in the past few days. I have to go home and make this right.

It was getting late so I decided to stay the night. Still no phone calls.

I got up the next morning and had breakfast with my granddad before getting back on the road.

I am going to go home, talk to my husband, and we are going to fix this.

Thirty-Four

Jeremy

Friday

"PEEK-A-BOO." MY HANDS FAN OUT AND I UNCOVER MY FACE. Amelia giggles. I cover my face again and repeat: "Peek-a-boo." She giggles again. Peek-a-boo seems to be a popular game with her.

It's Friday. Livy has been gone since Tuesday evening. I haven't heard from her. The only reason I know she's not dead in a ditch somewhere is because Maxwell called me last night and said she was there.

She had told him everything that was going on, in her mind at least, and he had convinced her that she needed to come home.

Livy is coming home today.

I should be overjoyed. I should be thinking about how much I've missed my wife who has been gone for four days.

I should be. But I'm not.

Instead, I'm angry. I'm angry because Livy left. She just left. She left me and she left Amelia with no regard to how this would affect either of us.

Since I got home on Wednesday, I've been trying to juggle Amelia and work. That has not been an easy task.

There was still paperwork to be signed and plans to be drawn up on the new project in Chicago, not to mention the project we were wrapping up here. I had inspections and walk-throughs to do. I had to postpone two appointments that were critical to closing this project. Mom has come over to help some, but she still works too and can't be here as much as I need her.

But Livy is coming home today. I don't feel any real happiness about that fact. I feel relief that I'll be able to go back to work. But other than that, I genuinely have no other positive feeling about Livy coming home.

The woman I love walked out on me three nights ago, and I wasn't even here to witness it. I'm not sure who is going to come walking through that door.

Just as I'm deep in thought while playing peek-a-boo with Amelia, I hear the deadbolt turn. Livy is here. I pick up Amelia and head toward the front door. Livy comes through the door and looks at me. "Hi."

"Hi," I reply.

Amelia reaches for her and Livy takes her from me. Just like that. It's as if she was never gone. At least according to Amelia, anyway. "Hi, sweet baby," Livy says and kisses Amelia's face. Amelia giggles.

Livy looks back at me. "How are you guys?"

I look back at her and slowly say, "We're…fine."

Livy has a smile on her face. A smile I haven't seen in a really long time. A genuine grin. It should make me happy. I should feel happy that my wife is happy after months of seeming tired and run down. I should go over and hug her and tell her it's good to see her smile. I should smile with her. We should smile together.

But I don't do any of those things. Instead, I say, with a frown, "Well, it seems as though you've had a lovely time away."

And instantly her smile disappears. "I was smiling because I was happy to see you. I was glad to be home because I wanted to talk to you and figure things out. But you're obviously upset."

"You left, Livy. You've been gone for four days and you didn't tell me where you were or when you were coming back…if you were coming back."

"Of course I was coming back. I told your mother."

"Yeah, you told her. But you didn't tell me anything. *Your husband.* You just left."

"I had to. I felt like if I told you anything, you would convince me to stay. I had to leave. I had to." Her voice is shaky.

Definitely not smiling anymore. And I should feel bad that she is on the verge of tears. But, I don't. I am angry. I am so angry that there is no room for any other emotion.

Livy walks away, carrying Amelia into the living room and setting her on the floor. I follow her.

"Why did you have to leave, Livy? Why did you *have* to?"

"I don't want to talk to you about this when you are angry, Jeremy."

"Well I don't think I am going to *not* be angry anytime soon. Not until you tell me why you left."

My voice elevates to a higher decibel.

"Jeremy, please don't yell."

There is a knock at the door. It's probably my mother. I asked her to come and get Amelia for the night so that I could get some answers from Livy without distraction. I open the door and the look on my mother's face is apparently a direct response from the look on my face. I'm pissed. *So pissed.*

"Is Amelia ready to go?" is all she says, still standing on the other side of the door.

"Yep." I turn and walk into Amelia's room to grab her overnight things. Walking through the living room I say to Livy, "My mother is here to take Amelia for a sleepover."

"What?" Livy gets up and picks up Amelia and follows me to the front door. "What is going on?" she says. I don't answer her.

"I'm going to take Amelia for the night so you two can have some time…to yourselves."

Livy looks confused. She looks back and forth between Mom and me. "How did you know I'd even be home today?" I don't know why, but that question pisses me off even more. She has the audacity to ask a question like that?

Does she not think we had the right to know where the hell she was?

Mom leaves with Amelia.

As soon as the door closes I ask Livy the same question I asked before: "Why did you leave, Livy? How could you just leave?"

"Are you serious? Do you not remember what I said on Saturday? I'm not your slave, Jeremy. I'm not here to keep your house clean and cook you dinner every night or to raise our child alone. You made me a promise and you broke it just like I told you that you would. I can't take it anymore. I feel like you don't appreciate what I do every day. You think Amelia and I just sit around and laugh and have fun all the time while you have to go to work and do your hard, tiring stressful job. But here's the reality. My brain is turning to pulp because all I do all day is baby talk. Until Tuesday, I hadn't read a book above toddler reading level in months. I never see you. Amelia never sees you. And also until Tuesday, I hadn't had a decent night's sleep in at least a year. And the only reason I did sleep was because I was assisted by half a bottle of whiskey. "

"What?"

"I checked into a hotel room because I wanted to be alone. I tried to sleep but I couldn't. So I went and bought a bottle of Jim Beam and drank half of it before I passed out."

"Livy! Are you fucking kidding me? What if something had happened to you? I would have had no idea where you were!"

"Relax, I'm fine. I went to Maxwell. We had a good talk and it made me feel better. And I was going to tell you all of that until I walked through the door and was greeted by your attitude."

"Attitude? You fucking left!" I'm yelling now. And I don't intend to stop. There is no baby in the vicinity and I'm angry as hell. "You don't just leave! Why didn't you tell me you felt this way? You promised me that you would talk to me if you ever felt overwhelmed or sad or whatever the fuck it is you are feeling right now."

"Oh, so now *I promised*?" she interrupts, also yelling, "*I* broke a promise and it's the end of the world but I tell you the same thing and you act like I'm fucking crazy! And I guess since you decided to break your promise to me I figured what was the point? And I haven't had an opportunity to tell you because you are nev-er fuck-ing here!"

"Jesus Christ, Livy. How many times do I have to tell you that I'm working on being home more?"

"I don't know, Jeremy, how many? Because you've been saying that shit since before Amelia was born. After a while hearing you say that gets old."

"Why didn't you say something Saturday morning? I was here."

"I don't know. It was four a.m. I was tired! And I was just trying to tough it out because your project at work was almost over. I thought if I just toughed it out, I would get my husband back and we'd be okay. But then you left for Chicago and I knew that it was all bullshit."

"Bullshit? It wasn't bullshit. I've been training people to do what I do so that I don't have to work so much. I even have a team in place for Chicago. I'll only have to go back like twice! Why do you assume the worst about me, Livy? I thought you knew me better than that."

"I don't think I know you anymore at all! You are never here!"

"Stop saying that!"

"It's the truth!"

"But not because I don't want to be! I'm working hard now so I can spend time with you and Amelia later. When she's bigger. When you need me more."

Livy opens her mouth to speak, but before she does, she looks at me like I suddenly have an alien coming out of my face somewhere. "What the fuck? *Need you more*? I need you now! She needs you now!"

"She doesn't even know that I'm not here!"

"Like hell she does! She cries for you all of the time. And I need you, dammit. I'm fucking stretched thin. So fucking thin! I'm trying to do everything right and I don't know if I am. I don't know how to be a mother, Jeremy, but I'm doing my best. I hate asking your mom because she makes me feel guilty that I'm not perfect like her. Not on purpose, but I still feel it all the same. I need you. Amelia needs you."

"She cries for me?"

"Oh fucking hell! Is that all you just heard? What is the point? You aren't even fucking listening."

"Jesus, Livy! Why are you being such a b—" I stop. My brain is thinking it, but I don't want to say it out loud. I don't want to call my wife a bitch. I'm pissed but I know name calling is pointless. But it's too late. I said enough for her to piece it together. When Livy realizes what

I was about to say, she's shocked and she scoffs.

"A bitch? That's what you think of me right now? You think I'm being a bitch? "

She's talking low and calm and that is deadly. I really need to diffuse this situation, but I don't know that I can. Plus, I'm still just too angry to even really care. I want her to apologize or admit that she was wrong to just leave. If I ever did something like that she would have murdered me.

"I am raising a child on my own. You have no idea how difficult that is. You have no clue. And you want to just step in later and do the easy shit? When there's no dirty diapers or middle of the night temper tantrums or giving her a bath just to have her pee all over herself, *and me*, moments later when I'm struggling to get her dressed? And you are going to stand there and call me a *bitch*? I left because I needed a break. I needed to be alone. When I walked through that door I felt better. I was going to apologize and tell you how I felt. But you didn't even give me a chance. You instantly came at me with anger and you think *I'm being a bitch*? You are different, Jeremy. I don't know why, but you are. You are so distant. Literally and emotionally. The last time we had sex it was like I was only there for your pleasure. You didn't even try to get me off. I just feel like you care less and less about me every day. And thirty minutes ago I wanted to try to make it right. Figure out what's wrong. But you know what? Now? Now, I could give a fuck."

She turns and walks away into Amelia's room and slams the door. And that is where she stays all night.

I make no effort to go in there and talk to her. I don't have anything to say. She said she had intended to apologize but I didn't give her a chance. That kind of makes me feel like a dick. But I'm also still mad that she left. I don't know what to do. I'm so tired. I'm tired of working and I'm tired feeling the way I feel right now. Like no decision I make is the right one. Like I'm failing.

The next morning, I wake up and decide to try to have a civil conversation with Livy before Mom brings Amelia back. However, all I find is an empty apartment and a note taped to the front door:

Went to get Amelia. Don't go freaking out. I will be back.

Yeah, she's still mad.

Thirty-Five

Livy

One week later

I HAVEN'T SPOKEN TO JEREMY SINCE THE NIGHT I SLEPT BY MYSELF IN Amelia's room. When I came back with Amelia the next day, he tried to talk and ask a lot of questions but I gave him the silent treatment until he gave up.

Real mature, I know, but I couldn't get over the fact that he had the nerve to even think I was being a bitch. I knew if I said anything to him, I would yell. So I just said nothing. After that day, I avoided him. Also juvenile, I realize, but until I can think about him almost calling me a bitch, without a rush of heat and anger bubbling inside of me, I just need to stay away from him. He's still working his regular schedule so it's not like he's here to avoid much. Rosalie has called me a million and one times asking if I need help or if I'm feeling okay. I've only answered a handful of times to reassure her I'm not a flight risk.

I'm better than I was last week. I'm still tired and I'm sad that I feel alone and that I can't think about my husband without wanting to throw something across the room. The difference now is that I've since had a realization that I am where I am because of my choices. I chose this. I chose to get married and I chose to have a child, whom I love so much. I went against my better judgment and this is where I ended up—in a marriage with a man I don't think I know any more and a baby that needs love. I'm not going to break this family up. It's not fair to Amelia. She will not grow up in a broken home. So I will do whatever I need to do to make sure she knows she is loved. I'll be miserable if I have to be, I don't care. I'm good at hiding emotions from people. I can put up a good front for her. And if Jeremy never slows down with work, I'll tell Amelia every lie I can make up so she'll think her father hung the moon for her. I will not disappoint her and have her become an adult who feels unloved and worthless.

It's close to two o'clock in the afternoon when the doorbell rings. I pick up Amelia from her play mat and go to answer the door. It's a delivery man with a box. "Sign here, please."

I crinkle my brow at him, this man with a beer belly and hideous shorts who is demanding things from me. "What is it?"

He raises his shoulders, "I dunno. But it requires a signature, ma'am." He stretches the electronic stylus out further to me. I huff and shift Amelia on my hip so I can take the stylus from the man's grubby hands. I didn't order anything and if Jeremy is expecting something, he would have told me.

Except I'm not speaking to him and I'm avoiding him.

Well, Jeremy should have left a note!

"Have a good day," the potbellied man says.

I'm investigating the box. It's pretty significant in size. "Yeah, you too," I say, still focusing on the box. The delivery man walks away and I move out into the hall. With Amelia still in my arms, I nudge the box with my foot, over the threshold and into the apartment. It's somewhat heavy, but manageable.

I set Amelia down in her high chair and give her some snacks to occupy her for a moment while I take a closer look at this package. It's addressed to Jeremy and me both. That gives me full license to go ahead and open it. I pick up the box. It's heavier than I originally thought and the size makes it awkward to lift. I give it a good heave and elevate it up to the breakfast table. I grab some scissors from a drawer and slice open the tape from the top and sides of the box. I open the flaps. Underneath the flaps, is a folded piece of paper sitting on top of packaging paper that is covering whatever else is in the box. The piece of paper says,

"Read this first". I pick up the paper and unfold it. On the inside, there is a typed message that simply states:

> `Jeremy and Livy, review the contents`
> `of this box together.`

Seriously?

Great. I have a mystery box from a mystery sender with mystery contents and I have to wait for Jeremy to come home before I know what it is?

I stomp one foot on the ground like a five-year-old. I turn to Amelia and I see she's all done with her snacks. I pick her up and take her back to the living room for some more play time. I try to forget that there is a big box of something on the table in the kitchen. But of course, I can't. For the whole afternoon, it's all I can think about.

What's in the box?

What's in the box?

What's in the box!?

I give Amelia her dinner while I sit next to—and stare at—*the box*.

I take Amelia in for a bath and settle her into bed.

Box. Box. Box!

I go to the kitchen and sit, again, next to *the box*. For three hours. I know I could peek and later pretend that I hadn't looked before Jeremy did, but I also find myself a little fearful and hesitant about what is in the box, and what the consequences might be if I do look inside without Jeremy.

I hear keys rattle and the lock turn. Jeremy comes through the door and looks over at me and the box.

"Hey, you're still up?" He points to the box. "What's this?"

I stand up and take the note I read earlier out of the box and hand it to Jeremy.

He reads the paper. "Who is it from?" he asks.

I shrug my shoulders.

"Livy, are you still not speaking to me? This is ridiculous."

"No. Jeremy, it's not that. I wasn't meaning to…" I don't want to start on some tangent of a conversation that will delay me any further from knowing what is in this box. "Never mind. Look, let's just see what's in the box, please. I've been staring at this thing all night!"

Jeremy lifts the packaging paper. Underneath, is a plain white envelope with both our names on it and the phrase, '*Read this before opening anything else*' beneath our names. The envelope is sitting on top of what appears to be a large container of some sort. From what I can see of it, it's wooden, somewhat dark in color and has two leather straps going across the top, parallel to each other, from back to front. It looks like a treasure chest. No. I think on it more. It looks more like a traveler's trunk.

Jeremy looks at me and then looks back at the box. He picks up the envelope and rips it open. Inside is a folded piece of paper. Jeremy unfolds the paper and begins to read it. To himself.

"What the fuck?" is all he says.

Thirty-Six

The Box

Jeremy and Livy,
You are receiving this package
because your relationship is strained
and in trouble.
The items contained in this trunk
are going to help you remember why you
are together in the first place and
they are going to help you find who you
once were.
In the trunk you will find a
series of envelopes, all numbered in
sequence. To begin the restoration
of the relationship that was once
indestructible, open the envelope
labeled #1 and follow the instructions.
Only open one envelope at a time
and be sure to follow all instructions
precisely.
If you don't, there is no guarantee
that this will work.
Keep in mind that the two of you are
kindred spirits who were not brought
together by accident. You were meant

for each other. You know that. All you
have to do is remember.

Best of luck to you both.

Thirty-Seven

Jeremy

Envelope #1

I REMOVE THE TRUNK FROM THE CARDBOARD BOX IT WAS DELIVERED in and set it on the table. It's slightly heavy. There is age and wear on the trunk and it looks like it had been put to good use in its early years. If I had to guess, I'd say the trunk looked to be at least one hundred years old. It gave me a strange feeling of nostalgia and I found myself wanting to know the history of the trunk and all of its owners of the past.

Livy and I sit at the table and stare at the trunk for what seems like an eternity. The note left no indication as to who sent the box. Who could it be? Mom? That's the obvious answer since she knows how stressed we've been lately. But why be so mysterious about it? And then, I think about how we got to this point, Livy and me.

How it came to someone anonymously sending us a trunk full of... whatever is in here, to fix our relationship?

Fix us. We were once *indestructible* and now I fear that it might take a shit load of duct tape to keep us together. I wish Livy would talk to me. I wish we could rewind a little and tell our pre-parenthood selves what was going to happen so that we might be able to prevent it. I wish I didn't have to work all of the fucking time. I wish Livy would let my mother help her.

A bucket full of wishes...
A bucket with a ton of fucking holes.

We've sat here too long. I finally break the silence. "So, are we going to do this? If not, I'm just going to go to bed." Livy doesn't respond. She doesn't even look at me. She's acting like I didn't say anything at all. She's acting like I'm not even in the room.

I huff out and stand to head to the bedroom. Without even turning her head in my direction she reaches out to me and grabs my arm. "Wait."

I back up and sit back down, elbows on the table, hands clasped. I lean in, "Livy? What is it?"

It takes her a moment but she finally looks up at me with a sullen look on her face. "How did this happen? Why?"

"What do you mean, Livy?"

"How did we get here? How did we go from us...to this? Why can't we figure this out?"

I shake my head. "I don't know. There are a lot of issues, but I don't know what to do to fix anything."

Livy stares past me for a few but very long minutes. "Let's look in the box, Jeremy. What have we got to lose?"

There are two clasps on the front of the trunk, securing the lid closed. I click them both open, simultaneously, and lift the lid up as far as the hinges on the back side of the trunk will allow. There are two brass brackets on either side of the trunk that scissor shut and then click into place, to keep the lid from falling, once it reaches its maximum height.

I look into the box and Livy is looking over my shoulder. There are a number of items in the box, but none directly exposed to eyesight. All of the objects are either wrapped in package paper or sealed in envelopes.

The first envelope, labeled simply as *#1*, is sitting on the top of all of the other items, in plain view. It is a large, yellow envelope with a clasp holding the flap closed. I fold in the clasp, open the envelope and glance inside. There are numerous, smaller envelopes inside. I turn the envelope upside down and empty it out onto the table. Livy shuffles through envelopes and picks one up.

"Each of them is labeled with a letter—A." She holds up the envelope she has in her hand. "B, C and D," she finishes, as she points to the others still on the table.

"This seems so complicated," I say. Who has time for this kind of meticulous detail? "So I guess we start with A?" I question.

"Seems logical." Livy shrugs.

Livy opens the first envelope and pulls out a folded slip of paper. "This one is typed also," she looks at me and says.

She reads the paper for about a minute and then I ask, "What does it say?"

She shakes her head. "I'm not doing this. This is pointless." She hands the paper over to me:

> To begin this process, you must first figure out why your heart is hurting. Only then can you begin to mend your wounds and heal. Inside the box, you will find two journals, one labeled for each of you.
>
> Your first journal entry will be a list of all the reasons you are angry at your spouse. **All of the reasons.** The list can be as long or as short as you want it to be but it needs to be thorough.
>
> These journals are for your eyes only so be as honest as you need to be.
>
> Sometimes the best way to express how you feel is to write it down on paper. Once it's out there, it's no

longer bottled up inside and you can fill that new empty space back up with good things.

Don't write this in front of each other. You need to take this opportunity to write everything down, rather than waste the entire time focused on what the other is writing.

Do this in solitude. Once you are done, move on to envelope B immediately.

"Why do you think this is pointless?" I ask, once I'm done reading.

"If I start writing stuff down, Jeremy, it's just going to make me angrier."

I wave the letter I have in my hand at her. "Or, it might make you feel better," I say, suggesting the letter's advice.

Livy looks at me as though she might throw something at me. She's looked at me like that a lot lately. It pisses me off but it also makes me sad.

"Look, if you don't want to do this then we don't have to. But the first letter was right. We are broken. You won't talk to me, and every time I say anything to you, you look at me like I'm an idiot or an asshole. I feel like everything I try to do is wrong."

"*Try to do?* Really? You don't try to do anything, Jeremy. You aren't here long enough to make an effort!" Livy snaps at me.

I have a kneejerk response to defend myself. "Well if I wasn't so worried about trying to provide for my family and its future, I wouldn't have to work so much."

Livy's face tightens harder. "Don't raise your voice. And stop saying stupid shit like that! You don't have to work so hard, Jeremy. It's your fucking company. You are the boss. You get to tell people what to do. You can do that from home."

"It's not that easy, Livy, and you know it. The company isn't ready to function without me being in the middle of everything."

"Oh, for the love of God, Jeremy! You've had that company for long enough now. You're expanding the business, for crying out loud. You mean to tell me that you are going to expand when you don't have all of your ducks in a row *here*?"

"You don't know what you're talking about, Livy. You have no idea..."

"I have no idea? What, you think I'm stupid? That I don't know anything about running a business? I went to college, Jeremy. I took the same damn business classes you did. Get the fuck over yourself. How about you stay at home with Amelia all day and I'll go run your goddamn company?"

"What the fuck, Livy? You aren't even making any sense. You are just saying shit to be hateful."

Livy's scowled face instantly turns the other direction. Her brows are raised and her eyes are big and immediately glass over.

I used the wrong word. She once said her mother was a hateful person and I've just used that word to describe her. It came out before I thought about it. But, it's not entirely untrue. Livy's demeanor towards me has been brutal since she came back, when I can get her to talk at all. And when she talks to me that way, it's like taking an arrow to the heart. She just insulted all of my hard work and my company. I try to just let it roll off my back, but there is only so much one person can take before the words fester and spoil and all you begin to think about is retaliation. I called her hateful to get her to stop saying things she didn't mean. I should have used another word.

Livy looks over at the trunk and as she does, a tear falls to her cheek. She reaches into the trunk and rummages for a moment. She lifts out an object wrapped in packaging paper, with a typed label attached that says *"For envelope A"*. Livy unwraps the paper. Within, are the two journals. Livy inspects them for a minute. They are quite nice as far as journals are concerned. They are leather bound with silver-edged paper, and outfitted with a leather strap, securing each book closed. Tucked into the straps are very elegant silver pens. Someone really put a lot of time into this trunk.

Livy hands me my journal. "I'll be in the bedroom," is all she says. She turns and walks away and as I watch her do so, I see her wipe her face. When she's angry, I'm angry. And when she's sad, I'm also sad. I suppose it's a good sign that at least I still have emotions towards her other than just anger and frustration.

I guess I'll put that in the journal.

Thirty-Eight

Livy

WRITING ABOUT WHY JEREMY MAKES ME ANGRY DID, IN TURN, make me angry. And it made me cry. Jeremy calling me hateful also made me cry. I know that he was in no way comparing me to my mother (or should I say comparing me to the perception I gave him of my mother, considering he'd never met her), but just him using that word stung. It was like he'd pierced my heart with an arrow.

But after I went through the anger and the tears and after I'd finished writing all I had intended to write, I had found that the trunk was right.

Yes, I did refer to the trunk as an animate object, as if it had come up with this idea all on its own. But I have no clue who sent us the trunk. My suspicions lie with Rosalie, but I feel like she would make no effort to make it anonymous. She'd shove it in our face and try to feed it to us like pie. Rosalie isn't a game player.

Or is she?

But until we figure it out, I will carry on as if the trunk is the sole provider of all of the wisdom being bestowed.

Because the trunk was right. Writing *was* therapeutic. I did feel better. And I also did feel empty.

It was past midnight when I came out of the room. And I realized that somehow, miraculously, Amelia was still asleep. Or quiet at least. I rushed over to the baby monitor to check it.

"She's fine. She's been asleep the whole time," Jeremy says.

"Wow. I cannot believe that she's still sleeping."

Jeremy is sitting on the sofa, flipping through TV channels. "Did you finish?" I ask.

"Yeah," he says flatly, not even turning his eyes in my direction.

"Want to see what's in envelope B?" I ask, silently begging him to look at me.

"I'm exhausted," he huffs. "But those are the rules right? We are supposed to open envelope B *immediately*?"

I nod and head to the kitchen table. Jeremy follows. I look through the remaining envelopes that are on the table to find B. It's larger than the other lettered envelopes, and heavier. I unseal the envelope and look in.

"What on earth?"

Jeremy leans in towards me, up on his tip toes, "What is it?"

I pull out a large stack of photographs. They are wrapped with a piece of paper that says:

> Sit down together and look through these. But before you do, pull out the other two items from the trunk that are related to this envelope.

I set the pictures down onto the table, still wrapped in the paper. I look into the trunk and find two square items labeled *"For envelope B"*. I pick up both squares of packaging paper and hand one to Jeremy. We unwrap each at the same time.

In my hands, is a medium-sized box. But I immediately realize that it's not any regular old box. Taped on the top of the box, there is a small, white record slip cover. There is a label on the cover that says "Play this." I remove the slip cover from the box and pull out the small, 45 record from its jacket. I take a glance at the writing on the label of the record and I find myself stunned a bit.

"Jeremy," I sigh. I look his way and hand him the record. It's the Janis Joplin single that he used to love to hear me sing. I look down at the square box that is still on the table and take off the lid. Nope, not a regular old box at all. It's a record player.

"What was in your paper?" I ask Jeremy.

He lifts up two glass, cylindrical containers full of wax, one with an index card taped to the front that reads "Light these."

"Candles," he says, not amused.

"I feel like we've fallen into some rehashed version of Alice in Wonderland," I say. I take the candles from him. They are both the same color—white. But I smell them and they smell distinctly different. And insanely enough, they smell like...*us*.

"Jeremy, smell this." I hand him one of the candles. He tilts it and takes a whiff. His eyes grow big.

"Peaches." He smiles.

"Yes. And this one. This one smells like you. It's earthy and smells so clean. It's just like the cologne you used to wear."

Used to wear being the operative phrase. I don't even think Jeremy wears cologne anymore. And I ran out of my peach conditioner and hand lotion months ago. I just had not had the chance or really the thought to buy any more recently. When Jeremy told me two weeks ago that we were going out on a date with each other, I knew I had a sample packet of the conditioner shoved away in my bathroom somewhere. When I finally found it in a drawer, I was so excited. However, given how the end of that day turned out, I'm not even sure Jeremy noticed that I had used it.

I walk over to the kitchen and pull a box of matches out of a bowl of random things that I have on the counter. I set both candles in the middle of the table and light them. In seconds the room is filled with the scents of Jeremy and me. It's as though he and I are swirling and floating around the room—dancing with one another. I close my eyes and inhale deeply. Emotion hits me and I have to sit down.

I look at Jeremy. "Do you feel that?"

He tilts his head upward and breathes in. "I don't know if I'm feeling what you're feeling. But I feel something. And it's good." He smiles.

I pick up the 45 record from the table. I place the record onto the player and set the needle. I turn on the record player. Cracks and pops come from the speaker just before the instrumental of the song begins. I adjust the volume a bit, so that it's not too loud. Then, Janis' raspy voice enters. Jeremy places a hand on my shoulder.

I look down at the pictures. With the fragrance and the music setting the ambiance, I pick up the pictures, remove the paper and begin flipping through. "These are all of us. You and me." Jeremy sits beside me and we begin looking through. There are some of before we got married. God, we looked so much younger and it was only a few short years ago. There are pictures of our wedding. We look so happy. Pictures of our first Christmas as a married couple, pictures of when Amelia was born. The three of us. So happy.

This is Rosalie's handy work for sure.

We continue to look through and I then realize that there are some pictures that I took myself with my phone.

"Wait a minute. This is a picture I took of us. On my phone. When we went to the space needle in Seattle. I never showed this to anyone. Especially not your Mom. This can't be Rosalie. She doesn't even know this picture exists."

"Wait, you think my mother is up to this?"

"Well yeah of course. Didn't you?"

"I suspected."

Well at least we agreed on something.

"But look. All of these last few pictures are of us on trips. They are pictures I took with my phone. No one knows about these pictures but you and me."

The wheels in my mind begin to spin. I point to the trunk and look at Jeremy. "You didn't come up with this did you? You are the only other one that's seen these pictures."

"No, Livy, it's not me," he says with a little condescension is his voice. "I'm not this clever. Plus, if I had the time to come up with something like this, I would have used that time to spend with you and Amelia."

"Well, this has taken a creepy turn. That means someone, perhaps Rosalie, hijacked my phone somehow."

"Are you sure you didn't share them? Text them to someone?" Jeremy quizzes, with a little more condescension.

"Positive," I responded, confidently.

"Hmmm," is all he offers back.

We continue looking at the photos. In each of them we are smiling, hugging, kissing. We are *loving* each other.

Something we haven't done in a long time it seems.

"So are we just supposed to move on to envelope C once we are finished looking at the photos?"

Jeremy looks at the paper that was wrapped around the photos. He flips it around. "There aren't any more instructions." He shrugs. "Odd, considering how specific everything else has been so far."

I grab the C envelope. "Ah ha! Here we go!"

On the sealed flap is a label with a typed message.

> Once you have thoroughly enjoyed your trip down memory lane with your aromatics, melodies and photographs, open this envelope.

And that is exactly what I do.

Another piece of paper:

> The pictures are to remind you of why you are married in the first place. You were once two young lovebirds that looked at each other with nothing but passion, admiration and respect. You are still young. And you still love each other. You just have to find it. Sometimes life gets in the way and you lose each other in the murkiness of it all.
>
> For your next step, use the pages of your journal to write down what you remember about what you used to feel.

How did you feel when you first met? Your first date? First kiss? First time you had sex?

"Um," Jeremy stammers, "I don't think this is from Mom."

"Why? Because of the word *sex*? I think your mom is familiar with the term."

"Yeah, but I just don't see her typing up a letter asking us to write about our first time."

"Let's worry about that later. There's more to read."

Write about all of the things you used to love about one another. As much as you can possibly remember. You don't have to write this in a room by yourself. You can write together. But you must follow two rules:
1) You must hang up all of the pictures before you start writing
2) You absolutely, no matter what, cannot have sex until further notice

"Further notice?" I question. "This trunk is very demanding."

"The *trunk* is demanding?" Jeremy asks.

"Well, I have no idea who is up to this. So I'm just going to blame the trunk." I motion my hand toward the trunk. "I mean, look at it. It's old. A little creepy. For all we know, it could be haunted, and we could be in the middle of some twisted horror movie. What if the spirit of the trunk hacked my phone, printed out these pictures, put all of this stuff inside the trunk and mailed it to us?"

Jeremy squints his eyes at me. "Livy, don't be ridiculous. Someone, *alive*, is behind this. But you are right. Until we know who to blame, it's best just to blame the trunk."

I read the last sentence of the instructions:

You must complete these instructions
immediately and proceed on to envelope
D.

"Yeah, well the *trunk* doesn't know we've begun this in the middle of the night. How are we going to hang all of these pictures? We don't have any frames?" Jeremy states.

Whoever put together this trunk knows that we are very scant on hanging pictures of ourselves. We have a ton of pictures of Amelia hung everywhere. We have one of the three of us and one of our wedding. I have no reasoning behind why we don't have more of us up; we just never did. Anyone who's ever been to our house knows this.

Which is everyone we know, practically. That narrows it down a lot.

"I know," Jeremy says. He walks over to one of the drawers in the kitchen and shuffles things around. He pulls out a small, white tube and lifts it in the air.

"Is that putty?" I ask.

"Yeah. We can stick it to the back of the pictures and stick them to the wall. At first, I thought tape but that could ruin the paint on the wall, so we should use putty." He smiles, basking in his creativity.

I can't help but smile too. "Okay. Putty it is."

We take the pictures into the living room and begin hanging them. With each picture we pick up, it seems we begin a *"Do you remember when"* story with each other. It took us a good half hour to hang the photos. We laughed a lot. We smiled a lot. And once we were done, we even hugged each other. And it was one of *those* hugs. The *lost in our own universe* hug. We hadn't done that in a long time.

"So since it looks like we'll be up for a while writing, want some wine?" Jeremy proposes.

"Sure," I say.

Jeremy pours us some wine—the kind we had at the restaurant on our first date; it's the only wine we drink. I turn off the record player, but leave the candles burning. We sit on the sofa, journals in hand, and lightly clink our glasses together. "Shall we begin?" Jeremy asks.

"We shall."

We write for a while.

We are sitting on opposite sides of the sofa, both neatly tucked into the corners. Every now and then, we peek up from our journals and look at each other. Smiling. Snickering. Even blushing. Finally, Jeremy puts his journal on the coffee table and leans over to me. He hovers for a few moments and then grabs my journal and pen. He lays them on the coffee table as well. Jeremy leans down and kisses me. Softly at first, but strengthening in power by every second that passes. I run my fingers through his hair. Writing about how we used to be helps me realize I miss this kiss and apparently it helped Jeremy remember too. It's refreshing.

Refreshing? Jeremy is laying on top if me, kissing me and trying to get his hand up my shirt and the only word I can think of is *refreshing*?

Jeremy's hand grazes my stomach and I immediately think of my stretch marks. And then I remember what the trunk said— *"no sex."*

"Jeremy, stop. No sex, remember? The trunk said so."

Jeremy leans up. "Yeah. Dammit. I just feel like we haven't been in this position much lately and writing all of those wonderful things about you just made me want to be closer to you. To kiss you."

"I know. But we have to listen to the trunk, right? I mean, it obviously knew this would spark something in us. It wants us to *not* have sex for a reason."

Jeremy lays his head on my chest and exhales.

"Are you done writing?" I ask him, playing with his hair.

He nods his head into my chest.

"Well then, let's get going. It's almost three. There's no telling what's in the D envelope. We might be up all night. Not to mention there is no telling when Amelia will wake up."

I am astounded that she has slept this long. It's as though the trunk delivered upon Amelia her own set of instructions to stay asleep while Mommy and Daddy sort it out in the other room.

We head over to the table and Jeremy picks up envelope D. He opens it to find yet another note. He begins reading it out loud.

> You've written down the worst.
> You've written down the best. To
> complete Envelope #1, you'll have to
> be brave enough to read what you've
> written out loud to one another.
> Previous instructions stated that
> these journals were for your eyes
> only, but it was stated as such in
> order to get you to put how you really
> felt onto the paper. And no one but
> you will read it still. But you now
> have to read it out loud. To each
> other.
>
> At this time, you will only read
> the things you wrote regarding why
> you are angry. The second part will be
> read at another disclosed time.
>
> Once you've read your entries to one
> another, you can go about the rest of
> your day as normal. But remember, no
> sex. And do not open the next envelope
> for at least twenty-four hours from
> the time the last word is read from
> both journals.

"This trunk is a fucking asshole," I murmur.

"Indeed," Jeremy agrees. "So let's get to reading," he adds.

"I put those words on paper in hopes that I could leave them there and forget about them," I whine.

"Well, the trunk had other plans. And we have to follow the rules. Are you worried about me hearing what you wrote?"

"It's not pretty," I confess.

"Well, maybe I need to hear it." Jeremy places his hand over mine.

"Even if it is harsh, I'll be ok."

I inhale and exhale quickly. "Okay. Well here goes nothing."

I look at Jeremy and look at my journal, then back at Jeremy. I've said most of these things to him before, so I don't know why I am hesitant now. Maybe because I'm not in the heat of anger. Maybe because when I look down at the page at the things I wrote, I feel guilty for having written them, even though it is how I feel. Jeremy has been working his ass off, but we don't communicate about anything anymore. I have to say what I've written. I've never been a chicken in my life so why start now?

You used to be my best friend. All we've done lately is argue because we don't see eye to eye on our current situation. I miss talking to you. I'd rather be talking to you. Not arguing, but talking.

I haven't seen you smile in a very long time. Before you started your business, I'd never seen you frown. Now, that's all you seem to do. And worry. It makes me want to keep all of what is going on with me bottled up inside because I don't want to stress you out anymore than you already are, but it also bothers me that you don't step back from your work every now and then, and see how Amelia and I are doing.

You've missed a lot of Amelia's firsts. I know you said that it wasn't important to you, but it should be. You don't ever get those back. Every first I've witnessed has been so precious. She's growing faster than I could ever imagine a tiny human could grow and you are missing it. She needs her father here, even if you don't agree.

When I found out I was pregnant, you told me it was going to be ok. I have changed my whole life for Amelia. My whole life right now IS Amelia. You haven't changed a thing about your life to accommodate her. You still get up do your same routine every morning. You go to work, come home whenever and do the same thing over again the next day. Even on weekends, you are so consumed with paperwork

and phone calls that you don't even notice that Amelia is
playing on the floor trying to get your attention.
   I feel like a single parent.
   You used to make me feel beautiful, but I don't feel that
way anymore.
   I used to have confidence in myself, and now everything
I do is riddled with guilt and doubt.

I look up at Jeremy. The last few lines are going to be the hardest to
say. I don't know if I can do it. I look back down at my journal and take
a deep breath.

   I love Amelia so much. She is the most precious gift I
have ever been given.

I begin to cry. To say the last sentences out loud may just kill me.

   But, some days, when it gets really hard...when I'm up
to my elbows in shit and running off no sleep and I have
dried, pureed carrots stuck in my hair...I wish...

I have a golf ball sized lump in my throat. The final words have
bundled up in my windpipe, refusing to come out. I clear my throat.
I have to start what I finish. I am staring directly down at my journal,
tears hitting the pages. I can't look at him. I'm sniffling and my hands
are shaking.

   Sometimes, I wish I would have just been strong enough
to tell you to leave me be that night at the bar. Because I
wonder if you could have found someone else that was better
suited for you and this lifestyle you want me to have.

I drop the journal on the ground and sit on the sofa and put my
hands in my face and cry.

Thirty-Nine

Jeremy's letter

You are stubborn. Usually I like that but now that we don't spend as much time together, I find myself not having the patience for it.

You are terrible at communication. Aside from your past, you used to just say whatever was on your mind. But now, getting information is like pulling teeth. You shut me out and that drives me insane.

I miss your smile. I miss your laugh. I've only seen either of those a few times in the last six months. I know you are tired and worn thin. Even when you smile with Amelia, it's not the same smile I remember from the first day I met you.

You left me. And at first, it terrified me. But then, when you came back, I was so mad at you and all I could think was how long was it going to be before you took off again and how I would have to worry if when I wake up every morning if that day was going to be the day that Livy couldn't take it anymore and just leave. And then I thought, what was the point of living like that?

I know I made a promise to you, to always make you happy. I know I work too much, but I wish you could understand that I'm trying to do this for us. You told me that I've broken my promise, and I'm sorry that you feel that way. But, you aren't my Livy anymore. In this few, six short *months, you've let whatever issues you have with me and yourself brew and grow and you never once told me that you weren't ok. You won't let my mother or anyone else help you to relieve the stress when I'm not here. I know you love Amelia. I see the way you are with her. You are amazing. But you are being stubborn and you want everything exactly your way and it's not how a marriage works. It's not how a family works. And aside from letting go of my business when I'm not yet ready to, in order to be here more often, I don't know how to fix this.*

Forty

Livy

L ISTENING TO HIM READ HIS LETTER, I FEEL AS THOUGH JEREMY IS belittling me. Like he is shaking his finger at me while mouthing, *"tsk, tsk, tsk, shame on you."*

Instead of trying to understand the point he is attempting to make, his words just make me angry all over again. I said all of those things to him, feeling ashamed that I even wrote them on the paper and he didn't even respond, while I sat there crying, pouring my heart out, begging him to understand my point of view. In return, he stood there as stoic as he's ever been, with a tight jaw, and read those words to me as coldly as if he were reading a book report about *War and Peace*. He had no emotion. He made eye contact with me the entire time, never wavering, never blinking. The words he had written on that paper were ingrained into his memory like he had said them in his head a hundred times already. When he spoke his last word, he snapped his journal shut and placed it on the coffee table. He turned around and ran his fingers through his hair.

I straighten my posture, going into defense mode. I sniffle and wipe my eyes of the wasted tears. "So that's it? I am wrong, you are right? You are the big grown up with the adult job and financial responsibilities that you can't seem to find any way to walk away from to spend time with the family you so desperately wanted? And I'm the one who is the spoiled rotten child who is throwing the tantrum because I'm not getting my way? That pretty much sums up what you wrote, isn't it?"

"Livy, that is not the point. Why can't you stop being so stubborn for two seconds and just understand my side of things for once?"

"And why can't you do the same for me, Jeremy? Why can't you understand what I am going through?"

Jeremy huffs. "Jesus Christ, what the fuck was the point of this? These stupid envelopes and directions? How is this helping us?" He walks over to the dining room table and he slams his hands onto it, on each side of the trunk. He peeks in briefly. "This is bullshit." Then he stands up straight, grabs his jacket that is hanging off the back of a chair and his keys that are by the door.

"Where are you going?" I ask.

Jeremy turns to me, but he looks near my feet. "I just can't believe you said you wished none of this ever happened. Us. Amelia. I can't believe you'd rather be alone with no one to love you."

I begin to cry again. "And this is what you call love, Jeremy? Walking out on your wife who just laid all of her cards out on the table and has never felt more vulnerable in her life? You're just going to leave?"

Jeremy opens the door. "I just can't look at you right now." He walks out the door and closes it behind him. I crumble to the floor and sob. My face is turned to the wall where we hung all of the pictures not just half an hour ago. Pictures of two people, smiling. Laughing. I don't even know who those people are. It's hard to remember those feelings. It seems like a lifetime ago, or even a life I never lived. Just maybe a life that I dreamed. I notice my wine glass still sitting on the coffee table. I want to pick up the glass and throw it at the wall of pictures that are mocking me while I'm sobbing here on the floor. But I don't because it'll just be a mess that I have to clean up.

I hear Amelia stir in the monitor. I have no time to feel sorry for myself. I head to the bathroom first to rinse my face. I look at myself in the mirror and wonder *where is the Livy that had no fear? Where is the Livy that never let anyone get to her? Where did she go?* The Livy in the reflection before me is afraid of everything. Afraid that she is going to screw up her daughter's life. Afraid that her husband will leave her or that she will run away from him.

I don't want to get a divorce. God, even the thought of that word makes my stomach churn. I just want Jeremy back. And I don't know how to make that happen. This trunk was supposed to help us, but so far it's only making our situation worse.

I wipe the towel over my face one last time and revert to mommy mode. There's no time to care about myself, or my marriage, when I have a six-month-old who requires all of me.

Forty-One

Jeremy

I'M LYING ON THE BED, THE SOFTEST BED *I*'VE EVER FELT, ON MY SIDE, *facing Livy. She is smiling her gorgeous smile. The one that makes her eyes sparkle. I tell a joke but I can't hear the words coming out of my mouth. But when I finish the joke, she laughs. Her laugh. The one that encapsulates you in such a manner where you can't help but feel anything but happiness. While she's laughing, the earth begins to shake. She is still laughing. Why is she still laughing? Am I the only one who is shaking? I do not understand...*

"Jeremy. Jeremy. Sweet boy, wake up. What on earth are you doing sleeping in this chair? Wake up!" My eyes are still closed, but I realize it's my mother's voice. I open my eyes and finally understand that I'm not in my bedroom, listening to Livy laugh. I am curled up in one of the lobby chairs of my apartment building. And my back hurts so badly. So does my head. What the fuck am I doing here?

I take a second to retrace my steps. While doing so, I acknowledge Mom. "Hi, Mom. What are you doing here?" My sudden recollection of my last actual encounter with Livy makes me jump out of the chair in panic. "Oh God, is Livy ok? Amelia?"

"Shh. Hey, I guess you had a rough night, huh?"

I smooth out my clothes and rub my head, making an attempt to straighten out my hair. "Yeah. Did Livy call you?"

"No. I'll explain upstairs, okay? Let's just get you out of this lobby.

You look like absolute shit. I'm surprised someone hasn't kicked you out on the street or called the cops."

"Gee, thanks, Mom." I'm quite surprised by my mother's language. I must really look like a complete mess.

We head to the elevator and make our way up to our floor. I reach our door and put the key in to unlock it when a thought that I had not yet considered crosses my mind. "What time is it?"

Mom looks down at her watch. "It's about five minutes until nine."

I wonder if Livy has up and left again. I am very hesitant to open this door.

"Well go on, then," my mother says, recognizing that I'm stalling. "What are you waiting for?"

I open the door finally and instantly hear Amelia's voice. I look into the living room and she is playing on the floor, lying on her back, playing with her feet. Livy is lying on the floor beside her, mimicking Amelia's moves, looking at Amelia. They are giggling together. This is by far the most adorable and heartwarming sight I have ever seen. It makes me wish I was lying on the other side of Amelia, playing the same game.

"Helloooo," Mom rings out, lingering the last syllable. Livy sits upright immediately and just as instant, her smile is gone. I witnessed a moment that I wasn't supposed to see and it was gone in a fleeting second but I wish I could stay in that moment forever.

"Uh, hi," Livy says, remaining seated by Amelia. She's checking her hair, as if my mother's presence suddenly requires her to be perfect.

I expect her to say next something like, *"Where the fuck were you all night?"* or *"How could you just walk out on me like that?"* But instead she says, "So you had to bring in your mother as reinforcements? You can't fight this battle on your own, Jeremy? Are you going to make Rosalie kick me out of my own house?"

Holy fucking Christ she's gone off the deep end.

My mother looks at me at the same time I look at her. Her eyes go wide, shocked by Livy's accusation. "I see you two are still at each other's throats. This all makes sense now."

"What makes sense?" Livy and I ask in unison.

Mom looks into her large, Mary-Poppins-sized bag and rummages through for a few seconds. She pulls out two envelopes.

"I got these two envelopes in the mail yesterday. The first one was addressed to me and it specifically stated that I was to come here today at nine a.m."

"And? What are you supposed to do when you get here, Mom?" I ask.

She pulls out the typed letter from one envelope and reads: *"Jeremy and Livy are in much need of some forced time alone together. Please go to their apartment at nine a.m. on Saturday and take Amelia to your house for the weekend. After Sunday, Amelia will remain at your home for the rest of the week, where Maggie has agreed to take over the babysitting duties until Friday."*

"What the fuck?" Livy exclaims.

Mom looks up at Livy and signals that she isn't done reading: *"They may protest you, but you must insist. Inform them that this is part of their instructions for* **relationship restoration** *and they must follow all of the rules in order to succeed."*

The trunk strikes again.

"So, you didn't send us this trunk?" Livy asks Mom. She points to the trunk, still sitting on our kitchen table.

Mom looks at Livy and then at me. And then at the trunk very curiously. "No. I didn't send you anything. What is in the trunk?"

I look at Livy to suggest whether we should tell mom and Livy shrugs and looks at me as if saying, *"Why not, you are going to tell her anyway."* So, I decide not to disclose. This is business between Livy and me. Well, and the trunk, of course.

"Nothing, Mom." I side step in between her and the trunk before she has a chance to look in. "It's just a package that came in the mail with no return address. We haven't really looked at it much. We just assumed it was from you since you are the most likely candidate to send us something." I look at Livy and she seems satisfied that I didn't give my mom all of the details like I usually do. I look back at Mom and she is giving me an arched eyebrow, readying herself to ask more questions.

"Rosalie, will you help me get Amelia's things together?"

Mom's stance softens and she turns around. "I most certainly will, sweet girl."

Livy and Mom spend twenty minutes or so in Amelia's room packing for her weeklong vacation. I don't know what the trunk has planned, since I still have to work next week, and probably most of this weekend. Maybe it's just an opportunity for Livy to get some breathing room. A break that she was too stubborn to ask for herself.

I sit on the floor and play with Amelia until Livy and Mom come back. "She's looking sleepy," I say to Livy or whoever wants to listen. "Good," my mom replies. "Maybe she'll get a good nap in the car."

"I'll change her so she's good and dry for the ride," Livy says. While Livy is changing Amelia, Mom finishes up gathering all of Amelia's one-hundred-thousand items into the dining room. "This may take more than one trip," she says. I look at her and before I can offer help to take things down, she snaps her fingers at me as if she's remembered something. "Oh, I am so glad I didn't forget. There were *two* envelopes."

"What did the other one say?"

"I don't know. That one was addressed to you, Jeremy."

"Me?"

"Mmhmm." Mom reaches into her bag again and pulls out another envelope, sure enough, with nothing but my first name on it. She hands it over and I eagerly work to open the flap. Once I have, I pull out yet another letter. This one is typed, but on my company's letter head. What the fuck?

> Dear Jeremy,
>
> I've been instructed by a source that you and I trust, but I've been sworn to keep anonymous, to tell you the below announcement in writing. I've also been informed by this source that failure to send you this letter will result in detrimental consequences on your livelihood. I am guessing this has something to do with you and Livy, or you just working too damn much, but

here are the instructions:

You, Jeremy Waters, are not allowed to report to work for seven full days. Specifically, beginning the Saturday that you are reading these instructions, ending the Friday following.

I, along with the help of project leads, Don and Lewis, will run the ship until you return. I promise you that we will care for your business just as you do. We will ensure every facet of this company continues to fire on all cylinders 24/7. Trust us, Jeremy. It is the only way you will truly know whether you can loosen the reigns and finally just be an owner rather than the everyman worker bee.

I swear to you that if there is even a slightest of hiccups, I will call you. We've got this. We will not let your business fail. We would never do that to you after all that you have done for us. Just let us do what we do.

Trust us.

I hope you take this time off to reflect about what is really important in your life. Please keep in mind that those important things can vanish in an instant, at any moment. Cherish what you have. Don't take it for granted.

My best to you, my friend.

Marcus

PS - I am sorry that I forced you to go to Chicago. But I think it is going to be good for us.

I look at my mom and then Livy. "How the fuck am I supposed to stay away from work for seven days?"

"What?" Livy responds. She rushes her way over to me and snatches the letter out of my hand.

"Hey, that is my letter," I gripe. She gives me a dirty look and I back down.

Livy proceeds to read the letter. And then she starts to smile slightly, but only briefly. "Well, I guess this would be a good thing if you could actually stand to be around me, Jeremy. It would be nice to have some time alone with you, but you made it quite clear last night how you felt."

"Livy, stop," I beg.

"Rosalie, thank you for taking Amelia. It's going to be hard to be away from her, but apparently the trunk thinks this is going to help somehow."

"What do you mean, the trunk? Why do you keep talking about the trunk?"

Livy holds up her hand, dismissively and shakes her head. "Never mind."

Livy grabs her keys. "Jeremy, I am going out. I'm going to give you some alone time. Because you need it. I'll be back soon. We can't open the next thing until tonight." Livy kisses Amelia on the cheek and walks out the door.

"What is going on here?" Mom asks.

As much as I want to tell her every weird thing that has happened the past few hours, I decide to just keep this mystery for Livy and me. "I'm not sure I even really know, Mom. But we'll tell you all about it when it unfolds. If it happens the way it's supposed to."

Mom places her hand on my cheek. "Don't waste your days off. Make the best of them."

"I'll try, Mom."

Mom leaves and I have no idea what to do with myself. I'm thinking about all that's transpired, and what exactly happened last night and why I woke up in the chair in the lobby. Before I realize I'm doing it, I find myself pacing in my kitchen. I stop pacing and go sit in the living room. Think, Jeremy, think. I place my head in my hands. I remember reading our journals to each other. I remember leaving because I was angry. And then I went to a bar two blocks down where I assume I proceeded to consume quite an amount of alcohol. I know I love Livy. I do. But I just don't have the same feelings for her as I once did. And she's not the same as she used to be. Why did it have to change? I even wonder if we're salvageable at this point. I don't want her to leave but I can't live like this anymore. The trunk has a plan, so I guess we'll continue to give it a shot.

I sit on the sofa for a while and flip through channels to find absolutely nothing to watch. I get up to see if the kitchen needs cleaning. Nope. I go to the bedroom to see if the bed should be made. Nope. I sit back down and flip through more channels. Still nothing. Check the kitchen again. Still clean. The bed. Still made. I find myself in this ostensibly infinite loop for some time. I have to stop. Maybe I should go out. But where? And Livy said she'd be back. But when? Does she even want me here when she gets back? I finally decided to leave, when the door opens. It's Livy. She's gone shopping.

"Hey," I say first.

"Hey," she says back.

I nod my head up to her and look at the single, small bag she has in her hand. "Whatcha got there?"

Livy sets the bag on the table and lifts out the contents. "Whiskey."

"What are we going to do with that, Livy?"

"We are going to spend the day drinking it, Jeremy. We are going to relax. Whether we speak to each other or not. We are going to try to exist in the same space until we can open the next envelope. We are going to drink this and either tolerate each other or kill each other. Either would be better than the state we're in now."

I look over at the trunk. "Did the trunk tell you to do this?"

"No. Just figured I'd try something on my own. I don't ever want you to look at me the way you looked at me last night. I'm not sorry for what I wrote, what I said. It is how I feel, sometimes. But you have to know that deep down, on ninety-eight percent of my days, I don't feel that way. Sometimes, I just get so weak from exhaustion that I have feelings like that. Like I set us up for failure. That I knew I was going to fail, but I did it anyway."

Livy goes to the kitchen and pulls out two glasses. I don't know what to say in response. She didn't say it with meanness in her voice, but she was very matter of fact. This whole time I thought she was being stubborn and immature, when in actuality, she is just trying to fight her demons of self-doubt. The demons she's always had but was able to manage to push aside until the stressor of being a mother superseded her strength.

Livy opens the bottle and pours two glasses. She screws the lid back onto the bottle and grabs the glasses. "Come on," she says and nudges her head over to the sofa. She walks to the living room and I follow. Livy sets the glasses onto the coffee table and then she sits on one end of the sofa and tucks her legs underneath her. She grabs the glass closest to her and signals for me to do the same. I raise my glass and we bring our glasses together, clinking for a toast. "Here's to whatever the fuck happens in the next fifteen hours. We can only pray that the outcome favors us."

"Here, here," I say and we both take a sip.

8 hours later...

"He looked for four hours to find out where the paperwork was before he realized he had already submitted it to the courthouse!"

Livy and I erupt in laughter and roll on the floor. I've been telling her stories about work. Stories that were stressful circumstances at the time but pretty funny in hindsight. I don't think I've shared a story about work with Livy since Amelia was born.

We are half a bottle into the bourbon. We've been laughing at my business antics for well over an hour now. Once I got her laughing, I told every story I could think of to keep the smile on her face.

When Livy first opened the bottle, we sat on opposite ends of the sofa, in silence, for an awkward amount of time. Then, Livy got up, went into the bedroom and emerged with a book. She curled up in her corner of the sofa and began reading. So, I pulled out my phone and began playing a game that one of the guys at work showed me. I don't understand the point of it, but it is an entertaining distraction. We sit on either side of the couch well into our second glass. It is only when Livy goes to pour us a third glass, she begins talking to me. She starts talking about Amelia and how she can roll over and if you let her, she'll roll from the kitchen, to the living room, right on into her bedroom as long as she has a clear path. She's also trying to crawl and she can hold a spoon on her own. None of these things I knew. I feel like such an asshole. Every time one of the guys at work asks about Amelia, I just give a generic response like, "*You know, she's growing.*" I seriously had no idea just how much. I mean physically, I see that she is getting bigger, but the things she is learning on a daily basis is astounding.

And I'm missing it all.

I smile and I listen to all that she tells me about Amelia. When Livy talks about her, it is with pride. So much pride. Livy isn't much of a hand-talker but with regards to the topic of Amelia, Livy makes bold hand gestures when in descriptive mode. Her eyes sparkle and her voice projects excitement and love. I've never seen this side of Livy before. Probably because I've never taken the time to look.

At one point, Livy looks at me and pauses mid-sentence. It's as though she is trying to decipher my look towards her. I don't mean to make any sort of odd facial expressions and I don't really know what it is she is analyzing.

She leans forward and touches the side of my face. "I miss that smile so much," she says. I was smiling. She was looking at me funny because I was smiling. I was smiling and I didn't even realize it. "I'm sorry," she says. "For everything."

"I am sorry too," I say. "For not being here more. I know I have my reasons, but those reasons aren't an excuse and I do realize that."

"Thank you," Livy says. "And I'm sorry for leaving. I just…freaked out and I felt so helpless. Like I didn't have a choice."

My heart sank. She felt helpless. Which makes sense because I wasn't around to help. And she won't ask for help from anyone else. It's her biggest strength and weakness, all rolled into one.

Now that we are rolling around on the floor giggling like school children, all I want to do is touch her face or run my fingers through her hair. I roll over to face her and catch her glance. Her beautiful green eyes that have been dull for so long are now sparkling, just as they used to. I scoot closer to her and reach out and take her hand and put it over my heart.

"I don't know what that trunk will make us do next, but if it's anything like the last envelope, I want to quit."

"But look where we are now. Right now. The trunk did that," Livy says.

I kiss her hand and place it back over my heart. All of the negativity I was harboring this morning has left my mind. I do still have feelings for Livy—all of the same feelings that I used to have. Maybe they were just dormant and I am beginning to think they are coming out of hibernation. "I love you so much, Livy. I am so sorry." I look at her for a brief moment before closing my eyes, not waiting for a response.

"Jeremy, wake up. It's time for the next envelope. Jeremy. Jeremy." I'm shaking again. Someone is shaking me. "Jeremy, wake up." I place my hand on my head. This is the second time in less than twenty-four hours that I've had a hangover. This is a bad pattern. I open my eyes. Livy's hair is encircling my entire face and I look up to see her eyes and her smile. "It's time to open the next envelope."

"Do you think we really need to? I mean, we are doing okay, right? We talked and laughed."

"We aren't quitting the trunk. Let's see what's next. She leans down and kisses me on the side of the face. My heart skips as I think about how I used to do that to her. *Used to.*

I raise up. "Okay, let's look." We make our way over to the trunk and pull out envelope *#2*. Livy looks very eager, so I let her open it. She rips it open like a Christmas gift. "Careful," I say, "You don't want to ruin anything inside."

She pulls out the contents. It's another letter and a paperback book. Livy hands me the book and begins reading the letter:

Dear Livy and Jeremy,

You may have forgotten what it is like to be new loves. To have mystery. To have passion. You need to remember those things about each other. It is the reason you are together. Now that you've been together for some years, there is no mystery and because of that, perhaps the passion has faded. Not just sexual passion, but general passion to make each other happy. Read this book and perhaps it will help you remember how your young love blossomed and perhaps it will reignite a spark that'll keep your flame burning. In the essence of saving time, it may prove most beneficial for you to read the story together. Livy, since you are such the literary expert, narrate the story to Jeremy. You may find that some parts are hard to read aloud but it is important that you read it cover to cover. Once you have, Livy, discuss with Jeremy what parts of the book were important to you.

After you discuss, wait twenty-four hours before opening the next envelope.

And don't forget: no sex.

Enjoy.

"What kind of book is it?" Livy asks.

I flip it over and read the summary. "Two people from different walks of life are thrown into a situation that forces them to interact with one another. When interaction becomes common practice they realize that their circumstances may have brought them together for a reason. This gripping tale runs the gambit of emotions. It shows that through all, love can prevail."

"What. The. Fuck?" Livy says "A fucking romance novel? Seriously? Let me see that." She reaches and takes it from my hand.

"You read romance, don't you?" I ask.

"Classic romance. Jane Austen. Bronte Sisters. Not this contemporary pseudo-epic-love-story bullshit."

"How is that really any different from classic romance?" I ignorantly ask, I think. However, Livy ponders this question for a moment. She flips the book over a few times herself. "Well, I don't know. I guess, that is a good question."

"Really?"

"Yeah. I mean, you can't judge a book by its cover, right? And really, going on the cover, there isn't much to judge. Let's see what it's about. You up for it?"

"So, you're going to read me a story?"

"Well, we can start it. If it's stupid, then we'll stop."

I look at her. I mean, what else do we really have to do? No work, No Amelia. Why not?

"Why not?" I repeat my thoughts out loud.

"Want some more bourbon, or are you all *whiskey-ed* out?"

"Uh, I think I'm good for now."

"Yeah, me too. But I am going to go pee and put on some pajamas."

"Okay."

Livy is excited to read the book, I can tell. It's a book she's never read before, which is rare considering I was sure she'd read all the books ever written at least twice.

He presses her against the wall and raises her arms above her head. He leans in close. Their eyes are connected, neither wanting to blink. He hovers over her for an eternity. She is anxiously anticipating his lips to meet hers but he is holding steadfastly to not make contact. He can tell that her breathing is growing heavy. She wants him to kiss her, or perhaps do more. However, he knows that if he gives in at that moment, he will be hers forever. There will be no going back. He ponders for a second and then says, "Oh, fuck it." He presses his lips firmly onto hers. Their pulses race against each other. Her arms still restrained above her head by his hands, she struggles to reciprocate the kiss. She wants to curl her fingers into his hair. She wants to run her nails down his back. She wants to feel the taught muscles of his chest as they tense to be closer to her.

As Livy is reading these words out loud, her own breaths are growing heavier. I think this book is turning her on. Which, in turn, is turning me on. Who knew that romance novels could be so hot?

'Never could I have imagined that I'd be in love with a girl like you. You are a serious pain in the ass. But it is totally worth it. I almost lost you and it scared the shit out of me. I honestly don't know now if I can live without you. When I thought you were gone I felt like my lungs forgot how to breathe. My heart forgot how to beat. I didn't want to exist if you didn't exist. I am so grateful that we got a second chance to realize what we have. I can only pray you feel the same way or I am sincerely fucked.'

She glances at him for a long time, her face expressionless. He is anxious to hear her response.

'When I thought my life was over, all I could think about was you. I wanted more minutes with you. I wanted to hold your hand one more time. I wanted to kiss you one last kiss. People say that their whole life

flashes before their eyes when they think that they are approaching their last moments on earth. But that wasn't true for me. All I could think about was you.'

He leans in to kiss her and she wraps her arms around him, hoping that she never has to let go.

With the last words read, Livy closes the back cover of the book and begins to cry. "This is the dumbest fucking book I have ever read. But oh, my God! The trunk really gets it. The trunk *really* gets it."

I think Livy has lost her mind. "Uh, what the fuck are you talking about?"

"The trunk, or whoever the fuck chose this book, is a genius. Essentially, although I'd like to believe that our story would be better written, this book is us. I mean, neither of us has faced near death, but just in the past few days, both of us have considered leaving one another. Don't you get it?"

I shake my head.

"You see. At the beginning, they were apprehensive about being together, like us."

"Like you," I correct.

Livy nods in agreement. "And then, once they did get together, it was like fireworks and symphonies and crashing waves. Remember? We couldn't keep our hands off each other. We were like wild animals at every opportune moment. You know, we were really like that even after we got married. Except..." Livy bows her head.

"Except what?"

"Well, you started working more...and, granted the traveling with you was exciting and the middle of the night wake up sex was pretty amazing, but it just got less and less frequent."

"But our life together isn't just about sex, Livy."

"No, it's not. You are absolutely right. But we lost what we had. The communication. The passion. The desire to be with one another. We don't have that anymore, Jeremy."

"So, what about the rest of the story? She gets shot. He thinks she's dead. How does that relate to us?"

"Don't you see? It's not the point that she almost died. It's that they almost lost one another. And, I think, Jeremy, as hard as it is to admit, we were on a road to destruction. I don't know what you were thinking, but I honestly had no idea how things could possibly get any better. I mean, I was just going to suck it up for the sake of Amelia and endure just being a miserable housewife. I had already accepted my fate because of the choices I had made."

"Because you chose to love me? And trust me? You think that because you made those choices that you were doomed for misery?"

"It's not like that. I mean, because I went against my better judgment about how I wanted to live my life, I ended up in a situation that I wasn't happy with and I was willing to endure for the sake of Amelia's happiness."

I seriously have no words. I think that my wife is either clinically certifiable or astutely genius. "Livy, that is the most idiotic and selfless thing I think I have ever heard anyone say."

She huffs out a laugh. "I guess. Like I said, I felt helpless. I mean, what were my choices? I don't want to break up Amelia's family. I don't want her to feel unloved for a second in her life."

Livy begins to cry and my heart breaks for her. She endured a childhood of feeling unloved and unwanted and now her singular goal in life is to make sure that Amelia, my daughter, never for a second feels that pain.

I move the book from her hands and bring her into me. "Goddammit, Livy, you are the fucking most amazing woman I have ever met. I am such a fucking prick for ever taking you for granted for even a second. And to think that I made you feel even a semblance that I didn't care about you anymore…I am such a fucking idiot. I am so sorry, baby."

And now I'm crying, "I am so sorry." We sit there, embraced in one another for some time. Finally, Livy sits up and wipes her face. "Holy fuck, what just happened? The trunk made us read a romance novel and we just had some kind of secular episode here. I am beginning to think this trunk may be from an alternate universe."

"That is perhaps a possibility. So, we've got like twenty hours before we can open the next envelope. What shall we do? Are you hungry?" I ask Livy.

Livy smirks at me. "I'm starving. What time is it? I know it's almost morning, but do you want to order Chinese and put our feet on the table?"

"Hell yes."

The food arrives. The delivery man gives us a peculiar look for ordering Chinese so early in the morning. But what is the point of twenty-four-seven delivery if you can't take advantage of it whenever you want? We situate in the living room and dig in. I'm not sure when the last time we had a meal was. "So, do you want to watch TV while we eat?" I ask.

"Well, we've got time. We should catch up on our DVR," Livy suggests.

"We have stuff on the DVR?" I had no clue.

"Uh, yeah, like one hundred fifty hours of stuff. I've been waiting to watch it with you."

Livy's face saddens a little at the realization that we've cluttered up the DVR with episodes that have gone unwatched because I wasn't here. Then, she faces me and gives me a smile. I inhale and smile back. "Well, let's see what we've got."

Livy begins flipping through our recordings. "We've missed like two seasons of *Walking Dead.*"

"Alright, let's start there."

And that's what we do. We eat Chinese with our feet propped on the coffee table, and we binge-watch *The Walking Dead* until we both fall asleep on the sofa, tangled up in one another.

Forty-Two

Livy

WE SLEPT FOR HOURS. HOURS! I WAKE UP ON THE COUCH. MY neck is cramped and in agony. But, as I am groaning at my throbbing sore neck, I do notice that Jeremy's arm and leg are wrapped around me and I am snuggled into him. This is really nice. *This is so nice.*

My movements cause Jeremy to stir and he in turn begins rumbling about his aching body parts. But then he too realizes our position and he leans in and kisses the back of my neck. Chills run the length of me. I lay there for a moment and lean into him, taking in our awkward but loving embrace. Then, I roll out and plant my feet on the floor. I stand up and stretch every extremity in hope that I can begin to feel a little normal again. Jeremy stands up behind me and mimics my stretching motions. Then, he wraps his arms around me and hugs me tighter than he ever has.

"That really was the dumbest fucking book ever," he chuckles out.

"I completely agree. But it got the point across."

And that is all we say about that for now.

"Why don't we get out of the house?" Jeremy suggests. "We could just go for a walk, maybe get some coffee or some..." he looks at his watch to see what time it is, "Some whatever meal you want to have."

I laugh. "Sounds good, but I really think I need a shower first."

"Okay, yeah, sounds good. You go ahead first and I'll check my phone for messages."

"No working, Jeremy Waters!"

"Yes, ma'am."

I come out of the shower feeling invigorated. I don't know what it was about reading that book out loud to Jeremy. There were quite a few sex scenes in it. And it wasn't really just about the sex scenes. It was about new love. About passion. About something we used to have that has faded. I wanted it back. That passion awakened me. I remembered feeling like I was living my life just fine until I met Jeremy and then I realized that every second with him was what life was worth living for. I want that back so badly. *So badly.* It makes me want to run into the living room naked and straddle him, doing to each other whatever we want to do until we can't breathe another breath, until we can't move another muscle. That used to be us. And I would be on that plan like melted butter on a hot cake but the trunk said *no sex*.

Stupid fucking trunk.

I dry my hair and get dressed. I walk into the living room to see what Jeremy is up to. He's on the phone. I begin to get angry, thinking he might be talking to someone from work. Before I say anything, I listen to the conversation a bit.

"Did she sleep okay, Mom? Is she eating okay? Livy says she likes to roll a lot. Please make sure you watch her."

He's checking on Amelia. Oh my God, I seriously want to flip the trunk off right now. With both hands. *Fuck you, trunk,* I'm going to go jump my husband's bones right now because the simple fact that he's checking in and showing love and concern right now is seriously turning me on.

But as I convince myself to do just that, he hangs up the phone and turns to me. "I just called, Mom. Amelia is doing just fine."

I tamp down my urges and maintain my self-control. "That's great. Thank you for checking."

He walks over to me. "Of course." He kisses me on the side of the face. "I am going to jump in the shower and I'll be right out."

"Okay."

Maybe I'm going to get my Jeremy back after all.

We grab some coffee and just stroll around the city. We point out restaurants that used to be clothing stores and abandoned areas that used to be restaurants. We come up on Joe's old bar. We just stand there. It's still thriving as a chain restaurant. It sickens me, but Joe and I really did benefit from it. And thinking about all the time I spent at that bar, at a time where I thought that was all I wanted to do with my life, really makes me appreciate how it all turned out.

"Jeremy, I'm not really sure where I'd be today if you hadn't come into my bar that night." I look up at Jeremy and he smiles.

"I'm not really sure where I'd be either, Livy. But, I'd like to think, even though we've had this bump in the road, that I did us both a pretty big favor walking in when I did."

I laugh. "Yeah, I'd say so."

"So, do you think our bump in the road is over?" I ask. For the sake of my sanity, I hope so.

"I don't know. I mean, I do still have a business to run and we do still have a child to raise. But you know what I have realized? I realized that I think I thought I had this whole adulthood thing figured out. And now? I feel like I don't have a fucking clue what I'm doing. I want to go back to where we were when we met. I was just a worker bee. You were just a hot bartender. Things were so easy."

I laugh. "Yeah, they were. And funnily enough, I thought everything was so hard. If only I knew then what..." I don't' even finish that stupid cliché phrase. But sadly, it's true. People say that shit for a reason. You look back on your younger self and you want to kick your younger self's ass for not knowing any better.

"But, look, Jeremy. We are here now. We are back at where we started. And even where we started isn't what it used to be. Everything changes. It can't stay the same."

"Then what about us? What do we do? Can we make change okay? Are we going to be ok, Livy?"

I shrug my shoulders because it's the only answer I can give. "Jeremy, I really do hope so. We suck at being adults, but I do still love you. I really do. And I really, truly think that if you still love me too, we can figure something out. I mean you and I have the whole rest of our lives. *The whole rest of our lives.* We might both live to be seventy-five. That is fifty years. We've only lived a little over half of that so far and we've only known each other for six years. Are we really going to make it fifty more years together?"

"Yikes. That is really substantial, Livy." Jeremy looks me in the eyes and places his hands on my shoulders. "Livy, when I stood up there with you at that altar, every single word I said, I meant. I know that I've fucked up by letting my workaholic-self overcome me, but I promise you, I meant those words. Every single word. I love you, Livy. We have lost each other but if we both live to be one-hundred-and-thirty years old, I want to spend every day of that knowing that you are my wife. I don't want any other reality than that. We have got to figure out how to make this work."

I look at the back alley lot where Joe's bar used to be. My insides cringe at the thought of where I would be if I hadn't met Jeremy. If I hadn't met him and Joe sold the bar still. I'd be a twenty-seven-year-old bitter woman, all alone in this city that doesn't give a fuck about anybody.

"Jeremy, I don't want any other reality either. I love you. And I trust you, even though I may have had some lapses in judgment on that front. But I don't want to be alone. I want to be with you. But I want the old Jeremy back. The one who used to love being with me for who I was. The one who cared enough to organize Christmas for the shelter children. The one who was thoughtful and patient. You aren't that Jeremy anymore, you know that, right?"

Jeremy nods. "I do know that. And you aren't the same Livy anymore. Granted, you did grow a kid and then push it out of your body, so I have no reason to blame you for your changes. But you used to be so confident in yourself. You used to speak your mind. Now you are so self-conscience and you never let me in. Why?"

"I'm just going to blame hormones. And being alone for so long. I'm in my head all of the time. And nothing I could ever put into words would be able to adequately explain to you what it is like to be a mother who has to put the needs of a helpless human before everything else. Even having to pee, Jeremy. Do you understand that? If I have to pee, but Amelia needs to eat, Amelia gets to eat."

"I guess I really never thought of it that way before. I mean, sure I know you sacrifice a lot, but I've never considered just how much. I just thought I was doing my part of the sacrifice at work."

"Jeremy, I don't want to live like this anymore. Having Amelia *has* changed me. So much. Before she was born, I thought that I understood love. I thought what you and I had together was true love. And maybe it is, Jeremy. I do love you, I know I do. I always had doubts that maybe what I was feeling was just being happy that someone was even willing to give me love. But when Amelia was born and I looked into her eyes for the first time, Jeremy, that is when I really understood what love was. I know you tried really hard and you did a great job getting me to trust you and love you. But all that tiny little baby had to do was look at me and I was consumed by a power that I had no control over. I didn't have to try to love her. I just did. And until the day I take my last breath, I will do everything for Amelia to keep her safe and to make her life the best life she could possibly have.

I want you and I to have a connection again. We used to have it and now I'm kicking myself in the ass because I doubted it. I doubted how you felt about me. Even after we got married, I doubted myself and worried if I was really good enough for you. And you are right. I was confident in myself because I knew *me*. But now, everyday changes. Every day is a new challenge and a new adventure with Amelia. Sometimes I can hardly keep up. It's overwhelming and fascinating all at once. But I don't want to do it alone anymore. Jeremy, we promised each other our lives. We only have one life. Amelia only has one life. We have to make this life together, all three of us, the best life we can make it or we may as well not even try at all. I want us to be together. All of us. I want to travel and show Amelia things that I've never even seen before. I want to live a full life and have no regrets."

Jeremy looks at me and cups my face in his hands. "I want that to." Then, he kisses me.

After Jeremy and I return home from our reminiscing of the city and our edifying talk about the future, we decide to spend the remaining hours until we can open the next envelope watching more recorded shows from the DVR.

I find myself cocooned by Jeremy's body, on the sofa, just as the day before. I have no recollection of how we got into this position, but I'm not complaining. And even though we've been crashing on the couch, it's the best sleep I have had in a long time. I think I could probably sleep another full day if it weren't for the fact we had to continue on with this mysterious trunk and its instructions.

I reach over to the coffee table to look at my phone to check the time. It's Monday, close to noon. Jeremy lifts his head and kisses me on the back of the neck. "What time is it?" he asks.

"Almost noon."

"We are way past our twenty-four-hour mark."

I get up and stretch and begin walking toward the trunk. "I know. We best get to it."

I reach in and rummage through the trunk for envelope *#3*. I find it. It is a small, yellow envelope with a clasp. I look at Jeremy, eager. I open the clasp and lift the flap of the envelope and peek inside. I pull out…a DVD case with a piece of paper wrapped around it. I removed the paper and look at the words typed on it. All it says is *ENJOY*.

Confused, I look at the DVD case and react to the cover. "What the fuck?"

"What is it?" Jeremy asks.

"It's…it's a porno."

"Porn?"

"Yeah."

"Wait, what are we supposed to do with that?" Jeremy asks.

I flutter the typed message around. "Apparently, we are to 'enjoy.'"

"So, we are supposed to watch that? Together?" Jeremy is very put off by that notion.

"Jeremy, don't act like you've never watched porn before."

"Well, I've never watched porn with my wife!"

"It's just porn."

"No. It's porn with my wife."

"Oh, grow up. It's really no worse than some of the shows we've watched before on cable."

"Yes, it is. It's porn."

"Whatever. I'm watching it. You chicken?"

Jeremy stiffens his posture and clears his throat. "Of course not."

"Great. I'll put the movie in. Should we make popcorn? Is that appropriate for porn?" I ask, facetiously.

"There is no food appropriate for porn."

"Right," I say with mockery.

I open the case of the DVD and there is a Post-it note attached to the disk. "*No Sex*" is all it says. But it is hand written which is interesting. However, the lettering is very boxy so I'd never be able to guess who wrote it if I wanted to.

No sex. Seriously? Like I'm going to want to have sex with my husband after watching porn? *Sure.* I'm no porn expert, but I've watched a few. It did nothing for me in the arousal department.

I punch the DVD into the player and the cheesy music instantly fills the room. No *Coming Soon* attractions on this flick, I think, and then I snicker at myself for the pun. As I sit down on the sofa and the title flashes across the screen in the fashion of some mid-nineties digital artistry, I look up at Jeremy who is still standing by the trunk. I pat my hand on a sofa cushion. "Come on, you big wuss, let's just get it over with."

He comes over. He sits. We watch. For thirty-five minutes we both observe with undulating eyebrows and heads tilted to the side, as though doing so might make the angle of the scene a little easier to understand.

At one point, I say, "Huh, I never considered doing that."

"Uh, I have," Jeremy replies. This coming from the evident porn aficionado.

As we are sitting there, I'm not sure what Jeremy is thinking but I am not the least embarrassed about watching actors, physically well endowed, not so much with the gift of acting, fuck each other's brains out. It actually reminded me of Jeremy and me. Not with the cheesy break away clothing and the terrible attempts of faking orgasms, of course, but how we used to be relentless toward one another. There was a time where we could hardly function in our daily activities until we spent a good forty-five minutes satisfying each other. There were days where we wouldn't get out of bed at all. Those days were frequent, before Jeremy opened his own business.

These days though, I wonder what my husband's penis even looks like anymore. Certainly it didn't change. But I haven't seen it in a while so I don't really know. But of course not for Jeremy's lack of trying. On the rare occasion that he is home, he always wants to have sex. But he wants to have sex just to have sex. Not because he wants to ravish his wife and make her world spin into oblivion. Those days were way in the past. Now he's just a man with a need and I'm his contractual obligation.

When the closing, less than captivating music begins and the credits appear, we both just sit there in silence. I'm not sure for how long, but Jeremy breaks the silence by clearing his throat and squeezing my hand. He's aroused. Of course he's aroused. He's a man that just watched a porno.

"You know I don't want to shoot you down, but I have to. The trunk told me so." I hold up the Post-it that I've had stuck to my fingers the whole duration of the movie. Jeremy lets out a huff.

"Then what the fuck was the point?" He's so frustrated. I shrug my shoulders and turn my head to look in his direction.

"Maybe when we actually do get to have sex again, we can try that sideways thing they did. I might even be able to get a hold of some leather, like that one girl had on, if you're interested." I'm really half way teasing because I know I'm giving Jeremy visuals and there is nothing he can do about it. We have to obey the trunk. But I do have to admit, teasing him like this is kind of turning me on as well. Perhaps that was the whole point. Seeing Jeremy get hot and bothered always had an effect on me. I'm beginning to wonder if whoever sent this trunk knows us as a couple better than we know ourselves.

Or maybe the trunk is just a cruel son of a bitch that likes to see my husband squirm. *Poor Jeremy.*

"So, now what?" Jeremy asks. "Do we have to wait before we can open the next one?"

"There weren't any instructions saying we couldn't."

Like a child, Jeremy runs to find the fourth envelope. It's a regular, greeting card sized envelope. Jeremy rips it open and finds a single piece of card stock.

"What does it say?"

"How the fuck am I supposed to do this?"

"What?" I'm whining. Now, I'm being the child. He hands me the card and I read it.

> *Undress each other.*
> *Take a shower with each other.*
> *Kiss each other.*
> *Touch each other.*
> *Lather, smell, caress.*
> *Take your time. It's all you've got.*
> *When you are done, lie in bed naked*
> *with each other.*
> *Hold each other.*
> *See each other.*
> *Sleep with each other.*
> *No sex.*
> *When you awake, you may open the next*
> *envelope.*

Forty-Three

Jeremy

Shower

H OW THE FUCK AM I SUPPOSED TO TAKE A SHOWER WITH MY WIFE without the end game of sex? I just watched a goddamned porno and I haven't had sex with Livy in a long time. That is just cruel and unusual punishment. The trunk is a sadist.

"There is a point to this, Jeremy. I'm not sure what, but there is a point. It's going to be hard…"

"Oh, it's going to be hard, all right."

"You are such a perverted teenager. It's going to be *difficult,*" she rephrases. "But let's just do it and see what happens. The trunk is like Mr. Miyagi. It is wise. We don't understand its logic and probably won't until the lesson is over. So, let's get started."

Livy begins walking toward the bathroom, motioning with her hand for me to follow, which I do reluctantly.

I get to the bathroom and Livy is standing there, waiting for me to make the first move. I don't want to do this. Not because I don't want to see Livy naked. I wish she was naked all of the time. But I don't want to see her naked and not be able to do anything about it.

Livy and I are standing face to face, inches apart, staring at one another. We are having a high noon stand off on who is going to make the first move. After standing there for a very long time, Livy begins to dip her eyebrows. Is she angry? Confused? Disappointed? I can't tell. She lets out a sigh and her face softens. Then, I feel her hand go under my t-shirt and touch my stomach. I'm so tense about the situation that I flinch. Livy's brow furls again but she keeps her hand under my shirt. It moves up my chest and then her other hand is under my shirt.

Livy smiles. "I sure do miss these abs. This chest." Her movements are slow and I'm frozen.

I feel like an idiot. Like she's never touched me before. But I'm afraid to move because I know when I do, my brain is going to shut off and I don't know what will happen after that.

Livy gestures to take off my shirt. I'm even hesitant to raise my arms to let her do it. Livy rolls her eyes and removes her hands from my chest.

"Jeremy, what is the problem here? Do you not want to see me naked in broad daylight?"

Her absurd question breaks me out of my nervous trance, "What? Why would you think that? That is the most ridiculous thing I've ever heard. Of course I want to see you naked."

"Then why aren't you moving?"

"Because I know once you are naked, I will want to do things to you that the trunk says I can't do."

"The trunk said we could touch." She proceeds to put her hand down my pants. And then she brings her lips to mine and kisses me hard. She pulls back, "It said we could kiss." She smiles which causes me to smile. Livy places both hands back under my shirt to retry taking it off. I lift my arms this time and she removes my shirt. She places her hands on my shoulders and runs them down the length of my torso until her fingers land on my belt, never once breaking eye contact with me. The feel of her fingertips gently touching my chest makes my heart pound. I can tell I am seconds away from my brain relinquishing all responsibility of thought and it makes me anxious.

"Livy," I start. I'm going to tell her I can't do this. We have to quit.

I begin shaking my head but before I can get any words out, she says, "Hey, it's just you and me. Husband and wife. Just getting soapy together."

I exhale. She's trying to calm me down. Convince me this isn't a big deal and she has no idea how sexy she is being right now. "You saying words like *soapy* is not helping me right now."

She smiles bigger and laughs. "I'm sorry. I'm not trying to tease you. I just want you to relax. Come on. It's just us. An old married couple, getting naked and cleaned up."

"You can't say *naked* again."

"Am I allowed to say anything?"

"No."

Still smiling, Livy begins unbuckling my belt. "Okay, well then, I will shut the fuck up and…"

"Ahhhhh! Don't say *fuck*!"

Livy laughs again. She brings her hand to her closed lips and makes the zipping motion. She turns to get the water for the shower running. She's leaning over the tub checking the temperature of the water and all I see is ass. *Sweet mother.* The combination of having just watched a porn, Livy saying words, her putting her hand into my underwear and now her ass in my face, is going to make me pass out. I cannot take this pressure anymore. Once the shower is going, Livy turns back around to me. She's looking at me questioningly but she doesn't say a word. I pull her close to me and I kiss her. Hard. I lift her up and sit her on the counter. Before I even know what I'm doing, I remove her shirt and bra. I'm on autopilot. I'm kissing and touching her everywhere, just like she and the trunk said I could do. Livy moans but she doesn't say a word. She puts her hands in my hair and tugs. God, I love it when she does that. I run my hands down to her stomach; my next goal is to get her pants off.

However, as soon as my hand touches just above the waistband of her pants she withdraws and instantly covers her bare skin with her arms as much as she can manage. "You were right. This is stupid. I don't want to do this." She attempts to maneuver to get down from the counter but I stop her.

"Livy, what just happened? What did I do?"

"Nothing, I just can't do this."

"You can't take a shower with your husband?"

She shakes her head.

There's a shift in dynamic. Thirty seconds ago, she was all on board and I was the hesitant one. Now, somehow, our roles have reversed.

"Why? Please tell me."

With the smallest of whispers she says, "Please don't make me say it out loud."

I take a step back from her, exasperated. I hate it when she does this.

I motion my hand toward the door. "Fine. I can't make you talk if you don't want to." I grab my shirt from the floor and walk out of the bathroom. I run my hands through my hair and down my face. I'm completely confused and frustrated. I have no idea what I did and because of that, I have no idea what to do to fix the situation. So I lean up against the wall next to the bathroom door, raise my eyes to the ceiling and say out loud the first thing that comes to my head. Loud enough for Livy to hear.

"We are supposed to be following the trunk's orders. We are deviating and it's probably not a good idea."

Livy's response is to cry.

Livy never cries.

Never used to cry.

Goddammit, what the fuck?

I exhale, even more frustrated and head back into the bathroom. Livy is still sitting on the counter but now she has her knees to her chest and her head is hidden. Her shoulders are shaking. I approach her as delicately as I can, knowing that anything I say or do right now potentially could be misinterpreted in a negative way and the aftermath could last indefinitely.

I watch her for a second, before I intervene. She's still topless. And even though she's crying and I can't really see anything but her bare shoulder and side, I still think she is so beautiful. I want to touch her. I want to run my hand over her shoulder and trace the line of her collarbone. Her skin is so soft; I just want to touch it. But I resist. My brain is back on, thinking its logical thoughts and I know if I try to touch her anywhere that's unclothed right now, she'll somehow take it the wrong way.

"Livy." I touch her knee instead. It's still covered in pants. "If you want me to leave you alone I will. But if you tell me why you are crying right now maybe I can help."

Livy shakes her head into her knees. "You won't understand. You'll think I'm being dumb."

This shit aggravates the hell out of me. Why can't she just fucking say what's on her mind? I know I need to handle this delicately but I just can't tolerate it. The more I baby her, the more she's going to act like this. So, I decide to be direct with her. At least if I piss her off, she'll say what's on her mind. She never holds back when she's pissed.

"Livy, I think what you are doing right now is dumb." She shoots her tear stained face up from its hiding place and glares at me. *Oh yeah* that pissed her off good. "You are crying, and I did something to make you cry and you won't even give me the courtesy of telling me what I did so that I'm sure not to do it again."

Her eyes narrow and her look is slicing right through me. I don't know what hurts worse. Seeing her cry or looking at her when she's looking at me like that.

"Livy, just tell me what it is. Since when do you care if I think what you do is dumb? So what if that's what I think. Obviously, it's bothering you enough to make you cry, and that is what I care about. Why don't you get that?"

With her arms still wrapped around her knees, Livy leans her head back against the bathroom mirror. She closes her eyes and takes a moment to compose or figure out her next move. When she opens her eyes, she looks at me again this time with resolve. She removes her arms from her legs, and lets her legs fall down over the edge of the counter.

Yep, she's still topless. I look at her bare chest. It's an automatic reaction. I cannot help it. A man can't stand in a room with a topless woman and not look at her chest. It's male nature. I remind myself that if Livy is about to speak, I need to focus on her face and listen.

Livy wipes her eyes. I don't think she caught my moment of weakness or the fact I nearly drooled all over myself when she put her legs down and revealed her half naked self to me. I knew she was naked. I've seen her naked before. Hundreds of times. But none of that matters. Every time I see her naked it's as breathtaking as the first time.

Livy motions off of the counter and stands. She looks at me but doesn't say a word. She hooks her thumbs into the waistband of her pants and pushes them down and removes them. If she had on underwear too, they must have gone with the pants because now she is completely naked.

Completely naked.

She stands there for a long moment without saying a word. I look at her. All of her. I just want to touch her everywhere.

Finally, she speaks. "Look at me, Jeremy."

"Uh, I am looking at you, Livy."

She places her hands on her breasts and lifts them up. Then she lets them go.

Holy fuck, she's naked and she's touching herself. I reach behind me to find something solid to prop myself against.

"Look at my boobs, Jeremy."

"I am."

She lifts them up again. "This is where they used to be." And she lets them go "This is where they are now."

"Okay."

She moves her hands down to her stomach and traces over her stretch marks. "Look at these. They are going to be there forever." She grabs my hand, which was helping me brace against the wall. I nearly fall. She runs my hand over the stretch marks. "Do you feel that? How can that possibly feel sexy when you touch it?"

I can't respond.

She spins around and leans over the counter slightly. "Look at my ass, Jeremy."

"Can't help but not." My throat is so dry.

"It's saggy."

"No, it's not."

She looks at me through the reflection of the bathroom mirror. "Yes it is. I haven't worked out in a really long time. Look at my arms." She raises one up into a flex position. "I used to have tone. I don't even know if I can even do a pushup anymore."

"Okay. So workout."

Livy spins back around and narrows her eyes again. "Well, fuck. How ingenious of you to think that. What a spectacular idea. Except there is this full time thing I do called being a mother that takes every last ounce of energy I have that makes it so I don't want to do anything else." Tears well up in her eyes and her face contorts. She begins to cry again but she doesn't hide it. She looks me straight in the eye. "Becoming a mother made me look this way and being a mother is stopping me from making it better. And on most days, I don't really care. But right now, standing here in front of you, all I want to be is sexy. I want you to look at me with lust. I know that sounds stupid but it is what I want. I want you to look at me and think, *'Goddamn that's a fine piece of ass.'* I want you to look at me the way you were looking at the women in the porn. You don't look at me that way. I feel like you fuck me because you have to. You used to make me feel like I was irresistible to you. But I don't feel that way anymore, and I guess I'm afraid that one day, you'll find something more appealing. I mean, look at you. You look exactly the same as when we first met. And look at me.

"I'm just a hot mess. My body expanded and then just fell wherever it wanted to. I don't even like looking at myself in the mirror. How on earth does this turn you on? I can count on my two hands how many times we've had sex since Amelia was born and none of those times was anything like what we used to have. You don't look at me with passion. "

I'm speechless. I try to think of words and I clear my throat. "Livy," is all I can say. I move to her and wrap my arms around her. My heart is fucking broken. She is crying into my chest. I have to act fast. Say something. Do something. If I stand here with no reaction, she'll think she's right and that's irreparable. I don't think about what to do next, I just do it. I move her head from my chest and place both of my hands on either side of her face. I kiss her and I clutch her hair into my fingers. I move my mouth to the side of her face and down her neck. I'm kissing her hard, leaving red marks everywhere I touch. I kiss her collarbone, from one side to the other, touching her nowhere else. I look up at her and her head is tilted back, eyes closed, mouth open, tears running down her face. "Look at me, Livy."

And she does.

I touch her face again with just one hand. Then I use both hands to cup her breasts. "Your tits are gorgeous, babe. If you knew what was going on in my head five minutes ago when you stood up from the counter, you wouldn't have a doubt how much I enjoy looking at these. Touching them. Kissing them."

Which I proceed to do. I lower myself and put both knees on the floor so that I'm eye level with her stomach. I touch each stretch mark and I kiss them all. I look up at Livy. "You've got to own these. They are beautiful. You have these because you have Amelia. You shouldn't dare be ashamed of that. When I see these, it reminds me of what you gave me. What you did for me. You sacrificed. These are your battle scars. Battle scars are sexy as hell." I kiss her stomach once more, looking up at her simultaneously. She smiles. I spin her around so now her ass is in my face. I take a hand full of each cheek. "And this ass. Fucking Christ. How can you think this ass is anything less than perfect? I just want to bite it."

Which I do.

"Jeremy!" Livy screams and laughs. She turns around and lightly smacks me on top of the head.

I stand up. "Livy, I am sorry if you see yourself that way. And I'm sorry that our past few sexual encounters have been lackluster. Totally my fault. We do it so little because of our circumstances and by the time I actually get the chance to have sex with my wife, I'm so out of control that I can't think straight and before I know it, it's over. Then, before I have a chance to make it right, it seems you always find a reason to get up and leave. And I'm so sorry that made you feel like I didn't want you. I do want you. So much that it's too much. And I think you are fucking gorgeous."

I know saying that is helping, but I have to show her. That is the only way to convince her. "Does the trunk have any limitations on kissing and touching?" Livy smirks and gives me a devilish look. The look she used to give me a lot. One I haven't seen in a long time. Among doing other things to my body, it makes my heart skip a beat.

I notice that after all this time, the shower is still running. I look at Livy and hold my finger up to her, "Don't move." I go to check the shower water, and sure enough, it's run cold. I turn off the water. "We still have to shower at some point. We have to follow orders, right?" Livy nods. "So, while we wait on the water to heat back up, I have other plans. I'm going to show you just how fucking beautiful I think you are."

I begin my kissing all over again, starting with her mouth and covering every square inch of her soft, naked flesh. Even all the way down to her toes. I'm kneeling on the floor, kissing her feet, as though I'm worshiping her. In a sense, I am and I hope she feels that way too. After I've made sure that I've covered every single spot, I lift Livy up back onto the counter and proceed to give her exactly what she deserves. Pleasure. I've been a selfish douche bag for too long. Maybe that's why the trunk won't let me have sex with my wife. Because it knows that's not what Livy wants. She wants to feel sexy. She wants me to want her, not just to want sex. So I try my damnedest to show her just how much I want her and only her.

Propped up on a counter top, waiting on the shower water to warm back up, I kiss and touch my wife until she nearly rips the hair out of my head and screams my name. Multiple times.

Forty-Four

Livy

Shower

JEREMY AND I ARE SITTING ON THE BATHMAT BY THE TUB ON THE bathroom floor, both of us completely naked. He's sitting with his back against the tub and I'm sitting in front of him with my back leaning against his chest. Our arms are entangled, wrapped around my chest. Jeremy has his face buried in my neck while I have my head tilted and leaned back against his shoulder. We are both panting and out of breath and holding onto each other for dear life. We might have bent the rules of the trunk a bit, but there were no specifications on the clarity of the definition of sex. What we just did to each other was not sex, but it wasn't something you'd see in a PG-13 movie either.

After Jeremy was done showing me just how amazing he thought my body was, which I'm fully convinced of now by the way, I felt the need to thank him and reciprocate. Although my legs felt like mush, I stood up from the counter and pushed him back against the wall and showed him just how appreciative I was.

When we were spent, Jeremy sat down on the floor and pulled me into him. He kissed me and stroked my hair and told me he loved me.

Now we are sitting in silence, trying to catch our breath.

I feel like such an idiot for not telling Jeremy sooner about the way I felt about myself. It's partially my fault for the mediocre sex we've been having. I didn't put forth much effort because I didn't want Jeremy to actually see me. I felt ashamed and embarrassed and I thought that if he actually took the time to look at me really closely, he'd see me as ugly and wouldn't be attracted to me anymore. The reality is that if I had just trusted Jeremy enough to tell him how I felt in the first place, we may have resolved this long ago.

When am I going to learn?

With our breathing and heart rates slowed down, Jeremy kisses me on the cheek and whispers into my ear. "Are you ready for a shower now?" I only nod. Jeremy stands up and reaches for my hands to help me up as well. He leans over to turn on the tub water and I can't help but to smack him on his ass. He jumps, turns and tickles me. I scream. He laughs. We kiss. A lot. Jeremy breaks our connection and says, "We should get in the shower, or we'll have nothing but cold water again."

"Well maybe cold water is what we need. What we just did was amazing but if I don't have sex with you soon, I'm going to explode."

"You are preaching to the choir, love. That was why I was so hesitant to begin with. I didn't know if I was going to be able to see you naked and not throw you over my shoulder, take you into the bedroom and have my way with you."

"Oh my God, please don't say that. You are making my insides tremble." I smile and stroke his scruffy face with my hand.

Jeremy turns on the shower head and throws back the curtain. He leans in to kiss me before he offers his hand to help me in the shower. "Good." He smiles back.

We are in the shower, doing the simplest of tasks: bathing. But there's something about being in a shower with your lover, who you aren't allowed to have sex with, and lathering each other up, touching soapy skin, watching the water fall over each other's bodies that turns the menial, hygienic chore into your own live porn show. We end up making a repeat performance of what we had just done outside of the shower twenty minutes before.

If that fucking trunk wasn't going to let us do what we both so desperately wanted to do, then we were going to utilize our own interpretation of the rules until we were told otherwise.

We stay in the shower until the water begins to run cold again.

"Fuck! That's cold!" I scream, me being the first to feel the change in temperature. "Oh my god, turn it off!" I yelp. Jeremy reaches and turns off the faucet. We laugh and kiss like teenagers who just snuck away to make out under the bleachers.

We stay in the tub for what seems like forever until I catch myself yawning right into Jeremy's mouth. It's contagious. Jeremy yawns right back. "Are you tired?" he asks.

"I guess," I respond. I don't know what time it is, but we haven't been in here too long, so I'm guessing it's middle afternoon or early evening by now. But I don't care what time it is. Any opportunity to sleep with Jeremy wrapped around me is one that I will not pass up.

Jeremy stands up and out of the tub and grabs a towel. He reaches for me to help me up. I step up and he wraps the towel around us both. He looks me in the eye. "Do you believe me? About what I said about your body? You are fucking sexy as hell and I don't want you to think any differently. You are *My Livy*. My wife. The mother of my child. I fucking love you and you are fucking sexy. Clear?"

I smile. "Crystal."

We dry off and head to the bedroom. We crawl into bed and, just as I had hoped, Jeremy drapes his entire body around me, exactly like he did when we were on the sofa earlier. "I love you, Livy," he says just before I drift off. "I love you too, Jeremy."

My heart is full.

The trunk is wise.

I thought I'd lost myself but maybe I really didn't.

I thought I'd lost Jeremy but maybe not.

At that moment just before I fall asleep, I think that perhaps everything is just as it should be.

We sleep for seventeen hours.

I wake in the same position I fell asleep. Jeremy is still wrapped around me. I don't think we've moved the whole time we were lying here. As soon as I open my eyes, Jeremy kisses me on the neck. His facial scruff brushes against my skin and gives me goose bumps.

"Good morning," he says. His voice is husky and it makes me want to roll over and sit on top of him. He uses the arm and leg that are wrapped around me to squeeze me into a full length body hug.

"Do you want some breakfast?" he asks.

"Sure."

Slowly, we get up and dress and head into the kitchen. I call Rosalie to check up on Amelia while Jeremy rummages through the fridge for something to cook. While I'm talking to Rosalie, Jeremy's phone rings. *His work phone.*

Jeremy looks at me as if asking me what he should do. "Rosalie, I have to let you go." I hang up before she has a chance to respond.

"Are you going to answer it?"

"I should. Marcus said he would only call if it was an emergency."

I huff and wave my hand. "Fine. Go." The high I had from the events of yesterday is immediately washed away by a stupid fucking ring tone.

Jeremy is on the phone with Marcus for twenty minutes. This must be really bad. When he hangs up, he walks back to the bedroom without saying a word. I follow him. I reach the bedroom and see Jeremy putting on jeans. "Where are you going?"

"I have to go to the office. Accounting fucked up and billed the wrong time to the wrong accounts. Multiple accounts. They are blaming the software or some shit, I don't know but they can't figure it out. I have to go help before it gets worse. Goddammit! I knew this was going to happen."

"You knew the software was going to break?"

"No, Livy that isn't what I meant. I knew something would go wrong. This was just too good to be true."

"Jeremy, if it's software issues, it would have happened whether you were there or not. You can't blame this on anyone. It didn't happen because you weren't there. It just happened."

"Either way, I still have to go fix it."

"But the trunk said no work. We still have envelopes left to open and you aren't supposed to go back to work all week."

"Livy! This is money we are talking here. My money. Our money. If I don't go fix this, our clients are going to be pissed and our reputation is going to get tainted."

He was right. I couldn't defend a stupid trunk over potential tarnishing of the business reputation.

But the trunk was working. At least I felt like it was.

"How long do you think you'll be gone?"

Jeremy is putting on his watch. "I have no clue, Livy."

The gentle man that loved me last night was gone. Jeremy was right back into businessman asshole mode. This business was stealing my husband away and there was nothing I could do about it. It might be time to decide that nothing in that trunk is going to work unless Jeremy is ready to let go.

"Okay. Fine. I'm going to go get Amelia. I miss her and I'm not sitting around this house alone waiting for you to come back. It was really idiotic to think a trunk full of instructions would fix us."

"No." Jeremy rushes over to me. I'm sitting on the bed. He sits beside me and wraps his arm around me. "No, Livy. We aren't done. I'm not giving up. I'm sorry I'm freaking out and if it were anything other than financial issues, I'd tell Marcus to figure it out. I swear. These last few days have been awesome. Well, except for the first part, of course, but even that was good, I think. We got it off our chests and I think I at least understand more about why you were so upset. I don't want to quit. We are almost done. Don't you want to see what's left?"

"Of course. But we're breaking the rules. You are going to work. We were supposed to open the next envelope when we woke up. We haven't even done that yet. Plus, I don't want to sit around here by myself staring at that trunk. It's too intriguing."

"Come with me."

"What?"

"Come with me. You've used accounting software before. Come help. Come with me."

I don't know what it is about those three last words. Jeremy wants me to help. He wants me to be a part of it. He wants me there by his side.

He wants me.

"Yes," is all I can say.

"Great. Get dressed. We need to hurry."

"Okay."

Forty-Five

Jeremy

Work

THE WHOLE RIDE TO WORK, LIVY DOESN'T SAY A WORD. BUT SHE'S smiling the entire time. A genuine ear-to-ear grin. I'm not sure what it was about me asking her to help that made her so happy but it did. And that makes me feel like a goddamn rock star.

I pull into my parking spot and look over at her. "You ready?" I ask.

"Of course," she says. I don't know how she forced words out of her lips, her smile is so big.

"I'm going to remind you that these guys are construction workers. I try not to hire douche bags, but they still have penises and you'll probably get whistled at..."

"Jeremy, hi, I'm Livy, have you met me? I can handle it."

"I know. But you've been different, you know, so I was just checking."

She stops walking and looks at me with a frown. After a moment of thought, her face straightens. "Fair enough. Thank you." And she leans in to give me a peck on the cheek.

We walk through the spaces, and there really isn't much whistling after all. Perhaps these meat heads have enough respect to not make moves on the boss's wife.

I head to accounting and look for Claire, the accounting manager.

We have three accountants working for us. There isn't really very much for Claire to manage, but she's been here the longest. She has two kids and her husband died nine months ago overseas fighting in Afghanistan. I gave her a fifteen percent pay raise, as much as I could afford, and told her to be a manager. I had to have justification for the raise to prove it wasn't favoritism. That shit is illegal, apparently, and will get your ass sued in a hot second if you get reported. However, no one has had any complaints about me promoting Claire.

"Hi, Claire, how are you today?"

"Not great, Jeremy. I don't know what happened. When I printed the logistics report this morning and reviewed it, I just happened to notice that Shaw overpaid their bill. I remember billing them last month and for some reason I noticed that the payment they submitted was more than what I billed. So, I checked it out and the bill that was sent out had the wrong amount. They didn't even question it and just paid it. So, I reviewed all of the other clients we billed last month, and only two received the correct bill amount. Everyone else either underpaid or overpaid."

"Shit!"

"I know, Jeremy, I am so sorry. We've been using this program for so long, and it's been so reliable. I don't even look at the bills anymore to verify. I just mail them."

Claire starts to cry. Fuck. I hug her and hand her a tissue. "We'll figure it out. You didn't do anything wrong. I'm not upset with you. But we do need to figure it out."

"I've gone over and over everything. I just don't know what happened."

"Okay, we just need fresh eyes to look at it. I need you to get a memo started that we can send to our clients, alerting them of the situation. Just make it generic. No specific details. Be very apologetic."

"Okay."

"Did you guys have any system updates of any kind recently?" Livy interjects. "Possibly between last month's billing and this month's billing? Did you check to make sure last month's billing was correct?"

Claire looks at Livy as though Livy's speaking a foreign language.

"Um."

Livy goes over to Claire and holds out her hand for a shake. "I'm Livy, Jeremy's wife. We met at last year's Christmas party, remember?"

Claire smiles and shakes Livy's hand "Oh yeah. I'm sorry I just didn't recognize you. You look...different."

"Yeah, it's what nine months of being pregnant and six months of hanging out with an infant will do to you."

Claire, laughs. "Tell me about it. Well it's nice to see you again. And to answer your questions, I'm not sure about any updates. That'd be a question for Bruce. He does all of our computer maintenance around here. He only works part time and he's not here today. I think Marcus tried to call him, but I don't know what happened with that. And I've been so frantic worried about this billing cycle that I didn't even consider last month. Oh God."

Livy, puts her hand on Claire's shoulder. "Claire, it's fine. We'll figure it out." She turns and looks at me. "Jeremy, you go find Marcus and find out what the deal is with Bruce." She spins around and points to Vanessa. "Vanessa, pull up last month's logistics report and verify the billing statements were accurate." She spins back around. "Claire, do you have a copy of this month's logistics report printed?"

"Yes."

"Good. Let me see it and pull up the system so I can take a look at what's going on."

"Ok."

Before I leave the room to go find Marcus, I watch Livy in action. Her full focus is on fixing the problem. She's gone into that zone where she won't quit until she makes it right. She's been given a mission and she won't relent until it's been completed.

Goddammit, I love that about her.

It's been four hours and still no resolution. The good news is that the billing last month was correct. The bad news is that no one can get in touch with Bruce. He's just a part time college kid who maybe doesn't have as strong of a work ethic as I thought he did. We may have to evaluate that when he comes into work tomorrow. Livy scoured over the software looking for any sign of where the problem might lie. After we gave up on trying to contact Bruce, Livy called the software vendor's help line.

"Okay, listen, *John*, is it? Good. Here's the deal. I'm twenty-seven years old and I've touched a computer before, okay? More than once, if you can believe it. I'm kind of seasoned on the whole *turning on the computer, opening up the software* process, alright? So, let's just go with what I've already told you and troubleshoot the actual issue, okay? I need to know if an update for our software was sent to us within the past thirty days and if you are aware of any bugs that may have been part of that update. Our system allocated billing inaccurately by $250,000. Do you understand how substantial that is? That's a quarter of a million dollars, John. So I would very much appreciate it if you would quit coming at me with that condescending tone and help me figure out what your software screwed up. And if you can't overcome your compelling, pathetic attempt to try to make me feel like an idiot, then put someone on the phone who can help me. Are we clear?"

There's a pause. Then, Livy begins writing something down on a notepad.

"Great. Where can I find that documentation, John?"

She writes more. "Good and where can I find the information about the patch?"

She goes to the keyboard and types in a few things. A few clicks of the mouse...

"Lovely. I've got it. And what happens if this patch doesn't work? Fantastic. That sounds great. And that'll be free of charge right, since it's your screw up? That's what I anticipated you'd say. Ok. I will be sure to give you a call back if that's what we need to do. Great. Thank you."

Livy hangs up the phone and looks up at me. "There's some documentation online that details an update that was released fifteen days ago. If it was implemented on our system, the documentation tells you where to go to look for the update serial number. If we have that serial number, John says there is a patch that we can download and install that will fix the existing glitch and prevent it from happening again. But if we don't have that serial number, or if the patch doesn't work, we can call back and have one of their tech members come out and take a look first thing in the morning...no cost."

That is my wife. My take-no-shit, get-the-job-done, wife. *My Livy.*

"So according to the documentation," Livy begins, clicking away at the mouse again. "I have to go to this tab under this setting and okay..." She's looking back and forth between what she wrote on the notepad and the screen. "Yep, okay, so we do have the latest update, according to the serial number, which means we should install the patch onto the server. Do you know how to log into the server, Jeremy?"

"I do."

"Good, that's what we have to do next."

"The server is in my office."

"Well let's go." She jumps up and is out of the door before I can turn around. I follow and jog a little to catch up. When we reach my office, I grab her hand and spin her around into my arms and kiss her. "You are so beautiful when you're working."

She gives me a smile and pulls back. "Thank you. Now, focus, Jeremy." She pats me on the cheek.

I walk over and log into the server. "There, now what?"

"Go to this site and download a file called this." She's pointing to her notepad.

I follow her orders.

"Okay, now, open the file so it can install itself. Okay, now we have to reboot the server and it should be fixed."

"Rebooting now."

It takes a good five minutes for the reboot to happen. Livy and I are both holding our breath for the entire time. I don't know what she's thinking but I'm praying this works. And it's not even because of the money. It's because I want to go back home and finish the trunk.

So I can have sex with my wife.

Because right now, I'm looking at her, leaning over my desk, anxiously waiting for the server to start back up. The intensity in her eyes and the way her hair is slipping out of its clip is making me want to send everyone home right now so I can take her on this desk.

I'm such a pervert.

But only for her.

Livy speaks and pulls me out of the fantasy I was having. "Okay, now we just need Claire to re-run the logistics report from this month and see if it's been fixed." She runs out of my office and down the hall. I stand and adjust myself before making my way down to the accounting office.

Claire is looking intensely at the screen. And then she screams. "Oh my God, I think it worked! I'm going to have to print it out to verify, but it looks like it worked!" She jumps up and hugs Livy, "Thank you! Oh my God, thank you!"

Livy hugs her back. "Not a problem. It was a pain in the ass, but not a problem." Livy looks over at me and winks. She mouths to me a "*thank you.*"

I put my hands in my pocket and rock back on my heels. I smile at her and mouth back "*you're welcome.*"

Forty-Six

Livy

Back at home

THE FEELING I HAVE RIGHT NOW IS EXHILARATING. JEREMY ASKED me for my help and I was able to help. That sense of being needed mixed with the pride of accomplishment gives me a feeling I haven't felt in a long time.

Once Jeremy settles the car into a space in the parking garage, my feet hit the pavement before he turns off the ignition. I'm sprinting to the elevator. I don't even know why I'm sprinting, but I hear Jeremy's foot falls right behind me. I'm giddy and I giggle like a school girl being chased by a crush on the playground. I reach the elevator and press the up button repeatedly, as if doing so will make the elevator arrive faster. Jeremy catches up to me and wraps his arms around my waist and kisses me on the back of the neck, sending goose bumps all over.

This is what we've been missing. The compulsion just to be near each other in an embrace. Smiles. We've been missing smiles for each other. The Jeremy and Livy of six years ago that met in a bar and impetuously grew a relationship based on trust and desire and respect. A relationship that grew hastily into love. Love that was broken by parenthood and a career. Remove those elements and we have Jeremy and Livy back. But what happens when those elements are replaced into their proper position and we have to go back to being who we were last week? The trunk helped us remember who we were but I'm really hoping that it won't end there. I'm hoping that the trunk will give us something to help us move forward so we can stay Jeremy and Livy from the past and still be proper parents for Amelia.

The elevator dings and Jeremy pushes me into the car. Before the door closes, he spins me around and places my face into his hands. He kisses me and inhales at the same time. "Livy, of all the sexy things I have ever seen you do, that, by far, was the sexiest fucking thing. We have got to finish this trunk soon so I can show you just how sexy that was."

I laugh. Pride swells in me again at the thought of how sexy he thought I was standing naked in our bathroom yesterday and again, saying it to me right now, fully clothed, all because of the way I handled the situation at the office.

"Thank you, Jeremy. Thank you for asking me to help. I can't explain to you how amazing that made me feel. I don't even know really why it made me feel that way but just you thinking to include me made me feel…significant."

"Is that why you've been so sad and closed off? Did you not feel significant?"

"Maybe. I don't know. I don't think I'll ever be able to explain to you what it feels like to go through what I've been through these past six months. For a while, I worried constantly if I was doing everything right with Amelia—sometimes I still worry about that. But then, after a few months something just clicked and I went on autopilot and I began not to really care anymore if I was doing it right. Amelia was healthy and happy and that's all that mattered. But then, I think I started to get bitter. Because, I was really proud of myself for figuring it out and not relying on your mother's or anyone else's help. I guess I was just waiting and waiting for the day that you'd come home and tell me you were proud of me for doing a great job."

A knot wrenched in my gut. I can't believe I just said those words out loud. Up until they passed my lips, I didn't even really realize that's how I felt. Deep down I'm not even sure if I was wholly mad at Jeremy for working so much. I was mad because I had accomplished doing the one thing I thought I would never be able to do—be a good moth-er—and no one was there to pat me on the shoulder and give me an *atta-boy.*

The elevator reaches our floor and I walk out without giving Jere-my a chance to respond to the epiphany I just blurted out. I don't blame him for not responding immediately, because I don't even really know what to say about it.

We make our way to our apartment and Jeremy unlocks the door. I feel as though our moods are a little deflated from what they were not just five minutes ago in the parking garage. After we are both inside and Jeremy closes the door, Jeremy starts, "Livy."

I turn to see Jeremy and the look on his face is heartbreaking. I al-most wonder if he is about to cry. I immediately rush over to hug him. "What is it, Jeremy?"

"I'm so sorry." He hugs me tightly. It's not one of our normal *get lost in each other* hugs. This hug is desperate, as if he is holding onto me for dear life. Like I'm dying and he's begging me to live.

"Jeremy?"

"I have thought a thousand times a day, ever since the day Amelia was born, that you are the most incredible mother Amelia could ever ask for. That I am so blessed to have found you to create and raise beau-tiful babies with. I can't even begin to imagine how many times I've thought how lucky I am and how amazing you are. And not once have I told you that. Not once. Oh my God, Livy, I am so sorry. I think I might get it now."

"Get what?"

"Why you were becoming who you were. Why someone gave us this trunk."

I sit down at the breakfast table. His words are too heavy for me to continue standing. Jeremy moves a chair over and sits in front of me. He grabs both of my hands into his.

"First of all, I'm an asshole and I'm sorry." I begin to shake my head. "Let me finish. You've been here day in and day out, raising our child, who is perfect. You thought I didn't see what an amazing job you were doing. You thought I didn't appreciate you and you began to question the point of it all. And on top of that, I made you feel ugly." I shake my head more. "I did. By not telling you how beautiful I still think you are and by not being attentive to your needs, physically and emotionally, I made you feel ugly. You were right when you yelled at me the other day. I did break my promise. I was trying so hard to get my business on track so I could finally come home and be a part of this family, I didn't see that I was breaking it apart in the process.

"Deep down, I knew that every day you were becoming less and less the Livy I married and I think you thought the same about me. And I never wanted to talk about it. I know I was never here, but if I had really wanted to talk to you about it, I would have made the time. I was scared, Livy. I was afraid that I was going to fail my business. And in doing so, I was afraid that I was going to fail you. I wanted to do it on my own because I didn't want you to worry about that on top of the distress from raising a newborn. I forgot that you were my partner and my best friend and I shut you out. And you did the same with Amelia. You shut me out about how hard it was for you because you didn't want me to have the additional stress. We stopped communicating and it landed us here. I want old Jeremy and Livy back. More than you know. I love you so much and when you told me you wanted to leave me, I felt like I'd been shot in the stomach. And when you did leave, I thought you were being selfish. But now I realize you weren't being selfish. You weren't even trying to prove a point. You missed us and you didn't know how to fix it. You felt like you were failing and it was breaking your heart. You are so determined to fix everything with no one's help, to validate your worth. And you don't do it on purpose; it's just how you are wired. But, Livy, you are worth more to me than you could possibly imagine. And I am so sorry that I haven't told you that every single day for the past six months."

We sat there staring at each other for a few moments, our hands entwined together. I try really hard to fight it, but I begin to cry.

"Jeremy, thank you. But it's not all your fault. You are right. I'm wired weird. But before Amelia, you made me feel ok about that. Even when you started the business and you worked all the time. We still made time for each other. And we just don't do that anymore. Jeremy, do you realize that we haven't had fun with each other, up until two days ago, since Amelia was born?"

Jeremy nods. "I realize that now. We both got so consumed at being responsible that we forgot how to be ourselves. That's the whole point of the trunk, Livy, don't you see? It was to help us remember who we fell in love with and bring that person back. At least that's what I'm gathering out of it. And hopefully, we can let old Jeremy and Livy and new Jeremy and Livy coexist somehow."

I smile. "Well the trunk isn't empty yet." I look inside, "There's only two envelopes left." I was slightly saddened by that fact. I was terrified really. I didn't want to go back to what we were just a week ago. I never wanted Jeremy to look at me the way he did when I came back from my granddad's. And I never wanted to feel the anger I had in my heart for the man that took a chance and taught me how to love.

"Well, we should probably get started. We are already half a day overdue."

Forty-Seven

Jeremy

Envelope #5

I PULL OUT ENVELOPE **#5**. I EAGERLY OPEN IT, JUST LIKE I'VE DONE with all of the others. I can see that there is more than one item inside, so I turn the envelope over and dump the contents on the table. There are three envelopes, similar to what was in envelope **#1**. I'm dreading this a little. I don't want to have to do anything else negative. Livy and I are past that point and I don't want to drudge up anything else. But if the trunk says we have to, then we have to.

The envelopes are lettered, just like the first ones—A, B, C—Livy grabs A and opens it. She pulls out the folded piece of paper, unfolds it and begins reading.

"Where did we put our journals?" she asks

"I think they are under the coffee table. Why?" I ask back.

She proceeds to read the instructions.

> Jeremy and Livy,
>   A few days ago, you wrote things in your journal that were good and bad. You told each other about the bad. And, hopefully, with all of the other

things you've done by now, you've moved on from the bad. Now, it's time to read the good to each other.

Livy places the letter on the table and smiles. Her remembering what she wrote about me is making her blush. She grabs my hand and walks to the living room. We sit on the sofa and she grabs the journals, handing mine to me.

"Who goes first?" I ask.

Livy shrugs her shoulders. "I don't care. I can go first."

"Okay." I lean into the arm of the sofa, preparing for her words. If she's blushing there is no telling what she's about to tell me.

Livy clears her throat and begins reading:

The first night I met you, you had my back, just in case. You didn't insist on being my protector. You didn't want to prove you were big and strong.

You never used any cheesy flirt lines with me. You were just yourself. All of the time.

You were patient with me.

You made extra efforts to make me feel comfortable in a relationship.

Your hugs were magical.

You always looked at the positive in a situation.

You put up with my bullshit.

You helped me understand that I deserved to be loved. That I wasn't broken or damaged. I was just Livy.

You treated me like a person. Not like a conquest.

You arranged Christmas for homeless children and you found my grandfather.

You made me feel beautiful. Something I never cared if I felt. But you made me feel that way, as exactly who I was.

You never asked me to change anything about myself.

Our sex was volatile. We were never shy with each other. Never questioned each other. We were always both

*assertive and sure of ourselves. We were experimental.
Kinky, sometimes even. We were never embarrassed. Never
hesitated. Never too tired for each other. We were the epitome
of passion.*

Livy looks up at me and stops reading. "And up until last night, I thought we'd lost that altogether. It really made me sad. To think that at one point in our lives we craved each other so much and three days ago, we couldn't even sit in the same room with one another and look at each other."

Pangs in my heart grip me as I think that if something—or someone…whatever—hadn't intervened, we still might be heading down that same destructive path that we were on three days ago. All because we are both so damn stubborn.

I nod at her in agreement to her last statement. "My turn." I smile and look down at the page on my journal.

*I loved everything about you.
I loved your voice
I loved your eyes and your hair.
I loved your scent.
I loved your bravery.
I loved your independence.
I loved that you rarely wore makeup.
I loved that you wore t-shirts and jeans.
I loved that you wore dresses and heels just for me.
I loved your determination and your perseverance about everything you cared for.
I loved how you loved everyone around you and you didn't even know that's what you were doing.
I loved the noises you made when we were naked with each other.
I loved how you weren't afraid to tell me what you liked and you weren't afraid to try new things.
I loved how you spoke your mind no matter the*

consequences.

I loved listening to you sing in the shower when you didn't think I was listening. Or even if you knew I was listening and you didn't quit because you weren't afraid to let me hear you sing.

I loved that you were a tomboy.

I loved your boobs and I loved your ass and every body part in between.

I loved your heart and I loved that you gave me a chance.

When I'm finished reading, I lock eyes onto Livy's eyes. She's smiling.

"I want to be all of those things you used to love. I miss that girl," she says, as a tear rolls down her face.

"You are still that girl, Livy, and I'm still that guy you wrote about, too. We just needed a swift kick in the ass to remember that."

Her eyes are searching for my trust. She wants to believe that we aren't going to go back to what we were a few days ago. I lean in and give her a hug. "It's going to be okay. I swear."

Livy doesn't respond with words. She just nods.

Forty-Eight

Livy

JEREMY HUGS ME AND I WANT TO BELIEVE HIM. AND I WANT TO believe that he believes it too. I nod to assure him that I heard him.

It's going to be okay.

I pull back and look into his eyes. The one thing that I know I'm not going to do is waste time dwelling on whether everything will be ok. Either it will or it won't and I understand that only time will reveal the outcome.

"Shall we open the next envelope?" I ask Jeremy with a smile.

Jeremy smiles back and brushes my face with his hand. "I don't see why not." His touch raises goose bumps the entire length of my body. It makes me happy to have that feeling again. Before the trunk showed up, it had been so long since I'd felt that way.

I walk over to the trunk to find the next envelope. It's a small plain white letter envelope. I open it and take out the folded paper. Unfolding the paper reveals the familiar typed font as previous instructions.

> Your first date was quite significant.
> Bring it all back by doing it all over
> again. From start to finish. When you
> are done, open envelope C.

This note saddens me. "We can't recreate our date. We started it with Porters at Joe's. We can't do that. What are we supposed to do?"

"We could skip the Porters, Livy. That's no big deal."

"It's a big deal to me Jeremy."

Jeremy rubs his chin with his hand and looks up into the air, as though he's trying to figure out an alternative. Finally, he looks back down to me and smiles. "You know how we were watching that cooking show once and one of the chefs made a deconstructed shepherd's pie—he took all of the components of the traditional dish and modernized the recipe?"

I tilt my head to the side and wonder where this is headed. "Uh, yeah?" I vaguely remember, but I just go along with it.

"Well, you know, architecture has kind of worked in that trend too, taking old style designs, picking apart the details and reproducing new styles with similar attributes of the old style in order to appeal to modern design enthusiasts."

I'm quickly losing interest and am growing impatient. "Jeremy, thank you for that educational tidbit, but what is the point you are trying to make?"

He smiles. "Sorry. My point is why don't we take our original date, pick apart the details, keep the important ones and make a brand new date?" He shrugs, "It could be fun."

I think over his suggestion for a moment. We can't bring Joe's bar back. But we can try to be creative and have fun with the time we have alone with each other. I grab Jeremy's hand and smile. "What did you have in mind?"

Jeremy walked over to the office desk we have by the window and opened his laptop. He sat down in the desk chair and began browsing the Internet. He did a fair amount of searching before speaking.

"So, here's the plan," he began. He pointed to his laptop, inviting me to look. "This bar has five-star reviews on its tap selection. We can start there for Porters." He looked at me and I returned his gaze and smiled.

With the click of his mouse, he showed me a new window on the laptop screen. "And here, this is a family-owned Italian restaurant that's uptown. They've been open since 1927 and they make their mozzarella fresh. And our wine is on their menu." He points to the online menu to verify.

"Sounds delicious. But do they—" I begin to question, but Jeremy quickly interrupts.

"Tiramisu? Yep."

I smile, knowing he knew exactly what I was thinking warms my heart.

"Afterwards," he continues, "we can walk a few blocks to here," he says, clicking and pointing to yet another window. "We can do some disco bowling."

On this, I become apprehensive. "Disco bowling? What the fuck is that?"

Jeremy laughs. "Starts at nine. They turn down the regular lights and turn on the black lights and strobe machines. And play seventies music while you bowl."

I think on this. This idea seems a stretch. I'm not so sure about being in a dimly lit area with a lot of people and loud music. It reminds me too much of clubbing, which is certainly not something I want to experience again. However, Jeremy's sweet, pouty eyes are asking me to trust him and give it a shot. It's really hard to say no to that face. "Okay, I'm in. Is that all?"

"No," Jeremy says, with a sly look on his face, "but the last part is a surprise."

"A surprise?"

Jeremy stands and wraps his arms around me. "Yes. A surprise."

I hug him back. We are lost in our own world with this hug. "When do you want to leave?" I ask, while Jeremy is still wrapped around me.

"Whenever you are ready."

"I think we should call Rosalie and let her know our plans. For emergency purposes. In case she needs to know where we are." My maternal instincts kick in, alerting that we should let someone know where we'll be.

"Okay. That's not a bad idea," Jeremy agrees.

After we notified Rosalie of our evening whereabouts and she responded with a delightful, *"Oh, that is so lovely! Have fun my loves. Amelia, Maggie and I are doing just fine,"* we took a cab and headed to the five-star bar.

The Porters were of a brand I'd never had and were delicious. And not to discredit our favorite little trattoria, but this new restaurant had the best mozzarella I'd ever tasted. Over dinner, Jeremy and I talked and laughed right up until our last bite of heavenly, delectable tiramisu.

The disco bowling was quite an event. It was a laborious task attempting to bowl in semi-dark with nothing but black light and strobes of fluorescent illuminating our lanes. But the music was entertaining and by our second pitcher of lousy, domestic beer—all that was available—we gave up on keeping score and took turns trying trick shots with the bowling balls. I started with trying to bowl with my opposite hand. I caught four pins. Jeremy's finale move was rolling the ball through his legs while facing away from the lane. He got a strike. *Lucky duck.*

Our cab ride home was filled with low whispers to each other and a great amount of giggling by us both. We were quite a sight for the cabbie. When the car stopped, I looked out of the window to take in our destination. Jeremy exited his side of the taxi and came over to my side to open my door. He took my hand, led me out of the cab, paid the driver and sent him on his way.

"Jeremy, why are we here?" I asked, while looking at the building that used to be Joe's bar. *My bar.*

"I'm walking you home." He smiled and took my hand again. I returned his smile and remembered how he had walked me home after our first date.

We began walking in the direction of our apartment. We strolled hand in hand for ten minutes in near silence. Not because we had nothing to say but because we were just enjoying the moment. When we arrived at our stoop, Jeremy stopped and faced me. "Livy, I just have to say I really like you."

Having imbibed on the Porters, the wine and the cheap beer, my brain's natural reaction is to let out a giggle. But I'm not too stymied to remember that those were the words he said to me, standing in front of my apartment stoop all of those years ago. The bad part is that I cannot remember what my response was to his proclamation, or even if I had one. So, I improvise.

"I guess I kind of like you too, Jeremy."

We smile at each other stupidly, like we're school children, just as we had done on our first date. Then, Jeremy leans in and kissed me on the side of my face and my body instantly felt hot from head to toe. I suddenly remember the feelings I had back then after he'd kissed me like that. The feelings reemerge and I feel like I am falling in love with Jeremy all over again.

Jeremy meets my gaze again and nudged his head toward our front door. "Shall we?"

The night had helped me remember myself. I felt like the old me. And standing across from me, smiling, was the old Jeremy. *My Jeremy.* I hook my arm in his and we proceed into our apartment.

Forty-Nine

Jeremy

Envelope C

"WHEN CAN WE OPEN ENVELOPE C?" LIVY ASKS, WITH A GIGGLE, as we walk into the apartment. The alcohol of the evening has gotten the better of us both. But we've laughed a lot and I have nothing to complain about in regards to that.

"The trunk said we could after we were done with our date," I say, trying not to hiccup.

Livy spins around to face me with wide eyes. "Are we done? Let's open it now."

I laugh at her expression and enthusiasm. And then I hiccup. "Okay."

I toss my keys onto the counter and then walk over to the kitchen table. Envelope C is small like the others. I open it slowly and pull out a piece of card stock.

Fuck.

It's there plain as day. I'm holding the card with both hands because I'm trying to focus and make sure it's saying what I think it's saying, and I don't want to drop it.

Four tiny letters, the first one capitalized, and one punctuation mark.

Fuck.

There is no explanation. It's just one word and a period.

Fuck.

I try to contemplate what this means. Is there a hidden message? Is it a clue? What am I missing?

Fuck.

I hone in on the word once again and I inhale.

"What is it, Jeremy?" Livy asks, high pitched and slightly slurred. "You have a very weird look on your face? What is it?"

Her voice shakes me from my thoughts. I'm over thinking this. If this means anything other than what I originally thought it meant, then the trunk can just go take a hike. I'm not some genius philosophical code cracker. I'm just a guy with a hard on for his wife. So, I'm going to take this card at exactly face value.

I look up at Livy. Her eyes are wide and they are scanning my face to try to get a sense of what the next move from the trunk is. With both hands, I drop the card onto the floor and I'm certain before it hits the ground, my hands are on Livy's face and my mouth is on hers, kissing her like it's life saving for the both of us.

I half expect Livy to pull away and ask about the card, but she doesn't. She melts into me and lets me take control of the situation. I think she instinctively knows what the trunk just told us to do.

Still kissing her, I begin to walk her backwards. I know there is a wall around here somewhere, and I just want to pin her up against it. I remember how bothered and flushed she got while reading the parts of that book where the male character would lead the foreplay with aggression. I know exactly what she wants right now. She wants me to take control and do whatever I want. She just wants to be a recipient right now and I am one-hundred-and-thirty-five percent ok with that.

Livy's back finally reaches a wall and we bump against it a little harder than I anticipated. I don't ask her if she's alright though. I know if she's hurt, she'd tell me. I don't want to break up this connection we have going right now.

I remove my hands from her face and reach down to find the bottom of her shirt. I lift it and remove it from her body, only very briefly unlocking our kiss. I throw her shirt somewhere and reach down again to find both of her wrists. I grab them and raise them above her head, pinning them against the wall. Livy groans and gives me the go ahead to ravish her just as I had fantasized about so many times in the past twenty-four hours.

With my right hand staying in place, securing Livy's arms above her head, I move my left hand down her arm, lightly brushing her skin as I make my way to her shoulder. My fingers continue to move down, along the side of her chest and continue past her ribs. I am finally met with the edge of her jeans and I proceed to unbutton and unzip them with one quick movement.

Still kissing her furiously, both of us already consumed with heavy breathing, I place my hand inside her jeans. Livy's hips push away from the wall and against me. She lets out a loud moan. I remember that moan. That moan along with the pressure between us is driving me to the edge. We need to get into a more compromising position.

The bed.

With one hand above and one hand below, I move my lips from her mouth to her breast. Upon contact, Livy lets a quiet whisper of my name. Hearing that has done me in so much further than the moan.

My lips continue to kiss and my fingers continue to move. Livy begins breathing even harder than before and making sounds that only I know how to decipher. She's almost there. I shift my head to pay equal and proper respect to her other breast. It only takes a few moments until Livy screams my name and presses against me so hard that I think she might float away if I weren't running interference.

I remove my hands from both positions and wrap my arms around her. I kiss her until her breathing slows. She places her hands in my hair and tugs. I love that sensation. I place my hand under her ass and nudge, the signal for her to wrap her legs around my waist. She complies. I walk into the bedroom, still kissing, her hands still clutched in my hair. I place a knee onto the bed and gently lower her onto it. Once settled, we disconnect. I stand to remove my shirt, but Livy kneels on the bed and comes over to me, eye level. She places her hands under my shirt and looks at me with that hungry look I've seen so many times.

"Let me," she says. I nod and she lifts my shirt over my head and then slowly removes my belt. Then my pants. Then boxers. She kisses my stomach and all the way up to my chest and neck, finally reaching the destination of my mouth. I place my hands in her hair and attempt to pull her as close to me as physically possible.

A thought flashes in my mind. I'm naked. She's not. This is a problem.

I unclasp her bra and motion her back down to a lying position on the bed. Livy takes care of the bra removal while I work on the jeans scenario. I'm pulling the pants off of her legs, when I realize there is no other fabric underneath.

I look at Livy. "Livy. You aren't wearing underwear?" I lift my arm and point beyond the walls, "The whole time we were…out there…in public…you were…"

"Commando?" she finishes my question. She shrugs and smirks that devilish grin of hers. "Mmmhmm. You said hurry, so I hurried. Your hand was just in there five minutes ago. You didn't notice?"

"That was hardly a time for noticing details," I quickly respond. I briefly try to replay the moment and actually wonder if I remember noticing the absence of soft fabric. And then my mind goes back to the matter at hand. *She's not wearing underwear!* Holy fuck, I don't know why but that is so hot!

"Is that getting to you, Jeremy? No panties?" She says the word panties with a pout in her voice. I get what she's doing now. *The porn.*

"Uh, yeah. Well played." I wink. "But you had no idea we would be doing this today."

"I decided to take my chances." She winks back.

Goddamn, I love this woman.

I finish removing the jeans and lean down to kiss her more. Our full body, skin-on-skin contact is fire and ice all at once. It's like we've never been naked around one another before, even though we were only just naked together yesterday. This is completely different. We are both writhing and letting our hands explore each other as if it were the first time. Livy is pulling and clutching and scratching at my skin like she's trying to rip me open and climb inside just to get closer to me. It's a little more aggressive than she's ever been and it is driving me absolutely insane. I can't hold out much longer. I start positioning myself for the next act of our performance when Livy places a hand on my shoulder and pushes me back.

"What's wrong?" I ask.

She grins again. "Nothing." She lifts herself from the bed and nudges me onto my back. "Me on top first," she says as she straddles me and lightly scrapes her nails down my chest. Her nails give me chills. I have a feeling she's about ride me like a mustang. I'm fearful and hopeful all at once. "Then, you can be on top." She leans down, our chests coming together and she softly kisses my lips. "Then..." she says, as she teases her fingers in my hair, "maybe we can try some of that other stuff we watched in the porno."

She winks and then makes her eyebrows dance, teasingly, by arching them up and down asynchronously. I can't believe this is the same Livy that was yelling at me and crying not just three days ago. It's not the same Livy. She's different. Different from a few days ago. And even different from when we first met. Maybe she is a phoenix, arisen from broken ashes. Whatever it is, I like it. I smile and smack her on the ass. She yelps with surprise and giggles.

"I'm all in," I respond, watching her eyes flicker with excitement and curiosity. I bring her face back down to mine and kiss her once more as we begin a night of ecstasy that neither one of us could possibly ever forget.

Fifty

Livy

I FEEL AS THOUGH JEREMY AND I HAVE TAKEN ALL OF THE PASSION and emotion from that stupid book we read and all of the lust and debauchery from the porn that we watched and merged it into one super cell of love. Before Amelia was born, Jeremy and I were always adventurous and experimental in the bedroom, (among other places). But even the things we'd done last night were on a level above anything we had ever contemplated doing. They were things I didn't know until a few days ago would be pleasurable if performed. All night, Jeremy and I played a constant back and forth battle of who could pleasure whom the best. In the end, I think we both went home with the gold.

The sun began to rise and we were both still awake, lying flat on our backs, completely spent. Muscles that I didn't even know I had ached. My lips ached. My nipples ached. I was afraid to look in the mirror to see the state of my body and what Jeremy had left me with. I felt a spattering of bruises and hickies everywhere.

Everywhere.

The thought of him marking me scared me. Not because he had hurt me. The thought scared me because I wondered if I saw what he had done to me, if I would ever let either one of us leave this bed again. We had tussled and taunted with each other for the better part of six hours and I still hadn't had enough. I was exhausted and sore and I wanted to go again. And again. I am not sure what exactly changed or transgressed last night but what happened was far beyond any sex we had ever had. *Ever.*

First time we had sex together? No comparison.

The assortment of *"we might get caught"* sessions over the years? Not even close.

Travel sex? Nope.

Honeymoon? A fraction of last night.

We had entered a realm, a vortex, where Jeremy and I connected in a way that we are never going to be able to let go of. Jeremy had once described the feelings between us as something reaching out from his chest and grabbing onto my heart. With all of the pain we had caused each other over the past few months, that grab had let go. But now, at this very moment, that grab has my heart clutched in a vice, holding on so tight that my chest hurts with the thought of it ever letting go again. That grab is pumping my heart, keeping it beating. If it ever lets go again, I most certainly will die.

I look over at Jeremy and he turns his head to look at me. "I love you so much, Jeremy. I know we've said our apologies already, but I am so sorry. For everything. For being bitter. For being stubborn. For leaving. I swear that I will stop holding everything in. I will let you know how I feel, just like I used to. I will stop worrying about whatever else might be stressing you out. Because in comparison to us being ok, nothing else matters."

Jeremy shakes his head in agreement and places his hand on my cheek. "I promise I will always be there to listen, no matter what." My cheek smiles into his hand and a tear of relief falls from my eye. We could have really fucked everything up. We almost lost each other. We almost gave up. The trunk helped us remember what we used to have and helped us turn it into something even better.

The trunk.

"The trunk!" I say as I sit up with realization. I motion to the dresser to find one of Jeremy's t-shirts. I throw it on. "We still have one more envelope!" Jeremy sits up with the same excitement. He slips on boxers and we head out of the bedroom, making way to the dining room table.

Both of us pause at the same time. Jeremy and I see it simultaneously. I feel like someone has kidnapped my child. I clutch my chest and run toward the table. "It's gone. The trunk is gone! Oh my God!" I look under the table. I look in the kitchen cabinets. I run to the living room and look under furniture and behind the television that's hung on the wall. "Where is it?"

Jeremy runs his hand through his hair, watching me look for the trunk in places that the trunk couldn't possibly fit. "I don't know. However, I am a little more concerned with the fact that if the trunk isn't here, that means that someone was in our apartment last night."

All of my moving freezes. I had not even thought of that. Someone came in and stole our trunk. "Oh, God." A panic attack begins to bubble. "That means, someone came in here…" as the thoughts enter my brain, I find it hard to spit them out into words because then those thoughts will be out in the open, lingering and true. "…came in here," I repeat, shaking my hands as if doing so will make the panic go away. "While we were in there." I point toward the bedroom. "Doing…"

"Yeah, that's exactly what it means. This is some fucked up shit, Livy. The fact that someone delivered us a trunk of mysterious instructions is weird enough. But to think that someone actually came into our apartment in the middle of the night and took it away is beyond creepy."

"But there was one envelope left. We weren't done. And other than that, the trunk was empty. Why would someone come in the middle of the night and take an empty trunk?"

"No. Livy. Look." Jeremy points at the wall. "The pictures are gone." He walks over to the coffee table. "The record player, the candles—all gone. The journals are gone too."

Now I feel like someone has kidnapped my second child. The one that doesn't even exist. "Oh my God!" I yell.

"Yeah."

"No one can read what we wrote. Jeremy! Those words were for our eyes only. Just for us!" I run my fingers through my hair and try to think about what to do. "So someone gives us a mysterious box of stuff and then takes it back? I don't even know where to go from here. Do we call the police? Do we forget it ever happened?" I am now in full on panic mode. My voice is at a piercing decibel and the panic is putting me on the verge of tears.

Jeremy quickly walks towards me and wraps his arms around me. "Shh. Hey, calm down," he says, as he clutches my head into his chest. "We are definitely not going to pretend it never happened." I steady my breathing with his and begin to calm down.

Finally, I have a rational thought. I look up at Jeremy. "Maybe we should put on a few more items of clothing and go ask the neighbor across the hall if he saw or heard anything strange last night."

"Good idea." We make our way back into the bedroom. I put on a bra but leave Jeremy's shirt on. I throw on some shorts, sans underwear—Jeremy notices—while Jeremy throws on some jeans and a shirt. We head to the front door, Jeremy taking lead. He reaches the door and pauses for longer than what it should take to unlock the door and turn the handle to open it.

"Jeremy, what is it?"

Jeremy reaches up and I peer around him to see what he is reaching for. It's an envelope, taped to the door. "It's the last envelope," Jeremy says.

"How do you know?" I ask.

"I remember it from last night. I glanced at it briefly before I opened the other envelope. I remember the handwriting and the fact that the ink is red."

The ink is red.

And it's hand written.

Very different from the hand written Post-it on the porno movie.

This handwriting is curly and antique looking. Very Charles Dickens-era.

Jeremy observes the hand writing and the envelope for far too long. "Well, open it already!" Maybe it's a ransom note for my two kidnapped children.

Jeremy runs his finger under the sealed seam of the envelope and opens the flap. He pulls out another piece of card stock, this one being larger than the one from last night, but similar in color. Still standing behind Jeremy, I peer over his shoulder to read the card.

Crown Plaza Hotel
Firelight Hall
Tonight
7pm

Fifty-One

Jeremy

Firelight Hall

LIVY AND I ARE AT OUR WITS END ABOUT WHAT WE'LL SEE WHEN WE open the double doors of the banquet hall we are standing in front of. When we arrived, we asked the concierge how to make our way to the Firelight Hall. He smiled as though he was expecting us.

"Ah, yes," he said as he motioned us to follow him. "Right this way."

Livy and I racked our brains all day, hypothesizing what was going to happen tonight in the ballroom at seven o'clock. Were we going to meet the ethereal creator of the trunk? Were we going to be drawn into a bright, white light from above and be abducted by aliens, never to be seen or heard from again? Perhaps someone came up with this entire elaborate plan not to help us, but to get us in a specific place at a specific time to serve us with legal papers over some frivolous law suit. After deliberating with Livy for nearly twelve hours, we had decided that any scenario that we had come up with was possible. There was actually even one that we kept going back to: one of those Nigerian bank scams actually being real. That we had a long lost relative living in a foreign country who was willing to part with a huge sum of money, but first we had to prove that we were both in our marriage for the long haul.

Anything was possible. Unlikely, but possible.

Livy and I are standing side by side, shoulder to shoulder. I turn my head to her and she mimics the movement. We both inhale a deep breath almost simultaneously.

"Are you ready?" I ask.

"As ready as I'll ever be."

We both reach for the door. Being that they are double doors, we each reach for a handle. I hesitate to pull the handle down, as does Livy. Neither one of us want to be the first. I find my balls and decide that I should take the lead. I slowly maneuver the handle to a downward position and Livy follows suit.

We look at each other one last time before we push the doors open, revealing the mystery and our fate.

"What the fuck?" Livy exclaims. With the doors open, we step into what seems to be an empty, dark banquet hall. I step back out and look at the gold etched plate above the doors.

Firelight Hall

"We are in the right room." I scratch my head. "I don't underst—"

Just then, the lights of the room flip on and blind me. Livy and I both shield our eyes with our forearms. There is so much light that it seems to be coming from every direction. We may have gotten it right with the alien abduction.

Very lightly in the background, music begins to play. It's the same song we were instructed to listen to a few days ago. *Janis.*

As my eyes adjust to the light, I lower my hand. Livy begins to do the same as soon as she hears the song. I take my attention away from the song to notice that there are people standing in front of us. My eyes aren't quite yet adjusted so while I can tell they are people, they are still blurry people. *Shapes of people.*

And then I heard Amelia coo. As soon as the sound reaches Livy's ears, she makes a dash in the direction from where the sound came. "What are you all doing here?" she asks.

What? Who? I close my eyes and shake my head to try to get my visual focus in check. I reopen my eyes and the people look familiar to me now.

Mom. Maggie. Jenna and Mike. Sara and Craig. Maxwell. Joe and Vicky. And Amelia, who Livy is now holding onto for dear life.

"Surprise!" everyone yells in unison.

"What? What the fuck is going on?" I didn't mean to say that out loud but I think I just did.

Mom walks up to me and gives me a hug. "Oh, baby boy, you look so confused."

"Uh, I am. Why are you all here?"

"We were invited. This is a celebration for you and Livy."

"Wait. What? A celebration? For what?"

"For figuring it out."

I don't know how much my mother knows about the trunk. If anything. Certainly, hopefully, not everything. If my mother gave me porn to encourage me to have sex with my wife, I may never be able to look at my mother again. I may never watch porn again. I may never have sex again.

"For figuring out that you two stubborn asses were meant for each other and that you love each other."

"Oh. Yeah, that. Of course," is all I can say in response. My mind is on overdrive trying to figure out how much she actually knows. My mind is also blown away by the fact that she just said *asses*.

"Wait," Livy says, quizzically. "I don't understand. All of you were in on the trunk?"

"Well, it wasn't our idea, technically," Sara chimes in. Livy and I wait but she doesn't offer any more details. From the feeling I have about the air in the room, I think we are going to have to coax every single detail out to find out the whole story.

"Mom, you acted like you didn't know anything about the trunk the other day," I accuse. She looks at me but doesn't respond.

Livy blushes. "Uh, do *all* of you know what was in the trunk?" She looks at Rosalie and then at Maxwell. I can tell in the expression on her face what she is praying the answer will be.

Sara grins and raises an eyebrow. "Everyone was asked to contribute *something*. We only know about what we offered." The look on Sara's face tells me that she knows about the porn. "And the journals. We all know about the journals," she continues.

"The journals?" Livy asks hesitantly. "Did you…read…?"

"None of us have read anything," Sara ensures. She seems to be the mouthpiece of the group. No one else has spoken. No one else will answer.

"So, if none of this was planned by you, then whose idea was it?"

Silence.

Awkwardness. Mike puts his hands in his pockets. Mom shifts her weight. I notice Maxwell look at his watch at the same time Sara looks down at the phone she has in her hand.

"Sara," Livy starts "What is going on?"

Sara exhales but says nothing.

Jesus, I am so tired of this game. If someone doesn't speak soon, I'm going to start shaking shoulders until I get some answers.

Just as I'm about to start with Jenna, a voice floats into the room from behind Livy and me. Someone has entered the room from the doors we just passed through not moments ago.

"Hello, Olive."

Fifty-Two

Livy

THERE ARE FOUR PEOPLE ON THIS PLANET THAT HAVE CALLED ME by my birth name.

1 – Jeremy, who is on my left. He called me Olive once and I threatened his life if he ever said it again.

2 – My grandfather, who is standing in front of me. He called me Olive when I was younger. Before I decided I just wanted to be Livy.

3 – The preacher who married Jeremy and me. He is not in my visible presence but I am more than one hundred percent sure that the person saying my real name behind me is not him.

Because the person who just spoke is a woman. That leaves only one option as to who it could be standing behind me. But I didn't have to guess anyway. As soon as she said the word *hello* my insides cringed and my stomach revolted against me, making me want to vomit on the spot.

All of the people standing in front of me remain frozen, awaiting my reaction. Jeremy doesn't move either. He's too confused. With Amelia in my arms, I slowly spin around. Even though I already know who the person standing in the doorway is, I still gasp in shock when I see her.

"Nancy."

Fifty-Three

Jeremy

"Nancy," I hear Livy say.

Nancy. Nancy? Who is…

Oh fuck. Nancy. Livy's mother.

I am immediately at Livy's side, my arm wrapped around her. She is shaking. I am terrified as to what might happen next. Livy might murder this woman. There is a very high probability that my wife may be about to murder her mother.

I take Amelia from Livy who hands her over willingly. Livy stands there motionless staring at Nancy. Nancy does the same but the difference between the two is that Livy looks ready to pounce and Nancy looks extremely nervous. She's clutching a bag in front of her with both hands, arms straight down. Her top hand is kneading and wringing the one underneath—the one that is holding on to her bag so tightly that her knuckles are white.

They stare at each other for a very long time. Above the music playing in the background, I swear I can hear the second hand of a clock ticking somewhere.

Tick tock, tick tock, tick tock. It goes on forever.

I take a few steps back and after kissing Amelia on the cheek, I hand her over to my mother. I may have to intervene in what's about to go down, and Amelia needs to stay safe.

I lean into my mother and whisper, "Why in the hell is she here?

What have you all done?"

My mother then leans into me. "We didn't do anything, love. We were just asked to help. It took some convincing but we decided it was for the best."

"Did Maxwell do this?"

"No, he's just a helper like the rest of us. He took more convincing than any of us. He didn't want her to have anything to do with yours and Livy's relationship."

"Wait. What? Her who? You mean Nancy? What does she have to do with any of this?"

"Everything. This was all her idea."

Fifty-Four

Livy

THE WOMAN STANDING BEFORE ME IS NOT THE WOMAN I REMEMBER Nancy to be. The Nancy I remember wore denim cutoff shorts and tank tops with no bra. The Nancy I remember had rusty orange hair that never looked to be brushed. The Nancy I remember always had a cigarette between her fingers.

This woman in front of me sounded like Nancy, for sure, but looked nothing like the Nancy of my childhood. This Nancy was holding onto a big leather purse, which looked to be somewhat expensive. She was wearing a violet pants suit and heels. And pearls—both around her neck and dangling from her ears. This Nancy had brown hair, like mine, and it was pulled up into a tight, neat bun that sat on the back of her head. This Nancy had on makeup. Mascara. Lipstick. She looked… clean. How the hell could this person really be Nancy?

"Olive?"

She says my name again and the bile resurfaces. Anger radiates through my entire body.

"Who the fuck are you?" Is my first instinctual question. I spit out my inquiry to her as though it were a piece of rotted food.

There is shock on her face and her hands tighten tighter around the strap of her bag.

"I'm…I'm, your mother."

"Like fuck you are," I throw back before her words completely leave her mouth.

"Olive, I…"

"Stop fucking calling me that!"

"Livy," Rosalie interjects.

I snap my head to her. "Did you know she would be here?" No response. I surf the crowd behind me with my gaze. "Did all of you know that she would be here?"

Crickets.

"Olive…I mean, Livy." The woman who just had the audacity to call herself my mother speaks. "They were all just trying…"

"Shut! Up!" I say, whipping my head back around in her direction. "You do not get to speak to me!"

My world is spinning. I do not understand what is going on. First we come to this mystery location and then we were supposed to be celebrating something and now all of a sudden Nancy is here. I try to steady my dizziness and ask the universe to help me make sense of things. I at least beg that it's not going to throw me anymore curve balls. Just as I'm done with my pleading, a man walks up behind Nancy and places his hand on her shoulder. She's still staring at me. The man leans in and whispers something into her ear. She shakes her head no. The man is tall. Taller than me, also with brown hair. He is also wearing a suit. And he looks oddly familiar. How do I know this guy?

"Who the fuck are you?" I ask. *Only one way to find out.*

"Olive," the man says.

Goddammit with that name!

"I'm Ronald. Ronny. I'm your dad."

My world goes black.

Fifty-Five

Livy

"L IVY, WAKE UP. LIVY."
         I hear Jeremy's voice. Thank God, I was dreaming. I must
have fallen asleep in the car or something on the way to the hotel. I
wiggle around a bit to signal to Jeremy that I am waking up. I have to
recover from the horrific dream I just had where Nancy was standing in
the doorway of a ballroom. *With my dad.*

"Livy," Jeremy says again and shakes my shoulder. "Wake up." I try
to open my eyes but it's difficult. Like when you try to wake from a
nightmare because you know you are dreaming but you just can't. You
fight so hard to open your eyes but the harder you fight, the further you
get sucked into the nightmare. I twist again and realize that either I'm
not in the car, or that Jeremy's car seats have been switched out with the
most uncomfortable, cold, hard seats in existence—all in between the
time we got in the car to go to the hotel and now. Jeremy lightly taps me
on the cheek. "Livy." My eyes pop open and I sit up fast. I am extremely
dizzy and nauseous. "Whoa," Jeremy says, "Slow down."

"What?" I ask confused. "What is going on?" My eyes adjust and
I scan my surroundings. A room. A big room. With decorations and
a table filled with food. There is music in the background. *Janis.* This
soothes me for a second until I remember that this is the exact setting of
the dream I just had. And then I realize something else. *I wasn't dreaming.* I dart glances everywhere in a sheer panic. There is no way what I

just experienced was real. It had to have been a dream. That is the only logical explanation.

Then my glances fail me and my eyes land on *her*. And *him*. I begin fanning my hand up and down in front of my face. "Oh my God, I think I'm going to puke!"

"Someone get her a cold rag and a ginger ale!" Jeremy yells. He hugs me and involuntarily I begin to sob. Hard. Loudly. "Shh, shh," he says and rocks with me on the floor. "I am so sorry. I had no idea," he whispers.

I don't acknowledge that I heard him. I feel so betrayed by everyone who I know with exception to Jeremy. Why would they do this? Why would they think this was ok? Why? The *whys* make me cry even harder and when I think that there are two people in the very same room as me, claiming to be my parents, witnessing my melt down, I cry even harder.

I feel something cold being placed on the back of my neck—the wash cloth Jeremy requested. "Livy," Jenna says, "Here, drink this."

"Is there bourbon in it?" I ask, muffled into Jeremy's chest.

Jenna replies, "No, but I'm on it. Here, take a few sips of straight ginger ale first to settle your stomach." I reach my arm out in the direction of her voice without looking up. I feel a solo cup being placed in my hand. I grab it and immediately sit it on the floor.

A few moments later, Jenna comes back. "Here, Livy what did you do with your cup?" I look up at her finally and see a bottle of bourbon in her hand. She was going to add a little to my ginger ale.

Fuck that.

"Just give me the bottle, Jenna." I reach out my arm and she reluctantly hands me the bottle.

"Livy?" Jeremy questions. He is afraid of what the outcome of this might be. I bring the bottle straight to my lips and take an elongated swig. Three or four gulps. Jeremy hugs his arms around me tighter either begging me to stop or telling me he understands. I'm not sure which but it keeps me from finishing the bottle which I am certain I could have done. I put the bottle down next to the ginger ale and wipe my lips with the back of my hand. I straighten my shoulders and take a deep breath. I have some scores to settle.

I stand up, a little unsteady. Jeremy quickly stands up with me waiting to brace me if I fall over.

I look over to Rosalie and everyone else crowded around her and Amelia.

"I don't know how any of you thought it would be appropriate to corral me here under false pretenses and expect me to celebrate anything with *her*." I point to Nancy. "I don't know what she's told you about herself and I certainly never told any of you about my past because I didn't want your pity, but this is in no way a celebratory occasion. Reuniting me with her?" I look over at Maxwell. "I am especially disappointed in you. You knew and you still let this happen. How could you?"

The bourbon is beginning to take effect.

I look over at Nancy and the man claiming to be my father. "And as for the two of you. I don't know why you are here but you can fucking leave. I don't know what you want, but I can tell you I'm not giving you any money and if you think you are going to lay your hands on my child…"

I can't even finish the sentence. I have no words for the graphic visual sketched in my head of what I would do to them if they thought they could come around just because they have a grandchild. Thinking of all the things Nancy ever did to me. All the harsh words she ever threw in my direction. To think those same hands and that same voice, touching and talking to Amelia made my whole body writhe with pain so much so that I wrapped my arms around my stomach and bent over slightly.

"Livy, are you okay?" Jeremy has his hands on my shoulders. I take a deep breath and nod. I look over at Nancy and Randy, or whatever his name was. "You should both leave. Now."

"Livy, maybe you should just hear…"

"Sara, I really don't want to be mean to you right now so please stay the fuck out of this."

My eyes still locked on Nancy. "Leave. I have no interest in whatever you want."

Neither of them budges. It infuriates me. This is a celebration for

Jeremy and me, dammit. I should be able to force them to leave. Call security or something. But this is a public place and I didn't reserve the space. I don't even know who did but no one else in the room seems to be on my side to get them to go away.

"Fine. Jeremy, get Amelia. We're leaving." He does as I ask. He's the only one who hasn't seemingly lost his mind. To my right, I notice there is another door for the banquet room. There is an exit sign above it indicating that I should be able to use it to escape this alternative universe we apparently have entered. There is no way I'm leaving out the doors we came in. Nancy and the man she brought with her are way too close to that door right now, meaning that if I attempted to exit that way, I'd have to get closer to them before I could get farther away. "Come on, Jeremy."

I make my way to the side door. Just as I am within reaching distance of the exit, a voice cries out in despair, "Livy! I love you!"

I halt my feet and stand there frozen. With the bourbon coursing through my veins, I am not sure if what I just heard was real. I look over at Jeremy and his expression indicates that it was. Before I have time to react to anything, Nancy repeats herself, but this time in a calmer, more peaceful tone.

"Livy, I love you. I know you don't believe me and you may never believe me. I understand that. I'm not trying to get anything from you. I was just hoping you'd hear me out. And when Dad told me you were in trouble with your marriage, I just wanted to try to help. Can you just let me explain? Five minutes? Ten minutes, max? And then, if you never want to see or hear from me again, I will go, because I know that is what I deserve."

I spin around on my heels and face her. I speak through my teeth. "You abused me. Physically. Verbally. Emotionally. You made me feel worthless. You made me feel like this world had no use for me. If I hadn't had any common sense, I would have ended up just like you, whoring it up all over town to score drugs. The only reason I am where I am today is because of my own good use of judgment. Don't you dare stand there and tell me that you love me! Why the fuck should I give you even a second of time to explain whatever it is you came here to say?"

Nancy stands there silent, giving me no answer to my question. Finally, she speaks. "Are you and Jeremy okay?"

"What?" I say after she asks a question that I never expected to come from her mouth.

"Are you and Jeremy going to be okay? Your marriage?"

I look back at Jeremy, who's still holding Amelia, and they both smile at me. "Yes. We are going to be okay."

"Good. I am glad I was able to at least do that for you. I am glad I was able to help. I'll go now, so you guys can continue on with the party. I am not really sure why I thought this atmosphere would ease the pain a little. Clearly, it was a bad choice." She looks over at the man who came in with her. "You should at least talk to Ronny, Livy. He didn't even know you existed until nearly a year ago. He hasn't done anything wrong."

I am beyond confused. Thoughts are swirling around in my head and I just cannot make heads or tails of what has happened tonight. It's really hard to speak right now. The alcohol has settled and has relaxed me. It's also got my mind running at five-hundred miles an hour begging for clarity and the return of normalcy. I suddenly have the urge to ask Nancy questions, the need to hear what she has to say and the curiosity to find out how she is involved with the mystery trunk.

I look at her face, just before she turns to leave, and remembered what it looked like the last time I saw her when I was seventeen. Her face then was sunken, rigid and angular. She always reminded me of the Wicked Witch of the West, minus the green skin tone. Now, her face is round, soft and tan. She looks a lot younger than she used to. She looks healthy. Throw a tiara on her head and she might even pass for Glinda the Good Witch.

As she begins to walk away, I'm stricken with regret. Why do I feel guilty for watching Nancy walk out of my life? She can't fix the past and I have no use for her in my life. What could she possibly do or say that would ever allow me to think of her in any other light than how I've seen her for all of these years? *As a monster.*

But she did have something to do with that trunk. And that trunk had a whole lot to do with the repair of my and Jeremy's relationship.

Monsters don't help people.

Everyone in the room is staring at me. Nancy walked out the door and went left down the hallway about five seconds ago. All of these people that I trust knew she would be here tonight and none of them thought it was a bad idea. They all even just admitted not less than an hour ago that they helped her with the trunk. Why would they help a monster?

Monsters don't ask people for help.

Why did Nancy come here? She said she had helped Jeremy and me. She brought me my dad. She told me she loved me.

Monsters don't love anything.

Now I feel like if I don't find out every single tiny detail of what she came here to tell me, I will have some sort of emptiness inside of me that will linger until my dying day.

I have to know.

I have to know.

I push into a full on sprint out the door and down the hallway until I see her waiting at the elevator.

"Wait!" Her head was down. She may have been crying. When she hears my plea, her eyes shoot in my direction and give me a look of surprise. There is a very small smile on her face.

I reach her end of the hallway. My heart is pounding, in combination of the running and the adrenaline of what I am about to do. *I can't believe I am about to do this.* I look at her and she looks back at me with hopeful eyes.

"Stay," is all I say.

Tears fall from her eyes and she wraps her arms around me before I have the opportunity to protest. Her hold is so tight and fierce that I can't even position my arms to reciprocate the hug.

Not that I would if I had the ability to.

"Almost three years ago, I got arrested after smashing a beer bottle over a guy's head at a bar. I was wasted out of my mind when it happened. I don't even remember much about what happened. Most of the details that I do know are from witness accounts that I had to listen to in court. Lucky for me, the guy I hit was a drug dealer...*my drug dealer*...and he was arrested too. He went to prison and will be there a while and because of who he was, the judge only gave me probation and forced me to enter into a twelve-week rehab program.

The first two weeks were the worst. I blamed everyone but myself for the position I was in. I was broke. Homeless. Pissed off at the world for the life it had handed me. But one night I had to do a group counseling session and one of the women was talking about how she would never forgive herself because her child almost died choking while she was high on meth. Child services took her child and she was forced into rehab too. Lying in bed, trying to sleep after that session, I thought about you, Livy. I had a clear head and I caught myself missing you and wanting to see you. I had just assumed you left after you turned eighteen but I didn't know for sure. You could have been dead for all I'd known and I was always too loaded to even bother to care. I cried for two days straight not knowing where you were. It felt like my heart turned on after being shut down for so many years and then someone ripped it out of my chest. I was so angry at myself for treating you the way I did. I wanted to kill myself for raising you that way.

"As the weeks moved on and I talked with counselors, I healed a little. And I vowed to stay sober, get my head and my life right and one day look for you. Even if just to see you from a distance. Just to know you were ok. After rehab, I spent about a year in therapy. Then I tracked down your dad and told him about you. It was part of the twelve steps of recovery. I had to make amends. I didn't know anything about what was going on in your life yet but I had to tell him you existed either way. If I had found out something bad had happened to you first, I might have chickened out telling him at all.

"Then, about a month ago, I finally worked up the courage to go see my dad. He told me about you and how Jeremy found him. He told me all about you and Jeremy. I told him I wanted to see you but he said it wasn't the right time because you were on rocky roads with your marriage. He told me that you had trust and communication issues with each other. And I don't know about Jeremy, but I feel one hundred percent responsible for your issues, Livy. I should have left you with my dad. I should have let him raise you to be a normal little girl. Hell, I should have pulled my head out of my ass and gotten sober so much sooner. But I honestly don't think I ever would have done that without that state forcing me to, threatening me with prison.

"You are so beautiful, Livy. I never, ever told you that. I remember the day you were born and how I felt that I never regretted for one second deciding to keep you. But I was broken and stupid and eventually my demons overcame me and I lost my way. And you are right. *Thank God* you had the fortitude to do the right thing, Livy. To leave and be better than me. I pray and thank God for that every day. Because if you had ended up like me…you know, I can't even imagine that. I am just so thankful you made the choices that you did and that you found Jeremy. No matter what the rest of my life has in store for me, I can be at peace with the fact that despite my seventeen years of being an idiot, you flourished and made a good life for yourself."

I am sitting at a table across from her, listening to her words. I am watching her lips move. I have so many thoughts and emotions coursing through me that it is difficult to actually concentrate on what she is saying. She is pouring her heart out to me and trying to explain her life to me. Her tragic past and her courageous recovery. All signs are pointing to her being genuine. However, I cannot help but think I'm being reeled in on some kind of scam. I let her speak and get it all out. I make no interruptions. I ask no questions. I do not give any opportunity to make this a two way conversation.

She is crying. The man she brought with her is sitting next to her and has an arm wrapped around her back, hugging her into his side. Even though I am not asking questions it doesn't mean I don't have a million of them. Like if this is my biological father and he's only just recently been informed of my existence why does he seems so personable and close to Nancy? Why is he obviously taking her side and supporting her? Why isn't he furious with her? Why didn't he come find me as soon as he found out?

And then I think that not once in my life did I ever have a desire to find or know my father. I had always just assumed that he was some deadbeat one night stand and that Nancy probably couldn't even point a finger in the direction of who might have provided my paternal genes. In high school, I did sometimes long to have a father. Someone to teach me to do things like change a tire or the basic standard of *righty-tighty-lefty-loosey*. Someone to encourage me to play sports and tell me that confidence is more attractive than lipstick. I had read about this kind of father figure in many books. I had always envisioned my grandfather playing that role. But before I met Jeremy, just as I had my speculations that there were no Prince Charmings, I also believed that there were no perfect fathers. And by the time Jeremy found my grandfather, I had learned all of the things a father should have taught his daughter, all by myself.

I feel like I should be rejoicing that Nancy is better and is apologizing. I should be elated that she made the effort to bring my father to me. This should be a happy, heartwarming encounter. But in all of those respects I feel nothing. I'm numb.

My only real feeling is anger. I am so angry. But I don't want to scream or fight. I just want her to finish what she came here to say so this night can be over.

"When your grandfather told me you were having marriage issues, I instantly felt I should do something to help. I didn't really know what to do, but when he told me that you were having trouble communicating, I naturally assumed that your issues with communication stemmed from our relationship—or lack of relationship, I guess I should say. I felt so guilty and I just wanted to help. When I was in rehab, we were encouraged to write down our feelings. Just write it out raw without even thinking. Just write. Then, we were asked to let what we wrote sit for a few days and then go back and read it. And I must say, that method helped me figure out and understand so many things that I'm not sure I would have otherwise. So, I told your grandfather what I wanted to do. He was strongly against it at first, but I suggested that I could still help, even if I was anonymous about it. He thought it over for a few days and then asked me what my plan was. It started out as just an unsigned letter suggesting that you write to each other. But dad had an even better idea. He said it wasn't just communication. It was that you guys had forgotten who you fell in love with because neither one of you were that person anymore. You were a new mother and Jeremy worked all of the time, both of you determined not to fail. But what you didn't realize was that you were failing each other. So he decided that we should get the whole family involved to help you two remember why you fell in love to begin with."

I turn my head and look behind me. Everyone else from the party is still here and shamelessly eavesdropping. As if scripted, they all nod their heads in unison, confirming what Nancy is saying to be true.

Rosalie speaks. "None of us wanted to help her at first, Livy. But she swore she was only doing it for your benefit. She promised that the only thing she wanted in return was for us to help her convince you that she was being sincere. I told her we couldn't make promises because you are pretty damn stubborn, but I told her we'd try. I know it will take time, Livy. But I swear to it that she has come here with true intentions. You are our family, Livy, and I wouldn't have even entertained the idea if I wasn't sure."

Rosalie just said *damn*, so she's serious.

Nancy chimes in. "Plus Rosalie told me that if I hurt you in any way ever again, she'd make me permanently disappear, never to be found."

"Rosalie!"

"Mom!"

Jeremy and I exclaim simultaneously.

Rosalie shrugs, neither confirming nor denying the threat.

Ronny begins to speak, and it startles me a little, because he's hardly said anything up to this point. "Livy, let's just put it all out there. For many years, I thought your mother was a heinous, evil bitch." Nancy winces but doesn't argue. "We dated a little over four months and one day she just left. I thought I loved her, and she vanished with nothing more than a note that said '*I'm sorry.*' It took me almost a year to move on and many years after that to trust anyone again within a relationship. So, when she came banging on my door, I didn't even want to let her in.

But she pleaded and so I did. She told me about you and I was furious. I had a child. A grown child. A girl. A child I never got to be a father to. I was heartbroken. And I wanted to go find you. Immediately. But she wouldn't even tell me your name or where you were. She told me that she didn't know where you were but she wanted to find you first. Then she left and gave me her number. She said she would be in touch but to call her if I wanted to. And just like that she was gone. I did call her a few days later. I wanted to ask her about you. Not about who you were, but just general things. Did you make good grades? Were you athletic? How old were you when you learned to walk?

"She broke down and cried for a long time. Because she didn't have answers to any of those questions. I asked her to have coffee with me somewhere and she agreed. I picked a place that was quiet and private so we could talk. She told me about you, what she could remember, and she told me about herself…what she could remember. She cried a lot. Told me how regretful she was about the majority of her decisions. And she told me why she left me."

Nancy starts crying and manages to speak through her tears. "I was going to have an abortion. I know that's not something you want to hear from the woman who gave birth to you, but it's the truth. And I couldn't do that and stay with Ronny. I didn't want him to know, so I just left. But when I got to the clinic, I couldn't go through with it. And I was too proud to go back to Ronny and too ashamed to confess to my dad at the time. So I just left town and settled where I could get a job to afford to take care of us. My pregnancy was great and I was adjusting to the idea of being a mother. I had high hopes and dreams for you and me. But then one night when you were around three-months old, I had some friends from work over. I remember that night like it was yesterday. It was the night that changed our lives. The night I will always regret. I was a social drinker and smoked pot occasionally but that night I was stressed about money and you were screaming because you were teething and I had just had enough. Some girl offered me a pill. Said it would make everything fade away. And it did. I was conscious and aware of everything but I was stressed about nothing. It snowballed from there. I found myself wanting to feel that way all of the time, which led to me partying more. The more I partied the more drugs I was introduced to." She wipes tears from her face. "I seriously do not even know how I took care of you at all. The last clear day I remember having before rehab was the day before I took that pill. I remember being so stressed out because I had no idea what I was doing with you. It was so hard taking care of you on my own. I was so young and stupid and stubborn. I refused to ask for help and eventually all of the frustration and anger and sadness that I hoarded won and I made a very bad choice. A horrible choice. A choice that I've wished I could take back so many times. I would give up my own life if I could go back and make the right choice for you."

Her head falls into her hands and her shoulders begin to shake from her sobs.

A tear falls down my cheek. She's not pleading to me, parent to child. She's not playing the apologetic ex-drug addict to her scorned, abused victim. She's not even professing to me, woman to woman. She's talking to me, mother to mother.

And suddenly, I get it.

I reach my hand across the table and lightly clutch her arm which startles her. She looks at me stunned. I draw in a deep breath. "I accepted a long time ago that I am who I am because of my past. And I like who I am. I'm flawed. Yes. But I still like who I've become. If it hadn't been for the path that my life traveled down I may never have met Jeremy. And even though we had some tough times, I don't want to imagine what life I'd have without him. I've hated you for a long time, Nancy, but I'm also grateful for your plan to help out Jeremy and me. I was on the brink of making a bad choice as well. Not with drugs or anything like that. But I had given up on Jeremy and me. I was tired and worn down. I couldn't fight anymore and I felt like Jeremy had already given up on us. I was too stubborn to leave because I didn't want Amelia to grow up in a broken home but I was also too stupid to realize that my plan to fake a happy marriage for the benefit of my daughter was never going to work either. It couldn't have. It wasn't until Jeremy and I were forced to spend time with each other and communicate and remember who we were that we realized what we'd really become. We've grown from that and I think we know better than to go back to that place. We've still got some things to work on but we'll get there." I wink at Jeremy.

I pull my arm back and I bounce my glance between Nancy and Ronny. "Nancy, I've hated you for so long, and I probably will never be able to forget what you did to me. But, I'm okay. And I get it. You were sick and now you are better and you are trying to right your wrong. It doesn't excuse what you did but I do have to recognize the fact that you had the courage to come here at all. You could have just let things stay as they were and never contacted me again. But you didn't, and I respect that. I don't know where we go from here." I look up at the ceiling to attempt to hold back tears. "But I do think it might be nice if you two stayed to help us celebrate."

They both smile. Ronny hugs Nancy and Nancy nods, "Yes, of course. Thank you."

I nod back.

Nancy stands. "I'm going to go find the ladies' room and freshen up."

"Okay," I exhale. I feel the weight of seventeen years of loathing slowly dissipate.

"I added the romance book. I knew that hot, sexy detective would get you stirring, Livy." The room erupts with laughter. Rosalie and Maxwell look at each other with furrowed brows and slanted grins. I think they are both trying to tune out parts of this conversation, but they are taking everything being said in the context of good fun.

"Maggie, you are a dirty girl," I say, "And by the way, I need to lend you some of *my* books. That shit was terrible!" I say as I take a swig of water, trying to avoid a hangover from my earlier binge.

"Whatever," Maggie argues. "It made the point, right?" I smile and nod. "Yes, it did."

"The candles were my idea," Rosalie says. "I still have a shirt of your father's, Jeremy, that smells like him to this day. That scent always takes me back to when we first met." She closes her eyes and tilts her head up a little in reminiscence.

Joe raises his hand. "I thought about the music. I remember a few times before I sold the bar, peeking out from the office. Jeremy would be sitting on that corner stool, watching you sing whenever someone played Janis on the jukebox." I look over at Jeremy. I thought the first time he had heard me sing that song was in the shower. Apparently, he had witnessed it at the bar as well, and I had been oblivious. Jeremy gives me a slight shrug and a smile as to say, *"What's a guy to do?"*

"I remembered you had a scrapbook of all the places you guys had traveled," Maggie says.

"Yeah but how did you get it?" I ask, still unsure.

Jenna chimes in. "I broke into your house one day when you were both gone. Well, technically not *broke in*, I mean, I have the key you gave me. I also hacked into your phone and stole all your pictures one afternoon while we were having lunch, Livy. You had to take Amelia to the restroom to change her. I knew I would have plenty of time to get what I needed. I knew if there were pictures on your phone that hadn't been shared with anyone else, it would elevate the mystery. I have to say that I am extremely grateful that you two aren't the sexting type." Everyone laughs again.

"Well, thanks for putting that out there, Jenna," I say with fake embarrassment. If Jeremy and I had been the sexting type, any reaction she had to seeing that would have been her own damn fault for snooping.

Maybe we'll *start* being the sexting type. It might not be a bad idea. I look at Jeremy and give him an eyebrow raise. He gives me a wink in understanding.

I look around the table at all of the people sitting with Jeremy and me. "Jeez, you are just a bunch of dirty, deceitful thieves. Remind me why I hang out with you all again?"

"Because you love us," Sara says. "Just so you know, I wrote all of the instructions." She winks. I know she knew we were waiting for that confession, specifically regarding the Fuck card. I smile and wink back.

"What instructions?" Rosalie asks. Sara clears her throat and looks at me like she's trying to find the right words. "Well, after we came up with so many good ideas, I knew if we just threw it all in a plain old box, they wouldn't get it. That's why I volunteered to organize everything and have it delivered. I had found an old trunk at a consignment store about six months ago. I loved it, but I had no idea what I was going to do with it. So, I just bought it and I knew I would put it to some use eventually. Then, I thought it was perfect to hold all of the items that we'd collected for you two. I put everything in the trunk and each item came with a list of instructions. I thought the order I put it in would help it all make sense." She shoots a devilish grin my way.

"Sara, you did a great job. Really. Thank you. But how on earth did you figure all of this out? I mean, no offense, but you aren't married." I notice Craig do a slight, uncomfortable shift in his seat.

"No, Livy. But I know you and Jeremy. That's all the knowledge I needed."

I smile at her. The fact that she put so much effort into helping us warms my heart. I've only seen her a handful of times since she moved to Connecticut, yet she cared about us so much that she took the reins on Nancy's idea and customized it just for us because she knew how to make it most effective. I am truly in awe.

"How did you even know about this, Sara?" I ask.

"Jenna called me. She said it was a family emergency. I came into town a few weekends ago. I'm sorry I didn't come see you. I only stayed the night to do my part. Plus, after I had found out what was going on and that your mother was involved, I knew I wouldn't be able to see you without spilling the beans. So, I came in on a Saturday. We all got together." She circles her hand above and around the table, implicating all of the involved parties. "Rosalie, Maggie, Jenna and I met with Nancy for dinner and we talked about what we were going to do. After Nancy talked about the journals, Rosalie mentioned we could add more items as well, to help stir up some good memories. So, I told everyone that I had a great idea and that they should all mail me within that week what they wanted to contribute. Nancy sent the journals, Rosalie sent the candles, Jenna sent the pictures, Maggie sent the book. I even called Joe to see if he had any suggestions. He sent me the record and the player. After I had everything, I started on the instructions to help put it all together."

She smirks. She didn't mention the porn. I'm dying to know who sent the porn. I'm looking around the table to see if anyone looks guilty but no one is letting on. I will have to pull Sara aside later and find out. I can tell by the look in her face, she is loving that she has one little fact that is still a mystery. *This girl and her drama.* I'm glad she hasn't mentioned it out in open forum though, or that any one has. I am hands down certain that neither Rosalie nor Maxwell knows about the DVD and I think more than one person in this room would be mortified if they found out.

"Wow, Sara, you really took my idea and ran with it," Nancy says.

"Yeah. I mean your idea was great. I just wanted to try to make it fool proof. I do medical research for a living. I like to put things in a particular, chronological format so that theorems work exactly as they should."

I find it amusing that she considered mine and Jeremy's relationship as a theorem—like we were some kind of social experiment. I guess to her scientific brain, we were in some sorts.

"Well, bravo," Nancy says. "Bravo to everyone." Nancy raises her cup of soda. "It seems as though we pulled it off." Everyone raises their cups in the air including myself and Jeremy.

I look over at Jeremy. I can see every ounce of love he has for me in his eyes and I hope he can see mine as well. He leans over and kisses me. "It seems as though you are correct," Jeremy says to Nancy.

With everyone's cup still raised, Joe pipes in, "To Jeremy and Livy. May they learn from their mistakes and stop being so stubborn and stupid. And may they have a long life of happiness."

"Cheers!" Everyone else says while laughing and smiling at Jeremy and me.

I take another sip of my water. I look over at Maxwell. "I do have one more question. Maxwell, Nancy said she came to you a month ago and you told her Jeremy and I were having issues. I only told you about our issues two weeks ago. How did you already know we were having problems?"

"The last time I came to visit, I could see it all over your face. I thought perhaps I was mistaken so I didn't mention it to you. But I called Rosalie later in the week and she said she was also concerned." I look over at Rosalie. She nods only slightly. Maxwell continues, "Rosalie and I tried to figure out what to do ourselves. Rosalie said she had tried to help you with Amelia, but you were so steadfast on doing everything on your own. And she told me that she and Jenna both kept telling Jeremy he needed to take a break from work, but he just kept brushing them off. We didn't know what to do. And then," He looks over at Nancy, and they exchange smiles, "as if some strange sign from above, your mother shows up on my doorstep. We spent a day talking about her and then talking about you. She said she wanted to know where you were and I was adamant that she shouldn't get mixed up in your business at the moment because you and Jeremy were struggling. I told her that she didn't need to add to any stress that was already there. But, she said she wanted to help and I told her it wasn't a good idea until she mentioned the anonymous letter. Somehow, she made it sound like a really good idea. But, since Rosalie and Jenna had already been trying to help, I wanted them involved too. And of course, they got Sara and Maggie involved."

I think for a second. "But you didn't contribute anything to the trunk."

"No, I didn't," he confirms. "Rosalie called and told me about sending stuff to Sara. But I couldn't think of anything to give you that wouldn't give away that I was involved in the plan. Sara made it clear that you two couldn't know who sent the trunk to you."

Sara smiles. "I thought you would take it more seriously if you didn't know it was just family trying to get all up in your business."

Everyone laughs. But she is probably right.

"So Sara called me one night and asked if I had sent anything. I told her no because all I could think to send were pictures of me and your grandmother and that would have blown our cover. She told me that she had enough to go with already and that when it was all over and out in the open, I could give you those things afterward."

"That's why I took the trunk back," Sara said. "I used Jenna's key and snuck in early this morning." She smiles again.

"So you…" I stop and think, trying to figure out how to ask her cryptically if she heard Jeremy and me in the bedroom.

Sara shakes her head immediately, knowing what I'm trying to ask. She created the Fuck card so she knew we'd be occupied in the bedroom and she could sneak in at some point and take everything, leaving only the final card. But how did she know we wouldn't be tangled up in the living room, or hell, even in the kitchen? And did she hear anything?

"I was in and out, five minutes, like a ninja," she says. "I came early this morning because I thought you'd be sleeping." She winks. Only Jeremy and I notice the wink. She's only saying that in front of everyone so she doesn't lead on that she knows what we were doing when she came by. And really I think the reason we didn't hear her come in was because we were too focused on each other. There's no way she didn't hear us. I have a lot of questions to ask her, one-on-one, later.

"So, I have the trunk here and we've all added some more things to it—more personal stuff. You'll have plenty of time to look at it when you get home. Jeremy, you still have the rest of the week off and Livy, Rosalie and Maggie may never give Amelia back," Sara jokes.

Rosalie chuckles. "Of course we will! But not until Friday, as agreed."

I look at Jeremy. "I think another two days alone with Jeremy will be ok." I smile. He returns a smile to me.

I look around at everyone. "I can't believe all of you did this for us." I grab Jeremy's hand, "Thank you. All of you."

This whole room of people came together to help us. And they did it in secret because they knew we wouldn't have accepted it otherwise. They knew us better than we knew ourselves. Even my own estranged mother knew how to help. And none of the rest may have figured out the right thing to do if she hadn't started the suggestion. My thoughts spin in wonderment over the reality of the entire situation.

I looked around the room again at our wildly disjointed, crazy family.

Jeremy and Amelia.

Rosalie, Maggie, Jenna and Mike.

Sara and Craig.

Joe and Vicky.

My granddad.

My parents.

Parents.

Jeremy showed me love.

Love that I was then able to share with Amelia.

Love that allowed me to heal from my past and move forward.

Love that may give me the strength, courage and trust I need to possibly consider having a relationship with my parents.

Parents.

That love is present within me and it is lingering and radiating throughout the room. Its force is greater than anything I've ever felt. Jeremy's love helped me become a better person and I will be eternally grateful. But the love in this room right now is by far the best type of love. The love of *family.*

As we are rounding out the night and beginning to say our goodbyes, Rosalie tells everyone to halt. "Wait! We almost forgot! The gift!"

Everyone exalts and gathers around Jeremy and me. Rosalie fishes an envelope out of her bag and hands it to Jeremy. "Another envelope?" he asks, eyeing her skeptically.

"It's good," she says. "I promise. Open it."

Jeremy tears open the envelope and investigates the contents. I take a peek and then we both look at everyone around us. "No. You guys. This is too much. We can't accept this."

"You can and you will," Rosalie says sternly. "You haven't been on a real vacation since you were married. Not even for an anniversary. It's time."

In his hand, Jeremy held a travel package for a seven day, round trip, all inclusive vacation to Aruba—the same place we spent our honeymoon.

"But when?" Jeremy asks.

"One week from Friday, your flight leaves. Non-refundable," Rosalie commands. "We all pitched in. All of us," she says, looking over at Ronny and Nancy. They both present small smiles. "And, Jeremy," Rosalie continues. "You and Marcus have some things to discuss about the business. He has a plan and you need to listen. You have next week to smooth out the details, and then you let him do what he suggests." She shakes her finger at him. "But no business until after Friday."

I can tell Jeremy wants to asks questions, but he just nods.

"And Livy, between myself, Maggie and Jenna, we will take very good care of Amelia. She will be in good hands and you have nothing to worry about while you are away."

And then I nod. "I know."

I look over at Nancy and Ronny, who are two steps behind everyone else. I walk over to them. I look at Nancy. "Thank you. For coming up with this idea. We have a lot to discuss, in time. If you give me your number, I will call you when I'm ready. I promise. Same to you, Ronny. I know you've done nothing wrong in this scenario, but it's still too new. I need to process all of this. But when I'm ready, I will call you both."

"That is all I can ask for," Nancy responds.

"I am looking forward to getting to know you," Ronny says.

When we are home, and I have Amelia settled in her bed, I look down at her and realize how much I've missed her. Rosalie agreed to let her spend the night at home because I missed her so much. She goes back to Rosalie's tomorrow, so that Jeremy and I can finish out our week together. I'll still miss Amelia, but I am looking forward to more time alone with Jeremy.

I also realize that despite all of the craziness that has happened in the past few weeks, I feel secure in knowing that I have people in my life that are willing to drop everything they are doing and step up to the plate to help me when I need it most. The weight that was bearing down on my shoulders and suffocating the life out of me, when I felt like I was alone and trapped and had nowhere to turn, has disappeared. I have a new outlook on my life, once again, and instead of being fearful and anxious about mine and Jeremy's future, I am hopeful and excited.

Fifty-Six

Jeremy

Three weeks later

"I'LL GET THE DOOR," I SAY TO LIVY, AS SHE FINISHES GETTING Amelia dressed. We're having guests for dinner.

Our trip to Aruba was exactly what we needed to reflect on everything the trunk, *a.k.a* our family, taught us. We spent the days paying attention to no one but each other. We recollected about our dating years and when we came to Aruba the first time. We also talked a lot about the future and what we wanted to do with it. We made decisions about that together. It was eye-opening because I had been so consumed with working and stabilizing the business for our future that I had never considered what Livy wanted out of that future. We talked about how we should invest our money and whether we'd buy a house. Livy even talked about going back to work. She wasn't sure if she wanted to go back to the shelter, or if she wanted to do some type of consulting. After helping me fix my accounting error at work, she thought she might be able to find a niche in that somehow. Nothing on that front was solidified, but I did tell her that I would support her in whatever she wanted to do.

Marcus and I did have a discussion. He made an offer to be my vice-president. He said that having the week to run things on his own, with the exception of the billing incident, he was confident that he could take on the majority of the workload that I had been dragging around for so long. His argument was strong as he pointed out that he didn't have a family that he would be missing out on and he was ready to get his hands dirty in work. He had no issues pulling the long hours that I had been doing. I took into consideration that he did do a lot of leg work with getting the business in Chicago and I trusted him more than I trusted anyone else that worked there—even some guys that had worked for me longer than he had. Marcus was a good man that just had a few years of hard luck due to tragedy and heartbreak.

Having Marcus as my VP and him taking on the responsibilities that he was proposing meant that I could be home with Livy so much more and I wouldn't miss out on watching Amelia grow up. I wanted to accept his offer on the spot, but I told him I would think about it. I thought about it for a solid twenty-four hours. I discussed it with Livy and she was completely on board. The next day, I told Marcus that I had accepted his offer and that I would have our lawyer draw up a contract for his new position.

I open the door and am greeted with two of the biggest smiling faces I have ever seen. Ronny and Nancy. After Livy's initial reaction to seeing Nancy at the party our family organized a few weeks ago, she never said another negative thing about Nancy. The week following and during our trip, Livy talked about Ronny and Nancy often. I think she even called Nancy her mother once. I asked Livy why she had softened up to Nancy so quickly that night and Livy simply responded that it was *just a mom thing.*

I assumed she didn't explain further because she didn't think I'd understand. I didn't press, because I wasn't that concerned over the reason. But I can say, that in true Livy fashion, she shocked the hell out of me when she asked me if it was ok to invite Nancy and Ronny for dinner at our place. When I said yes, without hesitation, she hugged me and called them both that night. Livy didn't talk to Nancy long on the phone, but she talked to Ronny for over half an hour. When she was done talking with him, she hugged me again, one of our classic hugs, where no one else exists, and she said to me, "I feel like if I hadn't met you, none of this would be happening right now. Even if they had found me, I would have been too bitter and closed off to have even given them a chance to explain. You showed me how to love and I think that is why it was so easy for me to give them the opportunity to get to know me. To know us. To know Amelia. Because my heart is full of love. It's no longer filled with hate or anger or doubt. Just love. And I know all of this transformation happened in me without you even knowing you were doing it, but thank you." She squeezed and gave me a little pinch on my ass.

I laughed. "You're welcome. And I knew exactly what I was doing the whole time, just so you know." I pinched her back.

I had my Livy back. And she had me back. And that was all that mattered.

Epilogue

Livy

Two years later

Amelia's third birthday

M Y GOD, HOW MY WORLD HAS CHANGED. THIS SWEET LITTLE chubby cheeked precious bundle of joy has turned into a never ending supply of energy that takes on the world like a tornado. I thought raising an infant was hard. That shit's fucking cheesecake compared to wrangling a toddler. She's a tiny little terror that never slows down and destroys everything in her path.

But she is beautiful. And she has manners, most of the time. And she eats her vegetables and sleeps well at night. We haven't quite mastered potty training yet, but we're working on it. I count every blessing that I have in regards to her. She's happy and healthy and after seeing how some of the other children behave on the playground at the park, I thank sweet Baby Jesus that Amelia is mine. Because compared to all other three year olds I've had the pleasure to encounter, she is an angel.

Everyone is here today to celebrate the birthday girl. Rosalie, of course. Maggie and Stanley, Jenna and Mike and their kids. Joe and Vicky—still together for over five years. I can't believe that woman has put up with his stubborn ass for that long. They even live together. Sara and Craig are here. They got married six months ago and are currently working on a family of their own. Maxwell is here as well.

And my mom and dad are here. Yes, my *mom* and my *dad*.

Things started slowly with them. I talked with them on the phone. They came over for dinner. Sometimes together, sometimes separate. I got to know them both very well.

I remember back when I first moved away from home and I told myself everyday that I didn't give a fuck if I ever saw Nancy again. But now, I find myself scared sometimes that I might lose her. That she might relapse and go back to who she was before. She has never given off any indication that she would, though. I'm just paranoid. I like *this* Nancy. She's kind and generous. She listens and she hugs. She sews and she cooks. I didn't get this Nancy growing up, but I am very glad that I have her now. I don't want it to ever change.

Nancy, Ronny, and I have become very close. Or I should rather say that Nancy and Ronny became very close to the rest of us. All of us. The whole family. Nancy and Rosalie go shopping together at fabric stores for crying out loud. Ronny and Joe, and Maxwell when he's in town, play poker together.

A few months after the party Nancy threw for Jeremy and me, she and Ronny began dating again. Just recently, they bought a townhome together, about an hour's drive south of the city. They aren't sure if they'll ever get married, but I have to say that it is pretty nice that Amelia has a set of grandparents that found their way back to each other once again.

"I cannot believe that Amelia is three years old," Rosalie says to me. "It seems yesterday that she was a tiny little thing."

"I know," I agree. "It's weird, but sometimes I just want her to stop growing. It's happening too fast."

Rosalie pats me on the shoulder. "Oh, sweet girl, I know. Just remember to take all of the precious moments in as they come and enjoy the ride. Sadly, before you know it, she'll be eighteen and ready take on the world."

I laugh and nod but my insides swirl with a little sadness. As much as I want Amelia to grow and learn and flourish, I also want to freeze time and keep her little because I know I'm going to blink and she'll be an adult and she won't be my precious little baby girl anymore.

"She'll still be your little girl," Rosalie says, somehow reading my thoughts.

"I know," is all I can reply. I feel like I'm going to cry so I try to think about something else because there's no crying at birthday parties.

We eat lunch and then watch Amelia open her gifts and blow out her candles. Her smile is as big as ever and it makes my heart melt. She's having the time of her life being the center of attention. Jeremy has taken a thousand and one pictures. He bought a professional grade camera about a year ago. His subject of photographical interest is always Amelia. Sometimes me, but mostly Amelia. He started a blog and writes about how Amelia is growing and how our family dynamic works. He's gotten quite an audience for his stories and pictures since he began. But he doesn't care about the fans. All he cares about is chronicling Amelia. He loves that baby girl so much and it makes me love him more and more every day.

We keep the trunk under our bed. From time to time, we pull it out and go through it. Maxwell put a lot of pictures of him and my grandmother in the trunk. He also put in a copy of the vows they had written to each other on their wedding day and some pressed flowers from a bouquet he had given her on their first date. All symbols of love. Rosalie added a lot of pictures of her and Jeremy's dad as well, along with some love letters he wrote to her. Jeremy and I have read those letters together many times. We've also read that stupid romance novel together again. Twice. And we've watched the porno together again, one weekend when Amelia was with Rosalie. We were trying to perfect some techniques and had to review the footage.

I did find out after our party that Sara had included the porn. I had called her the next day to find out. I had to know. She said it was Craig's idea and she said that absolutely no one else knew about it. I was relieved to know it was a secret, and I thought it was odd that it was Craig's idea, given his gentle demeanor. Sara said that Craig's suggestion stirred up a conversation between the two of them in regards to why he would suggest that to begin with. He said that it was a *"fun, couples' thing to do."* She took the hint he was throwing her way and told him to pick out two movies: one for us and one for them.

"Because," Sara said to me, "there was no way I was going to watch the same porn as you and Jeremy. That's just too weird." The whole conversation about pornography was weird, but I can't say I didn't disagree with her on that particular point.

Last year, Maggie and Jenna gave Jeremy and me a gift for our anniversary. We thought it was strange, but the card attached read *"for the trunk."* It was a new album of pictures that they, and other members of the family, had taken of us over the course of a year. They were all beautiful pictures of Jeremy and me smiling and laughing together. Loving each other.

That time in our life, when we thought it was the end of us, was very brief. But it taught us a lot about maturity, honesty and communication. We both went into our marriage naïve and confident that our love would be enough. And it was, until stress and adulthood hit us in the face. What we've learned is that we will be ok, and our love will survive, as long as we work hard at it and stay supportive of one another. Couples like us are called partners for a reason. Because by definition, partners work together to achieve a common goal, while sharing both the risks and the profits of that goal. And that is what we do every day. Work together. Every day hasn't been perfect. Some days are better than others. Our goal is to love each other and to love our family. And we've been pretty great at doing it for a while now. Everything is as smooth sailing as it should be.

The party is over and everyone is gone. Amelia is in bed. Jeremy and I are sitting in the living room, watching TV with our feet propped up on the coffee table, settled next to the containers of leftover food that we are stuffing our faces with. In all of the excitement of the birthday celebration, neither one of us ate anything.

"Do you want some wine?" Jeremy asks.

"No thanks," I say with a mouthful of food.

He looks over at me and eyes me curiously.

I look at him and smile.

"Livy?" It's been a long day and he knows I would never turn down a glass of wine. The jig is up. I turn to face him and swallow my food. I look into his crystal blues. "I'm pregnant."

Jeremy smiles. The same smile he smiled with the first pregnancy announcement. "Are you serious?"

I nod. "I am. The doctor confirmed it yesterday."

His eyes immediately go to my stomach. And then his hand goes there too. He looks back up at me. "You aren't freaking out," he says and smiles even bigger.

"I'm not freaking out," I repeat.

He leans in and kisses me on the side of my face. "Are you happy, Livy?"

I wrap my arms around him and we embrace in one of our epic hugs. "So happy."

Acknowledgements

For nine months, my husband has listened to me discuss story lines and plot angles that he couldn't probably care less about. He's spent many nights and weekend afternoons hanging out alone while I was burrowed in my writing cave, typing, editing and obsessing over this story.

To you, my dear husband, I thank you so much for your patience, your ideas and suggestions, and mostly for your love and support of me and the passion that I have to form words into stories.

To my lifelong best friend and sister from another mister, JV, thank you for giving me endless encouragement. I would have given up this crazy journey a while ago if I hadn't had you in my corner.

To Colleen Hoover: You started this. And if you ever read this book, I hope you love it. Or, maybe at least like it a little. Your writing gave me the motivation, confidence and courage to publish something of my own. You are a talented and creative writer, but my favorite things about you are your willingness to help others succeed, your humbleness amongst your fans and your generosity toward people less fortunate. You are incredible all around, and I am very glad that Amazon suggested that I read *Slammed* that one time in March of 2013. You and your books have made a major impact on my life not only as a writer but also as a human.

CPSIA information can be obtained
at www.ICGtesting.com
Printed in the USA
BVOW06s0006311016

466444BV00019B/213/P